THE FABER BOOK OF
CONTEMPORARY SOUTH PACIFIC STORIES

in the same series

THE FABER BOOK OF
CONTEMPORARY AUSTRALIAN SHORT STORIES

THE FABER BOOK OF
CONTEMPORARY CARIBBEAN SHORT STORIES

THE FABER BOOK OF
CONTEMPORARY LATIN AMERICAN SHORT STORIES

THE FABER BOOK OF
CANADIAN SHORT STORIES

THE FABER BOOK OF
GAY SHORT FICTION

The Faber Book of

CONTEMPORARY
SOUTH PACIFIC STORIES

Edited by

C. K. STEAD

faber and faber

LONDON · BOSTON

First published in 1994
by Faber and Faber Limited
3 Queen Square London WC1N 3AU

Photoset in Palatino by Parker Typesetting Service, Leicester
Printed in England by Clays Ltd, St Ives plc

A CIP record for this book is
available from the British Library

ISBN 0–571–16765–9

2 4 6 8 10 9 7 5 3 1

Contents

Acknowledgements

The editor and publisher would like to thank the following for permission to use the stories in this volume:

MARJORIE TUÄINAKORE CROCOMBE and *Kovave* for 'The Healer'; YVONNE DU FRESNE and Victoria University Press for 'Farvel'; VINCENT ERI and Jacaranda Wiley for 'Village, Church and School'; JANET FRAME and W. H. Allen for 'The Headmistress's Story'; MAURICE GEE and Penguin Books for 'Joker and Wife'; VANESSA GRIFFEN and *Mana* for 'A Double Life'; EPELI HAU'OFA and Longman Paul for 'The Glorious Pacific Way'; SHONAGH KOEA and Penguin Books for 'The Woman Who Never Went Home'; JOHN KOLIA and the Institute of Papua New Guinea Studies for 'For Sale at Koke Market'; GRAEME LAY and Polynesian Press for 'The Jacket'; BILL MANHIRE and Heinemann Reed for 'Cannibals'; OWEN MARSHALL and the Pegasus Press for 'The Tsunami'; PHILIP MINCHER and John McIndoe for 'Träumerei'; MICHAEL MORRISSEY and Penguin Books for 'Beethoven's Ears'; RAYMOND PILLAI and Mana Publications/South Pacific Creative Arts Society for 'The Celebration'; JOHN PUHIATAU PULE and Penguin Books for 'Letters'; JANETTE SINCLAIR and *Sport* for 'Outlines of Gondwanaland' C. K. STEAD and *Sport* for 'A Short History of New Zealand'; J. C. STURM and Spiral for 'A Thousand and One Nights'; SUBRAMANI and Three Continents Press for 'Kala'; MARGARET SUTHERLAND and Hodder & Stoughton for 'A Letter from the Dead'; ANNE TARRANT and *Landfall* for 'White Socracte'; APIRANA TAYLOR and Penguin Books for 'Carving up the Cross', 'Pa Mai' and 'The Kumara Plant'; EMMA KRUSE VA'AI and Price Milburn for 'Ta Tatau'; JOSEPH C. VERAMU and the Fiji Centre, University of the South Pacific for 'Kerekere'; VILI

ACKNOWLEDGEMENTS

VETE and *Mana* for 'For Change'; IAN WEDDE and Victoria University Press/Price Milburn for 'Paradise'; VIRGINIA WERE and *Sport* for 'Levuka'.

Introduction

This is an anthology representing contemporary short fiction in English from the South Pacific, chosen by a Pakeha New Zealander. Personal taste, for which there is no accounting, has some bearing on choices; but definitions set limits, so I will explain, as far as I am able, what I have allowed my terms to mean, and what they have seemed to require of me.

First, it is a more genuinely 'contemporary' selection than the Australian and Canadian anthologies in the same Faber series, each of which ranges over its whole field since the Second World War, and includes work of several writers now deceased. To have offered that kind of selection from New Zealand would have shown how very strong the tradition of short fiction has been and continues to be; but it would have crowded out almost entirely Pacific Island writers who are just now finding their way in what has been for most a second language, and whose work (with the exception of Albert Wendt's) has only begun to be published since about 1975. It would also have shown little of the South Pacific region, which seldom figured in New Zealand fiction until the influx of island migrants in recent years began to make us more aware of the micro-states to the north which are their homelands. A truly contemporary selection, favouring (though not exclusively) some form of South Pacific vision or consciousness, seemed called for. Other anthologies will give the kind of overview of modern New Zealand short fiction which this one does not attempt. This is the first to put New Zealand writing into a South Pacific context.

The islands now called New Zealand have had, and retain, several overlapping identities. Polynesian settlement began about one thousand years ago, and must have occurred in the form of unrepeatable accidents, since pre-European Maori consciousness of a larger inhabited world is entirely a mythological one. New Zealand's colonial identity through-out the latter half of the nineteenth century and on into the twentieth was anglophone British, though always with elements of Maori culture and language, the weight and significance of these varying with the fortunes of the native race.

There was a time when New Zealand and Australia were close. The Anzacs were a joint force; and 'Australasian' sporting teams competed against the rest of the world. But the opportunity for political union was allowed to pass when the Commonwealth of Australian states was formed at the turn of the century, and though Australia now attracts New Zealanders both to top jobs and to its dole queues, and the move towards economic union continues, the two neighbouring states remain regrettably wary of one another. Politically New Zealand has taken its South Pacific identity more and more seriously in recent years, partly because the island states look to Wellington for the Government support they need to survive as modern economies, and to Auckland as the centre of Polynesia.

New Zealand's dominant culture remains British; any pretence to the contrary is just that – and expedient. Narrow your focus in any urban market centre and you might think for a moment, until the harsher light revealed the peculiar mix of northern and southern hemisphere vegetation, that you were in an English provincial town. After a single generation island migrants, like their Maori cousins, have to work consciously to preserve their language. Nevertheless, strong elements of their languages, music, oral culture, food habits, dress, decoration and thought patterns, remain to give a distinct flavour to New Zealand life, especially in the north, and this is reflected in some of the fiction.

In the colonial and post-colonial mind there is always – must be – a division and shifting of identities which has both destructive and creative potential. This is not always acknowledged, and often hotly denied where it is most manifest. It is also difficult to analyse because it involves contradictions, and self-contradictions. The colonial is fiercely independent, sensitive to patronizing or possessive attentions from mother country or fatherland, proud of freedoms won and affluence achieved, yet at the same time loyal to and protective of the language, customs and institutions brought from the home country.

In my own case, a child during the Second World War, the contradictions were strong. Japan threatened in the Pacific while New Zealand troops fought in the northern hemisphere; and I recall that though I feared the prospect of a Japanese invasion, it still seemed to me that in some sense the 'real' war – the *serious* one – was the one going on in Europe.

Yet my childhood was charged with the aura of Oceania. My mother had spent much of her childhood on remote Pacific atolls – Nauru, Makatea, Ocean Island, Malden Island – where her father, a Swedish sea captain, had worked laying moorings and serving as harbour master. Her reminiscences were rich in nostalgia and romance, and our house was full of photographs showing groups of semi-naked brown men working under the supervision of my grandfather in white suit and pith helmet, coconut palms reflected in glassy lagoons, coral reefs and three-masted schooners. There were, it now seems when I reflect on it, three 'realities': that of New Zealand which was all about me; that of England, the arbiter, source of power, language and culture; and that of Oceania, the region of romance. All three have a place somewhere in the making of this anthology.

But the person who is seen from the homeland as the colonial, and who through two or three generations sees himself thus, is to the indigenous people the colonizer. Again there are ambiguities. Colonization is both sought and resisted, desired and resented. The new culture – superior in its technology and the affluence it can create – is eagerly encouraged by the same indigenous people who deplore its destruction of their own, and who at times are driven by it to loss of confidence and despair.

In small island states like Nuie, the Cooks, and Western Samoa, the indigenous population remains predominant, and much of their culture survives; but economic pressures and modern appetites lead to dilution at home as well as to emigration, usually to New Zealand.

Island politics often retain elements of conflict between

traditional ways and those of modern democracy. Samoa has passed from German colony through New Zealand Trusteeship to independence, while retaining more or less intact the old Samoa's aristocratic matai system of village social control. Tonga, whose king recently announced that he had seen (whether in a vision or literally was not quite clear) oil gushing from the lagoon in front of his palace, retains a system of absolute monarchy and privileged nobles, and it is not surprising that it should be the first of the island states to produce a notable satirist, Epeli Hau'ofa. Fiji's indigenous population is now equalled by the descendants of indentured labourers brought from India to work the cane fields, while the lingua franca is that of the British colonists. Ethnic Fijian advantages were written into the constitution at the time of independence; but when these were not sufficient to prevent an Indian-backed Government winning power, there was a Fijian military coup.

In New Zealand the Maori have been swamped, outnumbered ten to one by European (mainly British) immigrants, most of whom have long since lost all contact with their forebears' homeland and families. But Maori numbers and confidence have grown throughout the present century; and the assertion of Maori identity and rights has led in turn to a degree of politicization of their fiction.

The present selection of island and Maori writers' work reflects a little of all of this, if only as background. Fiction writers must deal with individuals and particulars rather than with the groups and statistics which are the concern of politicians. Abstraction and argument belong to other forms of discourse. The eye of imagination can shed tears, but seems always to close when blame is laid. Where there is conflict and social distress the best writers can do is find new ways to bear witness.

Among Pakeha New Zealanders Janet Frame and Maurice Gee perhaps best represent the broad main road of New Zealand fiction, in which New Zealand is, it might be said, *domesticated* – no longer either 'remote' from some more important otherwhere, nor fraught with anxieties about cross-cultural identity. Yet even Frame's story, which might have been written anywhere, still has subtle suggestions of what V. S. Naipaul calls 'a client culture', remote from its source. Father twiddles the knobs of the radio 'trying to get "overseas"'; while the wonderful traditional literary inheritance, made up entirely of British and American 'classics', which at first seems to protect the narrator from the pain of her sister's death, comes at the end of the story to seem a 'concealment'.

Most writers represented in this collection have been chosen for some experience or knowledge or vision of the South Pacific, the movement of its peoples and the mix of its cultures; or alternatively in a few cases (stories by du Fresne, Mincher and Morrissey) because in their different ways they represent the survival of a sense of Europe as a distant, almost mythological homeland, the Pakeha Hawaiki, which by implication suggests 'the Pacific' in its old sense of remoteness, vastness, romance and loss.

As for Pakeha visions of our South Pacific home, these are as various as the writers themselves, from Manhire's comic book history, through Ian Wedde's exhilarating image of 'Paradise', or Janette Sinclair's of 'Gondwanaland', to Marshall's rude Kiwis gathered on a beach waiting for the tsunami to come across thousands of miles of ocean from Chile, and Graeme Lay's factual recording of an island immigrant schoolgirl's difficulties coming to terms with a new life in Auckland.

A Note on Absences

An earlier version of this anthology included stories by the Samoan New Zealander, Albert Wendt, and Maori, or Maori–Pakeha, writers Patricia Grace, Keri Hulme and Witi Ihimaera. Permissions letters had gone out, and had been signed and returned. Then at the last minute, and in unison, these four asked that their stories be withdrawn. Strictly speaking they were bound by contract, and to take their stories out involved time, trouble and expense; but it was felt that authors should be held to their word by a sense of honour and propriety, not by law, and so the stories were removed. Pressed for reasons, Wendt and Grace offered none. Ihimaera suggested he was protecting Maori mana, and pointed out that he and Wendt were themselves anthologists with a special understanding of Polynesia. Hulme wrote to the publisher suggesting that there were others with 'greater expertise and experience in the matter of Polynesian literature (and New Zealand literature in general)' than the 'former scholar (with expertise on Pound I believe)', C. K. Stead. In a later note she wrote, 'unless you are aware of the extensive history of insult and attack that surrounds Karl Stead's relations with Maori and Polynesian writers, I doubt me very much that you will understand the current matter'.

Not lacking confidence in his 'expertise and experience' in the field of New Zealand letters, the 'former scholar' none-theless reviewed this 'history' as dispassionately as he was able, and could find neither insult nor attack, but only the application, to one novel by Hulme and one by Ihimaera, of the same standards of judgement applied to any work in the English language that came before him, irrespective of the race of the author. To give Maori or Pacific Island writers special exemption from all but favourable notice, which is what these four appear to want, and mostly to get, would have seemed patronizing. In 1985 I reviewed Keri Hulme's *The Bone People*. I described Hulme as 'a powerful and original literary talent' and said that this was 'abundantly clear' in the novel; but I added that what I called the author's 'imaginative complicity' in extreme violence against a child left 'a bitter aftertaste'.

In 1986 I reviewed Ihimaera's *The Matriarch*. My final paragraph reads,

> Ihimaera repeats Te Kooti's cry – 'We are all slaves in the land of Pharaoh'. It is strange coming from a man much honoured in his own country and now serving as New Zealand Consul in New York; but whatever the facts, in the mind it may be so. And if that is the case, freedom can only be won in the mind. No external power can confer it. My own view is that the kind of picking over old wounds and ancient evils that this novel represents is not the way to go about freeing the mind. The past does not have to be forgotten; but its rights and wrongs belong to those who lived them, not to us . . . Ihimaera owed it to himself to write a more considered novel – one which used the language more scrupulously. Everyone would have been better served by a more truthful image.

Prior to this I had questioned the inclusion of poems in Maori in the *Penguin Book of New Zealand Verse*, pointing out that its editors, like myself and most New Zealanders of both races, did not know the Maori language, and could not judge the poems they had included, which in translation seemed banal.

And (to complete the picture of my transgressions) in 1990 I wrote a column questioning current Government policies based on the 1840 Treaty of Waitangi, and the effects these were having, or might have, on New Zealand law.

All of these reviews and commentaries seemed to me the proper stuff of intellectual debate (would certainly be seen so in a more robust society) and I felt not the least twinge of guilt or regret at having been frank in the public forum. But I did not wish to behave defensively, or engage in profitless battles, and when the four writers withdrew their work I at once offered to resign as editor. The publishers made it clear,

however, that they did not want this; and that if I resigned
there would be no South Pacific selection in the Faber Contemporary Stories series. This would have meant in turn that
two dozen writers from around the Pacific region would have
lost the opportunity to see their work displayed on a wider
stage.

There have been many ironies, not least that of imagining
how bitterly these four would have complained if my selection had not included them; and how much more nearly it
would have matched their image of me if that had been the
case. There was also the spectacle of Witi Ihimaera protecting
Pacific values by fax from the South of France; of Keri Hulme,
whose reputation and income rest so largely upon her novel
having won the Booker Prize, asking 'Where is London? It is
not a centre, a node, for us'; and of Albert Wendt and Patricia
Grace, the one holding a Chair in a Department of English
Language and Literature, the other appearing as a female
icon in New Zealand's centennial Year of Women's Suffrage,
both unwilling or unable to explain their breach of a contract.

No doubt the intention was to cause a larger exodus, but
that did not happen. They have gone off in their little boat,
and the ship sails on. I very much regret the absences –
particularly of Hulme, whose work has a stunning directness
and force; and of Wendt, because his short stories, before his
recent two novels, *Ola* and *Black Rainbow*, which suggest
some kind of collapse of his talent, represent some of the best
in Pacific Island writing. But on the other hand, the final
selection is in many ways more interesting and less predic-
table than it would have been without this prompting. And
even the event itself is a reflection of the present state of the
Pacific, and indeed of the world, where the disappearance of
the single great power-bloc confrontation, and the conse-
quent lifting of that pressure, has led to fragmentation, and
the reassertion of older ethnic and tribal identities and
grudges.

C. K. STEAD

The Healer

MARJORIE TUÄNIKORE CROCOMBE

Mata was a witch. At least that was how Europeans translated our word 'ta'unga', which really means 'a specialist in the art of the supernatural'.

She lived by a small stream that L-shaped its way along. Her tiny house nestled under some coconut trees, and beside her cook house there were the usual mango trees, a clump of sugar cane, and a lemon tree. The creek was a useful one, for Mata's family fished there for prawns and eels. They also drank the water and bathed in it. We lived next door and we used to swim in a deep water-hole higher up the creek. Further up again, there lived another family who made similar use of the creek, but they also tethered their pigs by it.

Mata's family could not afford to install a tap. We felt superior because we had one, but now I come to think of it we were little better off with our upright tap outside our kitchen than Mata was with her creek water. The tap water originated in the same mountains as the creek, and in the rainy season both kinds became the same undrinkable chocolate brown.

'What do you expect?' Nero would say when we got periodic attacks of stomach trouble. 'We drink gallons of mud from the open intake and not to forget the shit of dear old Boss's cattle that roam around there. Maki was telling me the other day that they found some cattle bones in the water intake up there.' Then he'd amble off to write another letter of complaint to the Administration. It achieved nothing.

Mata's husband was Piri, a returned soldier with the distinction of actually having seen Egypt and the Red Sea during the First World War, when he had volunteered for service with the New Zealand forces, like many other islanders. Now

1

he could look forward every year to a free trip to town to take part in the Anzac Day parade. Piri would dress up in his long white trousers, white shirt, coat and tie, and he would pin on a couple of war medals. Then he would send his daughter to watch out for the truck.

'Papa,' she shouted as the truck veered round the corner half a mile away. 'Papa, hurry. It's coming – now it's passing Brown's place – whew it's going fast.' The driver stopped the truck with a screech of brakes and the horn beeping loudly. But there was no need for Piri to rush: he knew that the kavamani had sent the truck to get him and it would not leave without him, no matter how impatient the driver was.

There were many of his fellow ex-servicemen on the truck. Some of them old, toothless, grey-haired men. Piri immediately noticed that one or two were not on board this time.

'Where's Tua?' he shouted as the driver revved up the engine. 'In hospital,' he was told. 'Been there for six weeks now.' Piri also learned that Mani was dead, and that someone else was too old to march any more. 'But *you* look young, anyway,' said Tei. 'Must be the good bush beer that you have around this part of the island.' Piri didn't answer. He knew they were referring to his son, a notorious brewer whose name regularly appeared on the list of court convictions.

The parade was a short, sterile affair, but it could not stifle the feeling of oneness among the soldiers. The group was small and one would rub shoulders with prestigious men, both Maori and European. It rekindled in Piri an ember of glory that would help him through his other three hundred and sixty-four days of insignificance.

After a rather bedraggled march to the soldiers' memorial, several prayers, a Biblical text, and a hymn, a bugler who was long out of practice sounded a tinny Last Post. The men were dismissed. Then they went and drank cups of sweet tea and ate dry sandwiches. Soon it was all over for the Maori veterans. The truck took them home again to obscurity until the next Anzac Day service – if they lived that long. The European ex-servicemen would retire to one of their friend's homes and drink beer. It was against the law for Maoris to drink and it was on occasions like this that laws like that really hurt. Some Europeans took particular Maoris home to drink, but that only made it worse for the uninvited like Piri.

Piri shook every hand warmly as he left the truck to walk home. 'Not many old people left,' he would tell Mata later, as he struggled out of his restricting clothes. He sighed with grateful relief as he flung them on the mat and wrapped a length of pareu, a gaily coloured sarong-like material, round his waist. Then he sat down cross-legged and rolled a cigarette.

'After the service,' he said to Mata, 'we had pieces of bread with tiny bits of meat in them. Not enough to feed a hen! Got anything to eat?'

'Only this,' Mata replied, pushing a banana leaf parcel towards him. Piri's hunger vanished rapidly as he was confronted with a blob of dried-up, rubber-like octopus tentacles that had been baked in an earth oven the day before. He pulled out the smallest piece, dribbled some coconut sauce into his tin plate and dipped the meat into it. Then he swirled the octopus tentacle round, as though hoping to soften it. But it remained as hard as it had ever been and his worn-down molars refused to cope with it. Finally, in disgust, Piri threw the chewed remains of the octopus meat into the open fire and noisily drank the sauce from his plate. His wife just sat and watched.

Piri was a little sorry for Mata. He had had a very interesting day, yet his wife had never even been up to the village ever since they had been married. She lived a very withdrawn life.

Mata was known as the 'ghost maker', for she had power to call on her own special spirit 'Ka'u Mango', or 'Ka'u the Shark'. Because of this she was both feared and respected, particularly by children.

Mata, it seemed, knew everything that went on in the spirit world, but of course she kept up to date on what went on in the real world too. Keeping abreast of gossip and scandal was part of her stock in trade, and the spiritual answers usually reflected the material realities.

The screeching of wagon wheels on the sandy road and the whoa-ing of the driver soon brought Piri back to the present. 'That coming here?' Mata asked. 'Oi – Oi!' she was answered

3

from outside, as if the visitors had heard her question. 'Oi – Papa Piri e! E Mama e!'

'Oi – come!' Piri answered as he stepped out from the cook house. Then he stuck his head back inside to tell Mata who the visitors were. 'To see you, I think,' he added. A young boy was lying on a pillow in the wagon.

'Take them into the other house,' Mata called to Piri. 'I'll come in after.' Mata picked up the knife and finished prising the chestnuts out of their shells, carefully placing them on a tin plate.

Inside the separate sleeping house the leader of the party was telling Piri why they had come. She brought out a packet of tobacco from her basket and passed it to Piri. What a luxury it was for Piri to roll a cigarette with real cigarette paper. Normally he used nothing but dried banana leaves, which smelled just like those women smell who burn the rubbish by the road. Piri rolled one for Mata too, who was coming in now.

'Ae – we've come today because it is a holiday. We were hoping there wouldn't be many people here.' After a puff or two on her cigarette, she continued, 'My grandson here we took him to hospital. The doctor, a European, he tap him here; he tap him there; he listen to his chest and took a picture – aue – where was it, Mere?' She turned to her daughter trying to pick up the thread. 'Ae – ae – a picture of the chest, but he find nothing. They give us big bottle of white medicine, but he drink it all up quick – nothing happen to him. Still the boy is not well. The Maori doctor friend he say – Ae, try our own medicine at the ta'unga. Maybe she can fix him.'

Mata said nothing for a while. Nor did she examine the patient. She seemed to withdraw into herself and her eyes became glazed. Her body trembled and her mouth twitched as she fell into a trance. At last she asked Mere: 'Where is the boy's father?'

'Dead.'

'Where?'

'Makatea Island, digging phosphate.'

'He write to you? He send you things?'

'Yes, every ship from there bring something.'

4

'You write back?'

There was silence. The mother wept, blowing her nose. Mata said no more. The spluttering of the candlenut lamp cast eerie shadows in the house and the smell of the nut was very strong. The sick boy wanted so much to cough, but he was too scared to break the silence. Mata stared towards the entrance of the house as if she was willing something to enter. Piri, the two women, and the sick boy looked towards the door, wondering. It was getting late now. Then the silence was suddenly broken by a distant voice that immediately stopped the boy's weeping. The voice came from the direction of Mata.

'E Mere e! Can you hear? You know who it is – don't you? Listen carefully to me. Don't waste time weeping. My sweat – I wasted it in the mines working – to earn money for the European house you wanted. I sent the money – the plates – the glasses – the linen – and – and perfume – yet you lie to me – I didn't know you lie so much. My friend had a letter – from his wife. She say who you live with – that news made me angry. My gang was working that night – I fell from the top – top of the cliff. And I want – want my son – to – aaaah!'

'Aue, aue,' wept the mother of the sick child. 'It's true, it's true what you say.'

Mata did not move any more. She sat as if in a deep sleep. Then her eyes twitched and slowly opened. Still, no one spoke. When she was fully awake she said: 'I make some medicine for him to drink.' Piri got up and went outside to gather the stalk of the red sugar cane, a few leaves of a plant which grew by the creek, and some green guava leaves. Then Mata said: 'I think your son has cried for his father – he wants to die like his father. He doesn't like his new father. Ask him at home if that is true. You and he can help each other sort out what to do,' advised Mata. 'Then come again next week.'

On the way home, the young boy, Tei, thought about Mata's words. Indeed he had cried for his father to come and take him away. For he hated to see the new man around the place who would not even help his mother in the tomato plot, who wouldn't even cut the grass around the place. All he seemed to do was to get drunk on the weekends and sleep off the effects of his three-day bout for the rest of the week. Once he had thrashed Tei for answering back, and that day Tei had decided to die like his father. It had been his secret until that day but, as Mata knew, it was a common 'way out' among her people.

'Mamma,' he whispered to his mother after everyone had gone to bed. 'I did call Papa to come and get me. I wanted to die very much.'

'Why?'

Tei told his mother the secret. As his mother held him in the dark Tei felt for the first time that maybe he did not want to die after all. And Mere made up her mind to send away Epi, her lover. When she told him to leave the house there was a tremendous row, which attracted the attention of the neighbours.

'It's taken a long time,' one said. 'Why she kept such a good-for-nothing for so long I don't know. And now all of a sudden she gets rid of him.'

'It's because they went to see the ta'unga.'

'Is that so?'

'Oh, you and your tupapaku story. That's all you women think of.'

'What do you know about such things anyway? You who were born yesterday.'

When Mere returned to the ta'unga the following week, Mere's husband spoke to her once more through the medium of Mata, but this time he was pleased. 'Meitaki,' he said, 'Tei should stay with you.' And Mata added, 'Carry on taking the medicine I made for him, but no need to come back and see me.'

Mata's reputation as a healer was again confirmed, and she had a long line of visitors in the afternoons. She did not exploit her clients. Some brought her gifts of food, tobacco, and occasionally money. The police ignored her activities. The Maori policemen probably secretly believed in her powers. Even the Church ignored her. Many churchmen brought their patients there as a last resort. After many futile visits to the hospital, they came to try Mata's kind of healing.

One night my sister fell off her bicycle after she had been packing oranges for the monthly ship that called at the island.

'Get the benzine lamp,' ordered my mother. No other lamp would do, for the brighter the light, the less likely were we to run into a ghost on our way to Mata's home.

Mata did not need to go into a trance for such a simple diagnosis. 'It's the arapo,' she told us without hesitation. 'Look at the moon, it waxes full, and on such a night the chief Tepera walks. He comes down along the boundary of Brown's property and the Seventh Day Adventist compound. That's the way he always goes. Tonight he was chasing a slave who escaped out to the sea. He never catches him though, so he is awakened to repeat the performance every night like this for ever.'

'Why did Alice get hurt?'

'He doesn't mean to hurt anyone, but your daughter happened to come along when the chief was passing. She brushed against him, that's all. Lucky though she didn't run head-on into him or we would have had bad news for you tonight.'

Mata's clients continued to come and go. We knew most of the visitors there, because our mother was very friendly with Mata and she got the more personal details from her. Throughout the years Mata's reputation grew and she attracted many clients. Then, suddenly and unexpectedly, came her tragic downfall.

There was a visitor from the outer islands staying with Mata and Piri. One day, he went fishing in the lagoon. He did not return. The news spread through the village and the men went out to search for him up and down the lagoon. But they could not find him. Mata sought him by spiritual means without success. On the third day, Piri found Kati's body wedged in a rock in the harbour. Piri and his son wrapped the body up in a mat and they floated it home along the edge of the lagoon. Somehow it was a familiar sight – for Piri was always dragging something home: a piece of log he found on the beach, a dry coconut leaf for his fire, or a bundle of octopus on a rusty wire with its tentacles streaming behind. Now he returned with Kati, the epileptic, who had gone out fishing three days before on an equally beautiful morning.

'What's happened to Mata?' someone asked, as a group of curious helpers followed the bundle to Piri's home. 'Why she not tell Piri where to find Kati three days ago?'

'E'aa – what did you say?'

'You know, Ka'u the Shark. He knows everything.' Soon they reached Piri's place. He untied the rope from the mat and threw it into the canoe that had been drawn up on the beach. Silently the men stepped into the water and took each corner of the mat bundle. They heaved it up and walked up the beach to where some other men had already dug a grave.

'Didn't you send for the pastor?' asked Timi.

'He's inside with Mata.'

'I'll get him now,' said Piri, grateful for a chance to get away for a moment.

Soon the pastor came out, followed by Mata and Piri. Mata's hair was dishevelled, her eyes were tired. For the last three evenings she had tried to call upon Ka'u the Shark to let her know where Kati's body was. But Piri had found him merely by accident, maybe helped by his knowledge of the currents in the lagoon and harbour. Kati's death was a defeat for Mata and everyone knew it.

The pastor conducted a short ceremony. There was no wailing. No pigs were killed. Nobody bothered to perform more than the bare necessities for the underprivileged stranger.

From then on fewer wagons drew up outside Piri's house. Even we children heard the news that Mata had lost her power. We were now a little less afraid to pass her house at night.

Mata died alone one day, when Piri was out fishing in the lagoon. Ka'u, their son, who had been named after Ka'u the Shark, migrated to New Zealand to seek a new life. Piri was now too old to attend the Anzac Day parade. His daughter got married and moved to another village. Then some distant relation took pity on Piri and invited him to come and live in another village.

At long last the owner of the land on which Piri had been living was able to take it back with an easy conscience. Often he had been tempted to kick Piri and Mata off, for they never supplied their share of food gifts, even when requested, but he always feared Mata's supernatural retaliation. Now she was no more.

Piri's former home was burned to the ground and the site was ploughed up and planted with sweet potatoes. Only Kati's grave reminded us of the spot where the village healer had lived and plied her trade.

Farvel

YVONNE DU FRESNE

You know, all today they have been here. In my house. A door
opens by itself. A hand raps on the window glass like the crack
of winter ice breaking up in the old country. A hand touches
my shoulder and I turn ready to hear somebody say,

'Use the new jam for lunch. It has set so *nice*!' There is
nobody there.

Somebody touches my hair, absentmindedly, as they used
to, gazing out of the windows, looking at the sky, at the land.
Our land. It speaks, you know. Or a voice sings. Suddenly.
And you must listen, every sense alert.

Who touched my hair?

The door shut with no wind to do that.

The house is full of them. I hear tag-ends of words, laughter.
Then a wind pounces on the garden, the trees. Grass, leaves,
shiver, ripple with silver, with laughter, with calling voices.

'Hoy!' I call to them in Danish, 'you come now to your nice
lunch!' As if they *need* lunch, those ones. They have no desire
for this world's food any more. They are with God now.

Then I hear that one living voice from a month ago. Calling
from her farmhouse drive, with its trees leaning from a lifetime
of the north-westerlies. She as bent as her trees, out on the
Tainui Line.

'Farvel, mit eget kaere barn!'

'Farewell, my own darling child!'

I turn in the road. I know that cry. I call, with a laugh, you
know?

'Nej – nej. You are not saying farewell to me forever. No
death for you yet!'

But she is not laughing. Again comes that cry, bleak as the
wind –

'Farvel, mit eget kaere barn!'

And then she looks at my face. She is learning it all over
again. She is leaving us. Soon. She will know the time. She is
warning me.

'Nej!' I call. 'Not yet.'

I look at her face, not just her face, but all the faces that one
by one have gone. I see her stand, out in the road, watching
me as if she can never have enough of looking. Not just my
face, all our faces. We look the same, you see. So I do my
part. I wave. I shout.

'Farvel! Tante Helga Westergaard, you are *great*!'

She knows. She breaks into a broad smile and waves. I go,
but the figure left behind on that road never moves, never
blinks its sea-pale eyes from fear that they miss one last, small
glance.

She is being drawn back into that other country. From the
first breath I took, I heard its music; the men and women
singing. Remembering too, you understand, the thin soil, the
howling winter weather. But, being so young, I only thought
of that great multitude of our left-behind people, their faces
shining with love, singing in a world filled with light. And
that was Europe to me. That was my Denmark. There were
the singers, and the sacred dancers, moving rank on slow
rank. And now they come to claim her, those dancers, and
she goes to meet them, her hands outflung in greeting, so
tall, walking so softly.

The wind still blows.

'Ah,' I say to the voices in the rooms, to the laughter in the
trees, in the sky, 'you be quiet now. I have to think. I have to
be with her.'

Our language was spoken in a rapid, cold stream, like the
water rushing in its courses over the moors, and gleaming so
still in the marshes where we lived in Jutland. I was always
part of a group, a frieze of women, very tall, in the long grass
of a paddock, or looking out of a window. Always standing,
once or twice in the busy day, one hand on the hip, the other
used to help the meaning along – coming delicately down to
rest on certain words that mattered. They talked as they

danced, the movements spare and ceremonial, leaving things to be understood. Taking in, breathing in, the messages of the land and sky of the Manawatu. I learned the spoken words, and with my skin, my eyes, my senses, endlessly took in the signs, the changing light of sun and colour, and water, the line of hills and plains, the movement of birds. The signs were the magic signs learned by our people long ago in Denmark. They had the power, my Bedstemoder said, to see them, to use them in the new lands. They knew the secrets of food-growing, the places to find water, how to build shelter, and the pattern of the seasons. We learned all that so that our bodies and our spirits could grow, side by side. And they had the power to change themselves into the shapes of birds – the swan, the wild geese, the eagle, the falcon.

The first people here, said my Bedstemoder, had the same powers. Here it was that the sea birds and the ghost-herons became the souls of the people who had died. Who journeyed back to their home, to the sun at their death, as we do.

When I first saw those people, the Maoris, at the Recreation Ground in a huge gathering, long ago, I knew she spoke the truth. There they *were*, standing under the soft thunder of the macrocarpas. They wore the long mantles, and the birds' feathers, sweeping back in their hair; half men, half birds. As certain men and women in Denmark changed to swans, eagles, so did they. So I always saw that race and ours, able to read the signs, to haunt the sky on wings, an irresistible sweep of wings; sky-walkers.

Tante Helga is loosening the cord. Coming into my ears is a voice.

'My child, I need Thee.'

So I go and put on a more suitable dress and wash my face, making myself neat for Tante Helga. I brush my hair in front of the mirror, not looking into it, and then I do. I see the face of an ageing woman; the lines, the bones of my people. They have stamped me with their image forever. But also on it, the squint-lines of our summers here; the ridges and hollows left by the sun and dust of the new country, *my* country.

I go to the verandah and lean over. The sun beats down. The river is shrunken, its black banks glitter with mica that my Bedstemoder said was treasure, dragonfire, here as in Denmark.

Then, like a sigh, up the drying river bed flies a heron, that one that lives on the little island. A grey heron, but today changed in the flat light to black paper, a soul, starting its journey to the sea. That is my sign. So I walk out into the beating sun, to the fence that borders the paddock, that reaches to the river.

I stand and look at the land. The ghost-heron has vanished. And I *cannot* stop my grief, my tears that turn down my wind-furrowed face. I look at our land, and the river, and I cannot make sense of it, or hear Tante Helga's voice. All I can remember are her cheek bones, the blue northern eyes of our lost people. I weep like a little child. Out of my shameful gaping mouth I call,

'Tante Helga. Tante! We are lost forever.'

And her voice comes, deep in my ear, loosening the cord, but still gossiping on, as she did, one summer afternoon, on the lawn behind me.

'There your Bedstemoder, Abild Westergaard, lay on the second day of her death, in her room, in this house. And your Moder and I peeped out of the kitchen window into the farmyard and saw the Maoris, and she said,

'"Helga, they are here."'

'And they were. Some sitting, some standing, and the Chief standing looking out over the land. They were quite still; warfalcons at rest.

'Your Mother gripped my hand, so *tight*.

'"They are from the pa," she whispered, "where Moder went. She loved them all. Come now."'

'I stood in front of the Chief, the one with the long feather sweeping back from his head. We looked at each other. I greeted him in Danish, he greeted me in Maori. Then we turned and stood with his people, our neighbours. We touched their faces, in their way of greeting, and we stood here. Our hair blew about, but we stood so still with them, helping Abild Westergaard begin her journey to sun-fire. It was a great honour they did us that day.'

The old lilting voice dies away to a murmur, to silence, in my mind.

13

Who are left now? They and us, changed a little, but still knowing who we are. Using our old knowledge, and our new.

I look over the paddocks at my neighbour, Rangi Katene. Her house looks at me through the trees. I often stand in them in their circle of ancient trunks, and the wind hisses through their leaves and combs the grass at my feet. Sacred trees. Their roots reach down to underground rivers, dragon-lairs. The house and Rangi know those messages from the dark.

And now, you know something strange? The wind has dropped. There is a golden light, that light when the sun is spent, when the dust motes turn to golden bees in the air. Every grass blade in the parched earth you can see, golden wires. The head-dresses those ancient dancers wore in the Jutland festival, they were made like wheat-ears, red-gold, quivering over their still faces. Faces that knew everying. Like my Tante Helga. Somehow, the power of the Old Religion slipped into the New Religion in Jutland. God and the Old Magic mixed together. I have worked out that truth, by myself.

The golden bees of the sun swarm over the paddocks. It seems to me not a trick of light, but a gift from God that I see those Maoris and Danes and English, now clear, now blur-red, standing facing their lands. My house, like Rangi's, reaches its roots down to the heart of this land. Our roots are the same. We have our people, living and dead, round us forever.

Canoe, Viking ship, foam-necked, set out together on the last journey north, over the sea-roads to world's-end.

So I let go of the fence post I am gripping, scrub my face dry with a knuckled fist, and lift my eyes to be blinded by the light that welcomes Helga Westegaard at the end of her journey.

Oh, my brothers and sisters, see how our hands join together as we farewell our great Dead.

Farvel. Farvel.

Village, Church, and School

VINCENT ERI

The harsh rustle of the sago palms contrasted sharply with the slow gentle swaying of the coconut palms.

In the village below, clouds of dirty brown dust danced in and out among the forest of house-posts. The wind forced itself through the cracks in the floor and the holes in the walls. The dust clouds twisted and turned forming weird and wonderful shapes.

A fence five foot tall encircled the entire village. It was made of long bamboo tubes placed horizontally on top of each other. They were kept in place by saplings pegged into the ground. This fence had been erected on the orders of the government officers who said that pigs must be kept away from the village.

On the windward side of the village, outside the fence, stood a lone building. It stood in a north-south direction. The entrance was on the north side. Each wall had a blackboard nailed to it, the largest being on the south wall. There were pictures of Biblical stories, and an ABC chart that depicted many objects the children had never seen. A hungry cockroach had eaten clean through the first picture, which the teacher called 'Apple'. Three portraits looked down on the children: King George VI, Archbishop De Boismenu of Yule Island, and St Thérèse, the patron saint of the school.

No partitions separated one class-room from another. Everybody squatted crosslegged on the palm-wood floor.

The school grounds were always wet. The owners had allowed this land to be used for a school because it wasn't much good for building a house. Each flood scoured the area of food wrappings, human and animal excrement, and pieces of paper. During the day the children deposited more. At night the adults added to the collection.

Huge breadfruit trees towered above, cutting out much of the sunlight. The undergrowth around the class-room was so thick that the building was not visible from any direction, not even from the village. Swarms of mosquitoes infested the dark shadows and bothered the children.

There were no toilets. Why bother to build to house our waste? That is what the villagers would say to the medical orderlies who complained. The villagers agreed that it was necessary to build 'small houses' for the government officers and the white missionaries. Their beautiful white skins looked too delicate to be allowed to use the bush. The teachers and students used the bush. So did all the village people. The teachers themselves did not believe in the story of the worms that made people sick. Nobody had seen these worms of destruction. The bush was kept clean by the pigs, who grew fat on it and trailed their bellies on the ground.

Five days a week the children strained their lungs and vocal cords singing their alphabets and numerals. The teachers did not seem to be bothered by the noise. The parents heard their children's voices when they passed by on their way to the garden. To them it was evidence that their children were learning – though it seemed to have little significance for them *what* their children were learning.

There was a new boy in the preparatory class. He had been in the school for a week. He had recently been transferred from the Protestant school, run by the London Missionary Society, to the Catholic school.

In the Daily Attendance Register his name was recorded as Hoiri Sevese. His father, Sevese Ovou, was a deacon in the LMS Church. Hoiri was about seven years old.

Hoiri had a bulging stomach, quite out of proportion to the size of his legs. It was surprising that he could see where he placed his feet when he was walking. The other children nicknamed him 'taubada', which literally means 'big man'. Originally it had been a term of respect for all white people living in the district, but by the late nineteen sixties it had become more of a mockery.

Hoiri didn't look as if he was going to inherit the towering build of his father. He was short and stalky and some people commented that he was growing sideways.

Hoiri was shy in his new surroundings. Though he was familiar enough with the children in his class, who had been his playmates for years in the village, the school work was different and even the prayers were said differently in the new school. But gradually he picked up most of the tricks of his new class. He learned, for example, that by saying 'May I leave the room' he could have as many recesses as he liked.

Right now he was anxious to leave the room. He had hidden a stick of sago in a secret place between the bearers under the palm flooring, and was worried whether another child might have discovered it. All the children kept the remains of their breakfast in such secret places to be eaten later, and this made it necessary to 'leave the room' as often as possible. Noticing that many of his friends were 'leaving the room', Hoiri wanted to follow, but lacked the courage to utter the password. Then, without warning, the boy nearest to him popped up like a cork out of water.

'Please, teacher, may Hoiri leave the room?' he shouted at the top of his voice. What could the teacher do when four or five other such requests had come from various quarters of the class. Without even looking, he gave his consent.

Hoiri felt greatly indebted to his courageous friend. If his sago was still there his friend must have some of it. In a flash he had disappeared under the building.

One or two pigs raised themselves from their siesta and eyed him askance. Others rubbed their mud-covered bodies furiously against the posts. The children in the school had got used to the countless mild earthquakes every day.

Hoiri searched for his sago in vain. Someone had 'left the room' earlier, and had discovered the hiding place. He fought to hold back his tears. Lunch was still an hour or so away. Concentration was more difficult on an empty stomach. For the first time he questioned his reason for being in school. He had no clear idea about this, but felt vaguely that he wanted to learn the white man's language. Not because he wanted to get a well-paid job – for there weren't any such jobs for Papuans and New Guineans to fill, but because the ability of conversing with the white people would earn him a respected position in the eyes of the community.

Hoiri wondered whether he would find anything to eat at his aunt's house. Two weeks ago things had been very different. Then his mother was alive and even when she went fishing or gardening she had always left some cooked food ready for him. But now Hoiri wasn't too eager to clear the steps of the class-room when the last phrase of the prayer had left his lips.

'Aren't you going to kneel down, Hoiri? We are all waiting for you.' Faintly the teacher's voice penetrated his brain. Hoiri had been so absorbed in his thoughts that he hadn't been aware of the silence that had fallen upon the building.

Hoiri had not become used to the Catholic way of kneeling for prayers and of making the sign of the cross. In his old school the teacher spoke the prayer alone, everyone else stood with their heads bowed and their eyes closed. Here they all recited the prayer together with the teacher. Hoiri was surprised that in the Catholic school the same Father, Son, and Holy Ghost were mentioned in the prayers. Why was there so much antagonism in his village between the followers of the two missions? Whatever the arguments were about, the London Missionary Society seemed to be in the stronger position. They had been the first to establish themselves in the village. In fact Hoiri's grandfather had been a very small boy when the Reverend James Chalmers first landed on the beach of Moveave.

Hoiri made his way into the village under the cloudless sky. The sun made the shadows of the houses darker than they really were. Among the disorderly rows of houses, the elavo with their huge pointed gables towered impressively. Even though Moveave was one of the largest villages in the Papuan Gulf it looked fairly deserted now. A few women were gossiping and weaving mats under the houses. Others were patching holes in their fishing nets, or picking lice from each other's hair.

Out in the open the glare from the sandy soil was hard on the eyes. The air was heavy with the unpleasant smell of scorched earth. Hoiri wished he was taller than three foot six. He cursed the people who did not teach their children and their dogs to do their business outside the village fence.

Bands of ill-fed dogs roamed the streets. They howled

miserably in the hope that some kindhearted people might give them some titbits to eat. They appeared to have changed the usual order of nature: the bones of their ribs appeared to grow outside their skins.

Hoiri could tell that his aunt had gone out with the other inhabitants of the house. The only step to the house had been pushed aside so that wandering dogs could not enter uninvited. Hopefully Hoiri searched the food rack above the fireplace. Over the years the smoke of cooking fires had coloured the entire room a dirty brown. For a minute he couldn't see anything while his eyes adjusted themselves to the dark.

'Have you found anything yet?' The voice belonged to Hoiri's cousin Meraveka, who went to the LMS school. 'I've got a long stick of sago that will be more than enough for both of us.' Hoiri reappeared from the darkness of the house holding a whole roasted breadfruit and half a dried coconut – still in its shell.

The cousins exchanged food as they walked along together. The oil from the dry coconut made it easier to swallow the rubbery sago. The breadfruit was of the Samoan variety which had been introduced by early South Sea missionaries.

'How do you like the Catholic School?' Meraveka was anxious to find out what new knowledge his cousin was learning. 'I am not as happy as when we were at school together. I can't understand why my parents did not take you to stay with us when your mother died. Is it not customary for the father's close relatives to take care of the children when the mother dies? But look what happened. They let your aunt Anna take you with your brother and sister into their house. And now she made you become a Catholic.'

Hoiri was troubled by his cousin's talk. He knew that he himself had nothing to do with the state of affairs. His father hadn't explained anything to him either. In fact he had mysteriously disappeared soon after his mother's burial and Hoiri did not know where he was or what he was doing.

'It was my father who made the decision,' Hoiri managed to say. 'I had no choice but to go and live with Aunt Anna. She said that if I didn't go to the Catholic school, she wouldn't give me a rami to wear. I chose to keep myself covered, rather than exposing myself to all the girls.'

A long silence followed. Meraveka felt he shouldn't have asked in the first place.

'What sorts of things are you learning at the new school?'

'Oh, the usual A, B, Cs and 1, 2, 3s. The main difference is that the teachers speak to us in English most of the time.'

'I would like to learn that language too. I envy the village constable, the councillors, and medical orderly, who can speak to the government officers when they come to our village. The Samoan pastors in our school teach us well, but I don't like the way they speak to us in Toaripi. They don't even speak it properly.'

Hoiri felt elevated. He was learning something his cousin wanted to know. What is more, he told his cousin that in the Catholic school the children were not forced to make sago for their teachers, a practice that was common in the LMS school and a task that took up the best part of the day. Hoiri had often heard his father say to the 'Ekalesia' that the practice was undesirable but absolutely necessary. 'These Samoans,' he would say, 'have come a long way to bring the Word of God to us. They have no land here where they could make their gardens. It is our responsibility to see that they have enough to eat.'

'I wish I could come to the same school as you,' Meraveka said, almost to himself. Hoiri felt sorry for him. He knew what these sago expeditions were like and he knew the punishment for shirking them: most boys realized that it was wiser to go on the tedious sago expeditions than to face the embarrassment of being caned naked in front of the girls.

Together the cousins forded the creek that was the only outlet in the south of the village to the large waterways. The tide was low and the water was up to their thighs.

The cool smell of mud was a relief to their nostrils. Though the water was full of animal and human excreta, the two boys were not bothered in the least. They had been swimming in that same creek ever since they had been able to float.

Long parallel trenches on the mud marked the mooring places of the canoes. Now only a few unserviceable canoes were left lying around. But on a Sabbath day or on Friday –

the 'Government Day' – the same creek would be jammed with canoes.

'Did you notice that government officers don't usually come to our village at low tide?' Hoiri remarked. 'I suppose that with all this floating around they are afraid of letting the water touch their clean white feet.'

'I have never seen them brave the water in this creek,' Meraveka added support. 'Whenever they come their canoes are laden with so many patrol boxes, cartons of goods, and furniture – you would think they'd come to stay for months. With that kind of load at low tides the canoe can't get any-where near the normal landing places. So the men of our village have to carry them like small children!'

When they had crossed to the other side they could hear the laughter and chattering of other boys not far away. It was usual at this time of day for the boys to collect coconuts and for the girls to cut wood and fill the water pots ready for their parents' return.

The boys were joking. They talked freely about sex. Not that they had personal experience. But they had heard it discussed often by their elders and there was nothing myster-ious about what went on between a boy and a girl in a lonely garden. They knew which of the partners gets a dirty back.

Soon boys disappeared in the thick undergrowth, each heading for his family's coconut grove. Hoiri and Meraveka made haste, because they knew that they had to swim across the same creek nearer to its junction with a larger waterway, and crocodiles had been known to venture right up to the village with the incoming tide.

By the time the sun was level with the tree tops the boys had their bundles of nuts neatly tied up. They suspended the load on a stick between the two of them and marched off to the bank of the creek to await the arrival of some fishing canoes. They noticed the white bubbles in the water and knew that some canoes must already have gone past. 'Can you hear the tui calling? It is announcing the turn of the tide,' Meraveka said. 'Many more canoes should be here any minute.'

Soon a large canoe full of women and girls swung into view from the bend in the creek. Their chattering was out of step to the rhythm of the paddles. Already the two boys could recognize one or two faces in the canoe. They all belonged to the boys' fathers' clan, the Operoro. Therefore they regarded all the girls as their sisters and all the women as their mothers.

That night the full moon was out. It was still a period of mourning so the children did not boo and cheer. After the evening meal, they sat and told stories to each other in between the rows of houses. It was a special night. Boys and girls had to keep strictly separate. Mothers warned their sons and elder sisters warned their brothers. On no account were they to play with girls. They were told that grown-up girls and women menstruated at this time. The pale yellow circle round the moon was the sign. Should a girl's grass skirt touch any part of a boy's head, his growth would be stunted.

Hoiri didn't feel he should play and have fun. It would be unfair to his mother. Instead he sat near his aunt Anna listening to her mumbling to herself. She complained of the extra responsibility thrust on her shoulders by the untimely death of her elder sister. Not that she minded looking after the children – but what stupidity to terminate one's life when one has years of useful life still in one's body? Anna cursed the 'mesiri' men, the sorcerers. She couldn't think of one good reason why they had taken her sister's life.

'Who is "they"?' asked Hoiri, who had picked up Aunt Anna's last remark.

'Oh, some people are never satisfied with their lot,' his aunt answered, not wishing to go into too much detail. 'They've got to kill. I do not know what they get out of taking other people's lives. You find that these people are friendly to you, but that is only the surface.'

'But who are these people?' Hoiri interrupted, not put off easily. 'How can one tell they are preparing the deadly mixture?'

Anna realized it was useless to avoid the subject. Hoiri had set his mind on knowing the truth.

'There are some men well-known in this village. It is they who carry out the ground work. They collect the dirt of the person who is to die. Sometimes they cut off a piece from the person's dress. Fresh clean ginger is used. They make sure

22

that their own dirt doesn't get on the ginger or else they are as liable to die. Then they pass these things on to the experts, who are scattered in the villages of the Toaripi coast, or take them to far away villages on the Moiripi coast. These experts do the rest.'

'Have these experts any means of knowing who their victims are?'

Anna explained that they do. When the mixture has been kept in a bamboo tube over a fireplace for some time, the apparition of the victim appears. The bamboo rolls about the floor when the victim is critically ill and writhes about desperately trying to hang on to his life. The sorcerers have been known to throw the mixture away, when they felt sympathetic towards the victim.

Usually the victim doesn't know for sure. He feels unwell. When he goes fishing, the fish he catches fall back into the water as he is about to land them in his canoe. Some of his property disappears mysteriously. Sometimes it is his close relatives' things that disappear.

As his aunt talked, Hoiri remembered an incident that took place when he and his parents were gardening up the river shortly before his mother's death. That day the half-inch-thick cane vine that secured their canoe to the nearest coconut tree snapped and the canoe was dragged into the muddy waters of the Taure river and sank. More strange, the loose floor-boards, which one would have expected to remain floating on top of the water, submerged with the canoe.

Hoiri cursed his father. Why hadn't he noted this and acted quickly and wisely? If he had given his mother the correct juice of herbs, barks, and roots to drink, they might have counteracted the force of sorcery. But maybe his being a deacon of the LMS Church prevented him from taking such traditional measures.

During the third week of mourning, Sevese Ovou, Hoiri's father, suddenly walked into his sister-in-law's house. He looked a different man. His clothes were black; a scraggy beard covered his face. He looked miserable. Obviously he had not been eating much.

Hoiri had a lot of things on his mind that he wanted to clear up with his father. But his aunt would not let him bother his father yet. He had to eat first.

In the end Hoiri burst straight out with the question: 'Did someone really cause my mother's death?' His father looked surprised and uneasy. His son should not have been told this, at least not at his age. He made Hoiri tell him all he already knew about this matter. When he realized how much Hoiri had already been told and how eager he was to know everything he reluctantly agreed to pursue the subject.

'When your mother died, her body was buried. Her spirit did not leave us. She has been visiting the places where she went fishing and gardening. Every evening, as the sun sets behind the tree tops, she changes to her human form and weeps for us. It is at one of these times that we the living can find out from the dead the cause of their death.'

'So that's why you have been away for two weeks?' Hoiri asked. And he now recalled that ever since his mother had died a separate food dish had been set aside in a special room at every meal time. His father now confirmed that this food was for his mother's spirit.

'And did you see her after all?' Hoiri asked again, most anxious for his father to continue.

'You see, son,' his father explained, 'I was facing the setting sun near our cemetery, alone. I felt the back of my neck become cold, all of a sudden. The cicadas seemed to screech louder than ever. Night was already falling and now here and there were real pockets of darkness where a tall tree obscured the quickly fading sunlight. I found it difficult to focus my eyes on any one object. Images became blurred. Trees which had been victims of grass fires held out their massive black arms as if to strike. I felt chilly though there wasn't a breath of wind. Then my feet became weak. There was a thumping in my chest. A nearby tree seemed to bend down towards me. My legs gave way and everything became blank for a moment. Then your mother's familiar voice came to my ears.'

In a low voice Sevese Ovou told his son the cause of his mother's death. He also mentioned the names of the 'mesiri' men who were involved. He ended on a note of warning to his son to keep well away from the evil men.

Hoiri also learned from his father that his mother's spirit would still be with them until the day a feast was made to forget her. It was vitally important that this feast to release her be not delayed any longer than necessary. The earlier she arrived in the place of the dead the better for her. Besides it was not fair to keep the whole village in a state of mourning. They must be freed to beat the drum again. The children too must be freed to cheer and laugh again at nights, the men must be allowed to shave their beards, and the women to take off their black grass skirts and black armbands.

The great day came at last. Smoke from numerous cooking fires made the village look as if it was on fire. It was a day of many activities. The whole village was awakened after three Sundays of inactivity.

The squealing of pigs being slaughtered rang from one end of the village to the other. The long-silenced drums boomed. Their thunderous notes were carried high above the tops of the sago palms. The nearby villages of Heatoare and Savaiviri were warned of the feast.

The women and girls had put on their best grass skirts. Only the close relatives of the dead woman were not yet allowed to dress in bright colours.

By late afternoon all the food had been assembled. School-children had depleted the meagre supply of chalk in their class-rooms so that their mothers could mark their pots.

At a signal from Hoiri's uncle the crowd settled down. The food was already placed into heaps, one for each clan. With a young coconut shoot in hand, the uncle went from heap to heap naming the clans for whom the food was intended.

By night-time all the food had been eaten or removed. From now on, any reference to Hoiri's mother would be made in the past tense.

Hoiri was sad to think that his dear mother's spirit was to be leaving for ever early next morning. Once she had passed the villages in which people had known her during her lifetime, her body and spirit would be reunited. Hoiri was comforted by the knowledge that his mother lacked nothing to enable her to make her trip comfortably. His father had provided her with everything at the funeral. Before she was lowered into her grave she had been given a string bag full of roasted balls of sago and coconuts, a lamp, and a knife to defend herself with. The more Hoiri thought about the dangers that lay in wait for her in this journey the more he wished he could accompany her.

From his father he had learned about the cunning ferrymen and dishonest guest-house proprietors she was likely to meet on her way, who were only too ready to deceive and rob the unwary. But if she survived the journey, she would shed her dark skin and become a European. She would be in a land of plenty and one day she would send gifts to them.

From then on Hoiri kept trying to visualize this land of plenty his mother had gone to. Did she ever arrive there? And if she did, had she forgotten to send the goods to the loved ones she had left behind? Or were they intercepted before they reached their rightful owners? One day, he was sure, she would send these gifts.

The Headmistress's Story

JANET FRAME

You may be interested (she said) in the effect which a literary upbringing may have upon death and bereavement.

My first personal experience of human death happened when I was twelve years old and my sister, four years older and apparently in good health, died suddenly, giving me the opportunity to take part without restraint in the ritual of a 'death in the family', and at the same time to learn of the loneliness of a permanent absence in the family. During the weeks following the death the word 'loss' was used in letters of sympathy and in speech and I learned the heart-distinguishing difference between this loss and those repor-ted in the advertisement columns of the newspaper under Lost and Found, which presupposed an eventual finding if one searched far and wide enough. There was an element of searching in the passive waiting for my sister to reappear and there was also a certain kind of finding which could never have been the result of a newspaper advertisement for her life. At night I listened and listened until I learned that there was nothing to listen for, that what I hoped to hear had been receding farther into soundlessness.

This death gave me and my two sisters a feeling of import-ance, of newness and goodness. We bathed and were bap-tized in everyone's sympathy. We acquired the prestige of being in a family where someone had 'died young', a 'blossom plucked before her time', a life full of promise 'cut off tragically'. These clichés guarded the entrance to the lit-erary nature of my sister's death. In the midst of the con-fusion of loss and grief and change of status (my sister was raised from a laughing devil who could lie and cheat, torture with pinches and back thumps, to a heavenly angel who could have harmed no one), of departures without return, I took the path of escape already well worn in my life – the path to the literary death, my swift transport being a poetry anthology, *Mount Helicon*, required reading for that year at High School.

I discovered that by reading the poems I could put my dead sister where she belonged, that is, wherever I and the poets chose to put her, that I need not find words for her death, as others had found the words for me, to feed and expand my rather thin dull grief to an impressive maturity. Three poems spoke so directly to me that I was convinced they had been written for me and I was filled with admiration for the poets who knew yet could never have known my life. Browning's *Evelyn Hope* made an immediate statement of fact.

> *Beautiful Evelyn Hope is dead!*
> *Sit and watch by her side an hour.*
> *That was her bookshelf, this her bed;*
> *She plucked that piece of geranium flower,*
> *Beginning to die too, in the glass . . .*

One line of the poem gave her exact age: 'Sixteen years old when she died!'

Although the name and the setting had been changed it was clear that the poet knew every detail, and I felt that my sister would have relished the imaginative generosity which gave her a bed of her own to sleep in when she had always shared, a bookshelf of her own in a house where there was one bookshelf known by its definite article, *the* bookshelf, while the piece of geranium in the glass by her bed would have appealed to her as a romantic touch, for we knew and loved geraniums with their confident pose, their energy of being and their strong pure scent and colour. Not all the poem was devoted to my sister. There were references to the writer.

> *I have lived, I shall say, so much since then,*
> *Given up myself so many times, . . .*
> *Ransacked the ages, spoiled the climes . . .*

I had learned that 'giving up oneself' and 'surrendering' were not always confined to criminals and police, bandits and sheriffs, the sensitive way in which the teacher hurried over passages about 'surrendering' and 'giving up oneself' having given me a clue to the meaning. Again, my sister would have rejoiced to know that after her furtive reading of *True Confessions* and *True Romances* and the brief heartthrobs caused by the high school boys, she had at last been given a bounty of love with one who had 'ransacked the ages, spoiled the climes'.

In the next poem, Poe's *Annabel Lee*, although the name and the setting were changed it was again clear that the poet knew intimately our small seaside town where the roar and the hush of the sea sounded day and night in our ears, and it needed little adjustment of imagination, which is no use unless it is adjustable, to think of our town as the poet described it, 'a kingdom by the sea'.

> *It was many and many a year ago,*
> *In a kingdom by the sea,*
> *That a maiden there lived whom you may know*
> *By the name of Annabel Lee.*

Other lines revealed the truth of our lives. 'The angels, not half so happy in heaven,/Went envying her and me –'
Yes, I thought, that might have been so.
The mysterious reference to a 'highborn kinsman' who

> *. . . shut her up in a sepulchre*
> *In her tomb by the sounding sea*

would have appealed, I knew, to my sister's interest in the supernatural, while the 'many and many a year ago' brought to recent grief the balm of infinite distance.

With death and burial having been taken care of by the obliging poets I was able to use the incomparable facilities for grief and mourning given by Walt Whitman in the extract from *Leaves of Grass*,

*Once, Paumanok, when the lilac-scent was in the air and
the fifth-month grass was growing . . .*

I relived through the mockingbird my loss and mourning,
from the day when the bird 'crouched not upon the nest' to
its gradual abandoning of hope and its final exhaustion.

For years I spent these literary riches of my sister's death. I
pitied those whose death education had not begun and those
who did not know the advantages of a literary death; and
becoming so used to living on the proceeds of this one death,
never dreaming my store would be depleted, I was shocked
to find, ten years later, when another sister died, that after so
wasteful a poetic spending I was now faced with literary
poverty. Annabel Lee, The Lost Mate, Beautiful Evelyn Hope
had made a contract, as it were, with my elder sister's death. I
found this contract could not be revoked. I found I had little
to give the new hungry death. I had only one story, in all its
sordid detail – that of the *Gentleman from San Francisco* who
sets out on a long-awaited voyage around the world, only to
die within sight of Italy and to be transported home in a coffin
in the hold of the ship while his wife travels alone in their
stateroom. No romantic sepulchres, no mermaids, no pieces
of geranium flower beginning to die in the glass, nor envying
angels, and no sheltering within the grief of the mockingbird,

O heart, O throbbing heart, I am very sick and sorrowful.

My sister, Joy, and I, earning the first wages of our adult
life, were to pay for our mother's first long-awaited holiday
for many years, with her family in her home town two hundred miles north. Joy and my mother were to travel north by
train while my youngest sister, Helen, and I stayed home.

It was late summer. The weather was perfect. Everything
in the world shone with sunlight – the pine needles in the
plantation quivered with light, shaking off the excess in
showers of needle sparks; a gloss lay on the silver poplars,
the lombardy poplars, in the grass, the sky, the birds' feathers. The wire netting in the fowl run sparkled; while the
leghorns appeared to be wearing new white satin slimfit
cutaway coats, as they pecked at the hard-baked earth.

It was the beginning of an important year. Helen was in her first year at University, absorbed in poetry (*Epipsychidion*) and music (*Sonata* and *Symphony Pathétique*). Joy had given up teaching after a year and was thinking of applying to the Town Council for a job as a clerk which none of us had dreamed of being, as our lives were controlled not only by the literary death but by the literary life. Clerks, according to the poets we read (starting with Chaucer), were poor, pale, often tubercular. (In our home it was a virtue, somehow thought to be a matter of choice, to have 'rosy' cheeks, and in the days before our chests became breasts, to have 'fine little chests'.) In the world of the poets clerks occupied their working day in dreaming of sailing to the Spanish Main or the Golden Gate, and repeating nautical terms such as 'capstan', 'bulkhead', 'port' and 'starboard'.

I also had been teaching and during the holidays I had planned to do housework. I had put an advertisement in the local newspaper, signing myself 'Educated', and I was dealing with a number of replies ('Dear Educated') which chilled me with their unadorned reality. I spoke on the phone to some who had written and I was further chilled when I heard their hard experienced voices.

In the midst of this vocational turmoil our father went back and forth to his work each day with his lunch of onion sandwiches and salmon and shrimp and his stoppered bottle of milk and the jar of sugar for his tea. He was 'shunting' at the railway yards and therefore spent all day by the Engine Sheds and the Turntable, and sometimes I brought him a hot meat pie for lunch and the small vent in the top of the pastry would be steaming and the brown paper bag would be warmed and grease-stained when I gave it to him. He came home tired, the lines on his face creased with soot and coaldust, his blueys stained with coal and oil, and there'd be masses of oil-soaked cotton waste hanging from his bluey pockets. He would go into the garden and empty the crusts from his lunch tin, and peg his hastily washed blue-bordered hand towel on the rope clothesline, then he would come inside, his knees bent because he was too tired and stiff to straighten them, and he'd sit in his chair with his cup of tea on the table in front of him, spooning the sugar and stirring the twenty stirs that always made his etiquette-loving sister who had married into the family of a mayor give up hope of his social desirability.

There were as usual several cats around our house that summer. Big Puss, the great-great-great-grandmother and one each of her grandchildren who were by then grandparents themselves. All were black with mixed lengths of fur, and with literary names such as Fyodor, Myshkin, Blanquette. They roamed the hills, lay sensuously in the sun, mated in the hedge, the orchard and the pine plantation, and gave birth to their kittens in the empty broken-down pigsty; choosing one from each litter to present at the house. We had lately received Matilda ('who told lies for fun and perished miserably'), a scrawny black kitten with green eyes and a whining meow which said too early in her life that no one understood her and that she may have glimpsed something nasty in the pigsty. She complained day and night. The other cats attacked her and she would sit, lonely, on top of the gatepost at the foot of the hill, near the orchard, gazing at a spot in the grass where she had once seen a fieldmouse.

In this atmosphere my mother and Joy prepared for their holiday. Joy bought a pattern and some dress material and sewed a 'summer suit' and a 'sunsuit' which were fashionable then. Ever since we had learned by chance that life might not be worth living without a summer suit and a sunsuit we had been trying to make them, often unsuccessfully either because our energy wore out or because something irremediable happened to the neck-binding or the sleeve-fitting; or the darts puckered; or the hem dipped. Joy's summer suit, to go with her blond hair, was a success. Mother bought herself a blue silk floral dress with a navy blue straw hat to match. And at last, with the summer wardrobe and the travel arrangements completed, Mother and Joy set out on their train journey north, and we heard by phone late that evening that they had arrived.

'After all these years,' Mother said.

Satisfied, we put down the phone. In our reading, the literary life that paralleled our 'real' life, departures were not always blessed with arrival, and more often than not, the longed-for journeys remained dreams, with the clerk who dreamed of 'sailing to the Golden Gate' getting no further than his office,

> He is perched upon a high stool in London.
> The Golden Gate is very far away.

And there were others, with their unattainable Cathays and Carcassonnes.

And then, of course, there was the *Gentleman from San Francisco*.

About fifteen hours after that phone call we received another, from my mother's sister, Aunty Joy. Our telephone was old-fashioned, the kind the grocer and the butcher had, which we associated with giving and taking orders for bread and flour and meat. When the receiver was moved suddenly, and often in the midst of a conversation, the telephone would start an independent ringing, and then it would make droning noises like distant bombers, and crackling noises like a fire being started, and there would be thin faraway voices of other people having other conversations, giving news with Ohs and Ahs and I Say, and much inaudible detail. Aunty Joy's voice struggled through these interferences and at last sounded clear, and near, as she gave her news.

Our sister Joy, sunning herself on the beach (in her sun-suit!) had collapsed and died.

That was the news. There was no way of embellishing it or softening it or denying it or disbelieving it. It was just the news. Joy was dead. There was to be an inquest. After the inquest Mother would return home the following morning after travelling all night. My sister Joy would be on the train, in her coffin. They had phoned my father at work; he would make funeral arrangements.

The story of the *Gentleman from San Francisco* came to my mind. The longed-for journey, the arrival, the soul-sickening inconceivable return home.

By that afternoon the whole town knew of Joy's sudden death. The Lady Principal of the School came to visit us before we had time to clear away the telltale remnants of ourselves and our home life, and she sat in the small sooty kitchen speaking her words of sympathy, and giving us the first unexpected victory granted by Joy's death: we saw that our inhuman Lady Principal could be broken down into human molecules. Her visit was short. She left us tearful, waiting for our father to come home, and wondering how we could face him, for we knew that death is a time of apprehensive 'facing' of person and person when there's a calculation of how much love and grief it would be best to display, and a lightning reading of faces to try to compute the exact balance.

Fortunately, there was no need for calculated 'facing'. When Father came home we all sat in the kitchen and cried. Then Father went out to weed the dahlia bed and pour boiling water on the earwigs. Helen and I went to the suddenly hallowed bedroom to look at Joy's belongings strewn everywhere: scraps of sewing, unfinished hems and 'difficult' sleeves; collars abandoned on the dressing table, like half-prepared lace delicacies; lapels that had refused to stiffen; summer shoes cracked with layers of whiting; books; a collection of grasses and weeds which crackled in their dryness as we turned the pages – shepherd's purse, fat hen, rye grass, cutty grass, barley grass, feathery grass, twitch; a school workbook with drawings of faces and random remarks made on the prepared lessons; a jar of face cream; lipstick, powder, tweezers, all the aids of Joy's philosophy, 'Beauty must bear pain.' Everything was now memorable.

'She was hopeless at sewing collars,' Helen said, looking with reverence at the pile of spoiled collars.

'She stole that face cream from me,' I said.

We burst into tears.

We glanced at the pages of a letter strewn on the unmade bed.

'To the Town Clerk. Dear Sir, I wish to apply for the position advertised . . . '

Other pages were addressed to a penfriend who had suddenly become warm and sent her his photo and his love. 'Dear Albert. Albert dear. Dearest Albert. Darling Albert. My dear Albert . . . ' Each page had the same clever first sentence with words crossed out, inserted, substituted. We knew Joy's diary was under her mattress and it was understood that we would not read it until everything was 'over'.

All that day we kept returning to her room to inspect her 'things'. I went to the front bedroom and opened the box on my mother's dressing table, which held newspaper cuttings of our names in school prize lists, a picture of the first flying boat, a recipe for Date Pudding, Very Special, and the newspaper reports of the inquest after my elder sister's death. The newsprint had aged to match the ageing of the news; it seemed like a relic from a newspaper of last century. I reread the details which I knew by heart – the memories which the prompting of the coroner had forced into the minds of the spectators – 'Yes, she looked pale that day. I heard her say she felt tired.'

It was all so distant now. Beautiful Evelyn Hope, Annabel Lee

> *in her sepulchre there by the sea,* .
> *in her tomb by the sounding sea,*

the lilac scent in the air and the 'fifth-month grass' growing – all had made a paradise, a literary haven of that early death. It was fearful, now, to be cast out of paradise with only the depressing story of the *Gentleman from San Francisco* to use for comfort, with my sister in her anxiety over her summer suit and her sunsuit seeming to be as much a figure of fun as the Gentleman from San Francisco with his toothpaste and his toilet paper. My mother and my dead sister were parodying the story. My sister would be travelling in a lead coffin in the goods van of the train, with the mail bags, the holiday suitcases, cages of squawking hens and, perhaps, a sheep dog.

'She's coming in a lead coffin to stop her from smelling,' Helen said, in a kind of nursery-rhyme rhythm which recalled the end of the *Old Woman Who Lived in a Shoe*.

> *She went to the village to buy them a coffin*
> *And when she came back she found them aloffin'.*

Late that same afternoon my father, after polishing his shoes, for he never went anywhere without polishing his shoes, set off downtown to be seen and sympathized with, dealing with the news in his own way by being sociable, meeting his friends, and talking of 'old times'; and as his only hope at that time of day was to see his friends in the street he stood talking on the street corner, using it as the religious groups used it on Friday evenings as a place to 'save' and be 'saved'. When he came home bringing the evening paper, he had lost some of his panic.

'I saw Jimmy Woodall downtown,' he said.

And such was the intensity of our grief, running softly and secretly inside us, that it seemed as if he spoke like one of the pure in heart who had had the promise made to him fulfilled: *Blest are the pure in heart for they shall see God.*

'Jimmy Woodall? You saw Jimmy Woodall?' We spoke the name with reverence.

That night we sat around the big six-valve radio while father twiddled the knobs, trying to get 'overseas', and then gave up, and we listened to a detective play, *Inspector Scott of Scotland Yard, The Case of the Nabob of Blackmere.* We listened until the murderer was caught and the last ritualistic sentence uttered: 'Take him away.'

We set the alarm clock for five the next morning and we woke in the night-cold, peering out of the window at the mist and dew-covered grass where here and there a circular cloud of an early mushroom appeared to float. The railway station was cold too, facing the sea barely twenty yards away with no trains at that hour to act as windbreaks. Snowcoloured seagulls swooped above the platform or perched on the rusted rails of the old sidings, pecking at the gravel and the weathered grey wooden sleepers. Soon the train came rattling in. It was a 'slow' train, a goods train with trucks of sheep and other livestock, and one passenger carriage and light goods van. We had to leave the platform and walk on the gravel past the water tower and the signal box to greet our mother who was sitting looking out for us, resting her elbow on the sooty windowsill. She wore her blue silk floral dress and the navy blue straw hat to match, and her return so soon, in the clothes she set out in, seemed to be a ghastly mistake made by the railways. She was the only passenger on the train. As we caught sight of her and waited for her, the sinister fact of the death returned to us. Mother climbed awkwardly from the high carriage. She was indisputably alone. No one came down quickly after her with the luggage. There was no conversation and laughter about how wonderful the holiday had been and how good it was to be home.

My father kissed her. Helen and I stood apart, looking furtively about us, like plotters, trying not to glance at the goods van. We finally looked directly at the van. Mother saw us.

'We won't be able to see her in her coffin,' she said.

Again I heard in my mind the nursery rhyme refrain,

> She went to the village to buy them a coffin
> And when she came back she found them aloffin'.

The undertaker who had also met the train was supervising the removal of the coffin, waiting while the hens and ducks and dogs were unloaded on to the platform. The barking and squawking and quacking disturbed the sheep and cattle in the trucks; they began mooing and bleating and we could identify the beaded trill-like bleatings of the lambs, and the calves too, mooing in the uncontrolled way they have when there is nothing to answer them. My sister in her coffin was put into the hearse to the accompaniment of an animal chorus, and as I watched and listened, I felt that I was being released from the tyrannical comparison with the story of the Gentleman from San Francisco, that Joy's death was being dislodged from the literary world and housed, with the animal cries, among the first earliest deaths I knew before I was enticed into the concealments of literature, among the animal deaths that concealed nothing, that continued naturally beyond the act of dying through the cycle of putrefaction, maggots, sculptured weathered bone, to fresh grass and yellow buttercups.

My sister was buried the next day. Only the family and the weather attended her funeral. Noticeably absent were Annabel Lee, Evelyn Hope, one mockingbird, and one Gentleman from San Francisco.

Joker and Wife

MAURICE GEE

My mother watched me for signs of spirituality, and found one or two indications. She herself was open to things, she said, but was a late bloomer. She wanted an easier passage for me, no beating on doors already open – and she raised plump fists to show how she had suffered. I tried to say the words she wanted to hear, and can't be sure I didn't mean them. I manufactured a kind of sincerity. A precondition was that she face me the right way, which she did with relentless tenderness. Then I cried for squashed tea-tree jacks and spring lambs off to the works. So short a life. Such gentle trusting eyes. 'Such tender little chops,' my father said, but his remarks only pointed up her fineness and I liked the sad smiles she gave him then.

My sympathies travelled with ease along the chain of being. I grew damp-eyed at flowers wilting in a cut-glass vase. A cloud fading in the sky – 'like the soul of someone dying,' she said – made me drop my jaw, made me breathless. We were a little mad, my mother and I, engaged in a form of *folie à deux*.

It was not a dangerous state, for growing up in my family, in our town, I had come to know very well that conflict and ambiguity were the rule, and 'oneness' a room that could not be lived in. Alone with Mum, I believed myself special; but other voices sounded, shouts and yells. I stepped outside and there behaved in a proper way. I was inconspicuous and noisy. I stubbed my toes and wore scabs on my knees. I hugged the girders on the railway bridge while a train rumbled over, and skinned an eel and baked him on a sheet of tin over a fire. Subtleties were in my scope. The goody-good girls sat with pink ears while I defiled them. 'Open the window, monitor,' the teacher said; and haughty, pure of face, I opened it and let my fart escape.

In another room I was Dad's. He taught me how to keep accounts, do the books, balance up, not go broke. His speed at adding up and multiplying filled me with a kind of love.

'Seventeen twenty-fours?' I spring on him; but the blankess in his eye lasts only a second. 'Four hundred and eight.' 'Right! Right! One thousand six hundred and fifty-one divided by thirteen?' 'Hey, I'm not an adding machine. One hundred and twenty-seven.' 'You're a genius, Dad. You're better than Albert Einstein.' 'Who's this Einstein feller, then? I bet he'd soon go broke in my shop.'

'Must you always reduce things to money? There are other things,' Mum says.

Dad grins. He loves getting her on his own ground. He looks hungry, greedy, cruel, when he manages it. 'Money bought the clothes on your back. And the food in your belly.' *Stomach* is the word we use in our house, but Dad coarsens himself in his arguments with her. 'I got you a washing machine. And a fridge so the blowies can't bomb the meat. And now you want a lounge suite to park your bottom on. Well, that's all money, Ivy. That all comes from me selling spuds and cheese. You can't sell "higher things" by the slice. There's no demand for fillet of soul this week.'

Mum had no answer. Her mind was like a jellyfish, soft, transparent, moving with the pressure of tides. 'I won't argue with you. I won't descend to your level.' And by some act of will, she seemed to float; behaving exactly as he'd expected. He watched with a grin and wet his lips. It often seemed to me he meant to eat her.

I stood in a doorway between two rooms. I was drawn to him by his quickness and cruelty, his language, so full of spikes and grins; and to her by pity. I felt that my neutrality kept a balance, kept our family from going broke.

Yet I was moving to him all through my boyhood. It was no simple fight between the spirit and the flesh. To use one of my mother's metaphors, we had all come 'out of God's mixing bowl' and had our share of conflicting desires. A higher station was her goal, and she wanted it not only in spiritual mansions but in our street. She was also a greedy woman. She spoke of her 'sweet tooth' as though she were not responsible for it, as though it were an affliction and must be treated with scones and jam and another helping of sago pudding.

'Oh dear, what am I going to do about this old sweet tooth of mine?'

'Get my pliers, Noel,' Dad says, and Mum replies with a scream as she spoons out more pudding, 'You stay in your chair. Your father's got a funny sense of humour. No one wants any more of this? Mmm. Delicious.'

Dad tells us about the old Dalmatian up the valley, who pulled out his teeth with pliers when the dentist told him what the bill would be. 'He had them in a tobacco tin, rattling in his pocket. He had a grin like the meatworks.' But Mum cannot be put off. Eating pudding, she is deaf and blind. A trickle of milk runs from her mouth. She licks it with a sago-slimed tongue, and scrapes her plate as though it wears a skin she must take off. She sits back in her chair and sighs and smiles; and hears Dad now, lets his words replay in her mind, and says, 'That's hardly a topic for the table.' I think of the story of the pot that wouldn't stop cooking and think what a great Mother's Day present it would make, and see our town of Beavis awash in porridge and the cars throwing up bow-waves as they speed through it. I think of porridge squishing between my toes as I walk to school. Mum gives a lady-burp behind her hand. 'Pardon. What a tyrant the body is. But now at least I can face my night.' She means her Krishnamurti evening.

Nor was Dad any more of a piece. Mum described him fondly as 'a man's man', 'a lady killer'. He had a black libidinous eye, and I wonder which back doors he managed to slide through. I went on deliveries with him and heard a lot of cheek at doors and sensed meanings passing over my head. I saw hand slide on hand as the carton of groceries was transferred.

'Funny woman.'

'How do you mean?' With my father I keep on expecting the world to open up.

'She told me once Hell was here on Earth and we were the

sinners damned by God.' He grins and starts the van. 'She's got a screw loose. Another time she told me she was a little bird in an empty house with everyone gone. She was fluttering at the window, trying to get out. What do you think of that?'

I think there's hardly time for her to say it at the door.

'She drinks too much Dally plonk' – and I see him drinking with her at a table. Groceries in a carton sit on a chair and a room opens beyond, with brass knobs shining on a double bed. That's as far as I'll let myself go.

'She's a queer old world.'

'Yes,' I say.

I don't accept my mother's view that he can't feel what we feel. He would if he wanted to, I'm sure of that, but he thinks 'being open to things' is a game she's playing. 'It's how she fills her time instead of darning my socks.' Soon I want to hear the things *he* knows. He never tells me. Yacking is for women, that's his opinion.

On Saturdays in the season he takes me on the train to Kingsland station and we walk down the hill to Eden Park and watch Auckland v. Canterbury or Auckland v. Hawke's Bay.

'Go, go, go,' he yells. 'Beautiful. Beautiful.' On the train home he says into the air, 'A lovely try', making me blush, but I see other men smiling and nodding their heads, and understand he's speaking for them all, and I move closer to him on the seat. He's pleased not just because our team has won. It's the beauty of the cut-through that moves him, and the pass from centre to wing, and the run for the corner. The sun goes down as we walk home and the moon is in the sky. The dust road runs under swollen branches, night-black pines. He makes me stop and listen. The trees are sighing. There's a creaking sound high up as limb rubs on limb. He taps my arm. 'The creek.' It makes a muted hiss, a slide of water. Dad offers no comparisons. He uses no more words. When we get home he tells Mum, 'A chap was carted off with a broken leg.'

'That stupid game.'

'We won. We wiped the floor with them.'

'I hope you realize Noel there's more to life than football.'

I know that very well, and I lie in bed thinking of the water and the trees, and the darkness and the moon; and I understand something difficult, that brings me no ease: Mum and Dad know the same things, but know them differently.

It's unfortunate that just as Mum discovered Krishnamurti I was reading the *Arabian Nights*. I mean it was unfortunate for her. A bit of luck for me. I was set for other journeys than questings of the soul. Krishnamurti was a name I liked but I saw him riding on a magic carpet, opening caves, finding treasure. When Mum became ecstatic about his beauty, and the spirit shining in his face, I took another step away from her. Beauty of that sort was unmanly. I was frightened that she'd look for it in me. So I practised tough expressions, used tough words, I cut my sympathies back to what my friends at school might accept – and that wasn't much – and learned a kind of boredom with my mother. She blamed Dad, but he wasn't pleased to see me playing the lout. He took me aside and told me it was my job to keep her happy.

'Mine?'

'I've got the shop to think about. I'm the guy that keeps food in our bellies.'

'I've got school.'

'Well, Noel, pretend it's extra homework. Women get funny in their minds. They think life's passed them by. Let her talk about this Krishnamurky. Look as if you're floating on a cloud. That shouldn't be too hard for a clever bloke like you.'

It was too hard, and was made even harder by his winks of encouragement. And sometimes he'd get irritable and undo my work. Down went his paper and a little plosive sound came from his lips. 'Now Ivy, you can't say that. It doesn't follow.'

'He is. A saint. You can see it in his face.'

'Saints are Christians, aren't they? This guy's a Theo something. And if you're going to put him in the sum you've got to take in this lady here.' He hunted through a pile of magazines. 'Countess Elisabeth Bathory. She used to have her bath in human blood. And torture peasant girls to death for fun. How's that? I'll let you have your Krishnamurk, okay? But unless you look at this gal you're only playing games.'

'What I'm saying is, his teaching lifts us above all that. Evil. And appetites. And despair.'

'Appetites, Ivy? He hasn't seen you going at the pudding.'

My mother wept. She had eyes of such rich brown the pupil and the iris ran together. They gave her large eloquent expressions – of love, of soulfulness, of despair. She melted into tears and seemed to carry huge weights of grief. I was torn inside, and hated Dad. His little liquorice eyes grew round with mock incomprehension. But he came and patted her and stroked her arm, and he sent me off to make a cup of tea. When I came back they were standing by her chair. Her head was on his shoulder and she seemed to be sleeping. They rocked the way a horse rocks, and he was humming a tune in her ear. Vacantly he turned his eyes on me. 'You go off to bed now, son. Forget the tea, I'll make it.' His hand stroked her bottom. I watched him squeeze a bit of her like putty.

'Ow,' she whispered.

'Off you go. Leave her to me.'

I went to bed and imagined them, my mother and father, doing it. It was hideously disturbing, it made a swelling in my chest that hurt like an animal biting. It seemed they had betrayed me by suddenly being adult, and closing doors, and leaving me outside.

Krishnamurti. He was middle-aged by that time but his beauty was the sign he brought my mother. Many years later, in her little unit in a sausage block on the North Shore, she kept a library eighteen inches square from which, in memory, I chart her journey before spirit gave way to bridge and croquet and a spot of gin. Forgotten names on faded covers: Gerald Heard, Lin Yutang, the Oxford Group. And others that return a currency. Aldous Huxley. She grew cacti in earthen pots and broken-handled mugs but could not find courage to taste them. Huxley came after Krishnamurti (after the war) but never replaced him in her pantheon.

When she knew she'd lost me she embraced her faith with a passion that at last came close to being intellectual. Dad could not make any mark on her certainties, he could not get them fixed properly in his mind, so his shots struck nothing.

She spoke of 'the Beloved' and, familiarly, of Krishnaji, and it took him a while to discover they were not the same. In the end he grew tired of it and did not bother. He told me it would run its course. Now and then he roused himself to attack the members of her group: Mr Chalkley, whom he called 'the Colonel', Mrs Chalkley, 'the Begum', Mrs Brott, 'the draught mare', Miss Cole, 'the wilting violet', and so on. Mum smiled at that.

She went to her meetings on Tuesday nights, walking down our street and down the hill, and along beside the creek, under the pines, to the Chalkleys' turreted house (the 'Pleasure Dome') at the end of a burgeoning arm of the town. She let herself in at the back gate and walked through the vegetable garden. What went on inside I never knew. I imagined incense smoking in a bowl, and glowing crystal lamps, and fingers hooked together round a table inlaid with crescent moons. Ghostly voices whispered in the dark. 'You silly boy,' Mum said, 'We sit and talk.' Looking at the pink cheeks and magnified eyes, I could not believe it.

She was never late getting home. The Chalkleys, she said, were early-to-bedders. Dad leered like Groucho Marx, but she only sighed, and went to sit in the front room, where I found her scribbling in a threepenny notebook. I did not like her independence, or her familiarity with people outside our family, and I missed the days when I had been the one to make her happy.

I sat up reading until she came home. Sometimes I played Chinese checkers with Dad, but I had given up testing him with mental. Our companionship had changed to a sharing of Westerns. We argued passionately. I liked Zane Grey but Jackson Gregory was his favourite. I reckoned there was no one in Jackson Gregory who could beat Buck Duane to the draw, and Dad replied there was more to life than being fast with a gun. 'You sound like Mum,' I said. 'God forbid,' he answered, looking startled.

That was the night she came in late. We were both aware of the clock creeping round to ten past ten. 'You'd better get off to bed.'

'A car at the gate.'

We heard her feet, scuff scuff on the gravel, then she burst in panting. 'Oh Bob,' she said, 'have you got two and six?'

'Did you get the taxi?'

'No, no, it's for Mr Chalkley. He drove me home. He's at the gate.'

'He's charging you? And he couldn't even see you to the door?'

'Please, Bob. He's in a temper.' Her eyes grew dark and undefined.

Dad fished in his pocket for half a crown. 'You're no different from these Christians. All love and buttered tripe in church but as soon as it comes to making a bob . . . Here, Noel, you take it. I'm not having my wife running after him.' He spun the coin at me but I dropped it and it rolled under a chair.

Mum got on her knees. 'I'll do it.'

'No you won't,' Dad said.

I beat her to the coin and went out into the dark and down the path. I wasn't keen to face Mr Chalkley in a temper, and thinking of him as the Colonel didn't help. The car was a big black Vauxhall, shining under the street lamp. I went round to the driver's window and waited while Mr Chalkley wound it down. He had snappy eyes, very pale, and a little rat-trap mouth under a moustache with gleaming bristles.

'Are you the boy? Noel?'

'Yes,' I said. 'Here's your two and six.'

He took it and put it in a coin purse with snap ears.

'Stand where I can see you.'

I stood looking adenoidal while he glared at my face. I felt he was counting to see if I had everything, eyes and nose and mouth.

'Now your profile.'

'What?'

He reached out and took my jaw and forced my head round. 'Huh,' he said.

'Can I go now?'

'There's not the faintest resemblance. The woman's out of her mind.' He put his car in gear and drove away. The night pressed in on me and I ran up the path, stinging my soles, and ran into the kitchen to find Dad holding Mum by the shoulders, both of them laughing, and she half weeping with vexation too.

'Ha, ha, ha,' cried Dad, and he rocked Mum back and forth, making her head bounce.

'Stop it, Bob. Oh stop it. Go to bed, Noel. Your father's gone crazy.'

'Noel, Noel, do you know what she did?'

'Don't you tell him. He's got a low enough opinion of me.' She looked at me with a kind of delight in what she'd done, her anger at herself just a game.

'She saw a man watching her. He was in the shadows under the pines. Ha! Ha!'

'I told you, it wasn't a man.'

'He wouldn't answer when she called out. Just stood there watching. So she went back and the Colonel had to drive her home. And . . . and . . . '

'Bob! It wasn't a man, Noel. It was a post.'

'A post! A post! I wish I could have seen the Colonel's face. He should have charged you five bob not two and six.' He hugged Mum and danced her round the kitchen. 'What a loony wife I've got.'

I went to bed and heard laughing, shrieking, and heard him chasing her; and later on, of course, the creaking bed. What a thing that is, what a cliché, the creaking bed; and the moaning, and the cries stifled with a hand or pillow. The pleasure and relief and the grimness and disgust they worked in me.

'Was it really a post?' I said in the morning.

'Yes. It was in the shade but the moon was shining on the top of it. It looked like a man with a bald head.' She giggled as she stirred the porridge. 'I thought Mr Chalkley was going to burst.'

'He doesn't think I look like Krishnamurti.'

'Did he say that?'

'He looked at my profile.'

'The cheek of him. Just between you and me, he's soft in the head. His wife's the clever one.'

'I don't, do I? Look like Krishnamurti?'

'You look like a hooligan. Wear your shoes today. And put some iodine on your toe. If you bring me the scissors I'll cut that flap of skin off.'

We thought she would stop going to her meetings after

that. How could a skinflint like Mr Chalkley be spiritual? But no, off she went every Tuesday, with her notebook full of thoughts and her head scarf knotted under her chin. Dad and I played Chinese checkers by the winter fire. One night we made six-shooters by jamming wooden clothes pegs together. We put them in our belts and did fast draws. I beat him every time and he died extravagantly. He put tomato sauce in his palm and clapped it on his forehead and fell back in his chair with blood dribbling on his face. After that he said he had to go to the dunny. He put a new candle in the holder and went out with a magazine and I heard him treading up the path.

(Our lavatory was by the woodshed, hidden from the house by a willow hedge. The thing Mum wanted next, before a telephone, before new wallpaper in the bedroom, was a flush toilet. It was primitive going out at night especially in the rain, and having to carry a candle, and having the nightman running up your path! And she'd give anything not to keep a potty under the bed. Dad disagreed. People needed bringing down to earth. He claimed he was fond of the wetas in the dunny – the way they came out of the wall and looked at the candle flame. They had little black eyes like mice, he said. They were like devils waiting to skewer you on a fork. Dad always sat a long time up there, and I heard Mum telling him he ate too much cheese.)

After he had been away ten minutes I grew scared. The wind boomed round the house and made it creak. I went to the window and looked into the night and saw the fuzzy candlelight through the hedge. It was quarter to ten. I wanted him to come and people the house, whose other rooms, behind their doors, surrounded me with threat and emptiness. I went back to my chair and listened for his footsteps on the path. But the wind moaned, the house shuddered, the fire gulped and sucked in the chimney. I opened the back door and stood on the porch. 'Dad,' I yelled, and heard pines thrashing in the park and a window banging in the Catholic school. 'Dad, are you all right?'

I began to think someone had murdered him. Then, as though I'd grown up in a rush, I thought of his heart, the pills he took. His visits to the doctor, and knew he'd had a heart attack up there. People often died in the lavatory, he'd told me that. I sped up the path, running lightly, making myself non-existent in the dark. I stood, not breathing, in the chasm between the woodshed and the hedge. 'Dad, are you in there?' I was hollowed out with fright, and I pushed the door back with a dab of my fingers.

The little room was empty. The candle leaned its flame away from me. The wooden lid was on the hole, with Dad's magazine tucked in the handle. I glimpsed a weta, glossy-shelled, as I backed away. The door swung in the wind and closed with a thud. Willow leaves stroked my cheek and I shrieked and jumped away. Then I peered towards the bean-frames in the garden. 'Dad.' He would pounce on me. I grinned with terror. Then I gave it up. The game. His death. It was too much for me, and I pulled my arms round myself and ran for the house. I burst in and slammed the door and turned the key and ran to my chair and sat close to the stove, feeling the heat. Dad's chair, with his dent in it, was the strangest object I had ever seen.

Five minutes passed. I watched the clock so closely I saw the big hand move. It was too soon for Mum but I begged for her. And she came early. The wind fell silent, as though for an event, and a scuttling sounded on the path. I ran to the door and pulled it open. Her arms came thrusting in. Her face was blind like the moon. She tripped on the step and lurched at the stove; I thought her hands would burn on the fire-box door. 'Bob. Bob. Where is he?'

'He went to the lav.'

She gave a terrified look in that direction, and pushed at the door, ten feet away. Her eyes were leaking tears, her nose was wet. She came at me and clawed my jersey.

'Someone's out there. Someone followed me.'

Then Dad came down the path, whistling *Phil the Fluter's Ball*. He walked inside and did a little jig, with candle raised like a bottle and magazine slapping time on his trouser leg. 'What? What?'

'Oh, Bob.'

She gripped his shirt and cardigan and locked herself on him. She wanted to burrow in and hide herself. He put his arms around her, motioned me to take the candle. His face was hot beside her yellow scarf and his eyes were sheeny.

'Calm down, Ivy. What happened?'

She threw back her head to see him. 'A man followed me. He kept on walking after me. Oh Bob, he's still out there.'

Dad angled his arm and closed the door, turned the key. 'Now. We've locked him out. Who was he?'

'I don't know. I don't know. I got past the pines. And then I saw someone come out of the bracken. He followed me. Every time I stopped he stopped. And when I ran he ran. He wouldn't answer me when I called out.'

'Did he do anything? Show himself?'

'No. No. He ran round the edges of the street lamps. And when I got to the gate he climbed up the bank on to the lawn. I thought he was going round the house to beat me to the door.'

'I'll take a look.'

'Well, he'll have made himself scarce.'

Dad took her to a chair and made her sit down. He knelt in front of her and took her shoes off. Then he wet a flannel and washed her face. She closed her eyes so he could wipe the lids, but tears leaked out. She took the flannel and held it to her face and bit the fingers of her other hand. Dad stroked the back of her neck. He still had sauce in his eyebrows.

'Go to bed, Noel.' He knew from my look I had worked it out and his eyes warned me to mind my own business.

'Yes,' I said. 'Goodnight.' I went to bed. The mechanics of it, the reason, all was plain. But beyond that was another thing. I glimpsed it and it terrified me; enormous and dark and undefined, and yet with glittering features that I knew. I gave a little whimper and withdrew as it came close, and ran through litanies of school and creek; swimming and eel-fishing and games of cricket.

Through the wall I heard Dad in the scullery, running water in the kettle to make tea.

When Mum died I came up to Auckland to manage her funeral. There were mourners from the old folk's club and her bridge and croquet clubs, though she had given up bridge and croquet several years before. I was offended by their geriatric glee – a term I used to put them in their place – and only later remembered that cheefulness had been Mum's speciality. Her friends hee-heed and clacked their teeth, and told some spotty jokes; made mock assignations, had a good time. They drank to Ivy, one of the best. I gave her croquet mallet to a lady who asked for it, and gave them all something to carry away. They ran about like children, picking up this and that. Nobody wanted her books. When they had gone I put them in an apple box to send to some charity.

I was fifty-four, Dad's age when he died. Now Mum was dead. That opened up the way ahead. No one stood between me and my death. (The way behind was empty too, no wife or child.) I lifted down the books, leafing through one or two before I packed them. There he was, Krishnaji, with liquid eye and swollen mouth, wearing an embroidered Indian jacket; and a good grey suit in this one, overcoat on his arm, trilby in his hand. Mrs Besant, at his side, had a face not unlike my mother's.

She had never gone back to the Chalkleys', but had not given up books or her scribbled thoughts until Dad died. Then she put them away. After shifting to the North Shore she went back to Beavis only once. It was the time of the Gibson murder and the police were searching Beavis Creek for pieces of Mrs Gibson's body. Beavis was alive again in Mum's mind and she asked me to drive her out 'for a look-see'. First we went through the commercial part and she marvelled at the supermarkets, the new town hall – 'like a parrot's cage', she said – and the gift shops and craft shops and boutiques with names like *Fanny* and *Jilly* and *Snatch*. A fire station stood on the corner where Dad's iron and weatherboard grocery store had been. 'Dear, dear,' Mum said.

We went out through the factories and came to the creek. A notice at the entrance of Creek Road closed it to traffic. But Creek Road was not Creek Road at all. The pines were down. The blackberry vines were scraped from the bank and rows of liquid amber stood in their place. Houses had come over the hill and engulfed the Pleasure Dome. They crowded on its lawns and in its garden. It stood there broken, seedy, like a dolls' house when the children are grown up.

Along the road, by the bend, police vans and traffic cars

were parked. Men stood in groups and frogmen were busy in the creek. The spring sunshine slid on their cold black suits.

A trafficman thumbed us to clear out.

'To think I used to walk down there,' Mum said. I was thinking much the same – my days in the creek, my boyhood of swimming and eeling.

We drove up the hill.

'What makes a man do that to his wife?'

I did not know, and did not think about it. I had long ago stepped back from that sort of thing.

We came to our house. A little square room like a pill-box sat on top. The dunny and the willow hedge were gone.

'They certainly look after it.' Lawns as smooth as a putting green. Flower-beds shaped like hearts and diamonds. The front bank, where I had cut highways for my Dinky cars and trucks, was hidden under a mat of Livingstone daisies.

'Do you want to go in?'

We looked at it for a while, then I turned the car and drove away.

'We had a lot of fun there, Noel. Of course, I was always fluttering round, trying to get out. I was a quester.' She liked the word. 'And your father was a joker. He kept me down to earth.'

'He did that all right.'

'But in all our lives we never disagreed. Not one cross word.'

A Double Life

VANESSA GRIFFEN

Sometimes I have many worries, though no one would think so, to look at me, and I never let my friends know. We are not supposed to have these traits, us Fijians. Happy go lucky we are called, at least by the tourists that pass through here. Yet in the history books, we were once the most savage people in the Pacific. I know, because I read about that when I was at University. Yet it is remarkable now how we all go to church, when once we used to chase the missionaries, or so their history books say.

We are also thought to be strong – happy go lucky and strong. It is a hard combination to live up to. That is why, if you have any worries, don't show them too much. If you are sick or sad, or you are in a weak position, don't show it very much or for too long.

It is harder if you are a man, for we permit our women to be more voluble in their emotions. Actually, of the women in my family, I have always been secretly afraid, though I would never admit this to anyone. The women have a way of yelling at you or grumbling that I can have no answer for. I am a man, not a woman, so I am not so very voluble, except perhaps in drinking with my friends, and the end of the year celebrations at Christmas, when we might get very emotional as we meet again in the village from the city where many of us have gone. We also get very drunk and hold each other and sing very loudly, the men that is. The women at this time are loud too, but they may retire earlier, except for the young ones of course. Who knows where they may go?

I may sound very old, I even ramble when I write, or so my lecturers told me, but I am not old really, far from it. I have taught for many years before going back to University to get my degree. I am thirty-six, a serious man. At University, these young people about me think that I am old. They make fun of you there, these young ones, because we are slow, and they are so bright and fast. We are the in-service trainees, paid for by the government. But we get through just as well as they do in the end, and our views are more mature because we have had experience.

I was very proud to be at University and took my studies seriously. After years of teaching in a primary school, it was a pleasure to be a student and be taught by others much more learned than myself. I wanted to learn and improve myself and I hoped when I got out of University, that I would get a better job. I enjoyed University, but also it filled me with worries. I was among young people again and yet I was not young. I felt an old man. Perhaps that is the base of my difficulties.

I never worried much when I was young. I went into teaching after a bit of training. I did not have to think about it. My University days was a different experience. When I first went to the University, I, and my friends like me, the in-service trainees, were timid and careful. We did not want to make mistakes and look a 'fool' in front of all these young people. We did not know about essays, writing properly, our thinking was not fresh. Sometimes on the many things we were asked to write about, we had no thoughts at all. We did not know how to look up books to read on the subject.

It is funny to feel terrified of a building, but I was terrified of the library. Of course, we never let anyone know this. I thought maybe others of my colleagues shared my fears, but could never be sure, because we became secretive at the University, we compared how we were getting on. Sometimes, in the beginning, we older ones shared our fears and helped each other, but after that, once the first essays came in, and we began to see how we were doing, we helped each other less. It was every man for himself. I became alone then with no one to share my fears and worries.

I grew used to the library but always treated it with respect. I got to know the lecturers better, some anyway, but always remained quiet and reserved. I listened to them very carefully and tried to do what they said. I settled in to the University, in my own way. My colleagues did also, some even emerged as the gay and wise men of the class, with the confidence to make jokes; a friend of mine even became a playboy at the University, even though he is a married man. The University was a free place in social terms. We had no identity there except the identity we made. I did not change much. I made friends with some of the other students, but only through tutorials, and meeting in the canteen, or coming out of lectures. I am shy.

I always felt I was leading a double life at University. As I sat in lectures, taking notes (as I said it was a luxury for me to be taught) and listened to talk about politics and government, Nyerere and African states, China and its revolution, I felt like someone was pulling my head open, wider and wider. Courses on the family, social organization, other courses. English, where we broke up the language and when we read books, we talked about the psychology of the characters. Many thoughts went around in my head. We had to think and we had to talk.

In tutorials we had discussions. I sat afraid to move, to get attention to myself. All the things they were saying I did not know anything about. But many of us were like that. Some of the Indian girls, they sat like me, their hands clasped in their laps, their heads bent down. Some lecturers forced us to answer questions. I would smile and shake my head and say very little. If they asked me more I was humiliated. I thought only Europeans could blush, but underneath my skin I would blush. It is a burning feeling.

The young ones, I always admired them then. They could always open their mouths and talk. Even if they did not want to, instead of getting embarrassed, they could open their mouths and say things which were on the subject or nearly on the subject. I think they knew then how much people like me didn't know anything. To me, I was a man among children, with the lecturer sometimes my age, sometimes younger, but I did not know what they were talking about. I was afraid that one day the lecturer would look at me and say, 'You don't know what we are talking about, do you?' In the first semester at the University I spent all my time struggling so that no one would find this out.

I often wondered what would all these people say if they knew where I lived, how I sat in a corner, away from my wife and relatives talking, my children sleeping, and worked by a kerosene light to write an essay on my foolscap paper. The young students wondered why we worked so hard in the library, and late, where they went only to pick up books, some of them, and talk. It is because for some of us it is the only place to write our essays, the only place to read. We have families.

When we talked about the family in sociology, no one talked from experience. They talked about the mother's role, the father's role, about bringing up children and the effect of the environment. These times I felt like two men. One I left behind in my house, the man I was to my wife and children; and the other one sat in the tutorial room, and listened to talk about 'roles'.

I came to understand sociology sooner than I did the other subjects, though they used difficult terms for ordinary everyday things. But here I could make comments if I had to. It was then I really began to lead a double life at University. There, I left my family behind, and at home, I left University behind. So in tutorials, I made comments just like other students' comments, to show I understood what they were talking about in our lectures and in the books. We discussed the environmental effects on children's learning. That was always a good one, I was quite interested in it. Then at home, I did not think about anything they said, in relation to my family. I did not have time really to think about these things. I led a kind of double life.

I enjoyed my lectures and tutorials; they were a pleasure to me, though I was very quiet. I even became student enough to be bored and feel sleepy at times, and notice when the lecturer had not prepared his lesson well. My mind would wander sometimes to the scene I had left at my house that morning, of my youngest child crying with running nose and wet face on my wife's arm, while I left hurriedly to catch the bus with my black briefcase. I could hear my child's bawling, its mother telling it loudly to keep quiet now. Anything can enter your head when you are bored with a lecture.

Sometimes I even thought of my wife. But I did not allow myself to be bored for very long because I was a very earnest student, and I worried that I might miss something that I might not understand later. I was also very afraid of looking stupid in a tutorial.

Nothing is more terrible to me than to receive back my essays. It is a very private and painful thing. At the back of the last page the lecturer writes a grade or mark. It is always this that I look at first, before the comments. At first my grades used to make my stomach lurch. It is something terrible for a man my age who has been a teacher to see D, or D – on an essay which he read many books to prepare. Many times, in those first few months, when I wrote essays and got them back, I felt like crying. It is a shameful thing to admit. There seemed nothing I could do to make my grades change. It is shameful for me, a grown man, to feel like this over his pages of paper, but it is true. I can only write it here because we have been taught not to fear to express ourselves, to bring these things out. In tutorials they are always asking for our personal experiences, or our own ideas and opinions. Most of us prefer not to have them.

Only after almost a year had passed, did I get any rewards for my essays. In some subjects my grades were better, and I began to like these subjects more than I liked other subjects. But I always worried that I would fall back, that I would not understand enough, or correctly. I was more used to essays then. I sweated and tried to be inconspicuous in tutorials. I never made much contribution, but always attended them.

I have learned many things here. It is very difficult. I did not know it was possible for me to be so ignorant. In the village where I was teaching, I was the 'qase ni vuli', the school teacher. We do the teaching, we are the ones who know everything, after the church minister we are one of the most respected. We are just like everyone but because we teach, we are expected to be a bit more wise, because we have some learning. But, at the University, I was the stupid one. Some of my friends in the same position as me, they have not been able to take this idea of themselves being the stupid ones, the students. But for me, I was very humble in that place, because I had come to learn, and after we had had our first few lectures, I knew that my ignorance was very great. As I have said before, I enjoyed all my lectures. I was only ashamed of myself.

But that was at the beginning. I am much better now. I am more sure of myself. I have not done remarkably at the University, but I have got through at a steady pace, and in one or two subjects I have done fairly well. I am now working slowly towards the end of my degree. The University has become a familiar place to me but I still have a lot of respect for it.

I am still amazed at all the things that I have learned here. Sometimes when I go home and I sit down in my house and we are all talking, I think about these things. Sometimes I try to tell my friends the things we are learning, but it is very hard to talk about outside the place. They shake their heads and say 'Dina? True?', or nod at me and say 'Yes, many strange things they teach at University.' My family is the most difficult. Sometimes my wife does not understand why I must sit in a corner and write all night and this is hard work and our children must be quiet or I will shout at her to see to them.

I sometimes think about my family now. In tutorials we talk about relationships and the environment and how important it is for children to receive love and encouragement if they are to learn and later to get on well in life. For myself, sometimes I tend to disagree with this because looking at all the young ones on the streets in jeans with nothing to do, I blame them because they have not made use of the opportunities available to them.

My home is crowded and small. It is all I can afford, with rents so high. But even with a bigger house, it would still be crowded, because our relatives would come there. That is our family way of life. Yet in tutorials none of us talk of these things when we discuss the family. I know some of the other Fijians in the class, and even some of the Indian students, we all have homes that may be crowded, or shacks, poor, but we do not mention these things. How can we? Sometimes the lecturer says, 'But here in the Pacific,' (usually they are not from here), 'or here in Fiji, you have a different system, the extended family, where you have

greater interaction with your relatives, certain obligations
. . . Now from your own experience, what would you say
some of the features of the extended family are?' And then
she asks around the group, she is a New Zealand woman,
very shy 'Semisoni? Premila?' We feel sorry for her so we
talk about our relatives, how we look after each other in
time of need; reciprocity (that is giving without thought of
return). We list the features. I talk about our system, my
cousin's children that I have in my house while they go to
school. We talk about how our people are seldom allowed to
go starving, how the old are taken care of and not left to
grow old alone, or be put in old people's homes, 'Which is
what Europeans are more likely to do' the lecturer says with
a smile.

That is how we talk about the family. Sometimes as I
listen and talk, I think in the back of my mind about my
house, my wife and all my children, and I wonder what all
these people would think if they saw it. Because I have been
here long enough to know it is not a good environment. I sit
in tutorials and let these bright young ones talk about the
extended family and I nod knowingly (they begin to look on
me as the family man in the tutorials, because I am older).
But I don't let anyone know it is sometimes hard to fulfil all
those obligations, sometimes I even curse to myself my relatives; I have many worries to feed them all, but I leave that
to my wife. I do my duty.

Soon I will be leaving the University and I hope to have a
better job. I will still be in the teaching profession, but
maybe have a headmaster's post, or be head of a department. I shall be earning more money. I shall be sorry to
leave the University, it is a good life in a way, but for someone my age, it is better to be out working. The prospects are
good for me. I shall be able to apply for more posts now that
I have my degree, but no doubt I shall have to do some
teaching first, and it is a matter of knowing the right people.

But that is looking forward too much. I still have my
exams to pass and more work for me. When I graduate I
shall be a new man, my head at least will have more in it. I
shall be better qualified. I look forward now to getting a
better post, earning more pay, and perhaps a better place to

live for my wife and children. I shall still look after my relatives if they come, but perhaps fewer this time. It is only my right I think. After all, I have worked hard for this.

The Glorious Pacific Way

EPELI HAU'OFA

'I hear you're collecting oral traditions. Good work. It's about time someone started recording and preserving them before they're lost for ever,' said the nattily dressed Mr Harold Minte in the slightly condescending though friendly tone of a born diplomat, which Mr Minte actually was.

'Thank you, sir,' Ole Pasifikiwei responded shyly. He was not given to shyness, except in the presence of foreigners, and on this sultry evening at a cocktail party held in the verdant gardens of the International Nightlight Hotel, Ole was particularly reticent.

Through the persistent prodding of an inner voice which he had attributed to that of his Maker, Ole had spent much of the spare time from his job as Chief Eradicator of Pests and Weeds collecting oral traditions, initially as a hobby but in time it had developed into a near obsession. He had begun by recording and compiling his own family genealogy and oral history, after which he expanded into those of other families in his village, then neighbouring settlements, and in seven years he had covered a fifth of his island country. He recorded with pens in exercise books, which he piled at a far corner of his house, hoping that one day he would have a machine for typing his material and some filing cabinets for their proper storage. But he had no money for these luxuries, so he kept to his exercise books, taking care of them as best as he could.

His work on oral traditions attracted the approving notice of the Ministry of Environment, Religion, Culture, and Youth (universally dubbed MERCY), a high official of which, who was also an intimate of Ole's, had invited him to the cocktail party to meet the diplomat visiting Tiko on a project identification and funding mission.

'Perhaps you could do with some financial assistance,' Mr Minte suggested.

'That'll help a lot, sir.'

'We have money set aside for the promotion of culture preservation projects in the Pacific. Our aim is to preserve the Pacific Way. We want to help you.'

'Very generous of you, sir. When can I have some money?'

'After you've written me a letter asking for assistance.'

'Do I have to? Can't you just send some?'

'Obviously you haven't dealt with us before.'

'No, sir.'

'Things are never quite that simple, you know. We have the money to distribute, but we can't give it away just like that. We want you to ask us first. Tell us what you want; we don't wish to tell you what you should do. My job is to go around informing people that we want to co-operate for their own good, and people should play their part and ask us for help. Do you get me?'

'Yes, sir. But suppose no one asks?'

'That's no problem. Once people know that they can get things from us for nothing, they will ask. And besides, we can always send someone to help them draw up requests. By the way, who's that jolly chap over there?'

'That's His Excellency the Imperial Governor.'

'My God. I have something very important to tell him. I must see him now before he leaves. Come and see me tomorrow morning at ten at the MERCY Building. Think of what I've said and we'll talk about it then. I'm pleased we've met. Good night.'

Shortly afterwards Ole left for home, disturbed and feeling reduced. He had never before asked for anything from a total stranger. If Mr Minte had money to give, as he said he did, why did he not just give it? Why should he, Ole, be required to beg for it? He remembered an incident from his childhood when a bigger boy offered him a mango then demanded that he fall on his knees and beg for it. Hatred for Mr Minte surged in his stomach to be mixed with self-hatred for his own simplicity and for his reluctance to ask from a stranger while everyone else seemed to have been doing so without compunction. He needed a typewriter and some filing cabinets, not for himself but for the important work he had set out to do. Yet pride stood in the way. The Good Book says that pride is the curse of man. The Good Book also says, 'Ask and it shall be given unto you.' One should learn to ask for and accept things with grace. But he could not sleep well that night; his heart was torn – it was not easy to ask from a stranger if you weren't practised at it. He must do it nevertheless. There was no other way of acquiring the facilities he needed. Anyway, he supposed as he drifted into sleep, it's like committing sin: once you start it becomes progressively easier.

At ten the following morning Ole entered the MERCY office where Mr Minte was waiting.

'Good morning, Ole. Have you made up your mind about seeking help from us?'

'Yes, sir. I'd like to have a typewriter and some filing cabinets. I'll write you a letter. Thank you.'

'Now, Ole, I'm afraid that's not possible. As I said last night, things aren't so simple. We don't want to tell people what to do with the money we give, but there are things we cannot fund. Take your particular request for instance. My Minister has to report to our parliament on things people do with the money we give. Once politicians see that we've given a typewriter for culture preservation they will start asking embarrassing questions of my Minister. What's a civilized typewriter to do with native cultures? The Opposition will have a field day on that one. Most embarrassing. That won't do . . . '

'But in my case it has everything to do . . . '

'You have to ask for something more directly relevant, I'm sorry. Relevance is the key that opens the world,' Mr Minte said, and paused to savour the profundity of his remark before turning on an appearance of outstanding generosity.

'Look, we can give you $2000 a year for the next five years to publish a monthly newsletter of your activities. Send us a copy of each issue, OK?'

'But I still need a typewriter to produce a newsletter.'

'Try using a MERCY typewriter. You will have to form a committee, you know.'

'A committee? What for? I've been working alone for seven

years and no committee has been interested in me.'

'Oh, they will, they will when good money's involved. The point, however, is that we don't give to individuals, only to organizations. You form a group, call it the Oral Traditions Committee or something, which will then write to us for assistance. Do you follow me?' Mr Minte looked at his watch and lifted an eyebrow. 'I'm sorry, I have to go now to talk with the National Women's Association. Don't you know that your women are more forthcoming and efficient than your men? When we tell them – sorry – suggest that they form a committee, they do so immediately. It's a great pleasure handling them. Their organizations have tons of money from us and other helpers. Think about it and come again tomorrow at the same time. See you then.' Mr Minte went out and disappeared into a black official limousine.

Ole remained in the office keeping very still, as was his habit when angry, breathing deeply until he had regained his equanimity. Then he rose and walked slowly to the office of his intimate, the high MERCY official, who sat quietly and listened until Ole had poured out his heart.

'The trouble with you is that you're too moralistic,' Emi Bagarap said thoughtfully. 'You're too proud, Ole.'

'It's no longer a matter of pride, I've seen to that; it's self-respect.'

'Self-respect is a luxury we can't afford; we have no choice but to shelve it for a while. When we're developed, then we will do something about dignity and self-respect . . . '

'What if we are never developed?'

'We will develop! There's not a speck of doubt about that. You must cultivate the power of positive thinking,' said Emi Bagarap looking wise, experienced, and positive.

'You must keep in mind, Ole, that we're playing inter-national games in which the others have money and we don't. Simple as that. They set the rules and we play along trying to bend them for our benefit.

'Anyway, those on the other side aren't all that strict with their rules either. Take Mr Minte, for instance. He offers to give you $2000 a year for five years and all he wants is for you to form a committee and then the committee writes a letter asking for the funds and produces a newsletter regularly. But he didn't say anything about how the organization is to be formed or run. See? You can get three or four friends and form a committee with you as chairman and treasurer, and someone else as secretary. Get only those who're neither too interested nor too knowledgeable. That'll give you the freedom to do what needs to be done.

'Again, the letter asking for help will be from the Committee and not from you personally. Your self-respect will not be compromised, not that it really matters, mind you.

'Furthermore, Mr Minte didn't say anything about the size of your newsletter, did he? You can write it in a page or two taking about half an hour each month. And you don't have to write it in English either. And if you so wish you can produce two copies per issue, one for your records and one for Mr Minte. I'm not suggesting that this is what you do; that would be dishonest, you see. I'm only pointing out one of the many possible moves in this game.

'Most importantly, Mr Minte didn't say what you should do with the rest of the money. So. You pay, say, two dollars a year for your newsletter and with the balance you can buy a typewriter and four filing cabinets every year for five years.

'You see, Mr Minte is very good and very generous; he's been playing international games for a long, long time and knows what's what. He wants you to have your typewriter and other things but won't say it. Go see him tomorrow and tell him that you'll do what he told you.

'But you must remember that in dealing with foreigners, never appear too smart; it's better that you look humble and half-primitive, especially while you're learning the ropes. And try to take off six stone. It's necessary that we're seen to be starved and needy. The reason why Tiko gets very little aid money is that our people are too fat and jolly. I wish the government would wake up and do something about it.'

And so, Emi Bagarap, whose self-respect had been shelved for years, went on giving his friend, the novice, the benefit of his vast experience in the ways of the world.

When Ole left the office he was relieved and almost happy. He had begun to understand the complexities of life. Give me time, O Lord, he prayed as he headed toward the bus stop, and I'll be out there with the best of them.

'A word with you, old friend,' Manu's voice checked him.

'Oh, hello Manu. Long time no see. Where've you been?'

'Watching you lately, old friend. You have that look on your face,' Manu said simply.

'What look?' asked Ole in puzzlement.

'Of someone who's been convinced by the likes of Emi Bagarap. I'm worried about you. I know you and Emi have always been close, but allow me to tell you this before it's too late. Don't let him or anyone like him talk you into something you . . .'

'No one talks me into anything. I've never allowed anyone to do that,' Ole cut in with visible irritation.

'You're already into it, old friend; it's written all over your face. Beware of Emi; he's sold his soul and will have you sell yours if you don't watch out.'

'That's ridiculous. No one's sold his soul. We're only shelving certain things for a little while until we get what's good for the country.'

'No, no, old friend. You're deceiving yourself. You're not shelving anything; you're set to sell your soul no less. Do it and you'll never get it back because you will not want to.'

'You're wasting your time and mine, Manu. You belong to the past; it's time to wake up to the future,' Ole snapped and strode away.

Next day when he met Mr Minte he was all smiles. The smoothly seasoned diplomat raised an eyebrow and smiled back – he was familiar with this kind of transformation; it happened all the time; it was part of his job to make it happen.

'Well, Ole, when will you form the committee?'

'Tonight, sir.'

'Congratulations, Mr Chairman. Get your secretary to write me a letter and you'll get your first $2000 in a month's time.'

'Thank you very, very much Mr Minte; I'm most grateful.'

'You're welcome. It's been a pleasure dealing with you, Ole. you have a big future ahead. If you need anything, anything at all, don't hesitate to contact me. You know, if we had more people like you around, the Pacific would develop so rapidly you wouldn't see it.'

They shook hands, and as Ole opened the door Mr Minte called out, 'By the way, the INESCA will soon hold a workshop in Manila on the proper methods of collecting oral traditions. It'll do you good if you attend. I'll let you know in a few weeks.'

'Thank you again, Mr Minte.'

'Don't mention it. I'm always happy to be of assistance. Goodbye for now. I hope you'll soon get a typewriter and the filing cabinets.'

Ole whistled his way home, much elated. That evening, he formed the Committee for the Collection of Oral Traditions with himself as chairman and treasurer, his youngest brother as secretary, two friends as committee members, and the district officer as patron. The Committee immediately set to work drafting a letter to Mr Minte which was deliverd by hand the following morning. Within a month Ole recieved a cheque for $2000 and an invitation to attend a six-week training course in Manila. He went, leaving his house in the care of his elderly aunt, who did not understand what he was doing.

He found the course too confusing, but the throbbing night-life of Manila more than compensated for its uselessness. He enjoyed himself so much that on the third week he received a shot of penicillin and some friendly counsel from an understanding physician.

On his return journey he bought a duty-free typewriter in Sydney, where he also ordered four filing cabinets to be shipped home. He was much pleased with his speedy progress: he had secured what had only recently been a dream. One day, he told himself as the aircraft approached the Tikomaul International Airport, he would take over the directorship of the Bureau for the Preservation of Traditional Culture and Essential Indigenous Personality. Both Sailosi Atiu and Eric Hobsworth-Smith were getting long in the tooth.

When he finally arrived home his aged aunt greeted him tearfully. 'Ole, Ole, you're safe. Thank God those heathens didn't eat you. You look so thin; what did they do to you?'

'Don't worry, auntie,' Ole laughed. 'Those people aren't heathens, they're mainly Catholics, and they don't eat people. They only shoot each other.'

'You look so sick. Did they try to shoot you too?'

'I'm perfectly healthy ... except that I stubbed my big toe one night,' and he chortled.

'You should always wear shoes when you go overseas; I told you so, Ole. What's the matter? Why are you giggling?'

'The house looks so neat,' Ole deftly changed the subject. 'Thank you for looking after it; I know that I can always depend on you.'

'Oh, Ole, I cleared and scrubbed the whole place from top to bottom; it was such a mess. You need a wife to clean up after you. Why don't you get married? Yes, Ole, you were always messy, leaving things all over the place. You haven't changed, really you haven't.' She paused to dry her face. 'I threw out so much rubbish,' she said in a tone that alarmed Ole.

'You did, did you? And what did you do with my books?'

'Books? What books?'

'Those exercise books I stacked at the corner back there.'

'You mean those used-up filthy things? Oh, Ole, you shouldn't have kept your old school books. They collected so much dust and so many cockroaches.'

'They're the most important things in my life. I cannot live without them,' he declared and went looking for his books. 'They aren't here. What have you done with them?' he demanded.

'Sit down, Ole, and let's talk like good Christians.'

'No! Where are they?'

'Ole, you've always been a good boy. Sit down and have something to eat. You must be starving. What have they done to you?'

'Never mind that, I want my books!'

'Sit down and don't scream at me. That's a good boy. We're poor, you, me, the neighbours. And food is so expensive.'

'Where are my books?'

'Toilet paper is beyond our reach. It used to be ten cents a roll.'

'Yes, but what has that got to do with my books?'

'You didn't leave me any money when you went away, Ole. I had to eat and keep clean, and things are so expensive.'

'I'm sorry, but where are my books?'

'Don't keep asking me that question, Ole. I'm trying to explain. I'm your only living aunt. And I'm very old and ready to go to Heaven. Don't hasten me along, please. Don't you think that I'm more important than any old book?'

'What did you do with them? Where are they?'

'Ole, I had no money for food; I had no money for toilet paper. I had to eat and keep clean. Stop looking at me like that. You frighten me so.' She sniffed, blew her nose, then continued in a subdued tone. 'I used some and sold the rest cheaply to the neighbours. They're poor, Ole, but they also have to be hygienic.'

Ole stared at his aunt in disbelief. 'No, no. You're pulling my leg: you didn't really sell my books for toilet paper . . . '

'I did. Yes, yes I did. I'm sorry but how could I have known they were so important?'

'Oh, my God!' Ole choked in anguish. He sat very still, breathing deeply, trying desperately to stop his arms from lashing out. Then slowly, very slowly, he mumbled, 'Seven years' hard work down the bloody drain; shit!' Almost immediately the import of what he had uttered sank in and he burst into hysterical laughter, with tears streaming down his cheeks. It was also then that the brilliant idea occurred to him. He reached out and embraced his aunt, apologizing for his rudeness, promising never to do it again, and the old lady was so surprised at the transformation that she sobbed with tears of joy.

He recalled that he had Mr Minte's government committed to $10 000 over five years. That was to be the start; he, Ole Pasifikiwei, whose books had gone down the drain, would henceforth go after the whales of the ocean. If he were to beg, he informed himself, he might as well do it on the grand scale. He therefore sent Mr Minte an urgent letter and was soon rewarded with the arrival of Dr Andrew Wheeler, a razor-sharp expert upon whose advice Ole instituted the National Council for Social, Economic, and Cultural Research, bagging chiefs, ministers of state, top-flight clergymen, wives of VIPs, and his old friend, Emi Bagarap, into honorary office-holding positions, with himself as full-time secretary. Then Dr Wheeler devised a comprehensive four-year research programme and despatched professionally-worded letters to the INESCA, the Forge Foundation, the Friends of South Sea Natives, the Third World Conservation Commission, and the Konshu Fish and Forestry Institute for $400 000 funding.

A little later, and again with the skilled connivance of his indispensable Dr Wheeler, Ole expanded by creating eighteen other national committees and councils with specific, aid-worthy objectives, and designed irresistibly attractive projects and schemes to be funded from international sources. And he capped it all by succeeding in getting his groups placed by the Great International Organization on the list of the Two Hundred Least Developed Committees – those in need of urgent, generous aid.

After six years Ole had applied for a total of $14 million for his organizations, and his name had become well known in certain influential circles in Brussels, The Hague, Bonn, Geneva, Paris, London, New York, Washington, Wellington, Canberra, Tokyo, Peking, and Moscow, as well as in such regional laundry centres as Bangkok, Kuala Lumpur, Manila, Suva, and Noumea.

And the University of the Southern Paradise, whose wise, wily leaders saw in the man a great kindred talent that matched their own, bestowed upon him honorary doctoral degrees in Economics, Divinity, and Philosophy, although that learned institution had no philosophy of any kind, colour, or creed.

With fame and honour to his name, Ole Pasifikiwei immersed himself totally in the supreme task of development through foreign aid, relishing the twists and turns of international funding games. He has since shelved his original sense of self-respect and has assumed another, more attuned to his new, permanent role as a first-rate, expert beggar.

The Woman Who Never Went Home

SHONAGH KOEA

The man in the chamois-leather shirt was sitting on a high bar-stool, whisky on the rocks in hand, on the evening of her second day at the hotel. He was looking out over the swimming-pool with its cascades of bougainvillaea.

The likeness was so extraordinary that she dropped her bag and all the impedimenta women take to a tropical beach rolled out on to the floor.

The little dark-eyed maid who tended the foyer rushed forward to pick up the hairbrush, the lipstick that rolled under the receptionist's desk, the black bikini.

Was Madame tired? Had the sun been too much for Madame? Catherine waved her sunhat lazily at the maid and the porter and told them Madame was merely careless. Calm and clear as usual, her voice surprised her.

Halfway up the stairs she changed her mind and went slowly down again, taking now the left fork at the landing, the route that led to the mirrored Art Deco bar with its basket chairs, the lithe contemptuous barman and the man in chamois-leather who looked almost exactly like the man she remembered so well, a man who had been dead for ten years.

The barman stood behind his counter from mid-afternoon each day, shuttered eyes removing from his tired gaze the droves of Japanese tourists who photographed each other in exactly duplicated attitudes with airs of terrified excitement, and the other travellers who arrived, *en masse*, by bus from the airport.

They all carried plastic carry-alls emblazoned with the names of tour companies. Go-Along Tours, Best Tours, Sunset Tours (for the aged) had all passed through in the last two days. They came to see life, Catherine supposed, though if they had looked round instead of at each other they would have seen only the contempt of the sinuous barman.

'Won't you be bored?' her friends had asked before she left home. 'Fancy staying in Noumea for three whole weeks all on your own. Whatever will you do?'

She told them she would look at things and they gave her up as ridiculous. At eighteen she had been a wild, shy, ridiculous creature and had not altered greatly in twenty years. She had merely become more practised at it and more accomplished at hiding her tendencies.

But here indeed was something to look at, and like an amputee who thoughtfully fingers the stump of a limb in unguarded moments she charted a course for the mirrored bar where the man in chamois sat so silently, staring into his drink.

Almost on the parquet now, nearly at the bar entrance, her feet faltered on the last stair and she gave a scream, pointing to an ornamental fish-pool built into the wall. An enormous goldfish floated on its surface, eyes open, stomach distended, dead, and trailing a line of glutinous slime from its mouth.

The lady who looked after the gift shop by the reception desk rushed up, forgetting for a moment her look of ceaseless allure. The fish did not fool those sharp French eyes that divined the needs of the customers so well – French perfume and handbags displayed on a velvet cloth and other, less presentable things underneath the counter. She briskly tapped the glass and the old trickster fish rolled lazily over, swam again.

The maid from the foyer, the porter and the lady from the gift shop all screamed with laughter. Madame was so droll.

If she had banged a drum her arrival in the bar could not have been more noticeable but the man in chamois still sat on the bar-stool, self-contained and uncomprehending, as she slipped on to the stool beside him.

He was not as tall as the other had been but he had the same beautiful hands that now cupped his drink. From the toes of his shabby shoes of Spanish leather to his hair which grew in the same careless way he was almost an exact duplicate except that his eyes were the wrong colour. She studied his reflection minutely.

He and the barman began to talk with the easy familiarity of long acquaintance. She could not understand a word of their rapid French, though his voice was soft and pleased her.

The barman turned sharply towards her and she ordered a glass of mineral water, his palpitating disdain now becoming almost a living thing like a black cat with golden eyes sitting on the counter.

There seemed an air of intimacy between them as they talked. Perhaps they spoke of the government or racehorses, she could not tell. When the flush of early evening customers arrived the barman had to go elsewhere, tossing a few words over his shoulder when he could.

The man in the leather shirt settled on the stood, melancholy and unmoving. He drank with no hurry but with a dedicated lack of satisfaction. As soon as one drink was finished the barman, with no bidding, brought another the same in a fresh glass.

The sudden tropical night was now deeply upon everything. It seemed the only world was that in the little bar. Dinner was looming up and people began to consult the menu.

'I'm having frog's legs.'

'Mummy, David says he's having frog's legs.'

'Alec, will you speak to David and tell him he's not having frog's legs.'

It was the time of school holidays and the hotel was riddled with bold, charmless offspring who bleated loudly about the pleasures of Bondi, Wellington or Hornby.

Presently the man rose and, speaking sharply but indulgently to the barman, who smiled for the first time, strode away through the geranium-scented night. The barman wrote on a pad and it was a moment before she realized the bill had been chalked up. He had not paid.

The street outside seemed deserted. Where the road forked three ways the street-lamps shone only on empty pavements, shuttered windows and the softness of flowers. He had gone completely and, suddenly bereft, she wandered back into the hotel with distant laughter from unknown doorways echoing in her ears.

Now at last the stairs could claim a triumph, for they

claimed her completely this time, a full three flights. Alone, she dined in her room on an orange and a piece pulled from a French loaf and wondered where he came from. What was the reason for his air of past splendour?

Perplexed, she sat all the next day beside the swimming-pool like a pensive mushroom, dressed in the strapless black bathing-suit purchased in Honolulu the previous year and screened from other bathers by the immense size of her Rarotonga sunhat of two years ago.

Before the rising scents of early evening had even slightly blemished the late afternoon she was waiting in the foyer, casually flicking over the pages of a magazine and wearing a diamond horseshoe round her neck for luck. Would he come again?

A dozen times she looked up the forking road and then set off to walk the maze of streets, hoping to see him emerge from a flowery gateway, but although she passed along many blocks there was never a sight of the magical one she sought.

After this futile excursion she saw him again, sitting on the same bar-stool with the familiar drink in his hand.

His eyes contained a sudden recognition or rebuff, she could not tell which so she bolted away, in her wild shy way, into the dining-room.

He lapsed once more into a sort of melancholy after he finished his talk of politics or women with the barman. With the same shouted exchanged over the bill he disappeared abruptly into the night as the crowd thickened and she finished wasting some chicken and strawberries.

He would come again, she knew that now, and a sense of girlish skittishness came over her as though she had beaten death and destruction.

The following day she click-clacked into the bar as soon as it opened wearing a pair of French sandals with very high heels, a bikini made of black silk chrysanthemums and the large sunhat. Secrecy did not interest her. It was simply that she lacked the courage to carry out her quixotic plan and felt a need to boldly expose herself, thus becoming bold enough to act. Her shyness she carried with her, about the level of the third rib, and almost bent over to accommodate its swelling size.

The barman was alone and without preamble she began. The carefully rehearsed sentences, gleaned from her English-French dictionary the previous evening, fell easily from her lips.

The Monsieur who sat every evening on this very stool, she said, and with temerity actually perched herself upon it and sat there swinging her legs. This Monsieur was the exact image of someone who had been dead for ten years. The barman, teatowel discarded now, looked at the rings she still wore from habit and placed his hand on his heart.

No, she said, it was another one, not her husband. Her grief, she told him, had become unresolved and she bore it with her always like a silver plate in her head. She had not cried when he died. She had gone on calmly cutting star shapes out of shortbread and had said, callously, 'Dead? Who? What a sad accident.'

All this she told the barman in her halting French and he listened quietly with his hand on his heart. It was surprisingly easy to tell him what she had told no other and she thought that the reason was her use of another language. The words were strangers to her.

Nothing was required from the Monsieur, she told the barman. The pleasure of looking at that face was sufficient. But Monsieur, for the sake of his face, must not owe money anywhere and Madame would secretly pay his bill. He must never know who did this.

With one hand still on his heart the barman took her money with the other, quickly. They arranged for the bar bill to be sent to her room each evening on a tray and thus their conspiracy began and flourished.

Warned by the recognition in his eyes she widely skirted the bar area that evening and chose a shadowed seat behind a trellis for her observation of the man in chamois. His reflection was better value there because she could not only see it with a limpid clarity, it was mirrored in another glass. The price of anonymity in the shadows was a double image, a bargain.

An insomniac for years, she now fell at night into a gentle sleep which came upon her swiftly, as if she were a small falcon that rode on a prince's arm and had a velvet cover thrown over her head.

Waiting each day for evening, she spent her time on the beach observing crop-headed boys in military uniforms who watched sleek, exquisite girls. Even a deliberate seeker of evil could find no offence in their minuscule nakedness, she thought. Tourists lolled about in vile imitations of what they saw, the benediction of the sand never covering the folds of flesh. But they were happy, Catherine told herself, and their happiness was new and topical. Her sudden content was an old illicit enchantment, remembered from days past.

Each evening, as he rose to leave, the barman showed the man in the leather shirt the clear page on the pad. At first the man laughed in a mocking way and looked round the room with a sneer that the face she knew so well never wore in the lifetime she recollected. His privacy remained inviolate and his suspicion was followed by puzzlement. Each evening he walked away through the double doors with his hand upon his face, perplexed. She supposed the barman had told him of the mysterious likeness.

The barman warmed a little toward her now but he volunteered no information about the man in leather and she was too proud to ask for any. As for the man himself, unruffled, self-contained, an enigma, he spoke to no one but a black-and-white dog, which walked through the bar each evening, and the sinuous barman who remained the custodian of all secrets and the broadcaster of none.

She used to look for him each evening, threading her way through the blocks of houses round the hotel, shrilled at by resident poodles and chihuahuas whose *Chien Méchant* notices advertised only their toy ferocity.

He was always sitting on the same bar-stool when she returned, appearing from the entrance she never found.

The daily bill grew inexorably smaller. He began to look round with a veiled curiosity. Night after night his enveloping thoughtful gaze took in the plump Australian lady who favoured red and black spots, the old twins in pink cardigans, the sharp little blonde in a mauve velvet track-suit, the myriad of travellers who came and went.

*

There were only three days left of her holiday, so filled with her own invented charming business, when she saw him glance at her shadowy reflection in a mirror. He had never before conquered the trellis wall behind the roses.

She was dressed in her favourite grey, with a silver rope belt twisted round her waist and silver sandals that tied in bows like wings at her ankles. One of the Australians had just said to her, 'You're lucky you're so thin.' Indifferent, she turned away and met the eyes that were the wrong colour in the mirror, staring him out with what she hoped was an unseeing vagueness.

A gypsy violinist in a black velvet bolero and sleeves of ruffled silk came the following evening and played sad endless tunes.

Her usual fruitless search of the streets was accomplished swiftly so that she could be back earlier than usual. It was, she knew, an absurd contradiction.

She sped along, with purpose now, hardly noticing the chic that made the smallest garden charming. The spills of miniature lettuces growing in terra cotta pots beside secret, tiled doorways did not interest her, nor did her favourite garden, the one with the ornamental cast-iron wheelbarrow mounded with begonias and the scarlet blooms of impatiens.

He was at the bar, in residence as she called it grandly and wryly to herself, when she returned.

The melancholy climbing notes of the violin rose as the man in the chamois walked towards her secret trellised perch among the roses.

'Madame,' he said, 'you remind me so vividly of someone I knew once in Singapore. In 1961.'

She had never been to Singapore, she told him. In 1961 she was aged 18 and under her narrow bed in an unpalatable boarding-house she kept a green cardboard suitcase filled with a few shreds of clothing and linen, purchased at sales, in preparation for a marriage as unpalatable as that same boarding-house but more binding than its porridge.

He digested this piece of startling conversation for a moment, rocking back on his heels, and then he roared with laughter.

The other one had been exactly the same, she thought. She had always been able to make him laugh and that was how it had all begun.

For Sale at Koke Market

JOHN KOLIA

Koke Market (pronounced Koki in the Australian dialect) is now overlaid by a clean layer of red gravel but it was once more interestingly smelly. It lies east of Port Moresby harbour and of Ela Beach in the Central Province of the Papuan coast of the island of New Guinea, and has probably seen more years than either you or I, and has certainly had more visitors. Vegetables, fish and game have been sold there and perhaps more than that, for it is an exchange centre for language, marriage, customs, culture, politics, prostitutes, religion and philosophy. As in all other markets, prices eventually depend on demand and supply, although there are interesting obstacles occasionally to the process.

For instance, sometimes the Hula fishermen with memories of their recent labours among the dangers of the outer reef depths, refuse to allow their fish prices to be brought down even though the catch goes stale and unsold. Similarly, Miss Abaijah once declined most attractive offers of coalition at the market although this would have strengthened her Papuan separatist movement, and without that support, she could hardly hope to succeed in her aim. Mostly, however, the prices of goods and political parties tend to go down just before the market closes and the eagerness with which some politicians will press their stale fish on the customers is sometimes quite amusing.

But I have made up my mind to tell this story without tricks and shall drop the sarcasms. The story I have in mind concerns the widow Emma Skulate who was left a house above Koke Point and a pension of plantations by her late husband, and who did daily shopping as a sort of health-excursion at Koke Market, although I suspect she was really looking for friendly faces of long ago. Well, that's the matter I have in mind and perhaps something else might happen to come out of it.

Some tens of thousands of years before the birth of that female, the Koita people from the hills overlooking the market used to come down towards the market and on to the beach to collect water from wells there and to gather edible shell animals and shells for burning lime. They were not very interested in the products of the sea, however, and when epidemics preceded the arrival of the first foreigners (germs travel faster than the gospel), they decided that the wells had been malevolently enchanted and withdrew to the hills and dug new wells. The Motu newcomers by then had arrived in the Moresby area but they settled to the east and west of Koke, and having negotiated peaceful co-existence with the Koita, clung to beaches away from Koke and were joined by some of the Koita. Today, the Motu lingua franca has become dominant and if outsiders notice at all that some families are different from most of the Motu, they call them Koitapu which refers to the sago-growing of some of the Koita, using an old Vaimuru word for sago to so describe them. Later the Koita and Motu made famous if not notorious return trade-journeys to the gulf and the word for sago became other, but as a rather dry academic acquaintance once wittily said, 'I mention the fact merely to dispose of it and will not refer to the topic again.'

Later the white foreigners arrived, notably at the villages of Hanuabada to the west inside the harbour, then at Granville as the neck connecting Paga Hill to the mainland was called, then along Ela Beach and to Koke and inland. To get the trader Goldie away from the missionaries (on a hill overlooking Hanuabada), his near-village land was exchanged for land behind Koke and part of this forms the Koke-Badili area. Both missionaries and administrators rode their horses there on the beach and canoes from the east found a suitable resting place. The area developed slowly but during the last war a road shot up from Koke to the three airstrips and thousands of khaki-clad soldiers camped on the hillsides. Thus the area was worth developing after the war, as one pioneering mission (now increased) and one respected

Chinese man (now deceased) discovered. The market developed; the little island, once the site of a gaol, was joined and flattened; canoes came oftener and became stranded houses and one of the worst traffic bottle-necks in a city notorious for poor road engineering, developed. Cars, in the absence of an adequate public transport system, became so numerous that, finally, traffic could travel only west through Koke and had to return, even heavy trucks, via a dangerous hill-side road. More than one drunken driver became suddenly sober on finding himself flying down from the upper road towards the waves lapping the seawall of the lower road. Mrs Skulate's house sat dramatically between the two, and a more nervous woman might have wondered whether her life would not end with a truck through the ceiling or in an avalanche on to the reef.

But she was not a nervous woman. She was an old and calm woman. Not that she looked old, well not as old as she should have. As a younger woman she had selected a simple inexpensive appearance for herself (which mainly depended on controlled input and a protective film of fine oil) and dressed well. She could afford to spend money and time on trying always to look 'cool' (a usage which was not invented in the 1960s) so that a stranger entering her environment felt he had migrated to the moderate zone and one or two overheated gentlemen had even been known to shiver slightly. Given her age and her style, no doubt you have guessed that the role this dedicated actress adopted was based on great ladies of the screen, Gloria Swanson, Bette Davis, Katherine Hepburn, only in their non-hysterical scenes, of course. No Joan Crawford for her. So dedicated to this twenty-four hour image was she, even in private, that it would be untrue to call her an amateur. Pour scorn on her as you will, it was not such a bad pose with which to cope with life, as you will see.

At least Iani was impressed as his eyes followed her about the market that day, choosing herself a few choice pieces of native fruit, but mainly having her morning stroll. He wondered what it was she wanted, strolling about like the Queen at yet another tour of a Midlands factory. And quite a few villagers greeted her. But, no, she was not a missionary because she smiled at them from a height, nor held earnest conversations in the vernacular with them. In fact, when he got as close as he could and pretended to be absorbed in a nearby pattern of betels, pepper-bark and little puffed-up plastic bags of lime, all set out on a woven green-coconut-leaf mat, he discovered that she talked to everyone in a soft, slow, simple English which somehow ensured a communication of pleasant superficialities that ignored language barriers. These trivia appeared to concern a certain village, 'faithful old Sevese', and 'the late Mr Taubada', by whom Iani presumed was meant the white woman's husband.

'Well, here's one who's stayed on', he reflected. 'Am I also capable of finding a helpful protectress?'

Then he noticed that behind her, but quite a way behind, for he was delayed by more acquaintances and warmer conversations, came a tall, greying old fellow, still immensely strong-looking, with a woven shopping-basket on his arm. Iani did not doubt for a moment that this was the servant, but a plan occurred to him, for he recognized that the man was from his own area. The older man had not been back except for brief visits for a domestic-servant's lifetime, and Iani had not seen his village since he went away to a mission secondary school. But contacts have been established on less secure bases.

'Oh, there's my dear old friend Sevese', he announced to the space between himself and the lady. And he walked towards the unsuspecting subject of his sudden affections like a second-hand car salesman towards an unenthusiastic customer. Naturally he had the lady's attention, since he practically made the broadcast into her ear, and after all, he was a fine-looking and neatly dressed young man, even if 'university-dropout' was a constituent of his aura. Did she see through him at that moment? After all, who else would say it to nobody in good English? Why had he not called out 'Turagu' or 'Sevese' in excitement? Was she amused to recognize a fellow RADA-aspirant on the crowded market-stage of life? But probably she was mildly surprised and pleased to discover that faithful but foolish old Sevese could have a nephew (was it?) of such education and appearance. It might have been the son of one of the old labourers?

And having in her hands some golden citrus with which to make the daily sipora-drink for those guests who feigned sobriety, she had perforce to return to Sevese and the basket, to smile and comment patronizingly, 'Oh, have you found someone you know? How pleasant. Stay and talk to your friend, Sevese, I can walk home alone', the last part of the statement being of puzzling superfluity since it could never have been said that she had ever walked home not alone, that is never actually with Sevese. Rather she strolled smiling beneath her latest sunglasses and mock-floppy hat, while Sevese trudged watchfully behind. The only time he was not within her gravitational pull was during her annual absences from the country. And even then Sevese and his wife received postcards as regular as solar days and could demonstrate to friends her last position in the heavens, whether beneath a tall iron tower, on a ship gliding through suspiciously blue waves, or among white powdery hills; even if they had no real idea how to measure those positions longitudinally or latitudinally. They did know however which day the bank-manager's wife would call with exactly how much money for the week's wages and housekeeping. When they went home for their annual holidays (the wife's home) an idea that seemed to be more hers than theirs, she was adequately served and protected by replacement relatives chosen by Sevese. Chosen by him, that is, so that no harm would come to his well-paid position.

But she was about to escape and in a moment Sevese would be shrugging him off, so Iani was forced to ask, 'May – may I call on Sevese and ask your advice on something?' Now, one penalty of being always polite is that one cannot say, 'No', except indirectly. Therefore she was obliged to answer, 'Of course, if you wish'. Not as she wished, you notice, for of course she did not manage her late husband's extant fortune without having a financially suspicious mind which had little warning-signs like 'beggar', 'borrower' and 'confidence-trickster'.

In no way disturbed, not even by Iani's good looks, she carefully crossed the road from market to trading-company and rose towards her house like a relaxed escalator, but now of course she had two satellites a long way behind her. Not that she turned round to see them, but they were there nevertheless. One could perhaps tell by the shading on the contours of the more ancient of these satellites that its orbit was being somewhat affected by the entry of a new body into the system but, to return to earth and the human atmosphere, for the moment there was a calm front off the Gulf of Papua.

Iani looked at the trim figure in her ivory dress and beige shoes up ahead and wondered how she kept so clean. But then in his black trousers and embroidered Manila-shirt, he also looked tidier than dusty Moresby made likely. They were both practising the same device, in fact, wearing nothing that looked even slightly soiled. The difference was that her practice of it cost some hundred times a week what it cost him, and while she gambled in gilt-edged shares only slightly-tarnished, he played with unreliable cards with crumpled edges and wildly fluctuating fortunes. And, to complete the parade, Sevese wore a cotton shirt about width-feet wide at the shoulders, a pair of grey shorts which appeared to start approximately height-feet above the ground and a foot-sized pair of well-planted sandals. Iani being slighter, but with eastern Gulf height nevertheless, for the Toaripi are a tall group, could, by comparison, be more easily described in accordance with the introduced decimal system.

Thus, that is in one and two, they arrived at the upper and only entrance to the house, which was one of those where the back door is in fact the front, the lower giving on to a small terraced-balcony with impressive stone walls, these last made by a Wanigela man who could glance up any day from his canoe-house beyond the market and admire his own craftsmanship. He would have been surprised to realize that Mrs Skulate also admired the collection of beached canoe-dwellings, from a safe distance.

Iani realized that he might be about to find himself lost in the servants' quarters, which he later realized formed a flat under the main house. He therefore explained to Sevese, 'I want Mrs Skulate to help me fill in a form', a request with which Sevese had often approached his employer himself. Sevese's suspicions were thus somewhat lessened, although he stayed in the kitchen so that he would not miss a syllable of the ensuing conversation which had syllabic patterns he could hardly comprehend.

'May I come in?' Iani asked politely.

'Please do', said the gracious lady from Hollywood via lonely plantation.

At this point, I should perhaps explain that dropouts from the university were of two main types, the excited and the calm. The first were sincere idealists who wanted to change things or defend the village mores and who wrote fiery poetry and earned their extra-mural individual degrees in the discipline of worldly studies. Iani was rather of the other type, academically lazy, admiring of sophisticated urbanism as seen in unrealistic films, and eager for a suitable sinecure 'if only my second-cousin's brother-in-law gets in at the next election'; that is, an insincere idealist. He certainly was not going to stand about like a nervous servant, and sat down in one of the armchairs, producing at the same time his calculatedly shy smile.

'How may I help you; Iani, is it?'

'I wondered if you could advise me on getting a job.'

'I should hardly imagine so. Aren't there trained employment officers for that purpose?'

'But perhaps if you listened to my story . . . '

'Certainly', she answered, lighting a cigarette in a long holder, and thinking, 'He'll tell me a pack of lies then try to borrow money; I'll return him to Sevese, and that will be the end of it.'

But his next remark outmanoeuvred her. It seems he had once read Hemingway's dictum about producing only one true statement. If only all the other devious Papuans had emulated him, who knows what remarkable advances in racial integration might have occurred?

'I live by gambling', he told her, 'and would love to have an affair with a beautiful woman like yourself.'

Her eyes blinked in surprise and she laughed, 'Well, you are a remarkable young man. However, I neither gamble nor pretend to be younger than I am.'

'Oh', he countered with his prepared thrust, 'in that case may I be your acquaintance and have the pleasure of your conversation?'

'I am always pleased to meet Sevese's relations.'

'No, I am not asking permission to sit in your kitchen and eat your left-overs', he said, with only a slight tremble of indignation. 'I don't mind. You can treat me like another adult of whom you are not ashamed, or throw me out. If the former, we could be friends. If the latter, you are missing a chance to fit into today's Moresby. But, if you are that type of foreigner, how is it you are still here?'

'I mean in no way to offend you', she said, 'but at the same time I wouldn't want to mislead you into thinking I could be a possible source of money or gifts, and most certainly not a person with whom you could have a sexual relationship.'

'Why; d'you find natives beneath you?'

'Never; I find them around me. You are a handsome race of people, and you are very handsome, a fact you are well aware of. Be also aware, then, that I am an ageing woman who will not be having physical contact with anyone.'

'You look quite young.'

'I plan to continue doing so. In fact, I am neither young nor approachable in that way. I am quite happy to talk to you if you feel we can find any common ground for conversation. I daresay you would soon find me a bore with my books and my music – no rock-and-roll, I'm afraid. Would you care for a glass of sipora?'

'I hoped you'd offer me something stronger.'

'Sevese would be quite scandalized', she smiled. 'Sevese, may we have some sipora please?' And, with a scowl on his face he eventually brought them two tinkling glasses.

'I see', said Iani after a few sips. 'You save the strong stuff for the Europeans.'

'No, for the evening hours; it's my contribution to sobriety.'

'Why; are you frightened to let yourself go?'

'No, I'm reluctant to let the hours remaining to me slip by without observing clearly as many of them as possible.'

'You're trying to patronize me.'

'I regret not. But you mentioned a job. So far it would seem you would find employment only as a croupier or a gigolo. Since I can't assist you in either of those fields . . . '

'I also write.'

'Now, there is a way in which I could react. My life is reading. May I have the privilege . . . ?'

'Yes.'

'What have you written?'

'Well, I've written a book – about my home area.'

'Please bring it for me to read.'

'It isn't finished yet.'

'In that case allow me to be a merciless surgeon. You have not written a book, as you say. You are thinking of writing a book. And the aftercare instructions are brief. Go and get on with it instead of talking about it.'

'Are you throwing me out?'

'No, I'm throwing you in. And if you can't work where you are, you can use the study here.'

And so, Iani, thinking he had found the key to this strange woman's fortune (he thought of her as strange and imagined her to have a fortune when what she had was a comfortable income), did just that. He sat in the study and pretended to write. Each day, he scribbled away. And when she and Sevese were out, he also discovered that wherever the alcohol and money were kept, they were under lock and key and the key was not left lying about for him to pick up.

And he did show her a few pages once which after reading, she described as a 'weak effort', and exhorted him to be more ambitious and productive. She would obviously not have been popular as a tutor marking undergraduate assignments. However, one good thing did come out of the relationship, namely that he, at length, perceived the scope of her reading, himself borrowed some of her books and actually began to read, a practice that is not normally part of post-secondary school-life in Papua New Guinea. He almost felt the click when his brain one evening suddenly switched on to literacy. He experienced the new reaction of impatience at an intrusive conversation.

Ménage à trois not only described tri-spouses. Emma and Sevese certainly loved each other with the affectionate respect of years, even not speaking to each other once a year over minor differences such as whether or not Sevese's collection of empty bottles should be thrown out. And Mrs Skulate certainly liked Iani to a lesser degree than he liked her. Young men have that sort of awe of sophicated older women. The only thing is that Iani was frightened of Sevese who was highly suspicious of Iani. But a triangle has not got every point of its perimeter equidistant from a central point.

'Some of your judgements of the past are too hasty', said Emma after reading a further chapter of the great unwritten work. 'I notice such people as my husband and I get a special damning. Did you think we came here and were immediately wealthy? During the inter-war period before the Navigation Act was repealed, we lived on rice and bully-beef just as poor people do. We could not afford to have children and we worked like slaves.'

'But you did own a plantation.'

'No, we did not own it until after the war when we got sufficient war-compensation to pay off the bank-loan. For most of our lives we lived in mortal dread of the bank's foreclosing as they did to many others. One man I knew killed himself when he lost his holding. Once I did not buy a new dress for two years. Can any village woman say that? The average income of the villagers of Saroa for example – there's a UN survey on it – is today greater than my income in the 1930s. I could not buy a magazine let alone a book or a record. Hence my insatiability with both now.'

'But you exploited the natives.'

'We paid what we were told and for many years could hardly find the money to do so. We were so poor we could not have children.'

'Your husband was probably impotent.'

'No. And there were no contraceptive devices either or we couldn't afford them. We had no children mainly because we practised self-control. Ever heard of it? You should remind some of the villagers about it – many practised it traditionally – did you know? Then perhaps they will not bring babies carelessly into the world to suffer from malnutrition, TB, scabies, fungus, untreated sores and lack of schooling.'

Iani had already discovered that Mrs Skulate paid for the education of Sevese's children; and the eldest of these had even got to Lae University. And Sevese was to tell him later that she had spent her own money to run an excellent clinic on the plantation, not only for the labourers, which was required by law, but for all-comers. Many a time she had trudged to a village through the mud to aid a woman in difficult labour.

But Iani was determined to find the chink in her armour. So he finally got her to open the wine cupboard and after several drinks tried a mild caress. This produced the locking of the cupboard, the disappearance of the key and the enigmatic remark, 'I don't want you to end up in the swimming pool', which shows she was not invariably clear-headed, nor completely free from her *Sunset Boulevard* image. But at least he now knew where the drink cupboard was and decided on one glorious outburst. He would lose future benefit but just felt he must wound her deeply and end the affair. There was something of university-failure in it, something of inability to write a book, as well as a tumour of hatred of whites which he needed to have excised.

Consequently, one morning when the market excursion was about to commence (he often walked with her hoping to embarrass her, but she seemed to enjoy his company and he had to introduce her to any friends he met, and to their raised eyebrows) he pleaded muse-motivation as an excuse for not accompanying them.

He felt a sense of nervous excitement like a Portnoy in the toilet, when he got a bread-knife and prised open the door of the flimsy cupboard. He snatched a bottle and placed it to his lips. He felt very sexy. He went and lay on her bed and laughed aloud. He took off his clothes, rolled on the bed and then finally put some of her underclothing on.

'Christ; I'll go to gaol for this but it will be worth it. When she comes back I'll hide behind the door, lock Sevese out and rape her.'

As he staggered back to the living-room to get another bottle, he heard a squeal of brakes down at the market-crossing.

'They're always nearly getting run over down there', he thought, 'especially those Wanigelas.'

Then he went back and admired himself in the full-length mirror. Well, he was a splendid specimen, though perhaps not flattered by beige lace. Then he heard the ambulance.

'Hope it was a Chimbu', he shouted. Then he fell asleep on

her damask spread, liquor staining its pastel sheen from the neck of the overturned bottle.

'I've got plenty of time before they come back', he thought.

But he only woke up when he heard Sevese calling his name.

'What's the yelling about?'

He lurched drunkenly out of the bedroom. Sevese was leaning, wailing over the kitchen sink, washing the blood from the market-basket. Gloria Swanson had retired.

The Jacket

GRAEME LAY

June 24 I am going to use this big exercise book for my diary, and write down everything I feel and do. I brought the book with me when I left home. I used it for English at my school back home, and when I left there were still plenty of pages not written on, so it will be good for a diary. At home I read a story called *The Diary of Anne Frank*. It was a very sad story, but I read it heaps of times. Anne said that it made her feel better to write things down, it helped her to bear all those troubles she had, so maybe my diary will help me feel better too.

Tomorrow it will be two months exactly since I left home to come here. On the calendar, 61 days. Just two numbers, when I write it like that, 61 days, but it is the slowest and longest time I can remember. How can 61 days go so slowly? I still think of home all the time, of our house and the village and my friends, and I can remember every tiny thing about the island, except how warm it was. I can't remember that, exactly, because here it is so cold all the time, but when I lie here and close my eyes I can see my friends, and my family, and all my favourite places. Mama and Papa, and Mele and Metua, and Rima, and the big black rock where we swam in the lagoon, and the track from there that goes to the top of our mountain, and the freshness of the wind at the top. And if ever I can't remember properly, there are the photos by my bed, and my trochus shells, and my shell necklaces. One of the photos is of our guide troop. Me in the front row, between Metua and Ani, and everyone so neat in their uniforms. I smile when I look at Mama Raui, our leader, because she looks so fierce with her dark round face, but I know that she is only ferocious in the photo, she really laughs a lot. She is Mama's cousin. When I was a baby I was given to my grandparents, because I was the youngest in our family, and that is our custom. My real parents live on another island. Our village is called Vaipaka, and our house is a little bit back from the road that goes through the village, by the hill. When the last hurricane – Sharon – came, the waves from the lagoon came right over the road, but not as far as our garden, thank goodness. I have a photo of our house before the hurricane. There are flowers all over the tipani tree, and heaps of bananas on the palm by the front door. The house looks so pretty with the trees and the flowers and the lace curtains. Not like after the hurricane, when the big coral stones from the lagoon were washed up on the grass and the banana palm was broken. But at least the roof stayed on our house, not like at Mele's place. Some sheets of iron blew off their roof, and one sheet flew right over the house and cut their goat's head off. Not right off, but the goat was very injured, and Mele's dad had to finish cutting its head off with an axe. That was horrible, I couldn't look. There were some bad things that happened in our village, like Sharon, and some accidents on the motorbikes, but mostly there were good things, and I remember the good things, not the bad ones. School was good too, I liked it at the college, and I nearly always came top of my class. But I wish I didn't come top of the class now, because if I didn't I would probably still be there. We had exams in the first term, and I came first in English, History and Geography, and second in Accounting and Science. Mr Ashton, the papa'a teacher, came to our house after that and said to Mama and Papa that our school on the island wasn't good enough for me, that I should go to school in New Zealand. I wondered why Mr Ashton worked at our school if he thought it wasn't good, but he told Mama and Papa that they had a duty to get me a better education, and they talked about it to my Uncle George. When they talked about it I was worried, because I didn't want to go away, but my family and Mrs Ashton talked about it again, and all my family put in some money for the plane and sent me here to Aunty Vaine's. Aunty Vaine is my real mother's cousin, and she has been living in Auckland for over twenty years, so I never met her before, except once when she came back to the island for a holiday, but I was only a baby then. Uncle George arranged for me to stay with her, I think he rang his cousin in Auckland who went to see Aunty, and they met me at the airport. I took Aunty some pa'ua and some tipani and citrus, and we got a taxi to her house here in Sandringham. There's four of us here: Aunty, Ta (he's seventeen), Marlene and me. I share this bedroom with Marlene. She's six. The week after I arrived, Aunty took me to the girls' college to enrol, and she bought me a second-hand uniform. I've got to stop my diary now, the video's finished and Marlene wants to go to bed.

June 25   At first, Aunty was friendly. She asked me all about home and all the relations she hadn't seen for so long, and she told me the things she used to do when she was a girl on the island. Then she asked me how much money did I bring with me from the island, and I said I didn't bring any, and she got a bit angry. I told her Mama and Papa didn't have any money to give me, and they told me that Aunty had a good job and earned plenty of money. Aunty said she worked in the chicken factory, but she didn't get much money and most of what she got went to pay the rent. Then I asked her where was my uncle? He wasn't at the airport or at the house, and I didn't like to ask about him at first because I thought perhaps they were divorced or something. Aunty got very upset then and told me about the accident. Uncle Ben worked for an engineering firm at a place called Onehunga. He worked with big steel beams that they used for buildings and bridges, he used to load them on to trucks. One day the chain holding those beams came undone, and the beams slipped and fell on him. His chest was crushed, and he died in hospital. Aunty showed me a clipping from the newspaper, a paragraph about it. I told her I was very sorry I didn't know about the accident, nobody at home heard about it. She said Uncle Ben didn't come from our islands, he was from Niue, so she only told his family. She said one of the other Niue men told her she might get some money from the factory where Uncle Ben worked, but the factory manager told her that they wouldn't give her any money because they said that uncle didn't do the chain around the beams up properly and that's why the accident happened. She said they were going to get a lawyer to see if they could get some money, but the lawyer costs so much that they wouldn't have any left anyway, so they didn't. I felt really sad for Aunty then, and bad that I came to live with her when she didn't have enough money. She said on Sunday we are going to the cemetery to see my uncle's grave.

July 1   I haven't been able to write in my diary lately. I have had too much schoolwork to do. School is very hard here, even though the teachers are nice. My form teacher Mrs Price is best, she's choice, she introduced me to heaps of girls. They aren't from my island though, mostly they're Sa's, and their language is very strange to me. The school is so big, too, over a thousand girls, and so many rooms. It is scary, being in a school where there are so many strangers. Everyone seems cleverer than me, their English is so good. I try hard to keep up, but my marks are not very good compared to home. I never got such low marks, especially in English. Only a C for my last essay. I don't have enough time to do my work, that's partly the trouble. Aunty is on evening shift at the chicken factory, and I have to get the dinner every night. There's no proper place to study here either, only in the bedroom, and the noise from the video is so bad. Every night Ta gets some videos, and always they are noisy, full of shootings and wars and shouting. I hate that Sylvester Stallone. I think it's bad for Ta to watch just that sort of videos. Marlene too. Yesterday I went and asked Ta please could he turn the video down so I could work properly in my room, and he got angry and yelled bad words at me. I think he thinks he's Rambo himself. What a laugh, he's just a skinny dropout who can't get a job. He won't turn down the video. I'm going to bed now.

July 5   It's Sunday, but we didn't go to church. Aunty never goes to church. When I asked her why she didn't she said she didn't believe in God any more. I was very shocked when she said that, and I asked her why. She said it was because God took Uncle Ben away from them, and left them without anyone to take care of them, and not enough money, even though she always went to church before. I don't know whether that's right, but I can understand the way Aunty feels. Once I thought like that after Cyclone Sharon came to our island. I thought, everyone in this village always goes to church and prays and sings to the Lord, and He still lets the hurricane come and smash the houses and the crops. But then I believed the minister when he said that God sent the hurricane because someone had been wicked, and we must pray to Him even more. Now I'm not sure. If there is a God, He is very cruel sometimes, even to good people like Anne Frank, and Uncle Ben. Anyway, we got the bus out to the cemetery. It is huge, with heaps of hills all covered with graves. Uncle Ben's is a new one, of course, and it must have cost Aunty a lot of money, though she didn't say so. There is a smiling photo on the grey stone, and shiny black letters. BENJAMIN FILIGI, AGED 48 YEARS, DEARLY BELOVED HUSBAND OF VAINE AND FATHER OF TA AND MARLENE. We all cried at the grave, even Ta, when Aunty put the flowers on it. Uncle Ben looks like he was a nice man, looking from the photo on his grave.

July 10 I didn't go to school today. I wanted to, but it is such a long way that I have to get the bus, and the bus ticket costs a lot of money. Aunty said she didn't have any money left. She was getting in a mood, so I thought I will walk to school tomorrow instead of getting the bus. Today I tried to do my Maths by myself at home, but I got stuck. Maths is my hardest subject.

July 11 I am very tired tonight. This morning I got up at six o'clock and made some sandwiches for my lunch, and I left before any of the others were up. It was still dark, and very scary because there was hardly anyone else on the street. I walked right down Dominion Road, and gradually the sky got lighter, and I could see that Dominion Road went right to the horizon nearly. My bag strap was cutting into my shoulder, my bag was so heavy, and I was trying to remember which way the bus went from the time when I had a ticket. When I got to the corner where the bus turned I did remember, and I followed that street, but it took a long long time and I got to school too late for assembly and the prefect at the gate took my name and I had a detention. That was the first time I ever got one. The prefect told Mrs Price, and she asked me why I was late. I didn't like to tell her my Aunty didn't have any money for the bus, so I said I slept in. Mrs Price had a talk to me and asked me how I was getting on here, and the way Mrs Price looked I could see that she was a bit worried. She told me there was another girl from my country in her fifth form class and she would introduce us. At lunchtime she brought Moana to my room and introduced us, and we talked in our language. Moana doesn't come from my island, but she had some cousins who went to my school, and I knew them. I enjoyed talking to Moana, even though it made me very sad when I spoke to her in our language and about those people we knew, because then all those thoughts of home came rushing back and I couldn't think of anything else. Moana has been here since she was seven, so she hardly ever thinks about the islands, she said. When I told her how long it took me to walk to school she took me to the school library and showed me a street map. We saw that there was a much shorter way for me to come to school, I don't have to come the same way as the bus. Moana asked me if I would like to come to her place one day, but I saw on the map that she lives at Te Atatu, too far away from my place. Moana said she was out of zone, and the way she said it I knew that that was something special. I didn't like to tell her that I didn't know what that means. She said I should come to the Polynesian Club next year when they start practising for the festival, but that seems a long time yet. They don't practise in the winter, she said. I didn't get home from my detention until six o'clock, even though I walked that quicker way that I found on the map. I am very tired tonight, I can't write any more.

July 12 Aunty gave me two dollars this morning. I had to decide if I will spend it on the bus fare or some lunch. There was only fried bananas for breakfast and nothing left for lunch because Aunty doesn't get paid until tomorrow, so I decided to walk to school and buy my lunch. I went the way we worked out on the map, and I came to Haslett St. At the end of that street there was a bridge over the motorway that was just for pedestrians. Halfway across I stopped and looked down at the motorway. All those cars! The motorway was like a huge river, flowing into the city. It made me feel giddy, watching the cars all going together, all one way. But the worse thing was it started to rain while I was on the bridge. It rained and rained, very heavy, like it does at home, but very cold. I don't have a coat or a jacket, and there was nowhere to shelter, so I got wet through, on my hair, down my neck, on my legs, in my shoes. But I kept walking towards school, even though I was getting wetter and wetter and colder and colder. On the other side of the motorway there was a garage, and I waited in the doorway there out of the rain. A man came out and I asked him the time and he said five minutes to nine. That was way too late for school so I went back over the bridge and back home and I was so cold I had to get into bed to keep warm. I didn't get up till Marlene came home.

July 13   Aunty has changed to another shift at the factory, so she told Marlene and me to stay home from school and do the shopping. I made a list of the all the things that we needed, and we walked to the supermarket at Three Kings. There was some money left over and we were very hungry, so I got us some Kentucky Fried Chicken for lunch. It was so choice! I remember once one of my cousins from Auckland came to visit us on the island and she brought some Kentucky Fried Chicken on the plane in a big box. That was the first time I tasted it, and I loved that chicken then, but this was way better. And it is so neat the way they do it. I just went into this red and white building and there was a girl in a uniform just like the one on TV and I told her what we wanted and she talked into this microphone and only a few seconds later another girl brought it to her and she gave it to us. How do they do it so fast? Marlene and I took the chicken to the park next door and ate it there. When people went past us they stared. I knew they were thinking, why aren't those girls at school? I was worried that they might tell the police, so I said to Marlene come on, we'd better get home now. When we got home I put the groceries away and did some housework for

Aunty. I felt bad then about using her money for Kentucky Fried Chicken, and I told Marlene not to say we had it. I won't do that again. I went to bed in the afternoon, I didn't feel very well. My head feels all tight and my throat is very dry. I think I'm getting a cold from when I got wet yesterday.

July 18   I didn't write in my diary for a few days, because I stayed in bed. I had a really bad cold and I felt miserable. I've still got it but not as bad. I've missed quite a lot of school now, and I'm worried about how I'll be able to catch up. Exams are next month and I get very worried when I think about that. Always at home I did well in exams, but I can't here. It's still raining and cold outside, and the wind sounds spooky round the house. Everyone else has gone out, and all I can do is lie on the bed and stare at my photos and the trochus shell Papa gave me. When I pick up the shell and put it to my ear, I can hear the lagoon whispering to me. The trochus shells are very special to us. Once every year the people from the villages can get the trochus from the lagoon, but only a few for each family, so there will always be more the next year. Papa boils the trochus in a tin over the fire behind the house, to get the fish out before the man comes to buy the shells. Then they are polished for the tourists. But Papa polished this trochus just for me, and it is so beautiful with all the different colours, it is like holding a rainbow in my hand. Even the darkness here doesn't stop the trochus from shining.

July 19   I had a very bad day today. When I woke up I decided I must go to school and catch up my work so I will do well in exams and get a good report to send home to Mama and Papa. So I said to Aunty I'm going back to school, I'm walking but please could I have some money for my lunch? When I said that Aunty got very mad, and she yelled at me: 'I've got no money left for you!' she shouted. 'I haven't even got enough money for my own kids! Why did you have to come here anyway?' I told her I didn't really want to come, and I'm sorry for causing all this trouble to her. I said I don't like it here and I want to go home. Aunty got even angrier then and said she didn't even have enough money for the bus, so how is she going to pay for me to get the plane home? She said she didn't ask me to come here, she only said yes because she couldn't say no to her family. She said if I want to go back my family should send her the money to pay, and I said they couldn't because they spent all their money sending me here. I felt desperate then and ran out of the room, crying. Everything here is money. Money for food, money for buses, money for warm clothes, money for shoes. Back home we only need money for the motorbike, and a bit of food from the shop, everything else we get from the lagoon and the plantation. Every week Papa gets the flying fish from his boat outside the reef, we don't always worry about money. But here money makes me frightened, because there isn't enough, and I feel bad that Aunty has to get more because of me. There is a word for how I feel, but I can't remember it. *Guilty*. I found the word in my dictionary, I knew it started with G. I feel guilty, but I don't know what to do. There is no telephone here to ring, or at home. All I can do is lie on my bed and stare at my photos and hold my trochus. No school again today.

July 20 Raining again. I didn't go to school. I did some cleaning and watched some TV, and at about eleven o'clock someone knocked on the front door. I looked through the curtains, and it was a papa'a man with a briefcase. I didn't like to open the door to the man because I was alone, so I just watched while he knocked again, and again. Then he got out some paper from his briefcase, wrote something on it and put it in the letterbox. After he drove away I went out and got it. It was a letter, addressed to my Aunty. I opened it. It said that because I hadn't been to school, and no one had contacted the school about my absence, my Aunty should ring or visit the school immediately. I screwed the letter up and put it in the rubbish. I don't want Aunty to get mad again, but I'm worried about the letter. I know it's against the law to not go to school but I can't go back. I'm too far behind. Perhaps I could leave school and get a job in an office. That would help Aunty with the money.

July 21 Such a lot happened today, I never had such a day in my whole life. Ta gave me some money for the bus, and told me how to get to Downtown. I caught that bus at Balmoral, and it went right down Queen Street, the first time I have been there. All those huge buildings! It was like a TV programme. At the traffic lights all the people rush out into the middle of the street, and I thought they would bang into each other, but they didn't, they just kept walking. I got out of the bus at the bottom, by a big hotel, and I looked at the fountain. But there was a freezing wind there, the coldest I had ever felt, and then it started to rain, and the rain made it even colder. I left that freezing place and walked up Queen Street under the shelter by the shops. I couldn't stop staring in the shop windows. So many lovely things! And in one shop they were advertising holiday places, and there was a poster of home, a big one, showing the whole island! It must have been taken from a plane, because it showed the whole lagoon, and all the motus, just the way I saw it when I left. It was a very beautiful picture, the lagoon so blue, and the ocean all around so dark, and the white where the waves break on the reef. I wanted to say to people in the street, 'Look, there's my island, isn't it beautiful?' But all the people were just streaming past, not stopping, not noticing. I kept on walking up Queen Street, I was looking for a clothes shop, because I needed a jacket. The wind went right through my sweatshirt, as if I had nothing on at all. I came to a very big shop, all white inside. I walked around and looked at everything. There were racks and racks of coats and jackets, but as I looked through the jackets I could see a man by the counter staring at me, so I went back out into the cold. I passed a big concrete area where there were no cars or buses. I walked around it but there was nothing to see, not even a fountain, so I started to walk back to the street. But as I did I saw four kids sitting against a wall, three boys and a girl. Maoris, I think. They wore raggy clothes and funny hats, and they were holding a plastic bag up to their faces. When I saw that I knew that it must be glue in that bag. When I got closer one of the boys shouted at me, and another one got up and held up his fist. I started to run I was so frightened, and they laughed at me then and went back to their seat. Back on the street where there were people I felt safer. At school I had heard the other girls talk about shopping in Kay Road, and I knew that it was on the top of Queen Street, so I kept on walking. At the top there was a busy corner, and I asked an Island lady where is Kay Road and she pointed to where we were, and then I remembered I had been along that road on the bus when I went to school. I remembered there were shops with jackets too, and I walked along until I came to the biggest one. Through the window I could see the rack with jackets. I was very worried about what I was going to do, but I was so cold I didn't really care how wrong it was, just about how I could do it without getting caught. I went into the shop and over to the corner and walked behind the rack. I had a white super-market bag in my pocket, and I took it out. I couldn't stop my hands from shaking. I didn't even look at the size, I just took a blue one and put it in the bag as quickly as I could. I felt as if everyone was looking at me, and I wanted to run, but instead I walked around and pretended to look at some coats, then I walked out. I didn't stop until I got to the bridge over the motorway. I took out the jacket and saw the lable. $125! I put it on. It was so warm! It's got wool stuff inside and water-proof on the outside. I turned the collar up and wore it to just before I got home. Then I put it back in the bag, and when I was inside, I put it under my bed.

July 22   I couldn't sleep all last night. It was very bad to take the jacket from that shop. As the Bible says, Thou Shalt Not Steal, and even though we don't go to church here, I can't forget the ministers saying that. Thou Shalt Not Steal, I have heard that commandment ever since I was little. Now I feel that everyone is looking into my room and seeing the jacket. I won't wear it again. I am too ashamed. Anne Frank would never steal, even food when she was nearly starving. But what can I do with it? I can't think of anything else today except what to do about the jacket. I must make up for my badness.

July 23   Saturday today. Ta got three videos, all fighting and shooting. I can hear through the wall, and it sounds as if

there is a war on there. At home on Saturday night Mama
Raui and some of the others used to take us to the resort
hotel at Tokoa. Tokoa is just a little island across a channel
close to the reef, and because Sharon washed away the
bridge you have to be pulled across on a barge. I love that,
and the way you see all the coloured lights among the palm
trees as you come across, it looks like a magic land, all
coloured in the blackness, and so quiet you can hear the
waves breaking on the reef. We used to sit under the palms
and have fruit drinks, and watch the dancing on the stage
for the tourists. The hotel is *very* expensive, but we didn't
have to pay anything to watch. Mama told me that it didn't
cost anything for us because the hotel was so expensive that
not many people went to stay there, and the manager liked
the locals to come and watch so that all the tables would be
full and it looked like there were more people in the hotel
than there really were. But it was beautiful there, and I
loved the dancing and drumming. I want to dance at Tokoa
when I'm older. I decided what to do about the jacket. On
Monday I will take it back to the shop.

July 25   So much happened today that I will have to write it
all down very slowly and carefully to make sure I don't miss
anything out. When I woke up I put the jacket in my school
bag and told my Aunty I'm going to school. I walked along
Dominion Road, and when I got to the motorway I waited
under the bridge for about half an hour. It was very cold,
but not like before with the wind and rain, today it was still
and the grass was white under the bridge. I had to put the
jacket on to keep warm, and keep my hands in the pockets
to stop them hurting. When the cars stopped coming so
much I knew it must be after nine o'clock, and I came out. I
took the jacket off and put it in the bag again, and I walked
up to Kay Road. There weren't many people in the shop,
and I walked over to the place where the jackets were
hanging. I didn't look around, I just quickly started to take
the jacket out of the bag, but as I took it out my eyes came
up, and I saw that a little way away, on the other side of the
dresses, a lady was watching me. I started to push the jacket
back in the bag, but she saw what I was doing. She came

over and said, 'What are you doing?' She was quite old, with grey hair and false-looking teeth. I just looked at the ground, I couldn't speak. 'Did you take this?' she said. Her voice was very cross. I nodded. I couldn't explain to her that I didn't take it then, I took it before, because I thought she wouldn't believe me. She said, 'Come with me,' and she took me by the arm and we went over to the back of the shop. Other people were all looking at me and I started to cry. I didn't know what was going to happen to me. We went into an office, and there was a man in there, sitting by a desk. He was quite young, and he had a suit on. The lady told him she had found me taking the jacket, and the man said 'Is this right?' and I just nodded. I couldn't stop crying, so I couldn't explain. All I thought was now I will have to go to court and bring shame on my family. The man told me to sit down, and he rang someone on his telephone. He said, 'It's a shop-lifter,' and the cross lady was looking at me as if I was really dirty or something. Then the man asked me my name and where I live and if I go to school and I told him all those things, but I didn't tell him I was taking the jacket back either. He just looked at me really hard and his voice was very angry and he said, 'Do you know how much this store loses every year because of people like you?' Then a police lady came in, and the shop lady went out. The police lady was young and quite pretty, with dark hair. She sat down and when she asked me questions her voice was kind, not like those other ones. I told her what happened about the jacket and what I did, and my voice was getting better with her, and she said to the man, 'I think she's telling the truth.' He looked cross with her then, and he said, 'You know it's our policy to pros . . . ' (I didn't know that word.) But she said, 'I think we should talk to someone from the school first.' The man was tapping his pen on the edge of the desk, and he was frowning at her. Then he said, 'All right, I have to agree, it is an unusual case.' 'Very unusual,' she said. 'I never heard of a shop-lifter who took back what she stole.' She smiled at me a little bit, and she asked me, 'Who would you like us to talk to from school?'

When Mrs Price came in she looked just the same as she always did, not worried or anything. But I started crying again when I saw her because I was so ashamed, and she sat down by me and said, 'Don't worry Tuaine, we'll sort this out.' Then she and the police lady talked, and they seemed really friendly to one another, like they knew each other before. Mrs Price has got grey hair, but her face is young, and she talks in a very kind way. The manager of the shop just sat there looking angry, I don't think he liked the way the two ladies were talking to each other so friendly. Then Mrs Price asked me why I hadn't been to school, and I told her about the money, and Aunty and my uncle and how he was killed. And I told her about the exams and how I was worried about them and how I got cold when I went out and how I took the jacket. I said I was very ashamed for what I did and I knew that Aunty would give me a bad hiding, but I didn't mind because it was so bad what I did. All the time I was talking I was praying to myself that the police lady wouldn't make me go to the court, because to me that was the greatest shame. When my story was finished Mrs Price looked at the police lady and she gave a big sigh like she was tired or something. 'Well?' she said to the police lady. The lady looked at the manager with a very determined face. She said, 'This is a special case, Mr Jackson, I think you must agree. The goods have been recovered, and I really don't think this girl is a thief.' The manager didn't look at her, but he nodded his head. I said to him, 'I'm very sorry that I took your jacket. I will never do it again.' He stood up then, and he nodded again, and Mrs Price said, 'I'll take you home now, Tuaine.'

Mrs Price and I sat in her car outside our house. Traffic was whizzing past, it was nearly lunchtime. Mrs Price was talking slowly, it seemed to me she was thinking deeply about every-thing she was saying, trying to consider everything. She said, 'I think what we must first do is get you extra tuition with your schoolwork, so that you catch up what you've missed. And I'll contact Social Welfare about an extra benefit for your Aunty, she *must* be entitled to one. That will help with the clothing problem . . . ' Then Mrs Price stopped, and she looked at me for a long time without speaking. She has very clear, grey eyes, very kind and trusting, and her eyes seemed to see a long way into me. 'Or,' she said, in a very slow voice, 'would you just like us to arrange for you to go home?' I looked straight back into those grey, kind eyes. The way she said it, I knew it could be. Tears came back into my own eyes. Through them I saw a house, and faces, and the lagoon, shining and blue, 'I would like to go home,' I said.

Cannibals

BILL MANHIRE

We were sailing in the Pacific. Seeking out new lands: savages and treasure, sex and mineral rights, you know the sort of thing. Our weaponry very much superior to anything we might meet, the insurance company happy, the holds well stocked, all hands on deck, charts spread out on our knees, tang of sea in our nostrils.

Day after day. Uncle James reading aloud from the Bible.

The South Seas are sprinkled with numberless islands, like stars in the Milky Way. There are whole necklaces of islands, and each jewel on the chain is another paradise.

If the charts are hard to read, that is because of the wild, uncharted waters we are venturing into.

'I love you,' says the ship to the sea. 'We have always been friends, we two, and ever shall be.'

'Yes,' says the sea. 'But oftentimes, when the wind blows high and fierce, I have been greatly troubled for your safety.'

'Yes, dear sea, it is the wind, ever, ever the wind that is making dispeace between us, because it is seldom in the same mind.'

'True, that is the worst of the wind.'

'How beautifully blue you are today, oh sea, and what tiny wavelets you wear. I never care to go back to the noisy grimy docks when I think of you as you are now.'

'And how beautiful *you* are also, oh ship. Do you know that at a distance you might be mistaken for some bright-winged sea-bird skimming along in the sunshine. But who are these on your deck, oh ship, who make such clamour?'

'They are rough diamonds – sailors, explorers, missionaries. One or two stowaways. The occasional mutineer.'

'Oh well,' says the sea, 'nothing new there, very much the usual stuff.'

You see a peak in the distance, feathery palms and so forth, and you have to admit it's a pretty good feeling.

Our ship slices through the water, breasts the wave, on it goes through the opening in the reef, the *Tia Maria* is its name, I expect I forgot to say that earlier. I am writing on my knees, which is always difficult.

Maps all over the deck. Cap'n Tooth at the helm, old seadog. Excitement mounting. We sail in silver waters beside golden sands.

This island is probably uninhabited, so we will be able to give it a name, that's always a pleasurable thing. Maybe something from the list of names that Gerald keeps in his pocket.

Yes, the island certainly looks uninhabited. Nothing stirring. Any minute now we will lower the rowing boat and men will row ashore for coconuts and just generally try to see what they can see. The rest of us might swim a bit, or maybe sketch the extinct volcano.

'We haven't used Llandudno Junction yet,' says Gerald.

General derision.

Gerald blushes, I'll say that for him, but on he goes, he is totally undeterred.

'Let's see,' he says. 'How about Seattle? Pontypridd? Crofts of Dipple?'

But hold, who are these sinister black creatures who suddenly appear upon the shore, rank upon rank of them, three abreast, uttering cries that chill the very blood in our veins? They skip and howl, they wade into the surf and shake their fists above their heads . . .

Wait a minute . . . those black cassocks . . . those cadaverous smiles . . .

The priests of Rome! Here before us!

Break out more sail! Away! Away! While yet there is breath in our bodies!

*

Well, that was a near thing. Touch and go there for a while. Cap'n Tooth breaks out the rum, we decide to call the island Adventure Island, because of the adventure we had there.

'And to think it was so nearly Misadventure Island!' jokes Uncle James.

Gerald scowls below deck, murderous black sharks cruise about our little ship, but our spirits are high.

Tonight I discovered a stowaway in my cabin. It happened thus. I had knelt to say my evening prayers, when my right knee encountered something strange beneath the bunk. Upon investigation, I found a boy secreted there, a sprightly lad clad in denim, who made a dash for the door, one of those absolutely futile things for I caught him easily, even I was surprised at the ease of it, and I threw him forthwith to the floor. Upon which I had my second surprise of the evening.

The young fellow's shirt had torn a little in the course of our struggle, and as I gazed down, panting and victorious, what did I see, peeping out at me, but two quite perfect female breasts . . .

Well! My stowaway is a girl!

Her name is foreign, it sounds like Meefanwee, and gradually I believe I gain her confidence.

Meefanwee has black hair and green eyes, a really interesting combination.

I shall keep her, I shall be her protector, I shall certainly not let on to Uncle James.

The *Tia Maria* courses on through the vast Pacific. A few days ago we had the adventure with the pirates, that was at Pirate Island. And just after that there was the island where we couldn't find a place to land. It looked so beautiful and mysterious, just rising up out of the blue Pacific, but we sailed round and round it and failed to find an opening in the coral reef. The crew grew tired of our circular motions and fell to muttering among themselves, and Cap'n Tooth had to give them more rum. But at last we were able to sail on and we decided to call the island Mystery Island, because it would always remain a mystery to us.

I keep Meefanwee concealed in my cabin.

She is my little stowaway, that is what I sometimes call her, she looks up into my face trustfully.

Sweet Jesus, it is a look which brings out all the manliness of my soul!

I read to her from the Bible, I touch her private parts.

We have let Gerald name some islands. There were actually three islands together, a group of them, and it was just after the fight with the giant octopus, and of course we were feeling good about that, and we just sort of gave him *carte blanche*, a French phrase, it means literally white map, I don't think that had ever occurred to me before. I am afraid Gerald rather took advantage of us, and he named the islands after three former girlfriends of his, Yvonne, Sharon and Mrs Llewellyn Davies. The islands were all uninhabited, which Gerald says just makes the names even more appropriate.

Actually there were one or two natives, several of us noticed them, but they ran off when they saw us coming.

We dumped the nuclear waste on one of the islands – Sharon, I think, but I don't really remember.

Uncle James has a rather bad snakebite, which he got when he went ashore a few days ago on Mrs Llewellyn Davies. Mrs Appleby, my aunt, is fearfully worried. His leg has swollen to several times its normal size. He cannot enter his cabin, and must lie out on the deck until the swelling subsides. It is a real nuisance: crew members are always tripping over him and he is constantly having to apologize.

Today there was a message in a bottle, that sometimes happens, I didn't see it myself but someone says there was one. I helped fight off the sandalwood traders, though, that was easy enough, we just opened fire with the really big guns and let them have it. Then we found some pearls, big ones, worth millions apparently, though I personally didn't do any of the diving. But I suppose the real news is the mutiny. I should probably have mentioned it a bit earlier. The crew, led by their own obscure desires, have slain good old Cap'n Tooth and set course for Valparaiso. But not before first putting us ashore on a nearby island.

Uncle James says that we must call our island Fortunate Island – 'for surely good fortune awaits us in this Pacific paradise.'

The island has a lagoon, a coral reef, coconut palms and a mysterious mountain which could be honeycombed with underground passages, it is hard to tell. The island is probably deserted, but we will have to do some proper exploring in the next few days and find a place for signalling ships from and so on.

Meefanwee is safely ashore. I am passing her off as a member of the crew.

'Uncle James,' I say, 'meet Douglas. Douglas, this is my uncle, James Appleby. Douglas was the only one of that riff-raff, mulatto crew, Uncle, with spirit enough to stand by us.'

'Pleased to meet you, my boy,' says Uncle James. 'Sorry I can't get up. My leg is still playing me up a little.'

In fact, Uncle's left leg is now twice the circumference of his upper body, and very, very pustular.

'What a lovely spot this is!'

Uncle James has summoned us all together for words of encouragement. We cluster about him on the sand. He lies like a beached whale.

'Mark these coconut palms, they have borne their fruit year after year, have died, and others have sprung up in their stead; and here has this spot remained, perhaps for centuries, all ready for man to live in and enjoy.'

He pauses. You can hear the deep incessant boom of distant combers.

'Pray tell, Mr Appleby,' says my aunt, 'what are the great merits of the coconut tree?'

'Why, I'll tell you madam: in the first place, you have the wood to build a house with; then you have the bark with which you can make ropes and lines, and fishing-nets if you please; then you have the leaves for thatching your house, and also for thatching your head if you please, ho ho, for you may make good hats out of them, and baskets also; then you have the fruit which, as a nut, is good to eat, and very useful in cooking; and in the young nut is the milk, which is also very wholesome; then you have the oil to burn and the shell to makes cups of, if you haven't any; and then you can draw toddy from the tree, which is very pleasant when fresh, but will make you tipsy if it is kept too long, ho ho; and then, after that, you may turn the toddy into arrack, which is a very strong spirit. Now there is no tree which yields so many useful things to man, for it supplies him with almost everything.'

'I had no idea of that,' replies the astonished woman. And she goes off to the far end of the beach to peruse her Bible.

'The island is evidently of volcanic origin,' remarks Gerald. 'What is your opinion, William?'

Gerald is addressing me. He and Douglas and I have gone exploring. The others are building a house back at Castaway Bay.

'But remember the reef is coral,' I say. 'Though I suppose the one does not necessarily preclude the other.'

Gerald and I do not really hit it off, I expect that's obvious. I find much of his behaviour unsatisfactory. Welsh, I suppose.

We go along in single file. Hacking through the undergrowth.

Suddenly Douglas screams.

'Oh don't be a girl!' cries Gerald scornfully. 'It's only some old bones.'

'You must think what you will, Gerald,' I quickly interpose. 'But unless I am very mistaken, those are the rib bones of a man. And those ashes which you poke so idly with a stick, they are signs of cooking. It's as I secretly feared but didn't like to say: before long we shall have cannibals to contend with.'

Douglas snuggles against me.

Gerald stands off to one side and regards us oddly.

I have tried to tell Uncle James of my suspicions. He was sitting on a headland, gazing out to sea. I waved the rib-bone before him. He looked for a moment, but then resumed his inspection of the far horizon.

'Who would ever have imagined, William,' said my uncle, 'that this island, and so many more which abound in the broad Pacific, could have been raised by the work of little insects no bigger than a pin's head.'

'Insects, uncle?' I replied. 'Oh come now.'

Plop! A coconut fell from a tree.

'Yes, insects. Give me that piece of coral with which you are toying.'

I passed him the rib-bone.

'Do you see, William,' said my uncle after a moment, 'that on every surface there are a hundred little holes? Well in every one of these little holes once lived a sea-insect; and as these insects increase, so do the branches of the coral trees.'

'But an island, uncle?' I said.

Plop!

'The coral grows at first at the bottom of the sea,' said my uncle wearily. 'There it is not disturbed by wind or wave. By degrees it increases, advancing higher and higher towards the surface; then it is like those reefs you see out there beyond the lagoon, William. Of course it never grows above the surface of the water for if it did the tiny animals would die.'

'Then how does it become an island?'

'By very slow degrees,' said my uncle. 'And frequently the droppings of seabirds play a not inconsiderable part. But run along now William and read your Bible. My leg pains me. I promise we shall speak of this another time.'

Alas, it was not to be. Our time together on Fortunate Island had drawn nearly to an end. Indeed, Uncle James was the first of our number to be captured and eaten by cannibals.

A few days after the conversation I have just set down, Gerald, Douglas and I were out exploring. Gerald walking ahead. Douglas and I secretly holding hands.

We came down to a beautiful sandy bay. Something big, a tree stump or barrel, was rolling in the gentle surf. We ran towards it.

Sweet Jesus! It was the hideously distended leg of my uncle, James Appleby.

I realized at once that my uncle had been captured by cannibals, that these same cannibals had cooked and no doubt eaten him, yet had first removed his swollen limb as a precaution against food poisoning.

We were clearly dealing with a highly intelligent, if savage, people.

It was time to take command.

'Douglas,' I said, 'you are cool; while Gerald, you are fearless. But I am cool *and* fearless, a combination of the qualities you possess individually, and therefore I propose to be your leader, offering cool but fearless leadership. Now let us go at once and warn the others.'

Then rough hands seized me and I knew that the savages had crept up on us even as we talked.

PART THE SECOND

We have been prisoners of the cannibals for several days now. Few of us survived the initial attack; and those among us who have had the fortune (or misfortune!) to keep our lives must witness the savages swaggering past our palisaded compound, patting their bellies and saying the name 'James Appleby' in tones of gratitude and wonder. Our captors seem to be making a special point of fattening the three Appleby girls. The unfortunate young women grow visibly from day to day, probably the steady diet of breadfruit is responsible, and they anxiously inspect their figures in the dress-length mirror which Mange Tout has installed inside the compound.

The leader of the cannibal band is a big, rough man, who names himself Jules Verne, while his lieutenant, the afore-mentioned Mange Tout, is even more terrible to behold. Mange Tout claims to be the offspring of a shark and a witch, and when he smiles, the row of sharp, triangular teeth which glint along his jaw lends a terrible credence to his tale.

All the same, there is something likeable about the fellow.

I am resolved to find some way of teaching these people Christian precepts. The thing will be to win their confidence. Already a few of them gather each morning for my Bible readings, it's quite encouraging. But each night the drums begin to beat and then the terrible fires glow in the distance. The air fills with the aroma of roasting flesh.

I am deeply puzzled by the cannibals' walk. Often when a group go about together, with Jules Verne at their head, I observe that they will pause. Jules Verne will move his head from side to side and sniff the air; then he will lift his knee up almost to the chin, stepping forward in the same movement, and walk on as before. His men follow in single file, one by one making the same curious motion. It is as if they are stepping over some unseen barrier.

Each night the air fills with songs which chill the blood.

> *Strip ze skin! Quarter ze body!*
> *Skin, head, hands, feet and bowels –*
> *Set zem aside, oh set zem aside.*
> *We catch ze blood in a pannikin.*
> *We eat ze 'eart and liver first.*
> *Aha! Ho ho! Zut alors!*

We clutch one another for comfort. Douglas and I do, anyway. So do Gerald and poor Mrs Appleby. Also the two remaining Appleby girls. The eldest girl, Madge, has already been carried off to the cannibal kitchen.

Each day I am taken to visit Jules Verne in his headquarters, we talk together, we chew the fat. It is probably the fact that I have given him a jigsaw of Edinburgh Castle that makes him favour me in this way. Usually I help him find the four corners; then he sets to and makes it up during the day, destroying it again at nightfall.

Another thing that has happened is I have taught Jules and his closest advisers how to play Monopoly. They seem to have an instinctive understanding of the game. I may have forgotten to say that with all the confusion during the mutiny I managed to smuggle away a few things like that, things that would be good for trading. They have certainly come in handy.

We all make sure Jules wins, of course. By the end of a typical game, Jules owns most of London, while I have spent many rounds languishing in jail!

Strange to say, I believe I am beginning to win the respect of these rough, untutored South Sea Islanders. Gerald, always quick to offer an opinion, says that they are not South Sea Islanders at all, but French adventurers who have stayed in the Pacific so many years that they have descended to a savage condition. But this seems highly implausible.

The cannibals are certainly not Christians. They worship a mysterious creature whom they address by the name 'Zodiac'. After their evening feasting, they gather on the shores of the lagoon, a terrifying sight in the moonlight, and cry the name of their god. They make strange huffing and puffing noises, and their strange stepping motions.

Of course there is debate amongst our little party, but I am of the view that the cannibals are not entirely devoid of intelligence.

I dream of the day when these frank, unlettered creatures will bring me their idols and cry: 'Take zese zings, zese *Zodiacs*. Zey were once our gods, but now we are ashamed of zem. Take zem 'ence, for we wish zat we never more may behold zem again!'

But each night the cannibal drums beat out their messages of death. The second Appleby girl, her name slips my mind, has been taken away. And Mange Tout, when he came yesterday to clean the mirror, stared at Mrs Appleby for several minutes and said something about the annual widow-strangling ceremony.

I have taken to spying on Gerald and my aunt. Gerald is a regular rascal where a pretty girl is concerned.

They spend hours and hours together in the far corner of the compound. They believe they are unobserved.

Gerald lies on his back, and Mrs Appleby smooths back the curly chestnut hair from his temples.

'Would you like to have me for a mama?' she asks.

'I would rather have you – for – for – '

Gerald hesitates.

'Well, dear, for what? Speak out,' says Mrs Appleby in an encouraging tone.

'I was going to say, for a sweetheart, ma'am. You are so very lovely.'

'Am I lovely?' my aunt repeats, looking at her handsome figure in the looking glass. Running the palms of her hands across her hips.

The hot blood mounts on Gerald's face and makes it burn.

'How you blush! Why do blush so?' she says.

'I don't know, ma'am. It comes to me when I talk to you, I think. I have these stirrings in my loins.'

'Strings in your loins?' exclaims my aunt. 'Why, how very strange! But you cannot have me for a sweetheart, Gerald. I am a widow in mourning, and the aunt of your young friend, William. At all events, we shall soon be eaten by these cannibals.'

'Still, I may love you quietly and at a distance, ma'am. You cannot help people loving you.'

'You funny boy,' she exclaims. 'Come here, you funny boy.'

And soon, I am afraid, she is all over him.

I have solved the problem of the cannibals' walk. Jules Verne believes that there are deadly invisible rays stretched across the surface of the island, they are like wires drawn taut a few inches above the ground. When Jules pauses and sniffs, lifting his knee towards his chin, he is first locating, then stepping over, these treacherous obstacles.

I have all this from Mange Tout, who has begun to confide in me and is plainly sceptical of the mysterious rays. Yet he, and the rest of Jules Verne's savage band, follow their leader in every point. Occasionally one of them will trip, or pretend to trip, then fall to the ground howling. At such moments, Jules Verne laughs hideously; and all those still on their feet join in.

The cannibals take very great care in the preparation of their food. Perhaps Gerald is right after all, there is certainly a Gallic quality to that. They took away the last of the Appleby girls this morning, and Mange Tout tells me in confidence that, after she has been bled, she will be marinaded for several hours before the actual process of cooking commences.

They anoint Miranda – that is her name, Miranda – they anoint her with quassia chips and rue, with the root of tormentil and ears of barley, with slippery elm powder and the bark of wild cherry, with bladderwrack and pulp of the Banyan, olibanum gum and coltsfoot, with wood betony and extract of underquil.

In the distance, the terrible drums begin again.

Each day when I am escorted to Jules Verne's headquarters to play Monopoly, I find myself pretending to step over the invisible rays. It is surprisingly easy to get into the habit. Jules Verne is most impressed by my behaviour and has explained to me that the rays are most dense around the headquarters building itself. The closer you approach, the greater the number of wires.

Near Jules Verne's hut is the impaled head of my uncle, James Appleby. He gazes out to sea through sightless eyes, as though he is scanning the horizon for a sail. A sail he knows will never come.

These cannibals do not eat the heads of their victims, they preserve them, and the procedures are really rather elaborate. Mange Tout has begun to instruct me in the treatment of heads.

We are at the Monopoly board.

'If the head is very much larger than the neck,' says Mange Tout, 'you must cut the throat lengthwise to remove the head. It is immaterial whether the eyes are taken out before the head is skinned or after.'

Jules Verne passes Go.

'The gouge,' continues Mange Tout, 'should go well to the back of the eye and separate the ligament which holds it to the socket. Should the gouge go into the eye,' warns Mange Tout, 'it will let out the moisture, which often damges the skin. Some people,' he continues, 'crush the skull slightly to make it come out of the skin easily, but this I do not personally advise.'

Jules Verne puts a hotel on Mayfair.

'Remove the brains,' says Mange Tout, 'by taking out a piece of skull at the back as you cut off the neck. This we did in the case of your late uncle, James Appleby, and it really worked rather well. Then you must pull the eyes out of their cavity and fill up their place with wool soaked in arsenical soap. Anoint the head and neck well with arsenical soap, and place in the neck a piece of stick covered with wool, the end of which you must slip into the hole already made in the skull for extracting the brains.'

Mange Tout breaks off and grins with delight. He smiles with every muscle in his head! He has just won $10 in a Beauty Contest. Jules Verne looks somewhat put out, he is not really much of a sport.

But look – there! – how the smile grows fixed on Mange Tout's face, a rictus of despair, a rictus of defeat, and he falls, he falls suddenly across the Monopoly board, scattering all the houses and hotels of central London. A spear is embedded in his back.

The air fills with howls and eldritch screams. Another band of cannibals is attacking. Jules Verne and his men rush to join battle with the enemy, they are not afraid. But head over heels they go over their own invisible tripwires and are quickly defeated.

Cries of the slaughtered. The greedy earth drinks the blood of the dead.

It is hard to be sure what to make of this new development. Have we been rescued? And if so, who has rescued us? Or have we fallen into the hands of even more ferocious savages?

PART THE THIRD

It has been a time of pain and dark confusion, and I have lost all sense of time. I seem to be alone. Mrs Appleby was here, I think, my brief companion in captivity, but then was taken away. For a time I heard her cries at intervals. Then, after a time, nothing.

Time passes.

There has been no sign of Douglas/Meefanwee or of

Gerald, perhaps they escaped, who knows, perhaps they were killed during the fighting between the rival bands of cannibals, it is as if they never existed. For the moment I must assume that they are dead – as dead as Jules Verne and his unfortunate followers.

I pass in and out of consciousness. Sometimes I think I can hear Meefanwee's voice, its ringing, bell-like laughter. Oh, it is like the sound of water running over stones! Then I ache for all that was mine and now is mine no longer, I ruefully touch my bruises. Then I begin to believe I can hear the raucous laughter of Gerald. He sounds as if he is drunk, laughing at his own jokes.

I fear I am delirious.

The other thing is that I seem to be underground – there are damp rock walls. What meagre light there is, comes from flaming torches. Ghastly shadows flicker across the walls and roof. My guess is that I am deep in the heart of the extinct volcano.

But hark! Rough voices, footsteps, cursings in a foreign tongue. The door of my cavern rasps open . . .

I am being alternately pushed and dragged, I hardly know which, through a series of dark, winding passages. On and on, I do not think I can endure much more, but then I am thrust out into a vast underground chamber. At the far end of this immense cavern are a hundred cannibal warriors, all in their battle finery, prostrate before a raised throne on which sits . . . a woman. The sight fills me with terror.

Dark of hair, dark of eye. Shoulderless dress and elaborate tattoos. But surely her features are those of a European? How strange!

And who is that who sits at her right hand, laughing and grunting, the torchlight flickering cruelly across his face? The hateful Gerald! There he sits beside the savage queen. As cool as a cucumber. Like some denizen of Hell.

'Gerald!' I cry. 'Where is Mrs Appleby?'

Gerald looks shifty.

I feel the woman's eyes on me, her gaze travels up and down my body, it is almost immodest, a woman her age, she must be nearly 50.

'Well, my young friend, you present me with an interesting problem. Shall I let you go, or shall you be my victim? Ha! Ha! Ha!'

She breaks into peals of hideous laughter.

'For pity's sake, your Highness!' I fall to my knees.

Gerald chuckles. Pleasure fairly swaggers across his features.

'William,' he says, 'may I introduce you to Mrs Llewellyn Davies.'

PART THE FOURTH

Well, how extraordinary!

We have been talking excitedly all evening. I have not been a prisoner at all, just sick with a sudden fever, probably from drinking the cannibal wine.

How strangely things have turned out! It seems that Mrs Llewellyn Davies is Gerald's old landlady. Gerald named an island after her earlier in the story. Well, she was more than his landlady, I suppose that's obvious. She ran a rooming house in Bangor, and Gerald lived there when he was doing his teacher training.

Meefanwee is not Meefanwee. I had the spelling wrong, she is Myfanwy. She is actually Mrs Llewellyn Davies' daughter. It is not clear who her father was, but it seems that Gerald is an obvious candidate, at any rate Myfanwy calls him 'Father'. Apparently when Myfanwy was a child her mother vanished, but the lonely child never believed the story about her mother being dead, and after she left high school she began to search the broad Pacific, she never gave up hope. She had adventure after adventure, of course, the Pacific is that sort of place, and one day she disguised herself as a boy, stowed away on a ship called the *Tia Maria* and, well, the rest is history . . .

The only wrong note in all this is Mrs Appleby. I am afraid that Mrs Llewellyn Davies found out about her relationship with Gerald and at once gave her to her savage followers. They feasted on her flesh that evening. Gerald does not seem to mind.

*

'But however did Mrs Llewellyn Davies – sorry, your mother – come to be here in the first place? Queen of a cannibal island and everything?'

I am talking to Myfanwy. We are down at the beach, we have been swimming in the clear lagoon, there is one of those astonishing sunsets out beyond the reef.

'Put your hand there, William, yes there, that's it, mmm that's lovely.'

'Well?'

'Well what, William?'

'Well are you going to answer my inquiry about your mother?'

'Oh *that*! Well, William, I have not quite gathered all of the details yet, I am just so happy to have found her at last. But you will remember that years ago a Welsh rugby supporters' tour group went missing, it was after the tour itself had finished – traditional forward dominance had told against us, as everyone predicted – and they went on a Pacific Island cruise, the supporters I mean, not the team, it was part of the original package.'

I nod.

'Well, William, as you probably also know, the boat disappeared, just vanished off the face of the earth, it was in all the newspapers at the time, no one could make any sense of it. Oooh, that's so good, press a little harder, oh yes darling. Well, it seems that the cruise ship was rammed by a mysterious submarine – Russian, French, American, no one seems to know. But the ship simply broke apart. It was all over in a matter of minutes. Everyone went to the bottom.'

'Except your mother,' I interpose.

'Except my mother. You see, she had been playing deck rugby, and was fortunate enough to be holding the ball at the precise moment of collision. Mother clung to the ball for dear life, it kept her afloat, she simply clung to it, hardly knowing what she was doing, till eventually she was washed up on the shores of this island, just a few yards from where we presently sit. It saved her life, you know, that rugby ball.'

'What a piece of luck! How extraordinary!'

'Yes, this is one of those cases where the truth is very much stranger than fiction.'

'But how did she come to acquire such power over these savage islanders?' I asked. 'She does not seem to be especially Christian, yet it is truly wonderful, the way in which they are obedient to her. And why did she attack Jules Verne? Had she seen you and Gerald, do you think, and set out to rescue you, or what?'

'I cannot say, William. It may simply be the volatile politics of the South Pacific. But I have not yet pursued these matters with her, so for the moment they must remain loose ends. Surely you can cope with a few loose ends, my darling? Now, would you like me to put my hand somewhere on you, what about there, shall I touch you there, does that feel good?'

I have resolved to build a raft. Myfanwy is helping me, she is sorry to see me bent on departure but she understands when I tell her I cannot have Gerald for a father-in-law, it is simply out of the question. The raft is made from the trunks of that selfsame tree whose merits were expounded, so long ago, by my late uncle, James Appleby. How little we guessed what lay in store! And even Uncle James could not have known that I would one day find a use for the coconut tree which even he had failed to anticipate!

From time to time Myfanwy and I embrace as of old, but now there is a distance. The sadness of departure lies between us.

During the day I work at building my raft. At night we join the others and listen to Mrs Llewellyn Davies read from her Visitors Book, she does a few entries each evening, the whole tribe assembles.

'The weather exceeded only by the company' – Littleford family, Birmingham.
'Vielen Dank!' – Familie G. Prutz, Hamburg.
'Thank you, very nice' – Jim and Noeline Carter, Tasmania.

The cannibals think it is a sacred book. After each entry they gasp and applaud. They show their appreciation in the usual manner.

*

I look out at the lagoon, at the clouds of spray above the reef, seabirds diving and calling ... and beyond lies all the vastness of the blue Pacific!

My raft is ready, it is time to go.

I shall be adrift for days, maybe for weeks. But eventually some ship will spot my ragged sail, heave to and take me aboard, faint and delirious from the pitiless sun, full of a wild story, cannibals and a mutiny, poor fellow, look! is that a Bible he is clutching, take him below ...

I gaze on Myfanwy, my companion in so many trials. I take her photograph. I touch her lips, her hair, her perfect breasts. Then I turn to go. That is how it is, adventure and regret, there is no getting away from it, we live in the broad Pacific, meeting and parting shake us, meeting and parting shake us, it is always touch and go.

The Tsunami

OWEN MARSHALL

I remember it was the day of the tidal wave from Chile. 'A tsunami,' Peter had said yet again, angrily, as we stood by the bench at breakfast. 'Nothing to do with the tide, nothing at all. A tsunami's a shock wave.'

Yet there it was in the paper of the night before; all about the Chilean tidal wave and how it was expected to be up to twenty-five feet high, and might sweep right over low-lying areas. Peter was doing a third unit of geography, and he took it as an academic affront that even the newspaper talked about the tsunami as a tidal wave instead of a tsunami. Raf and I agreed, of course.

'A tsunami, right,' we said, but we still thought about it as the tidal wave. In all of us is the perversity to resist correction.

We had tacitly decided that the tidal wave would be a big thing in our day. This wasn't a compliment to Chile or the wave. As students we found almost every day some preoccupation to shield us from our studies. Even now I have a fellow feeling when I read of prisoners who tamed cockroaches, or devised whole new political systems in their heads to pass the time. Thoreau knew that most of mankind understood a prisoner's world.

The newspaper said that the wave was expected between noon and two p.m., and over the radio there were warnings to farmers and property-owners to be prepared. It was a compelling notion: the great wave sweeping majestically across thousands of miles of ocean, to fall with thunderous devastation on our New Zealand. It quite captured the imagination of the city, and before midday the cars were streaming out to the coast.

We bought pies and a half-gallon jar of apple wine on our way to the estuary. 'A carafe, you mean,' said the pale man in the bottle-store loftily. He still used hair cream and we mocked him as we went on.

'A carafe, you mean. Oh quite, quite.' We passed the half-gallon of apple wine from one to another, regarding it quizzically and twisting our faces to suggest the features of the pale bottle-store man.

By twelve-thirty the cars were parked in rows along the beach frontages, and their occupants belched comfortably and waited for something to happen. Many people were down on the beach, impatient for the tidal wave to come. Peter's logical mind was outraged. 'My god, look at these people,' he said. 'If the tsunami does come it'll kill thousands, thousands of them.' He gave a shrill laugh of exasperation and incredulity. But Raf and I were delighted; it accorded with the youthful cynicism we cultivated at the university. We drove up the hill and parked in a children's play area, with swings, see-saws, and a humpty-dumpty among the grass. We took our apple wine and round pies, and sat with humpty-dumpty on his wall, looking down over the houses on to the crowds along the estuary and beach. Raf stuck out his corduroy legs in delight at the unsought demonstration of human nature acted out before him. 'Look at them, Peter,' he kept saying, and drew further joy from the resentment with which Peter watched the crowd press forward to the tsunami.

Another car drove on to the playground, and a couple got out and stood with their backs supported by the grille, looking down upon the sea. Then the man wandered closer, and I recognized Leslie Foster. He sat on a swing with his hands hanging between his knees. He had a thin, Spanish face, with a beard to suit it, and his shoulders were slightly hunched in that typical way that I recalled from the years we were at school together. At school at the same time would be a better description. He and I had mutual friends, but we never found any ease in each other's company. I never trusted his sneering humour, and he considered me something of a milksop I think. Yet at university we gave each other greater recognition, for there our common background, always taken for granted before, was something of a link.

I went over and sat on the bleached, wooden seat of the other swing. I stretched my legs to pass the puddle in the rut beneath. 'How are things?' I said. He turned his head and gave his quirking, Spanish smile. 'I don't think that tidal wave's coming,' I said.

'Bloody tidal wave. Who needs it?' he said.

We talked idly for a time, but every topic seemed to release the same bitterness, and he didn't even pretend to listen to anything I said. He would screw up his eyes impatiently, and rock back on the swing. 'She wanted to come out here today,' he broke in. 'It wasn't my idea.' We both looked over at the woman still standing at the front of the car and staring out to sea. As if she realized she was the topic of our conversation, she glanced back at us, then came over towards the swings. Les introduced her grudgingly as Mrs Elizabeth Reid, his landlady.

'Nice to meet friends of Les,' she said. I wouldn't guess at her age, but she wasn't a girl. She had a lot of flesh on her upper arms and shoulders, and her hips swept out like a harp. I like a run in the car,' she said. 'Blows the cobwebs out and that; don't you think?' Les screwed up his eyes, and gave his mocking, lop-sided smile. 'I wanted to go down by the beach with everyone else but Les wouldn't.' She paused and then said, 'It's late,' as if the tidal wave were a train or bus delayed by departmental inefficiency. 'It's a run out, though, isn't it? A chance to have a breather.' She had an unpleasant voice: ingratiating, but with a metallic edge.

'Yes. Chance to have a breather,' repeated Les, mocking the idiom, but she didn't seem to realize it. She went off to sit in the car out of the breeze, and have a cigarette. Les and I were left swaying on the worn seats of the playground swings. 'Chance to have a breather,' said Les again, with morose emphasis. 'Well, I suppose that's fair enough. You'd laugh if I told you. If I told you what she's sprung on me today.' I didn't ask; I wasn't really interested in any of his confidences, but I knew he was going to tell me anyway. It was something to do with his loneliness I suppose; picking on me just because I was there and we had been to the same school. 'She's pregnant, the lovely lady. She told me on the way out.' He rocked back and forth, setting loose a distorted image in the water beneath the swing.

'You could get something done, I suppose.'

'Not easy,' he said, with a sneer at my vagueness, and the ignorance of facts which it revealed. 'Anyway, she feels that marriage is the best answer. She's divorced, but thinks in terms of marriage.' I made a feeble reply about how nice she seemed, and how things had a habit of working out. Les ignored it completely. 'I'll have to leave varsity. I can't see myself getting by in full-time study with her and a kid.'

'I suppose so.' It did seem a waste. Les was a clever student. Even at school he'd been a clever beggar, and he'd had straight 'A's since then.

'I can't blame her for it happening.' I admired him for saying that. In his own crabbed way he'd always seen things as they were. He was honest with himself. 'She's rather a passive person, really,' he said. 'Likes to talk more than anything else. It started last year, when she went on a citrus fruit diet. I used to go into the bathroom and joke about it when she stood on the scales with a towel round herself. Sometimes I'd put a foot deliberately on the scales, and she would laugh and jab back with her elbows.' Les was going to say more, then he broke off with a barking laugh. 'Funny how these things get started,' he said, and he pushed out with his legs to get the swing going again as a sign he'd finished talking about the seduction of his landlady.

I hadn't wanted to hear about it, but personal revelations impose an obligation, and I asked him if he wanted some apple wine. 'Love it,' said Les, and he came with me back to the wall on which sat the patient humpty-dumpty, smiling in the face of his imminent fall and the tsunami. Les knew Raf, and I introduced him to Peter.

'I don't think the tsunami will persist across all that ocean,' said Peter.

'The what?' said Les.

'The tidal wave. He means the tidal wave,' Raf and I put in.

'That bloody thing,' said Les with belittling contempt, looking not out to sea, but towards the car and his landlady. He tipped the apple wine down his throat without appearing to swallow. We could hear its unimpeded gurgle as it went down, and we began to drink more rapidly to keep up. Les cast a malaise over our group, interrupting the established pattern of our relationships. He was interested only in his own problems, and our wine.

His impatience seemed to extend to the people along the foreshore below. The tsunami had not come; promises of something different had failed once again. Some people began to leave for the city, and only those with nothing they wished to return to remained. A few roared their cars across the asphalt frontage of the beach, while others stood in the sand-dunes and pelted beer bottles with stones.

When the wine was finished, Les said he'd better take his landlady home. I walked part of the way towards the car with him to show a fitting sense of comradeship for a fellow old boy whose secret I shared. By now he wished he hadn't told me, of course, and not being able to say just that, he got in some remark about how heavy I was. I saw him cross the rough grass of the playground, walking in his round-shouldered, rather furtive way. I felt no loyalty whatsoever, and told Raf and Peter as soon as I rejoined them. We watched Les and Mrs Reid having a last look down to the beach. She was talking, and waved a hand dismissively towards the ocean. Her strong hips and jutting breasts seemed to accentuate Leslie's stooped concavity.

'Serve him right. Serve him damn right,' said Raf. It wasn't a moral judgement, rather a reference to all those nights on which Les had returned to his landlady, and Raf had frittered his time away with cards and bitter study.

Les and Mrs Reid drove quite close to regain the road. I could see her mouth opening and closing quickly as she talked to him, and Les glanced at me as they passed. It was his own smile though, inwardly directed and not for me; his tilted, Spanish smile which he still wore as he turned the car again and began to drive down the hill. Elizabeth Reid had turned sideways somewhat in the seat, the better to watch him as she talked, and her mouth opened and closed effortlessly. It was a recollection which I found hard to shake off as we ourselves left. Peter was in a good humour because the tsunami had failed as he had predicted, but the unwanted glimpse of Leslie Foster's life had chilled my mood, and Raf's too in a different way. He sat silently, holding the empty wine flask between his knees, and reflecting on his unwilling celibacy.

Before tea, as I prepared the vegetables, I listened to a government seismologist on the radio explaining why the tidal wave hadn't come. I suppose he was a different seismologist from the one the papers had quoted the day before. I called out to the others to say it was on the news about the tidal wave not coming.

'Tsunami,' said Peter.

'Right.'

'The tsunami certainly came for old Les Foster though, didn't it. Talk about a shock wave,' said Raf. How we laughed at that. Raf and Peter came into the kitchen so we could see one another as we laughed, and better share the joke. All youth is pagan, and we believed that as the gods were satisfied with their sport, the rest of us were safe awhile. 'Came for old Les all right, the tsunami.' Even as I laughed I saw again Les and his landlady as they drove away, and that inward smile upon his face. As a drowning man might smile; for they say that at the very end the water is accepted, and that the past life spins out vividly. In Leslie's case it may well have been the future rather than the past he saw.

Träumerei

PHILIP MINCHER

Aunt May lived with my grandparents in the twilight zone between two centuries. In the beginning, in the oldest memories of my grandfather's house, she was a classic beauty with striking bright eyes in the sitting-room photo with my father and her other brothers. The old man and my uncles all had clean young faces you had to look hard at to recognize, and Aunt May was a beautiful young woman looking right at the camera. The young men stood grouped around their sister seated at a desk, and you could tell they were a close family.

In those early days, visiting my grandfather's house, I didn't see much of Aunt May because of her being a business woman and working for a big firm in the city, whereas my other aunts were always at home during the day. Then too for each of my other aunts there was an uncle, and that must have added to the fascination she held for me. I guess I must have fallen in love with my Aunt May before I even knew her, or rather with her classic beauty in the picture from the other side of my world.

Then when I knew her she was a gaunt grey old lady who was always going somewhere else and never dropped a syllable from my given name. She was generous from a distance, with a range beyond Christmas and birthdays. Once she bought me *The English Struwwelpeter*, and that must have come out of the past too:

> *The door flew open, in he ran,*
> *The great, long, red-legged scissor man . . .*

She wouldn't have known about the nightmares. For balance, there were a couple of Bonzo books, and I remember a magnificent tin sword that would have put Wilkinsons to shame. But there was so much more.

For Aunt May, bless her imperishable soul, gave me music.

Her room was a velvet and lavender inner sanctum as old as her picture. There was a smell of musk and lilac like the inside of handbags, bric-à-brac and lace from another age. And there was a wind-up Brunswick gramophone standing silent in the corner.

One Sunday morning I was parading my cigarbox insect collection for my grandfather. We were engrossed in the study of wetas, sharing the magnifying glass over fierce heads and barbed legs and gleaming armour-plate, when somebody began to play a piano on the other side of the world. The notes came gently on the still morning air, pervading that other passion, charging our halls of science with the new energy of art.

Hearing and sight fought for mastery, the pinned wetas stared back at me with black soulless eyes. I looked ever so carefully and there was my grandfather listening too and not with his mind wholly on science. The record machine had been silent for so long.

The theme filtered mistily through the walls and down the clinging corridors of time. I didn't know what it was. I hadn't, consciously, even heard the name of Robert Schumann, and a title like *Träumerei* from *Kinderscenen* would have meant even less. But a wordless message crept into my soul, infusing utterly, a cipher for all time. And then there was silence again and the warming sun shimmering through.

I had to know.

'What would that tune be, Grandad?'

'I don't know. Pretty piece.'

'Is it old?'

'Ah.'

That was my lot. The tune was old, 'pretty', nameless. To his glory he'd given me the natural world; in this dimension he was deaf, mute. I was on my own in a new galaxy and my touchstone was a sad song, a message of loss and longing from Aunt May's record machine.

After a while my aunt came out of the silence on her way to church, with her grey gaunt beauty and her formality with my given name.

'What have you there, Philip?'

'Wetas.'

'Wetas!' She made a face. 'What are you doing with the lad, Albert?' She always called my grandfather 'Albert' and my grandmother 'Eliza'.

'That's all right,' my grandfather winked at me. 'This is for men only.'

'How are your people, Philip?'

'Fine,' I said. 'Aunt May – ' I groped for the question, roughshod on holy ground. 'Could you tell me please – what was that music?'

I felt her eyes checking me out.

'Music, now? That's an advance on bugs, anyway.' Then she named Schumann's *Träumerei*.

I put the two names away for safe keeping.

'Do you have a gramophone?'

'Ours is busted,' I said.

That was all. I never heard music from my aunt's room again and she never even mentioned the subject until the day she gave me her gramophone and record collection. Looking back on it later I guessed she must have been watching quietly and waiting for me to grow up, and that we never got back to talking about it because she was always going somewhere else.

By that time there was only the slightest hint of the classic beauty thing, a cosmetic whisper of the past a stranger would have missed. But my eyes always saw the same Aunt May.

'How goes it with music, Philip?' She caught me unawares fresh from my grandfather's other Eden of English wildfowl and Damascus shotguns.

'Oh,' I groped for words to justify her interest, 'I heard *Light Cavalry* on the wireless last week.'

She came to the point without fuss.

'Would you like my gramophone?' Her words struck a magnificent chord. 'You'll have to ask your father, of course.'

'Aunt May, do you mean – your records too?'

'Oh, yes. You'll add to them when you grow up, of course. Wireless might be a great thing but you can't choose what you want to hear.'

I wanted to ask her in that case what if she chose to hear her records again, but she was getting ready to go out and had already put the matter aside.

We went back next weekend in my Uncle Jim's car and I had that feeling of a first fishing trip, or even going to buy a microscope. Uncle Jim was my uncle on the other side and not Aunt May's brother and she said 'How are you keeping, James?' and ushered us in through the sitting-room with the old clocks and the memories. We went quietly and respectfully into her room and took away her gramophone and all that ready music in the faded paper covers. We lashed the machine on the carrier and stowed the records carefully inside and even when I said my piece to Aunt May you wouldn't have known she was giving away anything that mattered. She said 'Cheerio, Albert' to my old man and 'My love to Winifred, James' to Uncle Jim and we drove away.

At home there was the usual turnout when we put the gramophone in place in my room and everyone had a look as if the record titles meant something to them. I promised to consider other people with the sound, and then I just shut up and waited. My mother touched the top of the machine and said 'Poor old May' and they all looked as if they understood what she meant by that and went out for a cup of tea. And at last I was alone with Aunt May's gift.

The titles made their own music: *Träumerei* of course; *Pathétique*; *Humoresque*; *Andante spianato*. The lyric poetry of the arias sang for me before they were played: *M'appari tutt' amor*; *Che gelida manina*; *Ah! fuyez, douce image* . . . Even the artists' names made their own exotic poem: Schnabel, Kreisler, Gigli, Korjus . . .

Cataloguing was one thing, playing was another. The new-found dimension was a box of foreign sound to my people. Music meant songs like *Waggon Wheels* or *Honey, you play in your own backyard*, or military bands on the *Diggers' Session*: if you couldn't sing along it was noise. So I chose my times to venture into the uncharted territory Aunt May had given me.

Exotic voices sang for me alone, transcending language. Unseen fingers bridged chords of time and sonatas crept into my soul.

The catalogue included what you might have called extras – light songs I scarcely noticed at first: *Santa Lucia*; *Beautiful Dreamer*; *Ah! Sweet Mystery of Life* . . . These were to acquire meaning as my demand became less severe. One day I examined them more closely and brought into the light a vintage ten inch of Grace Moore singing *Whistling Boy*. There were four words written on the jacket in a florid hand. They said: 'Good morning, Miss May.'

The message was faded and only the tidy storage of the record covers had preserved it. The four words confused me beyond truth, half-meanings burst in my brain like those vague adult passages that worried me in films. A whisper of excitement trembled in my blood.

I turned the disc, searching. The flip side was Grace Moore again, with a song that should have been corny: *One Night of Love*. I listened with a new awe, a first sensual stirring. The vision burst in my brain like a movie flashback: a classic beauty with long dark hair, in a perfumed room on the other side of life. I was crushed utterly on a theme of longing, a soundtrack of loss.

I probed for clues with more stealth than Charlie Chan. Did Aunt May play the piano? Sing? My mother looked back for the controlled answer. 'No, dear. She used to have a friend who was very musical . . . '

I never knew the truth. Her song had been sung before I came, I shunned the sterile murmurings of critics. My mind was too clean for old maid jokes, my love unsullied by time. I never knew why she chose silence. Afterwards when she went deaf the silly adult world lamented out of sequence: 'Poor dear, her music would have been such a comfort.' As if they knew.

Over the next couple of visits to my grandfather's house the likelihood of Aunt May being home took on a new wonder. There was a blend of wanting to see her and needing to be careful about the way I looked at her, and then each time disappointment to find she wasn't home. But finally she was there.

She came in on the latest display of specimens, the old Sunday morning pilgrimage to my grandfather's kitchen table. There was a mixed haul and my grandfather was getting up to find his other glasses.

'Good morning, Philip.'

'Good morning . . . Aunt May.'

She came closer to examine the display, blending her aura with the glories of my other world: a baby octopus in an Agee jar; a mouse's skin tanned in cold tea; trout ova in formalin; a pickled embryonic rabbit. If she laughed . . .

She didn't laugh.

'So you're going to be a scientist?' She touched one of the jars.

'Yes.' I wouldn't have believed in anything capable of preventing it.

'Not a musician, then?'

'I . . . don't think so.'

'You've got a violinist's hands, Philip.'

So. A violinist. I couldn't look at her eyes.

'I've got a friend who plays the violin,' I said. Don's hands were smaller. He'd shown me how to hold the thing and the truth was my joints had ached just from trying to look the part.

'And you wouldn't want to learn?'

'I don't think I'd be any good,' I said.

There were so many things. I had a fear she was thinking about lessons and I wanted to save her the disappointment.

'Aunt May.'

'Yes?' She was looking at the jar with the sleeping unborn rabbit. I wanted to cry.

'Thank you for the gramophone.'

'Oh yes. What did you like best?'

'I think – the violin pieces . . . '

I felt her eyes searching, longing for that lost era. I loved her back through the melancholy façade of age. Beyond propriety, once and forever, she took my hands: lifted and looked long. My hands were my nakedness, my eyes welled truth. I flew to her classic beauty out of sequence, pressed to her pilgrim spirit out of time. I sobbed against her dry breast.

'Hush, child. What is it?' But she knew. She held me with

tenderness unbound, her gaunt cheek wet against mine. 'We'll just go out on the verandah for a while, then. We don't want to worry old Grandad, do we?'

I sobered rapidly in the sunlight, almost ashamed. Melancholy bells shimmered on the morning air. Aunt May waited quietly at the old distance until I was all right.

Back in the kitchen my grandfather had his other glasses on and was studying the baby octopus. After a while I stopped feeling conscious of my hands. When I looked up Aunt May had come in from the verandah and I guessed she must be getting ready to go out.

Finally the sweet sad violin in my head lifted into silence.

Beethoven's Ears

MICHAEL MORRISSEY

When Ludwig van Beethoven died on 26 March 1827, his ears were amputated by the eminent anatomist Dr Joseph Wagner and placed in a jar filled with spirits of wine. Beethoven had slowly been going deaf since 1801 and Wagner wanted to examine his ears and try to ascertain the cause. In his autopsy report, Wagner noted that 'the external ear was large and irregularly formed, the scaphid fossa, but more especially the concha, was very spacious and half as large again as usual'. He also noted that the great composer's liver had shrunk to half normal size and was of a 'leathery consistency beset with knots the size of a bean'; the spleen was double normal size and the excretory duct of the pancreas 'as wide as a good quill'; the stomach was 'distended', and the body 'much emaciated'. In short, Beethoven was a mess.

However, on examining the brain, Wagner found its convolutions to be 'remarkably white' and 'very much deeper, wider and more numerous than ordinary'.

But to return to the ears. They sat in the spirits-of-wine-filled jar for several weeks, but before Wagner could complete the examination, the jar mysteriously disappeared. No one is quite sure what happened to the jar, but it is thought to have been illegally sold by Wagner's servant to an English doctor and smuggled across the English Channel into the sceptred isle. Having been fruitlessly examined by the English doctor (the syphilitic cause of Beethoven's deafness then being unrecognized) the ears were returned to the jar and placed on display in his living room for the curious scrutiny of dinner guests. In 1843 an urchin chimney sweep stole the jar and sold it to a pawnbroker who eventually persuaded a baronet from Kent that they were indeed Beethoven's ears.

When Phineas T. Barnum made his triumphal tour of Great Britain with Tom Thumb and the mother-daughter team who had won American hearts by playing Topsy and Little Eva in *Uncle Tom's Cabin*, the baronet offered the colourful American entrepreneur the ears for ten guineas. Barnum accepted the offer. So Beethoven's ears joined the Feejee Mermaid, Chang and Eng (the famous Siamese twins), Lionel the Lion Faced Man and General Tom Thumb, the world's most famous dwarf. When the general lifted one of the ears from the murky preserving fluid and placed it over one of his own diminutive organs and pretended to hear messages from beyond the grave both of the Fat Ladies would invariably shriek – to a duo of thigh-slapping delight from the Siamese twins.

The ears subsequently went underground (as it were) and were not seen or heard of again until the World Fair in St Louis of 1904. Soon after, they fell into the hands of the Great Tosca, a turn of the century hypnotist and mountebank, who claimed that 'the ears of the great German composer Beethoven had peculiar psychic properties'. They could, said the Great Tosca, hear a person's innermost thoughts. Tosca, a tall bearded man weighing eighteen stone, would stand blindfold on stage with the jar balanced delicately on his head, and reveal the embarrassingly private thoughts of his largely female audience. He would tell people what they had in their handbags, where they had been in the previous week, and what they had eaten for supper. These spectacular feats would produce thunderous applause and Tosca's assistant, a French girl from Marseilles, swears that on good nights 'the ears would undulate ever so slightly' in appreciation of this crude symphony of hand clapping.

But now the fate of Beethoven's ears takes a forked path. According to the European theory, the ears were sold to an eccentric, an unsuccessful composer called Erasmus Windhover. Windhover was the creator of several leadenly dull choral works and a large body of chamber music that had never been performed (though he would often hum these opuses aloud for the benefit of Beethoven's ears).

Six months later, Gustav Mahler received a visitor claiming to have in his possession the Tenth Symphony of Beethoven and would he care to conduct it? Mahler was sceptical but accepted the score and studied it closely. An hour later Mahler called Windhover back into his study. He said it was always a pleasure to meet a representative of the nation that had produced Purcell and Elgar. Then Mahler coughed and said that though the work did indeed appear to be in the style of Beethoven, the third movement was almost identical to the third movement of the *Eroica* and the concluding movement was very similar to the concluding movement of the Seventh. In short, the Tenth symphony of Beethoven was a fake. Enraged, Windhover swore that he knew the symphony to be 'a true and original work of Beethoven', for had he not taken down every note, line by line under the dictation of the great composer himself? It was typical of Mahler, an Austrian, to be jealous of Beethoven a German, etc., etc. Mahler bowed and said curtly, 'Goodday to you, Herr Windbreaker.'

Undeterred by Mahler's scepticism, Windhover returned to his pastoral retreat near Salisbury Plain, where he composed an eleventh Beethovenic symphony. Out-Mahlering Mahler, he called it the Symphony of the Ten Thousand. It called for two thousand musicians (502 first violins, 502 second violins, 240 violas, 240 cellos, 200 basses, 80 flutes, 80 oboes, 20 clarinets in E flat, 60 clarinets in B flat, 5 bass clarinets in B flat, 8 bassoons, 4 double bassoons, 27 horns, 10 trombones, 5 bass tubas, 6 harps, 3 celesta, 3 sets of tympani, 3 cymbals, 3 tambourines) and eight thousand singers. The local parish priest was 'deeply impressed' by Windhover's dedication to the craft of choral and orchestral music but inquired politely of Windhover how it was they could accommodate so many visitors in their village of three hundred? 'The Lord will provide,' Windhover replied. But the Lord, it seemed, was intent on turning a deaf ear to this posthumous masterpiece of Beethoven. When Windhover met with no interest in London musical circles, it is said he went to the famous circle of stones at Stonehenge and buried the ears under the largest stone. Some now claim that Beethoven's ears tranformed Stonehenge into a gigantic listening device. Others maintain that the famous black magician, Aleister Crowley dug them up and hung them around his neck, deriving much of his horrible powers from having them so close to his villainous heart. It was rumoured that The Great Beast nailed the ears above the table near the door of his infamous Black Magick restaurant, where strong men were weeping into their daemonically hot curries. The ears, Crowley said, greatly enjoyed the peculiar atmosphere of sexual decadence and diabolic incantation, as well as the sound of strong men weeping. When Crowley died, the ears were cremated and co-mingled with his ashes and placed in an urn on top of the Rock of Cefalu, where they remain to this day.

The alternative or 'colonial' theory is that the ears passed from the Barnum show to a theosophist, who gave them to Annie Besant. When Besant visited New Zealand in the nineteenth century, she bestowed them upon the local branch of the Order of the Golden Dawn. After the First World War, they appeared once more on the shelf of a Mrs Eleanor Spencer, a Dunedin music teacher, who said 'they could always detect false notes'. It is said that they are in the possession of the most musical of Mrs Spencer's eighty-seven grandchildren, but, according to another account, they re-entered show business . . .

In 1905 the Fuller Brothers toured with Cleopatra, 'a fearless snake charmer'. Cleopatra, who caused 'strong men to experience a strange shuddering thrill' and women to 'shriek in horror' at her skilled handling of boa constrictors, anacondas and black snakes, swore that Beethoven's ears kept her from being bitten. When Cleopatra was approached to donate Beethoven's ears to a time capsule, she agreed, even though parting with them was going to put her life in jeopardy. Where the time capsule is buried, no one knows, but it was rumoured to be secured under the Largest Wooden Building in the World. It is feared that, should the time capsule be excavated it will be as corroded by water as the time capsule retrieved from a well beneath the former District Court in Auckland.

There is even a post-Colonial theory concerning Beethoven's ears (especially espoused at the University of Auckland). According to its exponents, Beethoven's ears never existed or if they existed 'we as ex-Colonials have no need of them. We don't need European ears anymore; we have our own.'

*

It is uncertain, perhaps, whether Beethoven's ears still lie beneath Stonehenge or with Aleister Crowley's ashes or with one of Mrs Spencer's musical grandchildren or buried in a Wellington time capsule. It is certain, probably, that the ears will be in some way listening to human endeavour through all eternity and that many of us will believe – and who can do otherwise? – that throughout the aeons to pass they will listen to the sounds of new civilizations as well as their collapse, which will be heard by those ever alert organs as a strange, exciting but somehow orderly music.

The Celebration

RAYMOND PILLAI

The sky all around had a lurid glow as cane fires lit up the December evening. It was the close of the crushing season and those who had not finished harvesting their cane redoubled their efforts while the more fortunate ones rested from their labours. The Gounden household was one of the lucky ones. With good weather, enough cane trucks and a hard working cane gang, they had managed to move out all their cane. Now they took their ease in the cool of the evening and chatted idly over their bowls of yaqona.

'We've had a good crop this year, amma,' Rama said to his mother. 'Twelve hundred tons at the very least. And the final payment on last year's crop was a good one too. I think we can kill a goat for Christmas and celebrate. Nothing very big, mind you. Just a small affair for the family members only.'

Rama's mother was taken aback. 'It isn't a year yet since your father died,' she said indignantly. 'What will people think?'

'People will always think the worst of others. But we have nothing to fear. We said all the necessary prayers after appa's death. And the *kriyakaram* was a big one. We killed three goats, didn't we? Nobody can say we didn't observe the period of mourning correctly.'

'It's the first Christmas since he died,' his mother persisted.

'Look, amma, it happened ten months ago. You can't go on mourning him for ever. You have to stop some time.'

'Ramu, is there ever a time when we stop remembering completely? There are some things which are not easily forgotten, because they have become part of us. Since your father and I were married, forty years have passed. That's a long time.'

141

Too long, thought Rama. He had never got on well with his father. 'It's different for you, amma. I don't have to remember him.'

'I know you never liked your father, but that's no reason to forget him now. True, he used to beat you harshly at times. But there was a reason for it. Your father wanted you to grow up into a strong, honest man. That's why he brought you up so firmly. And not just you only. We all felt the weight of his hand at one time or another. But we've all benefited. We are wealthy. We are respected in the whole district. And we are still a united family. So many families quarrel and break up after the father dies. But has that happened to us? And why hasn't it happened to us? Because your father showed us the right way. Even though he is no longer alive, his spirit is still with us, keeping us united and happy.'

Rama had listened patiently to his mother's homily. After all, she had earned the right to her illusions. But he could not check himself any longer. 'If his spirit is still with us, then I say we should celebrate Christmas the way he would have celebrated it – with feasting and drinking. He always enjoyed life. You know that well enough. He wouldn't miss his meat and whisky for anything. I'm sure he wouldn't want us to sit around like fools just because he wasn't alive to share the occasion with us.'

'I'm sure your father would be filled with sorrow to see you making merry so soon after his death. Wait a little longer, and then you can have as much feasting and drinking as you want.'

'But how much longer amma? We didn't do anything for Easter or Diwali. How long are we going to continue as if we were corpses ourselves? I say we should kill one goat at least for Christmas. And people can say what they like. I don't give a damn!'

Rama had his way in the end. He was the eldest son after all. But his decision was strongly resented. When he brought home the Christmas goat, the family showed not the slightest interest and this made Rama very sore. At the very least they could have asked him what the goat had cost.

The Christmas celebrations proved to be a dispiriting affair. With the exception of Logesan, who was the youngest and who dared not cross his brother, the others found reasons for not attending. The two sisters said they were unable to travel. Their damn fool husbands must have got them pregnant again, thought Rama. Govinda had to go and see his ailing mother-in-law. A likely story! That mother-in-law of Govinda's was strong as an ox and twice as stupid. Gopal gave the same reason as the year before – he was afraid somebody would set fire to his cane if he left his farm. All feeble excuses! Well, let them stay away if they liked, fumed Rama. If they wanted to be stubborn, that was their own affair, but he wasn't going to let them spoil his pleasure.

The goat was slaughtered early on Christmas morning. In the past, Rama's father would have conducted the job personally, wearying everybody with his imperious commands. Today that privilege was Rama's. He took charge of the operation as if born to the task and gave orders with the aplomb of a veteran.

Logesan held the goat down by the legs while Rama forced a drink of water into the goat's mouth – the final kindness. Then a deft stroke of the knife sliced through the animal's throat, releasing a jet of hot blood.

'Look how you're holding that basin, you ass!' Rama shouted at his son, Anand. 'You'll let the whole stuff spill on the ground.'

Anand did his best to hold the basin steady as the blood gushed into it erratically. The animal's eyes dilated in terror, its body heaving in spasms of agony. Uncomprehending, crazed with pain, it struggled to raise its head and look at its tormenters, but Rama's firm grip on its muzzle held it prisoner. Hot, tortured blasts of air snorted through its labouring nostrils. Its body arched in agonized convulsions. Desperately it fought to regain its feet, but the combined weight of the two men brutally quelled all resistance. The spasms slowly ceased as its life ebbed out. It sagged and went limp, defeated.

The basin was almost full – frothing, dark, sinister. The flow of blood dwindled to a trickle. Judging the right moment expertly, Rama motioned to Anand to remove the basin. It was not a second too soon as a stream of undigested food spurted from the severed gullet. Rama twisted the head round and sawed through the spinal cord. The goat convulsed once more, then subsided. The deed was done.

Rama stood up and flicked the sweat away from his forehead with the back of his hand. 'He's a big bugger, isn't he?' he said. 'Over a hundred pounds in my estimation.'

Logesan murmured assent but Anand said nothing. Anand was sickened by the slaughter, more so because it was quite unnecessary. Young as he was, he was still perceptive enough to see that the goat was only a sacrifice to his father's ego.

Rama was not pleased with Anand's squeamishness. 'Look at this boy of mine. He is nearly old enough to have hair on his chin, but he's frightened of a little blood.'

Anand was stung. 'It's not the blood. It's the pain that we give the animal when we kill it.'

'Nonsense!' said Rama. 'It doesn't feel a thing. It gets such a shock that it doesn't know what's happening to it. Look at that goat there. See how peacefully it lies. Do you think it feels anything? Not one bit. It's gone. Finished.'

There was indeed something peaceful about the way it lay there, looking calm and composed even though its head was missing. Flies started buzzing round the neck of the carcass, and as the blood on the grass began to thicken and grow dark, the violent scene of a few minutes before seemed more remote and less reprehensible.

The goat yielded fifty-five pounds of meat, which should have pleased Rama, but he was still furious because the whole family was not present. 'They should have come,' he complained to his mother. 'We always used to celebrate Christmas in a big way. It was fun for everybody. But this year they think they can have more fun by themselves in their own homes. Our neighbours must be laughing at us. They know we killed such a big goat, and now there's no one to eat it. Well then, if nobody wants it, I'll eat it all by myself.'

'All this is your own doing, Ramu,' said his mother. 'You had no patience. You could not wait for even one year to show that you are the big man of the house now. I kept telling you, but you are too big now to listen to an old woman like me.'

'Amma, that's not true. I just wanted to enjoy Christmas.'

'Since when have you become a Christian, Ramu, that you must celebrate Christmas?'

'Haven't we always celebrated Christmas? Christmas is not a religious thing. It's only a public holiday. It's a time for feasting and merry-making.'

'All right, then. You go ahead with your feasting and see how much you enjoy it.'

'I will enjoy it!' he said defiantly. 'Shanti!' he roared at his wife. 'Why isn't the fried meat ready yet?'

'I'm just doing it now. I have only two hands, you know.'

'Your tongue seems to be working more than your hands nowadays. Hurry up with that meat.'

A few minutes later his wife brought in a bowl of chopped meat and liver mixed with fat and blood. It was done just the way he liked it, with plenty of chillies. In a separate saucer lay the goat's testicles, lightly fried in oil and neatly quartered. When Rama's father had been alive, the first meat was always reserved for him. No one might eat until he had tasted first and pronounced himself satisfied. It was almost a seigneurial right, confirming him in his place of honour as head of the house. Now the old man was no more. His mantle had fallen upon Rama's shoulders, and with it all the prerogatives. 'Ah, it's a long time since I've had such tasty meat,' said Rama with exaggerated relish. In truth he was disappointed to find the meat a little tough, but he was not going to let his chagrin show. 'Here, Anand,' he called to his son. 'Take some of this meat.'

Anand shuffled to the table reluctantly and put a few spoonfuls of fried blood into his cupped hand.

'Have some of this too,' said Rama, pointing to the saucer.

'I never eat that,' said Anand hastily. The thought of eating goat's testicles repelled him.

'Go on, it's good stuff.'

'I never eat it,' repeated Anand dully.

'Well, you are going to eat some today, my boy.'

'Why are you forcing him?' Anand's mother intervened. 'He says he doesn't want it.'

'Stop molly-coddling the boy. He's going to do what I tell him. Here, eat this.' Rama picked up a piece from the saucer and thrust it at Anand.

Anand took the proffered morsel. With a tremendous effort of will he bit into it and tried to swallow, but the spongy txture and somewhat ammoniacal tang of the flesh made him retch. He rushed out to the drain which ran past the kitchen window and vomited until he was exhausted.

'See what you have done to the boy!' cried Anand's mother. 'Why are you being so stubborn?'

'He's just enjoying his Christmas Day,' said Rama's mother bitterly. 'He just wants to show that he's the big man of the house. And he has proved it by bullying his son.'

'Stop it!' shouted Rama. 'I've had enough of you people!' With a violent motion of the hand he swept the meat bowl off the table and stamped out of the house.

His wife looked sadly at the meat strewn over the floor. She had prepared it so painstakingly, the way her husband liked it, and he had flung it aside to be trampled underfoot. Tears of exasperation welled up in her eyes.

'It's no use crying, Shanti,' her mother-in-law said to her. 'Men never change. In forty years of married life I never managed to change the ways of Ramu's father. And I don't think you'll ever be able to alter Ramu either. He's too much like his father. Make the most of your happy moments, and pray that the hard times are few. That's the only way to endure a lifetime together.'

Shanti made no reply. There was practical wisdom in the old woman's words, but hardly a grain of comfort. Still, there was no point in lingering over her troubles. She brushed back her tears as if nothing had happened. Then she bent down and began picking up the pieces of meat one by one.

Letters

JOHN PUHIATAU PULE

[1]

My father,
In the name of our Heavenly Father who protects us, we are now in a city called Christchurch, and the harbour called Lyttleton. I have never seen so many houses all in a neat row, and in the middle are long black roads, with hundreds of cars. I pray to the Lord to be with us in this new world. We had to wait a very long time before the government man said it's okay to leave the *Maui Pomare*. I am not frightened as I know the Lord is with me on this journey. The streets are very busy with lots of shoes and things to buy in the shops, not like the small shops in Alofi and Apia. I post this today, and tomorrow we sail by another boat to the Capital and meet up with my husband. I will write again soon.

My love to my mother, may God bless you both and look after you both in this world.

Mocca Laginogi

AUCKLAND, FEBRUARY 1943

My mother,
May the Lord be with you and bring strength and love to you and the family. We have found a flat at Wellington Street. The trip up from Wellington took a long time. All the way up we passed many towns, more than in Samoa.

Auckland is a big city. The buildings nearly touch the sun, and the sea is very close to the road. We pay 7 and 6 for our little flat which is close to where Lapa works down at the wharf, and I have found myself a job sewing clothes.

There is great sadness here as many sons were killed in the war in faraway countries. They say the Japanese are not far away, and the NZ government is still debating whether to send one machine-gun to protect Niue from invaders. Something like eighty Niueans are in Europe and the Solomon Islands.

We have decided that I will go for my driving licence and learn to drive a car.

Mocca Laginogi

FAKATOLA, LIKU, FEPUARI 1943

My dear Mocca,
In the year of our Lord and Protector, he be with you in the new world. Your brother, Puhia, is leaving on the next ship. I have paid his fare, he is always in trouble.

Many of our men here are leaving the Island to enlist in the NZ Army. I remember back in 1915 when 150 men were sent to a faraway country called France and Egypt. Not many returned.

We now have two cars on Niue, you will be the first Niuean woman to hold a licence and drive a car.

Expect Puhia in March.
The Lord look after and bless you.

Puhiataha

WELLINGTON STREET, AUCKLAND, 1944

My father,
Thanking you for paying my fare to this wonderful country where people are equal and life is better for every man. May the Lord bless you.

I am staying in the spare room with my sister and her husband. He got me a job working down at the wharf and the money is good. When I save up I will bring you and my mother here to be with us as life is good to us and will be for you. I am working hard and not drinking.

God bless you all.

Puhia

SAVIOUR STREET, AUCKLAND CITY, 1944

My father,
Thanks to the Lord that we are all alive today!

I have to tell you, as Puhia would not, he has been arrested several times now, and each time they have warned him. I have to go and pick him up at the police station every time. I'm afraid they will send him back to Niue. I ask him to stop drinking because with the other men after work they spend all their money. This is not good. It is a bad name for our family and you.

We had to move house again. Lila and Kau have one room. Lapa and I have the back room, and Puhia is in the spare room. It is a bigger house, looking over the shops of the main shopping street, Karangahape Road.

Mocca

LIKU, NIUE, 1944

My dear daughter,
May the Lord be with you and keep you well because without the Lord's protection we will surely perish.

I am getting old and find it hard to walk around at the wharf lifting banana crates. This job of Inspector is very tiring. My legs are not young.

Puhia arrived yesterday, drunk. He is a disgrace to my name. The people say, 'See! that man was sent back from NZ, too much drinking.' He said you bought him four new suits before leaving NZ. Is this true? Because he is empty. I am ready to leave on the ship *Maui Pomare*, leaving for Samoa on Feb 6th, arrive Fiji Feb 28th, then to NZ March 6th.

Please be there to meet me at the airport as I've been told it's a hard place to find anything. May the God above bless you and look after you in this world.

Puhiataha

AUCKLAND, 1944

My father,
My heart is sad that Puhia had to be sent back.

Yes, we bought four new suits for Puhia but the last few days before he was to leave on the ship he was supposed to take them to the dry-cleaners. Instead he went to the pub, got drunk, ended up in jail and lost the suits.

Only in the morning when the police arrived at my house did we know, and we had to rush him quickly to the wharf as the ship was leaving that very morning. The government officer said he will not be allowed back into NZ. Still, he is my brother and I love him. Everything has been settled here, all you have to do is arrive safely.

I pray you arrive safely.

Mocca

NIUE, 1944

Dearest Sis,
I am very sad at what I did. Is it true they won't let me back to NZ? I am teaching at the school and helping build a new hospital called Lord Liverpool. Lihe and myself are building a house near our parents' house.

Mocca, we have decided to give Atalani to you. She is still young but since you are childless, you need someone to look after you when you are old.

Puhiataha left for NZ a few days ago. The watermelon field is plentiful. I put a crate of talo, one box of green bananas, one of yam, and one of breadfruit for you on the next ship. Please help me and my family get to NZ again. Here I will grow old looking after the land. No money, only hardship.

God be with you and Lila.

Puhia

AUCKLAND, 1944

Dear Puhia,
Our father has arrived safely in the name of our Lord. We got to the airport late and could not find him, and there he was drinking a free cup of coffee. After many years he has not changed towards my husband.

I also got my licence and felt very proud driving our father home. You know I am the first Niuean woman to drive a car.

Last night we had a feast of pig and talo. Lila and Kau have found a home in Kingsland. The government helped them. See, this country looks after many people. It is a big country.

You know our father still hates Lapa. I keep telling my father to let the past rest, let God decide. But he is a stubborn man and there is no way of changing rock.

I am also worried at the amount of beer these men drink after work.

How is your family? You must try and keep your children together, they are scattered like leaves over NZ and Niue. I will try and see the government again, they are also very hard. You must not forget that you were arrested eleven times, and you stopped the traffic by lying on the road everytime you went drinking. In this country you must go to church, have a job, because money is important. Nothing is for free. We work very hard although sometimes life is hard just eating sardines and one potato every day.

Kau is always drunk and never brings home the money. Lila is getting into it too, you know our sister, famous for home-brew and going to jail for it.

I am planning to save money and buy a house for our parents. I wish you were here to help.

Look after our land, God be with you and forgive you, my brother.

Mocca

LIKU, NIUE, 1944

My sister Mocca,
Lani is your daughter and Daviti is your son, and I hope they both grow up to respect me. I know I hit my son badly, but if I don't he will grow up to be nothing. You know me, Sis, like our father, hard and bad-tempered.

The hospital is ready and a white doctor and nurse are the boss. It is full already. I'm sure most of them are there out of curiosity.

I keep our sister's grave clear of grass. The breadfruit tree over her is heavy with fruit.

Write soon my sister. Is God punishing me because I am

not there to help you? We only have one mother and one father.

God be with you and Lila.

Puhia

LIKU, NIUE, 1945

My dearest sister,

Thank you in the name of our Lord for the shoes. My wife is with me no more, I sent her home.

They are building a church in every village. We tried to have a Christmas as in NZ, but it's not the same. A government man was here and was treated to a feast. He looked frightened. God be with you all.

Puhia

AUCKLAND, 1945

Dear Puhia,

Thank God the war is over. The old folks say it is time now to count our dead. It has been a busy month for us, hair-cutting and marriages. Why do Palagi men want to marry Niuean women?

We all went fishing at Devonport wharf and the next day gathered mussels at Maraetai. Daviti is planting trees at a place called Muriwai, then he goes to work on the ships in Wellington. He fights a lot and is starting to drink with the men. Lani is doing well at school. I hope they look after us when we are old.

We go to church every Sunday. We never miss. Lapa has a new job at the Westfield freezing works.

Have you planted more talo to send here?

It is now the cold season. Our father gets lost in the city so someone has to be with him all the time.

On the next ship expect two boxes of clothes.

Your sister Mocca, in the year of our Lord.

LIKU, 1945

Sis,

I worked all day yesterday breaking up the hard rocks. That's what happens if a man has no sons around to help. Daviti who I had hoped would be my strength is gone. He is your son now. Tasi was caught drinking home-brew, and was punished by the new white NZ Commissioner. I don't know why they send these overlords to look after our Niue affairs. Look at the war, what does that say about their own affairs?

We are building clubs for the NZ people to get together and socialize. They say every capital in the world should have a pub but we still haven't got one, as the church disagrees with it.

There are now three cars and one bus on the island, with one policeman in every village. Mr Larsen, the new Commissioner, gave the orders.

Have you seen the Government about my family and myself coming to NZ? Life is hard here and many men and women are leaving for American Samoa, NZ, or Tahiti. I want to come back and help you, also start a new life with my family.

I gave your bike to Ligi to look after. Giving your bike away, is separating us from our childhood. Remember when we first got them? We were the envy of every village that we rode through. Now I must crush rocks because this land is hard. I can't plant talo on to rocks.

Thank you for the clothes, we have given some away to our folks who have nothing on their backs, although the church tries hard to clothe every man and woman and child. Now they want to seal the road with the same blackstuff they use on NZ roads, to the villages Lakepa, Liku to Avatele.

Please go and see the Government.

Your brother, Puhia

AUCKLAND, 1945

Dear brother,

I am doing all I can for you and your family to come here. I think saying that you have a family made things easier, as they want to help.

Daviti is in Wellington and he soon sails around the world. I won 102 pounds on Saturday at the Ellerslie racecourse. I have also opened an account and save every cent I can to help pay your family over here. Soon our father has to go home. He thinks betting on horses is better than selling fish.

Take care the Lord bless you and the family.

Mocca

LIKU, 1945

Sis,
Our father is here and looking wornout from the trip. He is the storyteller on the island, and is a very important man. We had dancing and plenty of timala and fish.

I have cleared a large part of the land to plant talo. Thank you for the five pound note and the photos.

Puhia

LIKU, 1945

Mocca,
In the year of our Lord, he who protects us in the world and he be with you for ever. Puhia has worked hard while I was away, but he is always talk talk talk about NZ, and he hardly goes to church. He is back to his old ways of drinking and other things. Maybe it is best if sometime in the future he can go with his family to NZ, but right now Puhia is my only son here to work the land.

Life the Palagi way is easy and if God is really white then there is such a thing as mercy. I only want my children to be good and follow the ways of the Lord. Believe in God and nothing will go wrong. You know these are always the same words I have spoken to you since you were a child old enough to understand. You, Mocca, my eldest daughter, are doing well, except that husband of yours. But I see that you are strong in mind and heart that he is the man you have chosen to be with. Then let it be. It seems that our people are slowly leaving for New Zealand, where all is good and there is no hardship, where money is plenty and life is rich.

I myself can see this force taking our young men with a powerful new hope.

Your mother and I are getting old and if there is a better future for Puhia and his family, then you, as the eldest, must help him. I can see he would rather go to NZ than crush rocks. Puhia has many sons, only Togia is left here. Although he is young he is keen to work.

God bless you and Lila.

Puhiataha

[2]

LIKU, 1946

My dear sister,

We are all well and the sugarcane fields are as tall as our house.

Some of the men who went to the war in Europe have returned with nothing in their pockets, they are waiting at the village council meeting house to discuss with the elders and Commissioner about work. As usual, the elders go straight to the Resident Commissioner for advice. What is happening, is that the elders can't solve the problems. These men will leave for the other islands to find work, and we all know that many do not come back home.

Our father is still at the wharf but will have to leave soon as he is getting old and all that walking around in the heat is slowing him down. Our mother weaves mats all day. It has not rained for three weeks and the lemon trees are dead.

Thank you for the clothes and shoes. Can you send us a lamp next time?

Take care my sister, may the Lord be with you forever.

Puhia

AUCKLAND, 1946

My father and mother,

I pray to the Lord that we will soon meet, and that he, the Protector of us all brings us together.

We are now at 30 Upper Queen Street, very close to the city

155

and to where we work. Life is not all that easy at times but we eat bread and sardines.

Lapa has learned to play the drums and has formed a band with some Niue boys in Grey Lynn, so most Saturday nights he is out, whereas I go out myself to friends and play poker. It is totally different from suipi. This is for money, lose some, win some.

I send some shirts for you and material for our mother.

God bless you all.

Mocca

LIKU, 1946

Mocca Laginogi,
We are both getting old but we still have Puhia here to look after us. It is God's word that you should have Daviti and Lani as your adopted son and daughter to look after you both when the time comes.

Puhia works everyday with his son Togia. Nobody really likes the Commissioner and there has been trouble.

Well, Mocca, I end this letter and hopefully we meet soon.

In the name of our Lord, amen.

Puhiataha

LIKU, 1950

Dear Mocca,
I have decided to marry Loata at the end of this year, but it won't be in the church in Liku, it will be in the minister's office in Alofi.

I need to ask you if you can send a wedding ring and I will repay you when I come to NZ in the very near future. As you know Loata has two other sons, Mana and Vihi, having herself married twice as I did so we both have grown-up children.

Our old father has retired from his work as Inspector at Alofi wharf. My ex-wife Lihi is giving me a bad time, but she will look after Atalani and Kufani while Togia and Pelesita will live with our Magafaoa.

God bless you all.

Puhia

AUCKLAND, 1950

Puhia,

We are happy at the news, and I have started looking for a ring which should be in my next letter. I love Loata very much, she is a good woman.

You have many children Puhia, and I think back to when I hurried with your first wife, Lovena, in the doctor's car to Alofi, and soon after Daviti was born, and Lovena said, 'Here, Mocca, take this son as your own flesh and blood.' I was sad, as I knew the two of you had separated, but I did not say anything then as I was happy to take Daviti as my own son.

Soon after Daviti was born Lapa and I left Niue for Samoa, leaving Daviti behind with our parents. That was back in 1930, and while in Apia I worked hard at many jobs, washing clothes and looking after the expatriates' children, while my husband worked in the forest. When he could find work in the schools, he would do two shifts. When we spent time in Manu'a, where Lapa was born and his mother Kamasa looked after us. Even though Lapa was from a paramount family, we still had to live and work in poor conditions. In Pago Pago it was much worse and then we decided to return to Niue in 1936, four years after our sister Fapene died of typhoid. Daviti attended school in the capital.

You know, islanders didn't look all that hot in clothes in those days.

Now after eight years here we are comfortable. Life is easy, not like life in Niue, having to look for food in the forest and climbing over rocks by the coast. When Mairi was born in 1936 Noue gave her to me at five months. I took her as my own daughter as I knew then that I could not have children. Maybe it was my mother who kept saying to me and Lila, 'Don't you two go through the hardship of childbearing.'

Although I cannot have children I have two of yours and one of Noue's. Remember when you and I were told by our father that Noue was not his son but our mother's from another man, and still I dare not ask my mother who the father is, but I hope one day she will tell me everything.

Here is a little history. Did you know that I am the first

Niuean woman to ever have a driver's licence in NZ? We have a new car. Lapa is now working at the Hellabys Freezing Works and has been promoted to foreman, so a bit more money is coming in. Maybe when you come back here Lapa can get you a job working in the same works.

Thanks for the box of yams. May the Lord look after you and the family in this world.

Mocca Laginogi

ALOFI, 1950

Dear Sis,
Thank you for the ring. I am at Alofi Post Office having already opened the parcel, and straight away I write to say thank you.

The people are very angry at the Resident Commissioner Larsen, and the Rev Check is annoyed at Mr Larsen who gave permission for the Mormon Church and the Catholic Church to establish a congregation on Niue soil. I find this wrong, as Mr Larsen went right over the heads of the village elders. Did you know that Mr Larsen is also judge and jury? There was a petition to have Mr Larsen removed but he managed to bribe the Council. He is acting the iki, and is a cruel man. Something is bound to happen soon as this can not go on for too long.

Once again, thanks for the ring and the materials, Loata will be very happy.

Puhia

UPPER QUEEN STREET, 1950

Dear brother,
It is also known here among Niueans that Mr Larsen is a crook. Some of the elders are bribed and cleverly used by him. It is not only Larsen, there are also other certain expatriates that are cruel and should not be on the island.

My work with Jack Naea is keeping me busy and already we give strong support to the Labour Party.

God bless you all.

Mocca

LIKU, 1950

Mocca,
Many years have gone now and I need to come to NZ.

The old ban from last century on dancing is still in power. We are not allowed to dance, only on permission of Mr Larsen, who is a cruel man. His wife is a leaf blown about by the wind.

There is severe punishment for those caught making home-brew.

I go into the bush everyday to collect fa for our mother's weaving baskets.

Our father is not well. Loata and I were married in Alofi, just a quiet one. Afterwards had a feast. Loata is a good woman. When I was ill, Loata came to my bed in the shadows and looked after me.

Sis, I long to come to NZ, can you do something?

God bless you and be with you in this world.

Puhia

UPPER QUEEN STREET, 1950

Puhia, my brother,
I am still trying but these things take time. I will send a box of clothes and pots on the next ship. Daviti is now in Canada and Lani is living in a house with other people in Kingsland, she has chosen to do so.

I will write soon.

Mocca

LIKU, 1951

My sister,
Mocca, everything has been taken care of for our father. Puhiataha is buried at the back of our house in Kavaka. The land has been passed on to me, and with my one son we work all day.

Daviti has not written to me nor sent any money. He has no respect.

Loata and I are collecting stones to build a home the old

way. We would be grateful if you can send some material for us. We only have one father, now he is gone. We must find a way to unite the family.

I wait for your words.

Your brother, Puhia

30 UPPER QUEEN STREET, 1951

My brother,
I have decided to bring my mother to NZ so I can look after her where it will be easy on her health. If you like I can bring your daughter Atalantica over, which will ease the burden.

Give me a little longer to save the money. God bless.

Mocca

AUCKLAND, 1952

Puhia,
Our sister Lila and Kau are now living in Newmarket, both are drinking too much. We have been here ten years now and hardly have anything to show from working. It is important to own a house here.

On the weekend we organized a Mei for Mafola's wedding. It was a big wedding with well over 100 people. Here is material for you and Mala and the basket is for mum. We only have one mother in this world.

Mocca

LIKU, 1952

My dear sister,
We now have a son and we are naming him Falekila.

The hospital in Alofi is always full, and the roads are always kept clean. Those who are fined in the courts keep the roads in order.

There is talk of self-government but the elders are saying there will be too much disagreement among the fuata about who will decide the future of the country.

We got a good crop this month. Daviti sent me a letter but no money in it. My first crop has all grown up but no one has come forward to help on the land, only Togia. There is much work to be done.

Take care my sister, the Lord be with you.

Puhia

AUCKLAND, 11 JUNE 1953

My brother,
All the papers are ready and mother and Atalantica can come to NZ, all you have to do is get them ready. I have paid for the fares. Here are some warm clothes for them. God bless.

Mocca

LIKU, 1953

My sister,
They are on their way having left yesterday for Samoa and Fiji, and should arrive in NZ on September 21.

We prepared a small umu to last the journey. We pray they have a safe journey.

Puhia

LIKU, SEPT. 1953

My dear sis,
You probably have heard that on the night of August 14th the Resident Commissioner, Mr Larsen, was murdered at his home while asleep in his bed by three men who escaped from jail, Tama from Makefu, Tulo from Hikutuvake and Eli from Liku.

All were sentenced to hang, while the fourth, also from Liku, Pelle, who did not take part in the killing but held the torch, ran back to the jail straight after the killing. All three say they did Niue a favour by getting rid of a tyrant; the three were eventually caught by the people of Vaiea. The relatives of those three are angry and there is talk of war if they are hanged. There are notes pinned on the notice board outside the Alofi Post Office, as I have seen them myself, saying that if the three are hung there will be trouble.

There is also talk of getting rid of some hafa-kasi Niueans

who are on the side of the judge's decision. I say that any slave who kills his master does so in legitimate self-defence whatever the circumstances.

Their appeals will be heard in NZ at the end of October, after the Niueans here refuse to hang them. The reason they were in jail in the first place was for minor thefts, one got two years for breaking into a shop, one got eighteen months for stealing two dollars and the other for swearing.

There are many harsh laws for the Niuean yet the expatriates walk about holding hands with the devil. You must keep me in touch with the case in NZ.

Puhia

UPPER QUEEN STREET, NOVEMBER 1953

Puhia,

Their appeals were upheld by the High Court on the eighteen of this month, after being heard on October 29th. The Niuean Labour Party has set up a petition along with numerous organizations such as the churches and the unions, for a peaceful means to stop the bloodthirsty people who want them hanged; anyway these groups are calling on the government to stay the execution.

The four arrived here on October 10 on the *Maui Pomare*, and have been in the news ever since. Mrs Larsen was given 3,000 pounds, a compassionate gift by the government.

There are two reasons why the appeals succeeded. One, they were still considered savages. Two, because Mr Larsen was using his position for his own gain. I have recognized there are two laws, one for the coloured and one for the white. If a Polynesian commits a crime against a white he is severly punished, but if the white is the offender it is considered appropriate, and the Polynesian is seen as a curse from God.

Here is a booklet published by the United Committee, *To Save Three Niueans*, that records the testaments and the trials by the four accused. Keep in touch.

Mocca

ALOFI, 1953

Mocca,

There is much anger in the villages where the three young men come from. A revolution perhaps. The expatriates are keeping to their own side of the fence while some have left for NZ.

I heard that the army from NZ may arrive if there is trouble. Maybe now is our chance to become independent, but the hafa-kasi are helping the expatriates. It is wrong what is happening, the history of Niue is more complicated than what has been written and how the world sees us. Even on this tiny rock there are two different races of people. In the old days there was much hostility between the people from the south and the people from the north, or their names Tafiti and Motu. The Tafiti people were the foreigners and the Motu people were the fanau of the land. There is a language difference, every village having its own unique dialect, but we have managed to leave our violent history where it belongs, in the past. It is our way of life and our understanding of our own selves and our future which is in doubt, ever since the white law and church have rooted themselves in this soil.

When the three men went before the court here, the judge was white, just off the boat from NZ with no understanding of our ways and still in limbo, not from our ways but being in isolation.

No Niuean has a chance before a white court. How can the white man judge a Niuean when he is totally different in mind and vision? Do we really need a Resident Commissioner? What is his job? All he does is play that stupid game of golf. And who has to fetch the balls they hit sometimes deliberately into the bush? A Niuean sentenced in the courts for a minor offence.

The only time we are allowed to perform our dance is when there is a visiting party off the boat, of no great importance. Outside these events we are forbidden to perform or sing our songs of the past.

Are we better off than our ancestors before the missionaries arrived? When the missionary, John Williams, kidnapped two Niueans in 1842 there was no court, and I sincerely hope that God made his family suffer. The *Messenger of Peace* was in fact built by the Rarotongans. The Jesus they showed us was an unhealthy, sickly looking person, who wore rags and was the saddest example of white justice, and here we are, praising the Jesus who suffers from the same hope and faith.

If what I write here is read it will be considered the Devil's voice. The LMS who have been on this land since 1842 is in turmoil over Mr Larsen's decision and his permission to have the Mormon Church on this soil. The church did not go to the elders for permission because they see us as savages who cannot make decisions. I say bring back the ghost of John Williams and put him on trial, it can be held at the place where he was eventually killed at Eromonga.

Look around us, there are descendants on Niue from the union between pastors and our women. Let this be the last Commissioner! It is a chaotic way for the English to keep hold of the British Empire.

Puhia

30 UPPER QUEEN STREET, 1953

Puhia,
Niueans in NZ are not very well liked. Some have lost their jobs and there is much hatred of our colour because of the murder of Mr Larsen, with shouts of 'Savages!' and 'Go Back Home!' on the streets.

There is good news that the Governor General has stopped the executions but the appeal is still going through to the Privy Council. Many people still want them dead. It's shocking to know how much hatred can arise out of being a different colour. There are great people with a genuine love for human beings, and there has been a small celebration for the success.

There will also be an inquiry to the administration on the island. But what you say about the churches has to be left behind in the past, as it is now too late, and we have become part of its goodness, not its darkness. I agree with your mind and vision, and it's too late to change what the NZ government has in store for us. There is talk of going independent; but the main body holding power are the village councils, not the government itself. I would not be surprised if any of the hafa-kasi is elected to be Premier. That is many years away yet.

Mocca

LIKU, 1954

Mocca,
That is good news. I hate to think what would have happened if the hangings had gone ahead. There were rumours of war. Yet there is still to be another Commissioner, and much questioning from the councils.

Yesterday I caught a marlin for the wedding of Taufa.

Puhia

AUCKLAND, 21 SEPTEMBER 1954

My brother,
Our mother and Atalani arrived this morning and I am writing this while everybody is sleeping. My heart is staring at the heavens looking for God to thank him for this day when I am with my mother again. Already she wants to plant the back-yard with talo and bananas. She has never seen so many cars and buildings.

Tonight we had a big feast. Well Puhia, soon you and your family must come here so we will be together. This house is alive like a flying fox, peka, peka.

Mocca

LIKU, 1954

Dear Sis,
It is that funny month of Christmas. Over here we try and celebrate but it's just songs and prayers, nobody has any money to buy presents, but many people here get gifts from their magafaoa in NZ. Thank you for the shirt and the materials. I caught two sharks yesterday, which filled our bellies, and the peka is crowding the trees and sky.

Until next time. Take care of our mother.

Puhia

LIKU, 1955

Dear Sis,

Happy New Year and pray everything you do this year brings prosperity and harmony.

There is much talk of the new Resident Commissioner, who they picked very carefully, a certain Mr McEwen. The start of this year for us has been clearing the talo field for replanting, and we are planting passion fruit as well. On the next ship expect a crate of talo.

Thanks for the candles and clothes.

Puhia and family

30 UPPER QUEEN STREET, 1955

My brother,

Thank you for the box of green bananas and talo, it has been busy for all of us. Weddings and haircutting ceremonies.

The Niuean Labour Party has a membership of 208. Our office and hall where we meet every month is in Grey Lynn. The noise over the murder of Mr Larsen has quietened down. Now all the fuss is centred on his wife who I heard is in Avondale. Anyway these things are part of our life no matter where we are from.

Take care my brother.

Mocca

30 UPPER QUEEN STREET, FEB 1956

My dear brother,

How are you and the family?

Thanks for the photos. I have decided to buy a house for my mother, we are looking; also I have two jobs, both sewing in the day and during the night. It is hard work but that's what it's like here, we are happy. Tau Kehesifa is used to the cold. She is a strong woman our mother but she always talks about you and Loata and family.

Last week we went to Maele's and Lalau's wedding. Then we went collecting seafood, Lu got mussels off the rocks.

Thanks for the box of yam.

Mocca

LIKU, 1956

Dear Sis,
What has happened to Daviti? I have not heard from him for
a while, he has forgotten me.

This month we planted rows of timala, and four sacks of
copra which we sold for a good price. This new boss just
hangs out at the clubs. We hardly see him with the Niueans,
only with the expatriates.

We cleared a small section of our land for my son, Togia, so
he can learn early to take custody of the land. Well Sis, after
banning songs and dance for years, we can now do what
would have annoyed Mr Larsen. When he was alive he constantly told us that to work on a Sunday is forbidden, yet
when a ship came in on a Sunday we had to work. That's
where Larsen had a problem, he thought he was God to say
yes or no.

Well, that is past now, leave the past where it belongs.
Take care my sister.

Puhia

AUCKLAND, 1956

Dear brother,
Please brother do not upset yourself with the past. You are
sometimes too hard-headed and you know your temper has
been bad for you and also to the Puhiataha clan and to our
village. If there is trouble, praying to the Lord helps but not
when there is anger in your heart. You must not feel this
anger as you will become very ill.

The green bananas arrived a little over-ripe, our mother is
weaving mats and hats.

My brother, take care of yourself and family.
May the Lord above look after you all.

Mocca

LIKU, 1957

Dear Mocca,
We have a daughter and we name her after our mother,

Atehemotu. She was born in the hospital. Another year and life is the same. We've been clearing the land and breaking the rocks into soil. The crops this year have been fair but it is still hard work. We are building another home in Pia, as the old one is rotting. There is a case of talo on the next ship.

Thanks for the pants and ropes. God be with you and mother.

Puhia

AUCKLAND, 1957

Dear Puhia,
Things are better for us now, and we are able to save money towards the house. Daviti is now in England. He writes sometimes. Lani is doing well for herself. Our mother gets many visitors and she enjoys going shopping every week-end. Lapa is drinking as usual but that is his life. You have a big family now, yet they are all over the world. You should try and keep them together.

Mocca

LIKU, 1957

Dear Matua,
Are you well, my mother? Is the new world the way you dreamed it was? All the people and the many things that you can buy; and the roads that you walk on and become lost so that the police have to bring you home; and your English which breaks at the mouth and seems to cause laughter. Your own ears strain to listen to your voice speaking a strange language. And when the winter walks angrily across the land and the wind madly throws cold air into the skin, and you shiver, and you think back to Niue-Fekai, and the warm sun under some shady tree grinding coconut flesh for the fish. The children come giggling over to you and give you a mother-of-pearl necklace. You know the life cord has been cut, and only the ocean in your heart can remember the old days, the days of white people who told you dancing is the Devil's way of mocking God, and singing the ancient song that you learned from your mother

was considered blasphemy. Where was your voice then. It is too late, another world has you now.

Puhia

39 SECOND AVE, KINGSLAND, 1958

My dear Puhia and Loata,
We have moved to our new house. The cost is £3,700. It is in an area where many relatives live, and not too far from the city. The shops are only up the hill.

We have been looking for a house since last month, and we signed the papers last week. We have to save up for some furniture, so far there are only two mattresses. There is a friendly Palagi family next door and a Samoan family on the other side. Across the road is another Palagi family and next to them is a Maori family. We have already made friends with the Indian couple who own the fruit shop on Great North Road. You remember that road, Puhia, you used to stop the traffic by sleeping on the road when you were drunk? There is also a factory where I hope to get a job sewing.

Here are some shoes and material. God bless you and the family.

Mocca

LIKU, 1958

Dear Mocca,
I thought you said let the past be where it is supposed to be; I know I did some things that did not give us a good name. Anyway, we are rejoicing that you have now your own house, and we all pray it will be of good spirit and much happiness. I am very proud of you. Many people, young and old are slowly leaving this island, they all hear about the easy life and the money to be made in NZ.

I also hear that many work in factories and dig ditches on the sides of the roads, and mostly labouring work. Is that all we are qualified for there?

With sons to help we can live off the land that we have been living on for many years right here. I can see the future in the darkness of a cave, the villages will be empty and more will be in New Zealand than Niue. Let it be. Of course I am afraid, but if I have to go to NZ with my family I will, it is a powerful force and unstoppable. Take care my sister and of our mother.

Puhia

KINGSLAND, 1958

Puhia,
Brother, here in NZ life is different than Niue, you know Niue, you work hard to look after the land as if it is your only child. If you neglect the child that child will die. Here there is a difference, if the child is ill doctors look after it.

Come over with your family, I will help you. In Niue you work on the field till you grow old and bend over like a leaf. Think about it, but do come over.

Your sister, Mocca

[3]

LIKU, 1960

Dearest sister,
It is happy news I am able to come back. I want to leave for NZ first and work, and then bring my family over. It won't be until next year when I have sorted the land out with our magafaoa.

How is our matua? We are still recovering from last year's hurricane. We did not realize how bad it was, the gardens are taking longer to heal, the flying fox circles the island which old people see as another omen of diaster.

So we are waiting for something to happen but I am not looking forward to seeing it or feeling it.

Puhia and family

LIKU, 1960

Dearest Sis,
Well Sis, the old people were right. The day before the greatest hurricane crushed everything, the flying fox were not seen.

They did not come back until the disaster was over. Many lay dead in the gardens and the rooftops of houses, those that died out at sea pushed back by the tide on to the shore. The rookeries are silent.

Over 900 houses damaged. Many of the coconut trees are dead, and every garden on the island wounded. It is like the old days, back to the main hunt for food in the forest, for arrowroot and nupia, wild yam. In the eye of the hurricane Loata gave birth to a son, and we have decided to name him after our father and great grandfather, Puhiatau Falani Fisipalima Pulehetau. He was born in the timala pit. Loata nearly died.

It is like the beginning of the end for something good that I saw briefly as a child, and when I look out on to the village I see sadness, not only for now but for tomorrow, and the years faraway. What is it, Mocca, what is it that my mind is searching for in this soil. The air is not the same, even the ocean is silent. I cannot touch the Bible. The answer, I think, went when our father died. He was the last of our magafaoa who saw our dignity clad by strangers from other countries. I cry as I write this, and stare at the open door to the chaos outside, which looks like a photo.

Thank you for the shoes. Bless you all for the help. Food and clothes have arrived at Alofi wharf.

Puhia

AUCKLAND, 1960

My dear brother,
I am crying because you are sad at these events that haunt you. All I can say is, pray to the God to comfort you, leave the past where it belongs, there is no change if you change everything. Some things must stay the same.

Come to NZ and start a new life here. You have a big family, just make sure this one male child does not turn against you; you have sons all over the world. Loata is a good woman and I love her like my own sister. She looked after you when you were very ill and none of your girlfriends wanted to know you then. I love Loata, she is a good woman. When you come here please don't drink, it is bad for you. All the men from Niue just drink all night after work on pay day. It's disgusting. What's really bad is that they go to church on Sundays suffering from headaches from too much drink.

Mocca

39 SECOND AVE, KINGSLAND, AUGUST 1960

Dear Puhia,
Our mother has gone to rest in the home of God. She passed away peacefully. You should have been here to see her, but it can't be helped. It was sudden, in her sleep. On a hill at Waikumete Cemetery there was a harmony that only my mother's presence can sustain.

She passed away peacefully on August 6th.

Puhia, have you and Loata chosen the day for you all to come over. There is plenty of work in this country and nobody goes hungry. It will take years for the gardens to prosper over there.

I wait for your reply.

Mocca

LIKU, 1960

Mocca,
They are all talking about self-government here but afraid to lose the body of NZ, which some Niueans think holds up the Island; all the talk of basing our economic reliability and politics on NZ is taken from surveys done in the Cook Islands. If it works we will be a tiny nation with its own government.

We are still reeling from the hurricane which they say has taken us backwards several years. Even if we do become self-governed, who will remain to be governed? A few people and coconut trees and hundreds of empty houses strangled by the forest.

Self-government is a habit designed to castrate the indigenous people. When the excitement dies down to a flame, it will be drowned by loans from other countries. Then we will become dependent on NZ, a sad fish on a steel hook too ugly to be brought to the surface. Many Niueans are overseas, without the people there will be no government.

Did you get my last letter? The last years of our mother were happy, free from the hardship that goes with being old and still working in the gardens. We pray for her.

Puhia and family

LIKU, 1961

Dear Mocca,
The only trees that are healthy are the oranges; the breadfruit trees took a beating. I spend most of my time fishing to get away from the foul smell of village meetings and people asking for loans. The flying fox drift with the clouds, there is hope yet.

Expect a box of yams on the next ship, we salvage enough from the gardens to send some over.

Puhia

LIKU, 1962

Dear Mocca,
I am ready to come to NZ and work. I will be there in August. I stay in Pago Pago for a few weeks then it's the same route to NZ via Fiji.

As soon as I get to NZ I'll find a job and then send for Loata and the children, Pele, Ata and Fisi.

Thank you for the suit it fits well and the new shoes.

Your brother, Puhia

Outlines of Gondwanaland

JANETTE SINCLAIR

Today I can see it clearly, beyond the bleached shelves of
Baring Head where there were plans some years ago to site a
nuclear power station. Now I am sure of it, though there have
been days when it was only a shimmer over the white salt-
pans of Grassmere, a hulking shadow behind the round
boulders of Moeraki, a grey-blue hint of continental mass like a
southerly change advancing upon the shingle bar of Lake
Onoke. The drifting continent. Yet for some reason I think of it
as more like an amoeba, pulsating, forever changing shape,
reaching out a tentative foot here across the Chatham Rise,
withdrawing to consolidate in the depths of the Kermadec
Trench, spreading itself in the islandless expanses south of
Mangaia, Fangataufa, Marotiri, Rapanui. For it is shy, shrink-
ing from the prows of intruders, whether those in the carved
canoes with their chants of Tangaroa, or in the tall ships whose
sails, white like their faces, were stretched upon the sign of the
cross. Of course it contrived – their Hawaika, their Terra
Australis Incognita, their South Sea Bubble – to evade them.
They went island-hopping and they are still doing it: Hokitika
to Kapuni, Apia to Porirua, Aitutaki to Tokoroa, Nuku'alofa to
Otara, Tauranga to Coolangatta, Lautoka to Rongotai . . .

Yesterday I left my hilltop home on Hataitai (breath of the
ocean) and went down to visit Veena in Rongotai. She remains
unsettled. Prem, her husband, works in the corner dairy with
his brother. How readily he has adopted the snappy walk
shorts, the 'she'll be right' expressions. Veena is too shy to
serve behind the counter. 'I don't know New Zealand money.
I am afraid of making a mistake for a customer.'

'Talk some bloody sense into her, eh.' Prem swung past

with a carton of frozen confectionery. 'All this bloody moping around. Fiji's down the drain. Bloody good riddance to it I say.' He looked at me with bright cheerful eyes. He is slender like Veena, but in him the lithe Dravidian darkness is busy, birdlike, chattering and darting everywhere. Veena stays in the flat at the back of the shop, cooking dhal and pakhoras. She feels the cold, but wears only an acrylic cardigan of dismal maroon over her sari. She worries about her mother. 'It is her heart. She does not like the hot weather. If only I could have brought her with me.' But Prem and Veena got in because they are young and able-bodied. Three brothers and a sister were left behind in Lautoka to care for the old mother.

When the coup happened I tried phoning my aunt in Suva, but was unable to get through for another three days. Not that she is frail. She and my uncle, who lives nearby, are old colonial survivors. But naturally I was concerned; the reports were confusing and the TV news had shown unpleasant scenes, though there was no suggestion of anti-European feeling around. 'Goodness me no, Glenda dear,' said Aunty Mary. 'We're just keeping our heads down.' She laughed, an anxious throaty chuckle. 'You know I can't blame the Fijians. People were saying Bavadra was just a puppet. They had a right to be worried.'

Her remarks were so conciliatory, so careful that I wondered if the Fijian SIS or whatever they call themselves had the phones tapped. 'Was it very frightening?' I said. 'I mean when it happened.'

'Not really dear. I was working in the Red Cross that day and a lady came in and said the army has just taken over the government. I did feel a bit shaken up. "Do you know what that is?" I said. "It's a military coup. A military coup here in Fiji!" I rushed home and told Luisa and old Viliami to turn on the radio. We sat there in the kitchen listening and all they could say was "O sobo sobo, O sobo sobo."' Her voice had taken on the sombre note. 'It *is* a shame dear. The end of Fiji as we knew it.'

I thought of the TV images of the new Fiji: the warm grey stone of the buildings where Aunty Mary had taken short-hand and typed for the Public Works Department, now swarming with soldiers in mottled jungle greens; suspicious eyes beneath a balaclava mask; the rifle, steely, oiled, resting with deceptive casualness on the forearm. And I wondered if Semesa had been one of those soldiers.

Our meeting was entirely accidental. I was returning to Wellington on the ferry after a relaxing yet resolving week in Nelson. My family, my friends, and even the weather had conspired to make me feel whole again, ready to pick up the pieces from my so abruptly shattered marriage. But when we left Queen Charlotte Sound the northerly wind hit, raising the swell and flinging collars of spray back from the wave-tops. The sky clouded over as the ship lurched towards the steep scarred cliffs, the scaly beak of Te Ika a Maui. People were driven inside to the lounges. Conscious of my newly vulnerable, pitiable, slightly unrespectable status, I opted to stay outside. How I dreaded having to take up again that stance, those rituals of the mating market-place. So I wandered the decks and thought of the empty flat I was returning to, possessions to be sorted and despatched, lawyers to be consulted, explanations to be made. Now I regretted the secure well-paying job that held me in the capital city. I looked at the ocean and thought of Kupe who by some mistake or other was supposed to have discovered the place, and wondered if I might see a giant squid or even dolphins. Then I walked on round to the bucking rolling stern deck and its exposed rows of wooden seating.

They were not empty. Five men in army uniform were there, each holding a can of beer. One swayed towards me. Quickly he said, too quickly, as if guilty, 'Have a drink?'

I said no thank you, for I was afraid of many things. But one of the things I was afraid of was offending them. So I stayed, at what might be a safe distance, to talk. (Perhaps I did not choose it that way, for another had moved slightly and stood, almost cutting off my exit, glowering in what I felt to be a predatory manner.) Then I discovered they were not New Zealand soldiers, but Fijian. 'Oh, sa bula,' I said in relief, for surely this made me less of a captured alien female. 'I have lived in Fiji. My father taught at Nasinu Training College, and then at Queen Victoria School and Natabua High School.'

The faces relaxed. Fijian phrases, those familiar sounds, tumbled around my ears. But also recalled was that feeling of being the outsider. (Why do they smile, what is it they are saying about me?) At last, 'What is the name of your father?' . . . 'When he was at QVS?' Some of them, apparently, had attended Queen Victoria School. The one who had moved, as I thought, to bar my escape, then said softly, 'You not know *me*? But I remember you – yes, Glenda.' He pushed back his dark beret and I recognized Semesa, though it was thirteen years since I had seen him.

We talked for the hour and a half that it took to get into harbour. They were on their way from Burnham to Waiouru for another training exercise with the New Zealand Army. 'Waiouru is freezing,' I warned them teasingly. 'Such a cold wind, worse than Wellington.' And I believed it, for the moment, just as I would not have believed two hours before that meeting soldiers on the ferry could make me happy. When we disembarked they all shook my hand, but Semesa leaned forward and kissed my forehead. I carried the imprint of his lips, warm brown Fijian lips, on my pale brow out into the cold winds of Wellington and down to my lonely basement flat.

My last visit to Fiji was in 1979, the honeymoon trip. Martin tolerated the three day stay in Suva with Aunty Mary, the visits to the uncles and cousins, the cutter trip over to Levuka and the climb in sweltering heat up the street of steps to see the old church where my grandmother and great-grandmother had been married. Then we spent a week in a little beach cottage Aunty Mary had arranged for us on the Korotogo coast. Looking back it seems to me that Martin didn't enjoy that either, though it was particularly blighted for him by a coral scratch on his ankle. We had a few days left to look around Lautoka. By then Martin had found some good paperbacks and wanted nothing more than to read on our hotel room balcony under the purple shade of the bougainvillaea. 'Don't you think we've done enough exploring your past, darling,' he said. 'Well I certainly feel as though I have.'

So I went on my own to meet Veena in her lunch-break

from the insurance office. When I saw her I felt embarrassment at my 'touristy' appearance – the flimsy sun-top, the bright tropical-flowered sarong knotted so casually at the waist. Veena looked cool and elegant in a pale green linen suit with tiny red hibiscus scattered on the collar and pocket trim.

'Accha, accha, Miss Hibiscus,' I said.

She laughed. 'It is no good. Both of us too old and married.' Then her face grew serious. 'Anyway, an Indian girl does not become Miss Hibiscus.'

Of course: a properly brought up, well-educated Hindu girl would not go in for that kind of vulgar display, because she was still guided by her sense of caste and tradition and the authority of the family.

'Did you bring your wedding photographs to show me?' Veena demanded.

'They're not developed yet, sorry. They'll be waiting for us when we get back. I'll send you some, I promise.' It occurred to me that Veena would be unimpressed by the awkward-looking couple standing outside the register office in nothing more formal than good street clothes, a scattering of confetti on their hair and shoulders. I thought of the photographs she had sent me: garlands of white and red flowers on the dark suit of the groom, Veena in a spangled sari of crocus-yellow, her arms heavy with bangles, her shining face lit by the blood-red 'tika' spot on her forehead. And I remembered also my surprise at her reaction, not mere acquiescence but evident happiness, to this marriage arranged by her widowed mother and elder brother.

'Where is your husband?' asked Veena.

I found myself explaining that he was not feeling well, exaggerating the degree of his indisposition, in fact inventing for him an alarming case of heat allergy.

'He will be all right when you get home,' she said with conviction. 'You cook him good food, make him strong, soon you will have many sons.' How she reminded me of her mother; that joking, direct, comfortable way of talking about things that my family broached only with coy references, if at all.

But there was something strange about hearing this from

Veena, who had been married for five years. 'Veena, how come you have no babies?'

'My husband does not want children yet. He says he must build his business first. He is very clever. And my mother has plenty of other grandchildren.' But briefly her proud face looked disconsolate. 'I tell him business is not everything. If he tries to be too big they get jealous. They want to be the boss of everything, but *we* do all the work.'

'Who get jealous?'

With a quick sideways movement Veena looked around the coffee-bar, crowded mostly with tourists and Indians. But she lowered her voice. 'The Fijians.'

And I realized that this was what she had meant by her earlier remark: it was not permissible, 'they' would not look with favour on an Indian girl becoming Miss Hibiscus.

I didn't ask if she ever came across Semesa. I hadn't kept in touch with him myself, the way I had with Veena writing three or four times a year. Aunty Mary gave me occasional news of him, mainly from her dealings with his father who was now highly placed in government service. Semesa's family had always had an aristocratic air about them; his mother was the daughter of a turaga.

I said goodbye to Veena and walked through the dust and noise of the market. Fijian women sat cross-legged behind piles of hairy coconuts, green-skinned oranges, muddy dalo and tavioka, green and pink sugar-cane like rough-hewn candy sticks. Old Indian men with yellow-stained moustaches and white turbans sold paper bags of unshelled peanuts and hot crunchy curried peas. I thought of detouring further, going down the avenue of scarlet drala blossoms and past my old school. Was it still called 'Lautoka European School'? But the day was hot, and perhaps I had left my new husband for too long. After all, he was one of the newer waves of immigrant to the South Pacific, only ten months out from Edinburgh with his rosy cheeks and white body. So I quickened my steps and worried about the white man's burden, and hoped I wouldn't find Martin gone to sleep in the arms of a whisky bottle. Though in my father's case of course, it was gin: gin and tonic and slices of lime in the warm dark evenings of interminable poker games. 'Gin! Supposed to be mother's ruin,' my mother had remarked sarcastically. But it was my father who had to be repatriated to New Zealand.

At the time nobody mentioned the drinking. 'In these two years since Independence your father has felt there's no longer a place for him in Fiji,' my mother wrote euphemistically. 'And we have the extra cost to consider – sending your sisters to boarding school in New Zealand, bringing them back for the school holidays etcetera, the way we did with you.' I supposed I was meant to feel guilty for setting that precedent, and then leaving it unjustified.

I refused to return to school after the August holidays in 1970, staying in Fiji long enough for the independence celebrations. At the ceremonies in Albert Park the sun blazed down and that strangely tropical mixture of smells – everything missing in the land of the long white cloud – lifted to my nostrils: sweet lemon grass and frangipani and gardenia, the bitter oil rubbed into the skin of the meke dancers, incenses of fenugreek and sandalwood drifting in sari folds. I looked for my friends among the musters of school uniforms, but there were so many young Fijian men in clean white shirts and sulu, so many Indian girls with their black hair oiled and elaborately braided. Kaleidoscope patterns of dark busy heads wearing red hibiscus flowers, bright bula shirts and tropical sunset dresses swirled around me. The lali knocked and clicked its tattoo. Deep Fijian voices rolled in meke chants and hymns. Then the swell of sounds drained away to the silence of the yaqona ceremony, a silence so profound that the bare feet of the kava bearer could be heard as he shuffled along the woven mat towards the dais of the official guests. In the same hush, except for the slow clap-clap-clap of heavy hands, the Prince of Wales drained the kava bowl.

Later I joined Veena and Semesa for the evening festivities: we danced through the streets behind psychedelic Chinese dragons, stopping only to eat fried noodles and chop suey bought from the Chinese kana stalls. Then we went back to Semesa's home and listened to the Beatles on his parents' new stereo set. It was *Sergeant Pepper's Lonely Hearts Club Band*. We were seventeen, thinking we had a stake in this new Fiji as much as in the rest of the world. We vowed to keep in touch, and when we had earned enough money, we would make the pilgrimage to London and meet outside Buckingham Palace, where we'd wave to Prince Charles, because he was one of us.

'He was born on November the 14th, 1948,' I told Veena, reading out from my Coronation Scrapbook.

'So. Then we celebrate the birthday of Prince Charles *and* Diwali,' she announced. 'My mother is making sweetmeats, curried dalo biscuits, roti . . . Our first Diwali in Lautoka is your last Diwali in Fiji.' She looked severely at me, her eyes made even more melancholy by the dark rings of kohl. Her family had only just moved to Lautoka, after her father's retirement from the Training College.

But I had no wish to think about next year, when I must go away to high school. There was Christmas before that: the trip to my grandmother's house in Suva, carols at the Anglican Cathedral, presents to be given out under the nokonoko tree, plum pudding with Fiji sixpences inside. And for now this invitation to share with Veena's family Diwali, their Festival of Light.

My mother was dubious. 'You don't know *what* she'll see there,' she hissed at my father.

'Oh codswallop. Arvind's a steady sort of bloke. She won't come across any more mumbo-jumbo than what they get up to in your Church of England.'

Yet instinctively, with a strange excitement, I knew what it was my mother feared. I was twelve, as old as some Hindu child-bride. Veena's older brother was the same age as the boarders in the high school compound where we lived, boarders whose dormitories were forbidden territory to us, boarders who watched out of brooding eyes as my sisters and I splashed with water-hose and wheelbarrow on the lawn.

On Diwali night I was let out of the car at the gate to Veena's garden. The darkness clung to my party dress. Behind me in the street a dog-pack howled. Flying-foxes flitted and squeaked up in the mango trees. Mosquitoes hummed around my ears. Listening insects bristled with stings. Dry things snapped underfoot. I walked as far as the baka, the weeping-fig tree, then stood petrified under its cascades of vine-like roots. What if I trod on a flabby toad making its way toward the drains?

A door opened and Veena's mother stood in a soft circle of light, a tiny candle sitting like a shell in the palm of her hand. 'Veena! Ga-len-da is come.' She drew me inside through rooms where small candles were placed in corners, on shelves and window-sills. More candles stood before paintings and tapestries of people with plump silvery-blue faces like moons. In the flickering light of a large candle a statue of dark oiled wood leered and waved eight arms at me.

After the meal Veena painted a red spot between my eyebrows. Then Veena and myself, her mother and aunties and her younger sister took candles and went out into the garden. Warm wax dripped on our hands. We walked in a procession around the weeping-fig tree, flickering in and out of the twisting columns of roots. Silently we placed the candles on the ground between white stones; the garden flowered with soft glowing faces.

There was a night at Matuvatucou when the boys of Queen Victoria School put on *Macbeth*. Semesa and I, being ten years old and the eldest children of the two teachers directing the play, were allowed to stay up and watch. We sat together on white-washed boulders beneath the school flagpole. Semesa liked the soldiers milling around waving their swords of silver-painted cardboard, the murderers leaping out of the dark woods, the ghost sliding down vines on to the stage, the witches in their shaggy locks that my mother had made from strands of wool. 'Those old lady – tevoro eh?' he said to me.

'They're witches. They put the bad ideas into Macbeth's head.'

But so many speeches. How long to the part when the soldiers dressed as trees and Birnam Wood did come to Dunsinane? (I had read the plot in my little book *Stories From Shakespeare*, and heard my father's elaborate plans for this scene.) Unable to keep up with Semesa's excitement, I grew sleepy.

Then Lady Macbeth walked on to the stage in a long white dress. She held a candle close to her face and I recognized

Simeone, a tall light-skinned student from Rotuma. His voice was high and carrying: 'Yet who would have thought the old man to have had so much blood in him? . . . Here's the smell of the blood still. All the perfumes of Arabia will not sweeten this little hand. Oh, oh, oh!' His eyes were shut but his face writhed in the candlelight. I shivered until I felt Semesa's small warm shoulders leaning against mine in the dark.

In the hall of the old house at Nasinu, stuffy and dim with all the doors shut, there was a spiral labyrinth. We had rolled the long narrow mat from one end till it was coiled like a spring, then tipped it on to its side. Semesa held back. 'Sa butobuto,' he said. So dark. The whites of his eyes looked large and wary.

'I will go,' said Veena. 'I am not afraid.' She eased herself into the opening. The mat was almost her height; the top of her head showed as she worked her way in smaller and smaller circles to the centre. Then the head disappeared and the shuffling noises stopped. 'I have come to it.' The voice sounded a long way off. 'Very secret. It is the oldest place. It is Gondwana. Fifty years ago my grandfather comes to Fiji from Gondwana in the hills. The boat is very big. There is many Indians, many "girmitiya" in it. He works very hard for years. Then back to India to bring my grandmother.'

Then Semesa pushed into the narrow entrance. 'I not vaka rerea. My vu, my grandfather hundred and hundred of years ago, he is Degei. Degei, sailing in the great canoe Kaunitoni, coming to Viseisei. Degei the snake-god climbing Uluda the mountain to find the dark cave.'

He reached the centre. His muffled voice spiralled its way back to me, 'Lako mai Glenda,' then that of Veena, more reedy, more ancient, 'Hurry now, we are waiting.'

So I lifted my arms above my head and squeezed between the layers of mat. 'Here is Glenda, zoom zoom, flying in the aeroplane at night between the clouds and the sea. Please fasten your seat-belts. We will be landing shortly at Nadi Airport.' The sweet musty smell of woven pandanus leaf surrounded me; stray fibres tickled my cheeks. The walls of the labyrinth pressed tightly. I could not see over the top. How dark it was. How quiet my friends were. What if it was a magic place, like the wardrobe Lucy found? Veena and Semesa might have disappeared: I would find nothing but an empty space when I reached the centre? Then I caught the warmth and smell of the two at the centre – a Fijian smell of coconut oil and cheap talcum powder from the women who wove the mat and Semesa's mother who cuddled him; an Indian smell of spices and ghee and sticky orange sweetmeat. At last I reached them, carrying my own smell, the last comer. We scuffled and giggled and wriggled together, rocking the mat until it toppled and we tumbled over one another in the heart of Gondwanaland.

A Short History of New Zealand

C. K. STEAD

He was 52 and had that London look – dry hair (he ran his fingers through it, glancing at himself in the lift mirror), tired eyes, something unhealthy about the skin; the suggestion of less than perfect cleanliness, which, like Lady Macbeth's 'damned spot', no amount of washing would quite remove. Was there a word for it? 'Care-worn' sounded too Victorian and virtuous. 'Stressed' was its modern and equally self-serving equivalent.

Within himself he felt little of this – only allowed the recognition to run through his mind, thinking it was how she, a 26-year-old fresh from New Zealand, would see him. As the lift doors opened he caught sight of her sitting in Reception. It was her knees that registered first, primly side by side, in dark stockings, with neat knee-caps and a fine curve away from each side, cut off by the line of the skirt. Good strong Kiwi legs, he thought; and then remembered how when he'd first come to England it had seemed to him that young Englishwomen had no calf muscles. It wasn't true any longer. In the intervening decades Europe had become athletic.

She looked in his direction and must have guessed he was the man she was to meet, but he went first to the desk and said he would be out until three.

'James Barrett,' he said taking the hand she held out to him. 'And you're Angela McIlroy.'

Out in the street she'd lost her bearings. He pointed down the Farringdon Road to where the figure of Justice over the Old Bailey lifted sword and scales against the dome of St Paul's. The sun glared down through the haze, casting no decisive shadows. The thump of a 24-hour disco came up through a basement grating. Believing he knew how dingy and confusing these streets must seem to her, he hailed a taxi and gave directions.

They were settled at a table under a tree in a pub yard near the British Museum and had made their choices before he took the little tape machine from his pocket and propped it between the pepper and salt.

'You won't mind, will you?' he asked, and she shook her head. She was unassertive, making no attempt to impress him. Shy, he decided; slightly apprehensive, but self-contained – and he made a mental note of these descriptions.

No need to turn on the machine yet; no need to begin at once with her novel, which was the purpose of the interview. Better to begin – where else? – at their common beginning. She knew he'd grown up in New Zealand – left as a young man intending to return, but had married an Englishwoman and . . .

Yes, she knew all that. She'd been told. 'Interesting,' she added, nodding and smiling – but he could see it was something other than interest she felt. Disapproval, perhaps? Or was it just indifference?

'I've been back, of course, but only for short stays – three weeks at most. There were eighteen years I never set foot in the place. By then it was too late.'

She'd ordered a salade niçoise. He watched her struggling to cut the lettuce in its bowl. Her drink was mineral water.

'Quite sure?' he asked, lifting his bottle of Italian white.

She held up one hand, like a policeman. Her mouth was full of salad. He filled his glass.

'Oh dammit,' she said, draining the mineral water and holding out her glass. 'Why not?'

'Why not!' he agreed, filling her glass.

'I'm not abstemious,' she said. 'Not especially. But jet-lag and wine . . . '

He nodded. 'Here's to *A Short History of New Zealand*.'

They touched glasses and drank, but the naming of her novel seemed to bring back that wariness which just for a moment he'd thought was about to be cast aside. She fell silent, waiting for him to lead their conversation.

'I read a large part of it coming down on the train this morning. It's quite a grim picture.'

She inclined her head.

'And a true one, so far as I can judge.' And then, almost without meaning to, he began to talk as the expatriate. Once started, it was hard to stop. Some part of his mind was detached. Was this the way to go about it? But then, why not? Somehow he had to get a response out of her.

His view of New Zealand was almost entirely negative, and at first, from the way she met his eyes, nodded, murmured assent, he could see he was taking her with him. But then he went too far. He felt it himself, and saw it in her eyes. Even New Zealand's weather, it seemed, was now inferior. This was London's third good summer in succession. She put her hand over her mouth, and her eyes were smiling.

He looked down at the table cloth and thought for a moment. 'I'm a journalist,' he said firmly. 'Sometimes when I get a twinge of the old nostalgia I just let myself think what it would have been like working on the *Herald* or the *Dom* or the *Press*, or the *ODT* for God's sake – just imagine it! – dealing with local cow and sheep stories, while all the world stuff was coming in on the wire, written by someone else.'

She nodded, but with such a blank face he began to feel irritation. Did she want him to write about her book? Did she understand that he was doing her a favour? 'My paper has a million readers,' he said.

Her face softened, as if there was something she understood. 'You've done well,' she said.

Her novel, *A Short History of New Zealand*, began with these sentences:

'One's name is Brent and the other is Hemi. One is white and one brown, and they are running under the moon. Ahead and behind and in all directions stretches away the landscape of the plains. You could say they are the cop and the robber. You could say they are the colonist and the colonized. You could say they are the Pakeha and the Maori.

'They are running through most of a long night. Sometimes they stop for breath. Sometimes Hemi reaches the end of his tether and turns on Brent. Pursuer is pursued, back over the same ground. But then it resumes, the other way. They run and keep running.'

The novel is set in a very small town – what used to be called a settlement – in the North Island. It has one cop, a young man who belongs to the local rugby club and takes long training runs with his team-mates. One night he's taking a last look around when he hears something in a storage shed. He goes looking. There are some tense moments in the silence and darkness of the shed – he's sure someone's there but can't find him – and then the burglar, a Maori, makes a break for it, straight out and down the wide main street, the cop in pursuit. In a couple of minutes they've left the town behind. They're out on the open road, running under the moon through the empty landscape, sometimes on the road, sometimes across ploughed fields, through bush, along stream-beds, back to the road again.

The Pakeha sprints. So does the Maori. They slow to jogging, recovering breath. The Maori sprints and the Pakeha almost loses him – but not for long. Sometimes the pursuit slows to a walk, or stops. They talk back and forth across a safe gap, reason with one another, threaten, shout insults.

Then they run again.

With the Sunday papers tucked under one arm he walked back from the village, over ploughed fields, skirting the wood where pheasants, bred for the annual shoot, scuttled away into the undergrowth. The gamekeeper had set snares for foxes, simple loops of fine wire along the edges of pathways. James tripped them as he went. He liked the sight of foxes appearing on his lawn. Why shouldn't those handsome predators, as well as the tweedy kind for whose sport it was intended, have game for supper?

Anne was waiting for him on the gravel outside the front door. He could see by the way she held her hands, and then by her anxious expression, that something was wrong. There had been a phone call from New Zealand. It was bad news. His mother . . .

He flew non-stop. There was no choice if he was to be there for the funeral. It meant eleven hours in the air to Los Angeles, a stop of two hours, and then on again – another twelve to Auckland. His grief was confused with jet-lag and a dread of finding himself among relatives with whom he believed he could have nothing in common. But after the service, when they'd gathered at his sister's Mt Eden house, drinking and eating and talking on the verandah and out on the back lawn, it came over him how much he was enjoying himself. The hugs of cousins he didn't at first recognize brought surges of old affection. Trivial reminiscences gave him pleasure. It even pleased him to be called Jamie. He'd expected to find himself behaving in a way that would be judged aloof, unfriendly, superior, but it wasn't like that at all. In his strange, jet-lagged state it was as though he saw it all from the outside – saw a different self emerge and take over – warm, out-going, filial, fraternal, avuncular.

Once or twice in his life a death and funeral had had this effect. He hadn't wept. He'd become an actor on a public stage. But this time it was different – something to do with these people, and with the green of the plum tree in new leaf, and the white of pear-blossom, and the freshness of air and light and water. How long was it since he'd felt such uncomplicated happiness?

He remembered that when he was a boy he would meet his mother unexpectedly in a room or in the garden and they would smile – not anxiously, just with the pleasure each felt at seeing the other. The sadness of that thought didn't spoil his happiness. It was part of it.

Late in the day he was asked the inevitable question: How was he finding New Zealand? It would have been easy to evade – to say it was only hours since he'd stepped off the plane. But what came out was 'great' and 'super' and 'wonderful to be home'. He knew it was the right answer; but it was as if, at least for that moment, it was true.

His questioner smiled, glad to hear it, but then shook his head. 'This country's a mess, Jamie. I don't like to say it, but the fact is *you're better off where you are.*'

That night he crashed asleep while the others were still drinking and talking, then woke in the early hours of the morning. He was in the back room of his sister's house, with wide windows looking out on the garden that was overhung with pungas and cabbage trees. The silence was so complete he strained for something that would prove he hadn't lost his hearing. A floorboard creaked – that was all. These wooden houses shifted with the changes in temperature.

A light shower began to fall, whispering on the iron roof. In childhood rain on the roof had always brought sleep, but now he lay listening, soothed but wide awake, his body still on London time.

He turned on the bedside lamp and looked in his bag for Angela McIlroy's novel, and beside it his tape recorder. He put the machine close to his ear, switched it on, and put out the light.

'The framework of your novel's the chase, but in alternating chapters you go back into the lives of the two men – family history, childhood, schooling . . . Did you feel you could do that equally – I mean with confidence . . .'

'I don't think I felt confident about any of it. I just jumped in and hoped I wouldn't sink.'

'Well, clearly you didn't sink. It's rather unusual, from a woman novelist. Not about . . . Not the usual sub . . . '

'They have mothers and sisters.'

'Yes, but the central characters . . . '

'You don't find them convincing?'

'Oh yes, I think so. Sure. As for the, ah – the Maori background . . . Well, I guess – who knows? I think only a Maori could say.'

'I'm not sure . . . I don't think I agree with that. I mean anyone, Maori or Pakeha, could say they felt it was right. Or they felt it was wrong. If you're talking about feeling, that is. Of course if facts are wrong, that's different. But no one . . . '

'No, I'm not suggesting that.'

There was a break. In the background could be heard the clatter of plates, the murmur of other conversations, a burst of loud laughter.

'Look, I don't know how to put this – I'm just feeling my way towards something. It's certainly not a criticism of your novel which I think is well written and well shaped. But the way it's done touches on something . . . '

'Delicate?'

'Delicate – yes. But I think I mean . . . big. I'm not making myself clear, am I.'

'Keep going.'

'It's there in the title – a short history of New Zealand. That's quite a claim. Quite an indictment.'

'Oh an indictment. Is that what it is?' There was the sound of her laughter. 'I think I plead the fifth.'

It was no longer a matter of law and order, or crime and punishment. It had become a question of who was fitter, stronger, cleverer; who would out-run, or out-fox, the other; who would win.

Those roads are long and straight, and when Brent saw headlights in the far distance he thought here was his chance. He would flag down the driver and tell him to call in help. But even while he was thinking this there was the twanging of fence wire and the Maori was off overland. He got a bit of a break on there, and quite soon, after crossing a couple of paddocks, he was in a field of corn. Something had happened to the crop. It was head-high but it seemed to be dried out, dead on the stalk and unpicked. The Maori plunged into it and disappeared. Brent hunted and then stopped. It was such a still night you couldn't move in there and not be heard. If there'd been a wind the Maori could have moved under cover of the rustling, but there was none. And the moon was bright. So Brent waited and rested. When the Maori made a break for it the chase was on again.

They ran through empty fields, through flocks of sheep, through cow-paddocks, through stubble, through crops of swedes and potatoes and cabbages, always well clear of farmhouses. Dogs barked in the distance. A nightbird sounded as they ran through the edges of a swamp. They came back to a road and ran on it. Then there was again the twanging of fence-wire and they were off over a field of onions. The onions had been turned up by a mechanical digger – they were lying on top of the soil, waiting to be collected, and they made it hard going. The Maori seemed to go over on one. It must have rolled under his foot, his ankle twisted, and for just a moment he went down.

'Now you bastard,' Brent thought. And then he wondered, What the fuck am I going to do with him? How'm I going to bring him in?

When he got to him the Maori was up on one knee, holding a knife. 'Come and get it, Dog-breath,' he said.

On the tape they sounded at first hesitant with one another, wary. He'd known it was because she distrusted him as an expatriate, expected him to be patronizing. It had made it hard for him to get to the more difficult, and therefore more interesting, questions. But as the lunch went on, and she shared his wine, the exchanges had become more frank, less hesitant.

He ran the tape forward, and listened again.

'I keep coming back to your title . . . '

'Yes, it's bold, I know.'

'And it makes how the thing ends important.'

'Don't tell me about it. Terribly important. I spent so many months agonizing over all that. I kept rewriting the end – it never seemed right. Then I'd give away the title – look for something more modest. But that seemed the easy way out. The cowardly . . . You see I'd had the title in mind right from the start – before I'd written a word. That, and the basic story of the all-night chase, which was something that happened. I read about it in the paper, and straight away I thought this is a short history of New Zealand. But it had such symbolic force – too much. Pakeha chases Maori through his own land to enforce British law. Every now and then Maori rebels and turns on Pakeha, but then it's back to the old chase. That was OK in a way – as a story – because it was real. It happened, and it was believable. But if it was to carry that symbolic load . . . '

'That's why the end . . . '

'Yes, because it's not finished, is it? I mean the history's not. It goes on . . . So the end of the novel has to be – what's the word?'

'Tentative? Not definitive?'

'Yes, that's right, but . . . *Provisional*. That's the word. I had it on a piece of paper pinned over my desk. The ending had to be provisional. The first version ended with an arrest. They ran all night and then early in the morning Hemi just lost heart and gave up. Well, that might be how it would happen – but as symbol . . . '

'No good. I can see that. They haven't given up.'

'And then I had him get away. No good again, you see. Too easy. Sentimental. Because the real history . . . '

'Yes, it's tougher than that.'

'Then I had them fight it out. But how does that end? Pakeha kills Maori? Maori kills Pakeha? They're both killed? They make friends and walk off hand in hand into the sunrise? You see? Nothing seemed to fit.'

'Not as things are right now. But they're all possible, aren't they?'

'You mean in reality.'

'I mean – what do I mean? They're possible ends, most of them, if you think just of the two men. Maybe the problem is there's too much conflict, d'you think? The story sets them too much in opposition. After all, it hasn't always been like that. If you think of our history . . . '

'Our?'

'Yes . . . Oh, I see. You think as an expatriate it's not mine any more.'

And there the tape ran out.

'Come and get it,' the Maori repeated, holding the knife out in front of him. And then suddenly he was up and running, not away this time, but straight at his pursuer. Brent turned and ran.

The sprint didn't last long. They had run too many miles; but when they stopped the Maori must have felt he was on top.

'OK,' he said. 'Just fuck off and I'll let you keep your balls.'

He turned and walked in the opposite direction. It can't have been long before he heard footsteps coming after him, keeping a safe distance. Brent wasn't going to give up now. If he couldn't arrest the bugger, he'd stick with him until daylight.

It took a few runs this way and that before the new rules were established. When the Maori chased, Brent ran. Once it was so close he felt his shirt slashed, and a strange sensation – not pain, a sort of coldness – down his back. He didn't think the knife had cut him, but later he felt a trickle of blood. After that he kept his distance; but as the Maori turned and headed off, he followed.

Now the Maori ran again, effortlessly, as if he was doing it to suit himself. He didn't look back. They came to a stop-bank – it loomed up high and straight above the plain on one side and the river on the other, with a flat grassy path along the top. They went up on to it and kept running, heading down-river towards the sea.

After half an hour they ran off the stop-bank and down a road, and there, opening out in front of them, was the coast – dunes and sand all scattered over with huge white logs and driftwood that had come down the river over the years and gone out to sea only to be washed back by the westerlies. Under the moon it looked like a huge boneyard, with the sea thundering against it.

The Maori seemed to know where he was going now. He stopped short of the dunes and headed north over fields until he came to another road. It was there he went into a pine grove. Brent lost him briefly, and for the first time thought he should give up. He was now a long way from home, and nobody would know where. He might be ambushed and knifed. You could bury a body in the piles of needles and it might not be found for years.

But he kept going, relying on his ears and on the stillness of the night. He stood with his back against a pine trunk and listened. When the Maori moved, Brent went after him.

They came to a clearing and stopped. They were on either side of it, the moon coming through so they could see one another. They rested, sizing one another up. After a while the Maori said, 'You got a wife and kids?'

Brent told him he had a wife, no kids yet.

The Maori turned the knife-blade this way and that on his palm, as if his hand were a razor strop.

'What about you,' Brent asked.

The Maori said, 'Soon I'll introduce you to my mates. They're Rastas.'

Brent didn't reply.

'Where I'm taking you,' the Maori said, 'we got a big hole in the ground, like a cave, eh. We call it a tomo. You ever seen a tomo, Dog-breath? They drop the dead calves down there. Sometimes a whole cow. Not even the stink comes up.'

He turned, out of the clearing, and began walking through the pines. He came to a fence and climbed over it. Over his shoulder he called, 'Come on Pakeha. Let's get there before the sun comes up.'

She'd solved her problem by adding a second layer – the story of the writer writing the story. It was what James had liked least about her novel, but he could see why she'd done it. There could be no end, so there had to be many ends – many possibilities, all left open. It was called 'meta-fiction' these days and it was very fashionable, but how could you get around the basic human appetite that every story should have a beginning a middle and an end, and that to be enjoyed it had to be believed?

The rain was getting heavier. The whisper on the roof became a rustling, and briefly a roar. There was the sound of water rushing along gutterings and through down-spouts, and dripping from punga fronds on to the lawn. Then it died away again to a gentle hissing. He thought of his Northamptonshire garden, the roses and hollyhocks, the woods across fields with crows circling and crying. At last drowsiness returned, and sleep.

He dreamed that he was talking to Angela McIlroy over lunch, or rather, listening while she talked. She spoke in fluent Maori, though words like salade niçoise and frascati were mixed up in it. Now and then she paused in her monologue to turn the blade of her knife back and forth across her open palm.

He strained to catch what it was she was telling him, certain that he did understand – that he was capable of it – but never quite making sense of it. It was like something just beyond reach, or a word on the tip of the tongue.

A Thousand and One Nights

J. C. STURM

They spent the afternoon on the small front lawn under the gum tree overlooking the harbour. It was more sheltered on the side lawn but the grass round there was stiff and prickly and you couldn't see the harbour, so the woman spread the rug at the foot of the gum tree and sat with her back against the trunk and her knitting in her lap. And all afternoon she pretended they were simply warming themselves in the gentle autumn sun in front of an old house hidden away in bush with a harbour to look at, and all afternoon she knew they were simply pretending and none of it was real, not even the wanting and willing and pretending, nothing except the waiting. The little girl squatted on her haunches at the edge of a garden shabby with withered summer flowers and talked to herself and mixed mud pies in an old enamel bowl and put in gravel for sultanas and baked them in tin lids and iced them with daisy petals and laid them beside the woman on the rug. Are they cooked yet, Mummy? And the woman felt each one with a finger and said, what pretty daisy cakes, yes, I think they're cooked, but we won't eat them, they're too pretty to eat.

And when it was three o'clock and time to waken the toddler, they hid the daisy cakes first, just in case, and went up the gravel path and wooden front steps and down the long linoleum passage past the mirror in the old coat-stand that wasn't theirs, past the white china door knobs of the bedroom, sitting-room, breakfast-room, past the old ship's bell on a fretwork bracket hanging at the end of the passage, and round the corner and through the door that always stuck and had to be pushed. And there was the toddler pulling himself up by the bars of the cot and his cheeks were plump and pink and his eyes blank with sleep. They changed him and put on rompers and jersey and carried him out to the gum tree and he blinked and blinked in the gentle sunlight till his eyes were as round and as blue as the harbour, and the little girl laughed and rolled on the rug against the woman's legs and laughed, he's Hunca Munca, Mummy, he's turned into Hunca Munca.

They made a pretend picnic with orange drinks and biscuits and pieces of apple and the toddler rubbed his in his hair and got it mixed up with bits of grass and stones till it looked like a piece of daisy cake and the little girl watched him and said, aren't toddlers silly, Mummy, and ate hers carefully like a tea party lady. And then she pulled off the little white boots she wore to make her ankles grow straight and strong and galloped around the lawn like the horse she was and stopped at the far end where the bush began and held up her arms like branches. Look I'm a tree, you can't get me now, I'm a tree. And the toddler dropped his daisy cake and staggered and gurgled and fell and crawled and dribbled across the lawn. But when he got there the tree turned into a bird and flew away. The woman leaned against the gum tree and watched them and pretended it was all real, but the sun slipped behind the tallest trees in the bush and the shadows crept across the corner of the rug and it was four o'clock.

They gathered everything up except the daisy cakes and put them on the side verandah and went round to the clothes-line on the back lawn where the sun still shone and the little girl said, we don't have to go in yet, do we, Mummy, it's still warm and sunny here, but the woman shook her head, no, it's getting late, it's time to light the fire and put the dinner on, and she gathered an armful of soft fluffy napkins and dropped the pegs for the little girl to pick up and gave the toddler a nappy to carry. And while they were picking up pegs and folding napkins the toddler got his tangled round his legs and fell over and had to be untangled and picked up too – while they were busy dawdling in the last of the sun, the cold crept out of the bush on the other side of the house and hid in the darkened rooms waiting for them.

The little girl squatted on her haunches outside the wood-shed and peered in the corners for wetas, and the woman poked about inside the shed turning the wood over and feeling it to see if it was dry and keeping a lookout for wetas too, and the toddler climbed up and down the concrete steps and looked at them upside down between his legs like Eeyore. And when they had carried the wood into the sitting-room and filled up the wood-box and the coal-scuttle and found the matches, the woman stuffed newspaper in the grate and jumbled dry sticks on top of it and covered them up with the heavier stuff and lumps of coal and held a burning match to the paper at each corner and dropped it in the middle. But the wood wasn't dry enough and smoked, so the woman covered the fireplace with another newspaper and pressed the edges hard against the bricks and the little girl looked stern, now you Mr Fire, you just burn up that nice wood my Mummy's given you, and don't be silly. And the toddler sat very still and watched the newspaper and waited. And when they heard a low roaring behind the paper and something began sucking its middle inwards the woman pulled it away quickly because she never knew what to do with it when it caught alight, but there was only a small flame after all struggling against the smoke and the heavy damp wood.

By five o'clock the children were in the bath and while the little girl was showing the toddler how to make waves for the boats to float over and the ducks to swim over and how to spread your flannel out flat on your knees like this to rub the soap on, the woman set about cooking the meal. She cooked enough for four. And then she carried the children into the sitting-room in big fluffy towels and rubbed them down in front of the fire and put on their warmed pyjamas and dressing-gowns and slippers. The little girl struggled to do up her own buttons and pushed and pulled at them and pulled her face down to see them properly and asked the woman is Daddy coming home for dinner, and the woman turned away to look at the clock and shook her head slowly, no dinner's ready now, so he can't be. Can't we wait for him? He might be very late. Do all Daddies come home *after* dinner? Some do and some don't, and if they do, they can't help it. If my bunny slippers had teeth they could bite. And she moved her toes to make the ears wiggle and the toddler gurgled and tried to make his wriggle too. Don't forget to pull the blind down, Mummy. And the woman went over to the window and tried not to think of the face that had been there once, a terrible dead white face with everything dragged down – hair, eyes, nose, mouth – pressing to reach them through the glass, till the toddler covered his eyes with his hands and the little girl screamed and screamed and hid herself in her Daddy's coat when he came in soon after. The Daddy laughed and said it must have been the moon come down to see them, but the toddler wouldn't take his hands away till they played peep-bo with him. So the woman pulled the blind down carefully right below the sill and picked up the towels and went out to the kitchen. And when she had served up four dinners and put the biggest one on top of a pot of hot water on the stove and covered it with a plate, she took the other three into the sitting-room and they had their dinner round the fire, the little girl sitting on a cushion with her red table across her knees and her bunnies wiggling at her on the other side, the toddler safe in his low chair with a feeder, and the woman beside him, just in case, with her plate in her lap.

And when they had had enough and drunk their milk, the woman stoked up the fire and dragged up the biggest chair in the room and the little girl brought her favourite book and the three of them squeezed into the big chair and made themselves comfortable for the story of Tom Thumb and his wife Hunca Munca. The little girl liked the story so much she knew what was coming over the page and said it out loud with the woman, and the toddler wanted to pat the pictures and dribble on them and got so excited his cheeks puffed out and his eyes were as round and as dark as Hunca Munca's. And when they had finished the last page they read it again slowly and loudly because they liked it so much and the toddler didn't know it was finished and went on puffing and patting and the little girl gave a great big sigh and stared into the fire. But what was the use of Tom Thumb putting a crooked sixpence into the doll's stocking and Hunca Munca sweeping the doll's house every morning, Mummy, when they'd smashed everything up. Weren't they silly mice to smash up the doll's house just because some of the things weren't real. And the woman said, yes, very silly, but perhaps they didn't know any better, being just mice. She carried the toddler into his cot and tucked them both up as snug as a bug in a rug and the little girl said night-night, Mummy, and say night-night to Daddy when he comes home, and the woman said, yes, I will, night-night and sleep tight. And it was nearly seven o'clock.

She washed the dishes and put the things away and turned off the stove under the pot with the dinner on top and went back to the sitting-room and turned the radio on and settled down with her knitting. But that wasn't any good because she couldn't hear anything except the noise it was making even when it was turned down low. So she found a book and settled down to read but that wasn't any good either because when she'd read a page twice carefully she still didn't know what she'd been reading. So she found a pencil and tried again, underlining bits here and there and writing things in the margin and this time it worked – she could read and underline and write things and *listen* at the same time. And the later it grew the easier she felt because if he didn't come by eight o'clock it would probably be midnight or the early hours of the morning, that's if he came at all. So the reading got easier and she didn't write so much or listen so hard, but by ten o'clock the fire had burnt right down and the wood-box and coal-scuttle were empty and she couldn't be bothered going out to the woodshed because of the wetas. She thought of having a bath but it seemed a bit risky – a bath wasn't a good place to be caught in – so she made some supper instead and filled her hot water bottle and got ready for bed.

But she didn't want to go to bed in case it happened again. She put her book and knitting away and straightened the chairs and cushions in the sitting-room and straightened the towels in the bathroom and swept the hearth and made sure there were enough aired napkins for tomorrow and picked up the children's toys and put them in the box on the side verandah. And when there weren't any more things to do, she tip-toed down the passage and round the corner, and lifted the handle so the door wouldn't stick and jar and crept in, but there wasn't anything to do there either except gaze at the children so pink and plump and easy in their sleep. So she crept out again and stood in the passage and didn't know what to do. If she went to bed it might happen again, and if she stayed up she might be caught. She stared at the old ship's bell and wondered what would happen if she took it down and stood on the front steps and shut her eyes and swung it up and down up and down with both hands as hard as she could – no, that wouldn't do because the children might wake up, and they mustn't find out – then suppose she ran through the bush with it and stood in the middle of the road and rang it and rang it till she couldn't hear anything couldn't listen to anything except the ringing. Would the people in the brown house with the white facings and the sunken garden and the people in the one next to it with the tennis court and the people in the new two-storied home with the sun-deck and the people who lived at the end of the long wide drive, would they look at one another and say, listen, isn't that someone ringing a bell? Why would anyone want to ring a bell in the middle of the night? And if they left their houses and came out to her, cautiously, in the middle of the road and asked, what are you doing, what is the matter, and she told them, this is an old ship's bell that hangs at the end of the passage. It doesn't belong to me, but I'm ringing it now because I've been waiting a long long time and I'm still waiting and *I can't wait any longer* – the woman put a hand to her mouth – what would they say then, what would they do with her then? She turned away from the bell and got into bed and waited and listened.

And some time later, she didn't know what time and it didn't matter because the waiting was over, she felt the footsteps thudding through her sleep, down the steps from the road into the bush, under the macrocarpa trees, past the giant fuchsia peeling its brown paper bark in the dark, between the bamboos in the dip beside the stream, into the tree-tunnel that led to the house. She slipped out of bed and crept across the passage into the sitting-room and hid behind the door, and the footsteps thundered around the house and into the house and up the passage and stopped suddenly outside the door. *You don't know I'm here, go to bed, I'm not here.* But the door swung open and the footsteps came in and closed it and stood there for a time and when they turned round it was the face at the window, dead white and terrible and all dragged down, pressing to reach her and there wasn't any glass, *there wasn't any glass*. And the woman covered her eyes with her hands and screamed and screamed and tried to hide herself in the wall, and woke with the screams choking her and the bed-clothes pressing her down and her body shaking and clammy with the thudding of her heart.

And then she heard the footsteps again coming through the tree-tunnel, heavy and uncertain at the same time, and then she couldn't hear them at all. Perhaps he's making water against the gum tree, perhaps he's gone off the lawn and fallen down the bank – no, not the bank, I can't do it, it's too far down and too far up and the pungas get in the way, please not the bank – let it be the gum tree. And she waited and listened and the footsteps came back on to the path and around the house and into the house and tried to be quiet up the passage. And she lay like someone hiding behind a door and shut her eyes and breathed deeply and slowly, I'm asleep, I'm asleep, and listened to the fumblings on the other side of the bed and the clothes dropping and the hands groping and felt the pull on the bedclothes and the mattress sag and listened till the breathing beside her was slower and deeper than her own. And she lay for a long time in the small space between one waiting and next and felt everything but the tiredness drain away from her, and listened to the small night noises and the night wind and watched the gum tree through the window, moving its branches like arms against the pale night sky – if you could turn into a bird, you could fly away – and she watched the gum tree, waiting for the miracle, till her eyes ached and closed and it was over.

Kala

SUBRAMANI

The rainy season was over. This unseasonable June rain descended on the city unexpectedly at mid-morning, by some strange godly intercession, ending the spell of drought.

Black rain erupted suddenly on the buildings, slashed into shopfronts; soon both sides of the streets were filled with running water.

And she saw him again. There at the intersection, in the first flurry of rain, thrusting through the crowd that seemed like a herd of buffalo in a mirage. He was lost temporarily. Then he re-emerged. He paused under a shop awning, frowning a little, wiping the rain off the sleeves of his yellow shirt.

The rain had made everything seem unreal. She wondered if it was the rain or her habit of seeing extraordinary significance in ordinary things that caused that feeling. Everything she saw and felt took on a dream-like quality: the excited faces that streamed in the sticky heat of the shopfronts, the generalized dread as he strode in her direction.

For a moment she was immobilized and thought she wouldn't be able to bear the encounter. Short-breathed, her temples tautly drawn, she laboured under conflicting impulses: she wanted to meet his eyes, and at the same time avoid drawing attention to herself. She kept her gaze fixed on the pavement, believing, absurdly, that there was an intimacy between them that he would at once recognize, an intimacy that required no words or gestures.

Her mouth was dry, and her red blouse black with perspiration. Her face, tense and moist, gleamed with expectation. She felt a tightness building up at the back of her neck. She opened and closed her handbag nervously, rummaging

203

through it for a handkerchief to clear her nose. She felt an unseen shadow touch her, brush over her. The pressure behind her head became intolerable. She waited desperately for the moment to jolt back to ordinariness. She saw his feet slide past her with a vague limp in their stride. She looked about furtively; he had disappeared into the crowd.

Wheels skidded in the streets. Faces behind frosted glass emerged briefly, took shape, and disappeared.

The rain had broken the city's monotony, interrupting work and stirring excitement. Someone had found a rat in the water. A crowd gathered on the pavement by the helpless creature, until a gust of wind sent rain scattering on the pavement, driving the crowd into the shops.

Holding her sari down, Kala crossed the street with a nervous haste.

After the rain a silvery haze hung over the city. Kala gazed out of the kitchen window. The sky hadn't softened. There were patches of rain on the side of the hills, and lightning flashed in the distance over the sea.

She heard water drip from the roof on to the pawpaw tree outside the kitchen window which faced the lawn. The unkempt grass was laid flat by the rain, and pools of clear water collected on mats of green. Beyond the lawn, the houses looked drenched and huddled together.

She stood at the window for a long time. Somewhere in the house a door opened with a low creak. She turned quickly, and tiptoed to the adjoining room. The child, sleeping, resembled a large bird folded within its wings.

She turned to the lounge. It was warm there, and slightly suffocating. There was still that faint unease she had sensed all week long. Sukhen's book was open under the lamp-shade, his slippers on the frayed rug. She shuffled back into the kitchen. Briskly she gathered the end of her sari at the waist, cleared the table of cups and left-over food, and boiled some water for the sink.

She turned on the radio and caught the final news item. They were still searching for the girl who had plunged into the Rewa River. Now the river would be swollen, making the search difficult. She pictured the girl's body washing out to sea and sinking below a ring of foam.

Poor Sukhen. She regretted she had brought up the subject of her job. Her outburst about work and self-fulfilment must have sounded so hollow. She blushed with shame as she thought of that evening. She knew she had over-played the home-bound housewife. Anyway that was after her interview with that creature from the Ministry of Education.

She felt anger building up again as she recalled the smirking face of the official. She disliked him the moment she saw him. She knew the type: insolent toward those below him but obsequious and cringing in the presence of his superiors. He was bald and impotent-looking, socks pulled up to his knees, dressed like the white colonial he had replaced.

He ignored her completely, continued to turn the flimsies in red and green folders, and answered the telephone with a secretive grin on his face. She sat awkwardly on a wooden chair under a ceiling fan that whirred feverishly. The room was newly painted, and had a half-finished appearance. When the man lifted his head, it was to announce that *his* ministry had nothing for her, and dismissed her with a nod. She left the office trembling with anger. She felt dizzy when she stepped into the sun.

Later she wished that she had had the fighting spirit, a bit of the abrasive manner, to retaliate, or at least stand up to him. She directed all her indignation at Sukhen. She was a woman who had been let down by marriage, crushed by a patriarchal system. Sukhen listened to her without saying anything. She hated him for staring at her like that, appraising her, thinking, she imagined, that it was all part of her stubbornness, her four independent years in India, and a degree in English literature. He came close to saying that once.

She had regarded her marriage as a trap. It undermined her true self. She had believed that she married for love. She was beginning to doubt even that. Things had been a little confused from the start. Sukhen had come to see her father on some business in Sigatoka. She liked Sukhen. But it was her mother who presented her with an appealing image, pointed to the aura about Sukhen – isn't he a bit like Lord Krishna himself? she said. So, when Sukhen asked Kala, she said yes she would marry him.

From the beginning, Sukhen's opinions had governed their life. In a real sense she lived his life. But she admired his mind, admired what she saw as his gift of clarity, his ability to see general meaning below ordinary occurrences. This helped her to see many things clearly herself. She willingly submitted herself to his wishes. She was told she must live for others. She had lived for her parents, Mr and Mrs Shiu Nath – she enjoyed referring to them thus – and for Sukhen, now for the child. This was the role decreed for the Hindu wife. In fact she found much satisfaction in it.

But she had lost much. It is true she vowed she would live for love. Now she was thinking of work and independence. Well, she had told herself, hadn't Sukhen's own life been formed by his work at the Foreign Affairs office? And hadn't he himself said you are free to be something and you are free to be nothing?

She had changed. So had Sukhen. At one time he was so full of the beauty of her inner life, her innocence and authenticity, her *Indianness*. He even said that there was something of an artist in her. She felt her world rising; it gave her the feeling there was a real self curled up somewhere inside waiting to be born. But very quickly that feeling had atrophied.

This casting about for her own voice, these counter-arguments she produced, had given her great confidence. She thought she had regained her self-esteem. She spoiled everything that night by screaming that she wouldn't have another child. Sukhen shouted back. And they quarrelled as they had never quarrelled before.

She thought just a few weeks ago she was completely satisfied with this unexamined life; now through her own doings she had brought chaos into their life. She could never think unkindly of Sukhen. It wasn't Sukhen, it was the emptiness of her life that unsettled her. Still she had his love; that was one real thing in her life. There was also something else: her education had given her the ability to use other people's views; living with Sukhen had agitated her to find out things for herself. Somehow he made her feel whole. Sometimes she wished he didn't have such an influence over her.

When Sukhen returned from work she clung to him, over-powered by her tears. She didn't want a life in which their love wasn't the centre.

She prepared dinner while he read the paper. She watched him slumped on the sofa in his baggy work pants, his head propped on his arm. She had watched him like that often, always feeling great tenderness. I love him, she said, and I will die a thousand times for him. She crossed the lounge wiping her wet hand on her sari. She stood by the couch looking into his moist brown eyes. She tilted her head smiling, saw how awkwardly his moustache was perched on his face; she hadn't quite adjusted to the new image it produced. She kneeled on the floor, still smiling, thinking of the clumsy adolescent verse he had written for her:

> If you hadn't come in my life
> I'd have died
> Without anyone kissing my eyes.

She smoothed his forehead, ran her fingers through his tousled hair, and kissed his eyes.

She returned to the kitchen, happy with this sudden out-pouring of softness, this special closeness.

The sky was still hard. She saw there was barely any light there. Gradually the neighbourhood darkened. Somewhere children were playing in the dusk. A baby squealed from a house, and then a sharp female voice rang out.

Slowly luminosity returned, now from the lighted windows. Beyond the houses wings of darkness spread to the bleakly lit streets. She heard a car grunt, saw it move slowly on the shiny asphalt, and disappear around the bend. In the twilight of the lampposts, the silhouetted figure of a man hurried in the same direction.

Her gaze returned to the lounge. Sukhen wasn't on the couch. For a second she felt frantic, as if she had lost him for good. She called his name and rushed into the bedroom, pushed open the bathroom door, swerved into the adjacent room. He was kneeling by the child's cot, watching her soft, regular breathing. He looked up without saying anything. She pulled him roughly to her and clung to him.

The following morning she took the child to Sukhen's mother, and caught a taxi to the city.

A cold wind swept the half-empty streets. The city had a bright, scrubbed look; it glowed coldly in the midmorning sun. She strolled uptown, along shopfronts, gazing into shop windows, sickened by the sight of stale cake in a glass cage.

She entered a side street of old shops. A soft gloom hung over this part of the city. She picked her way along the broken pavement and dug-up mud, fearing knowing looks or lewd remarks from the two road labourers who leaned on their shovels and chatted with a tall Fijian in blue overalls and large mauled boots. She walked under a scaffolding, avoiding the rubble from a collapsed façade. The dreary shopfronts were about to receive a face lift. The Fijian grinned as she walked past him.

She cursed herself for taking this street. Farther on, a couple of men were knocking down a concrete wall. Their hands were covered with plaster. She stopped briefly to watch a black cat climb a flight of broken steps to reach a sunny spot. She hurried across the street when a shopkeeper, with dark bloated face, lips lined with betelnut juice, stared disapprovingly at her.

The shopkeeper turned to talk to the Fijian in blue overalls, who was now sitting at the bottom of a dark stairway that led to well-lit offices displayed behind French windows. She was conscious they were following her with their eyes. She looked back. The shopkeeper had gone inside. The Fijian was still grinning. She bit her lips and smiled back. The Fijian laughed explosively, shaking his grizzled head. A flash of white showed between her lips as she laughed unabashedly, a rich and easy laughter. The workmen stopped pounding the wall and started to gaze in her direction.

She smiled to herself at this absurd exchange, and strolled on through clusters of people at the busy supermarket. She paused on the bridge across Nabukalou Creek. The sour-looking stream, lined with black and green bricks and rusted iron, moved sluggishly with the refuse. It bore the stench of rotting mangroves.

She stood there for some time, her head in a daze. The lonely haunted face she had seen emerge from the black rain swam before her eyes. She saw a pair of bare feet on naked shingles slaked with rain. Again she experienced the strange spell of those feet that had ages of solitude moving with them. She wanted to touch them, wash them of their weariness and sorrow with her tears. When she became conscious of her surroundings, her face burned with shame. She wandered through the streets sobbing inwardly, afraid of the madness that was overwhelming her.

Her legs ached. She felt shabby; her hair was askew, and her face gleamed with perspiration. She looked for a place to rest, found an empty table at the less crowded end of a milk bar. She leaned back on her chair wearily, with half-closed eyes, wondering why she was there. She seemed to be pushed along as in a dream; she could not retreat, and what lay ahead seemed dim and frightening.

An elderly waitress wiped the table with a dirty sponge, without looking at her or showing any interest in taking an order. She dropped her elbows on the table, pressing her temples with her fingers, digging into her thick black hair.

Opposite her table two men sipped tea from large white cups. The man in florid shirt and shorts suffered from a bad cold. His companion, bearded, wearing dark glasses, was reading from a wad of pink papers. He had a tense expression. The other poured tea from a battered tin teapot. He had a witty mouth and nodded frequently. After pouring the tea, he pulled a newspaper from his pocket and, just as deliberately as he had poured the tea, he spread the newspaper on the table. He pulled the sheaf of pink papers to his side, marked a section with a blue pen, and drew his friend's attention to the photograph on the front page of the newspaper.

Kala watched the two men for a while, then abruptly crossed over to the counter for a newspaper and returned to her table. The photograph on the front page was of an accident: a man sprawled on the wet asphalt before a semi-circle of agitated spectators, seen through a skein of rain which glistened in the headlight of a car.

She stared at the photograph for a long time, then turned the page. The drowned girl had surfaced. She had left a note: she had gone to join her dark lover in Brindaban.

Kala read the story again on the bus. Her mind kept returning to the girl's story. It triggered her memory, sent it racing
into the past, into the bittersweet agony of her childhood
infatuation with the dark god. She saw the bent figure of her
Vashnavite grandfather, recalled his mocking smile, his vir-
ahdukha songs about the god and his herd-girls. One morning, when she had come to his side, freshly bathed for
prayer, her hair damp and loose on her shoulder, he made
her sit on his string bed and sing to him. She sang in her
plaintive voice her favourite song 'My Mate Is He'. Without
her knowing, the old man had invested her fantasies with
real emotions and feelings. And dressed in that role for the
school concert, of a rural lass forsaken by her god, she
actually felt affected by his fickleness. Her teachers said she
had real talent. She was so happy. She held the old man and
sang to him. She recalled laughing and running away when
he tried to hold her by his side.

She alighted at the bus stop in her street, and returned to
the house intoning lines from the old song.

The meandering in the city left her feeling tired and
unclean. She washed, put on an attractive sari, and waited
for Sukhen.

She gazed at the neat, whitewashed house next door. She
saw Sumintra and Gopal enter with bags of groceries. They
had finished work early. There was movement in the kitchen,
and, after a while, the house was surrounded by a suffocating
gloom. She wished she could talk to Sumintra, woman to
woman. But after her first overture of friendship, which
finished in a near-catastrophe, she decided to keep away
from her. She had seen Sumintra on weekends, sitting at the
door, legs spread out, as if seized by an incurable boredom,
and Gopal moving about looking sallow and defeated. Yet
they had married for love.

It is like this with life, Kala told herself. It either ends in
sterility and boredom or leads to daily torment. Looking at
the still house now, she wished it would explode and free the
couple from where they were so cruelly imprisoned.

Kala too had loved destructively. She saw it clearly. She
had told herself she was saving Sukhen from his clamouring,
clutching relatives; whereas, in fact, she wanted him all for

herself. But she had managed to overcome her fears, realizing that these fears could only stifle love, which had a chance only in freedom. Sukhen loved differently. He had suffered much as a child, and again during his studies abroad, and had come close to what he called 'the enticement of the great emptiness'. Sometimes she witnessed a disquieting aloofness which frightened her. Love assuaged his pain, diminished his anxieties. She loved him more because he needed her.

Sometimes she had wished for a special intensity, and was disappointed with his sober love. But his face had so many subtle expressions, so many moods. She wanted him to be simple, someone who would love and be loved. When she broke free of her self-centred, narcissistic love she started to appreciate the beauty of his friendship. She found him pure-hearted, someone who would love without wanting any reward. She did have many moments of intense happiness with him. During those early days they listened to music a lot, and talked most of the night. She loved listening to him. His words had the magical quality of lifting all their experiences above the mundane, of refining what was crudely lived. He called himself a colonial betrayed by history. She loved even his despair. Then there were those beautiful details about his childhood which made her laugh and cry at once. When they had their first car, they drove around the island and picnicked along the coast. Sukhen showed great patience during these outings and attended to every detail.

After her wanderings in the city, she felt her actions had betrayed their extraordinary intimacy. She wanted to tell him everything, talk to him about what was happening to her. She decided to wait until he returned from his trip abroad.

The two weeks Sukhen was away she returned to the city. She moved alone in the crowd, absentmindedly, among malingerers, hangers-on, tourists – all performing their rites. So many empty faces, so many people footloose in the streets. She returned home when the sidewalks started to empty, her face burning with shame. Standing by the kitchen window, while the child played in the lounge, she felt the sadness of early nightfall. She was never so lonely or lost.

She fed the child, eating very little herself. She locked herself with the child in the bedroom, and gave herself up to morbid thoughts about madness and death. One night she woke up, sweating, to the phantasmal stillness of the house. Her forehead was in a fever. She lit a table lamp. She leaned against the wall, slowly slid down onto the floor, and sat there clenching her fists, feeling that if she didn't do something she would be engulfed by emptiness. She would never be herself again. She made up her mind to call Bijma, her younger sister, who lived in Sigatoka. Bijma sometimes stayed with her when Sukhen went abroad.

The following morning was bright and warm. She stood before the red mirror, ran her fingers over the curve of her cheek, studied her eyes. Both her face and eyes had retained a girlish radiance in spite of her thirty-two years. She felt a youthful glow invade her body. She forgot about Bijma, and started to enjoy the freedom of her aloneness.

She had lived in Suva for over seven years, yet she hadn't seen the city fully. In fact she had avoided it, regarded it as featureless, existing only for money. It was unlike the cities she had holidayed in during university vacations in India. These cities were full of myth and history. Now as she broke free of her sheltered life, the city suddenly took on a romantic aspect; it seemed to contain an extraordinary amalgam of feelings and sensations. It started to open up, come under her control.

She did things she hadn't done before. On impulse she opened her first bank account. And overcome by an impetuous feeling, she dropped a coin into the metallic box of an acrid-smelling public telephone, dialled a number at random, and carried on a conversation with a perfect stranger.

She strolled by the market stalls and push-carts, laughing at the ritual mutterings of the peanut sellers at the grimy bus station. She stood in the strong wind at the harbour, and watched a ship decked with tourists wearing seashell jewellery. She didn't feel befouled passing through the ill-famed alleys of the city.

One afternoon she walked into the city library, told herself she'd read something really outrageous. She searched through the shelves, reading odd pages from books she picked up. She selected a volume, carried it to an empty table, and read through an entire segment entitled 'Diary of the Seducer'.

It seemed to her that, in the city, she had strayed into a hidden region, the dark underside of her existence, where she was taken beyond daily responses into another mode of feeling. But she was never far away from the elusive shadow. For some obscure reason she imagined him sick and dying, and needing her help. What if he had tried to contact her and she hadn't known? She expected a glimpse of him in the long mirrors in Cumming Street, in an empty parking lot in a brown overcoat, or sitting on the sea wall against a flight of gulls and a dying afternoon.

She found him in her dream on a red hilltop, crawling upward on the bare slope like a fugitive, and she slipping and falling, her face smeared with red earth.

She asked herself what if he should overtake her one day, halt in front of her, touch her hand? She would melt on the pavement. Perhaps he would shake her by the shoulder and wake her from her dream.

Then she saw him. He was in a bookstore at the counter, his back towards her at an angle. She stood by a shelf of books in a state of near-panic, without moving or even turning her face. For a breathless second, out of the corner of her eye, she saw his outstretched hand on the counter. A hand she had touched so many times in her mind, the arch of his wrist, bones of his fingers, tendons, veins, the soft flesh brazened by the weather. A strong masculine hand. It waited furtively to receive the change. She shuddered when he spoke to the attendant. She couldn't catch the words, but the voice was cracked and troubled, and seemed to emanate from some remote corner of his being.

Suddenly he turned towards the door. A quick surreptitious movement of her eyes, and she caught a glimpse of one side of his bearded face and head. His hair had a touch of grey. The next instant he hurried away as if fleeing from something.

She took a deep breath and stepped outside the bookstore. It was bright in the street. She ran to the sidewalk. She saw him moving quickly in the crowd, shielding his eyes with a news-paper. His rapid stride accentuated the limp in his right foot. Soon he was lost in the pavement crowd. She stood motionless on the sidewalk, feeling a flush of breeze sweep over her.

She waited for Sukhen at the airport. She felt nervous and

unsteady and thought what if he wasn't on the plane. Suddenly he was there at the exit by the flight attendant. He chatted energetically all the way to Suva, with a happy glint in his eyes. She was mostly silent, her mind drifting off, sometimes looking at his face, sometimes gazing out of the car window.

They had an early dinner. She took the child to her room, and washed and dried the dishes. Sukhen showered, and settled into bed with the fortnight's newspapers.

She sat on the edge of the bed stroking his feet. Gently she prepared him, careful at first not to say too much or too little. She told him everything, and how lonely and confused she had been.

He placed the newspaper slowly on to his lap, and stared into her face. 'I don't understand what it is all about, Sukhen, I really don't . . . Couldn't it be that it's all a daydream?'

'Tell me what you think,' he said, narrowing his eyes but without appearing to force her to respond. He folded the newspapers and dropped them on to the floor. She saw he had paled. She tried to avoid his gaze, afraid of those far-seeing eyes.

'Sukhen, you'll have to help me . . . ' Her throat was full. She was ready to burst into tears.

'But you had gone to the city several times, that much seems clear,' he said. She sensed the deep irritation in his voice. He was starting to look at her from an immense distance. Lord, how could he be so cold and objective. She had great difficulty controlling her speech. He continued to peer at her. She was relieved when he withdrew his eyes. A prolonged silence followed when the spectre she had created seemed to govern their thoughts.

She reached for his shoulder. His body flinched slightly. After a moment he disengaged himself without looking at her. She tried to hold his hand but he lurched past her. She saw him walk to the creek behind the house, and stand at the edge of the creeping wilderness.

She found her slippers, and went out to the porch. The night was dark, full of stars, and the grass moist with dew. She sat on the step, her face cupped in her hands. After several minutes she lifted her face. She clasped her elbows as a shot of chill pierced her body. He was still gazing into the black emptiness.

He walked slowly back, and crouched in front of her. He took her limp fingers into his hand without looking at her. She saw he was reaching out. She wanted to hold him and cry freely. He raised his eyes, watched the play of light in her eyes, in her nightblue hair. His lips broke into a half-smile. Unable to contain her tears, she wept openly, burying her hot face in his shoulder. He led her into the house.

She heard him sleeping deeply. She lay on her back, hands beneath her head, legs pulled up under the sheet. She was seized by a sudden desire to grow old, allow her flesh to frizzle and fade away. This would be preferable to witnessing the rapid corrosion of her love. Her face was wet with tears.

She got up early in the morning, washed, and combed her hair, not forgetting to apply red dust on the white parting in her hair. She prepared his breakfast. Sukhen took an inordinately long time in the shower, fidgeted in the drawers, which irritated her because she wanted him to eat his breakfast hot.

Throughout the week he was edgy. She had difficulty assessing his true feelings. When he spoke he was vague and uncertain. There was an air of irreconcilable strife in the house. At night, she listened to some music while he read, seated in his customary chair. They slept on the two sides of the bed, apart.

Saturday morning they remained in bed together. The child appeared at the half-open door rubbing her eyes, hesitated, then waddled to her room. When Kala looked in, the child was asleep again. After a few minutes she returned to bed. There was warmth and pleasure in the crumpled sheet. She pulled it over their bodies, propped her head on the pillow, and turned sideways towards him. He had that half-smile on his face. He rolled on his side, stroked her face, running his fingers over her nose, the lovely arch of her cheekbone, felt her warm hair, her warmly stirring body. He fixed his gaze on her kohled eyes. Her face was flushed and yielding, and he kissed her, drawing her to him. She recalled now that he had said to her once that we can love like humans and like gods. She felt they had come together after an interval of many months.

Suddenly her face burst to life. She pulled his face roughly towards hers. 'Tell me,' she said, 'what is that one thing for which you would give your life?'

He was silent for a second, surprised at the intensity in her voice. He grinned and leaned over her, one arm across her breast. Looking into her smiling face he said, 'You really want me to answer that?'

She nodded, pressing her lips.

'Perhaps for love,' he said. 'Because it wouldn't be for a place or any cause.'

'Do you still love me, Sukhen? I mean truly love me?' she asked abruptly.

'Do you *feel* that I love you?' he replied.

'Yes, I think you must love me . . . love me very much. I don't know why . . . ' Then she said, 'Do you love me enough to die for me?' She appeared embarrassed at having asked that question.

'No,' he responded, quickly, touching her nose, 'because I'd want to live for you.'

She made a coy gesture, wrinkled her nose, and inched away slightly. She gazed through the half-open window.

'What is it, Sukhen,' she asked when she turned to him. 'What is is that we want? Why am I so uncertain?' She broke off, covered her face with her hands, pulling at the sheet.

He held her hand on the pillow and said, 'Isn't it something like this: all we can know is that we are here now, and then there is nothing. And what we have between now and that nothing is our love. That is the only thing.'

Tears clouded the pink of her eyes. 'Isn't it our duty, then, to be happy?' She held him, crying inwardly. 'What will become of us, Sukhen . . . '

When she took hold of herself, she found both her heart and mind responding to his words as if she, too, through a different route, had arrived at the same meaning, and for the moment love, nameless, unutterable, whatever its total significance, seemed the natural anchorage, the only refuge from other illusions.

She waited for Sukhen on Monday. The child was by her side on the couch, in a clean dotted frock, rocking to and fro. She made Sukhen's tea, and when he was settled on the couch, she told him. There was an accident in the city. Early in the morning when it was still dark. They had found him face down on the wet asphalt, a few yards from the creek, down a skew. There was a slight wind; his brown overcoat flapped and billowed. That's how they spotted him. There was no sign of any wound on his body, only a trace of blood on his shoe. A small crowd gathered around him. Then it started to drizzle again. They took shelter under the shopfronts from where they saw his body put into an ambulance.

Sukhen kept his eyes on her face. Her nostrils flared with her breath. She did not say anything more. There was no need to explain.

What the derelict god meant to her required no naming. Like love. And Sukhen didn't say a word.

A Letter from the Dead

MARGARET SUTHERLAND

What an unpredictable climate it is, thought Mrs Lake as she watched the surface of the pool pit and water pour off the tropical vines. The rain stopped just then and steam began to rise from the terrace tiles. Mrs Lake wiped her neck with a handkerchief.

The dog which had barked all day still barked. It did not like being tied up. Each bark was as clear and expectant as the first.

All the town grew noisy at that home-bound hour. The horns did not sound impatient so much as determined. Each one implied a house and garden and waiting family beyond the working world. Mrs Lake enjoyed that time of day. She had so many landscapes mounted in her mental album of people, mountains, harbours, buildings, trees, birds, cities, strays: so many airports, waiting rooms, hotel rooms in her life: she liked the thought of family life with its untidy warmth and hoarded past and the hangers-on.

Don will soon be here, she thought, and was glad. They would sit outside a while, sipping sherries, sharing the day's news. She would smile or commiserate until he settled back, his gaze on the harbour, enquiring. What about you, Amy? A good day?

All her days were good. Unlike the dog, she had the sense to know complaints were rarely worth persisting with after a certain time. She felt it was up to one to be happy, and so she was.

Mr Lake looked depressed and hot when he came in. Gratefully he kissed his wife, who in standard hotel accommodation could somehow create an illusion of lamplight and drawn curtains, and swallowed his sherry fast.

'Did any shipments get away today?' asked his wife, who followed his work closely. She was raising a topic inclining her husband to coronaries, and tipped the sherry bottle with a placating look. They both knew a serene fatalism towards Mr Lake's third-world contribution was sensible. They had spent fifteen years moving from one economic problem to the next: this time he was to find effective ways to distribute emergency aid supplies and fuel to the numerous outlying islands devastated by the recent hurricane.

'Today, yes, I did manage to discuss the problems with some of those who take an interest in such things.' He nodded to the bottle. 'The Ministers of Finance and Economic Development are still at loggerheads – their business being money, they want to control all the funds. The Minister of Rural Development has his views, the villagers being the ones most affected after all. Before lunch I was interviewed by the Minister of Food and Agriculture. He expects a say, naturally. Then the Minister of Works and Transport considers his department should take over distribution but, as fuel's involved, the Minister of Energy disagrees. Tomorrow we all meet over lunch, probably to drink too much and set up a committee to commission a study. Meanwhile the rice rots and grafters siphon off petrol and stockpile the tinned goods to sell off on the quiet.'

'They don't want to implement your recommendations at all?'

'Be lucky if they read them, much less implement them.'

'Remember Kenya, Don,' said Mrs Lake calmly. She kept their past postings on file. Like an excellent secretary she knew exactly where to lay her hand on former near-disasters which, at the eleventh hour, were resolved.

'Kenya was a picnic compared to this place,' he grumbled, but she saw the lion in his breast was ready to lie down.

Above the harbour and the town, the sunset flung itself to the perimeters of the low, hump-backed mountains.

'Those hills remind me of a dinosaur, plodding on, searching for a mate,' said Mr Lake in his reflective mood. 'Poor old boy – no hope for him here.' The passionate sky made him sigh. 'God, these places are lovely. Amy! Would you ever see a sight like that in England?'

She had heard these ambivalences often and found them comforting. Things repeated were reassuring, she found. She wasn't a housewife in a suburb, who could predict the milkman would deliver at seven o'clock and the collectors would take away the rubbish on a Wednesday. Her life was an endless adjustment.

'A quick swim before we eat?' she suggested. He reached over and stroked her arm. 'Amy, you keep me sane.'

'And what would I be without you?' She went inside to change and turn down the camp oven. They carried it with them wherever they went and she made simple meals, saving restaurant fare for special occasions. Mince pie had an essential ordinariness in their rootless life.

Walking between wild orchids and hibiscus folding at day's end, they followed the path to the pool. He was a little taller than his wife, and she a little broader in the hips than he. Their stride the same in length, they went side by side down the pool steps and struck out at the same moment. Wide, slow ripples began to lap the edges as they proceeded in breaststroke to the end and back. Mr Lake turned over and floated, his face to the still-brilliant sky. Mrs Lake, who did not want to wet her hair, bobbed up and down, testing the bottom with her toe-tips and pulling up her shoulder straps which had a way of slipping since she'd lost weight. Recently her husband had put on two or three kilos; the same amount she'd lost. He looked rotund in his shorts as they went up the pool steps hand in hand. A large frog hopped along the path and a bat swooped. The air smelled of rain and some perfumed shrub.

The casserole wasn't quite tender. After they had changed, they sauntered down the hill and along the main street of town. The creek which crossed it, an oily, tidal inlet, was edged by an arched and colonnaded walkway – a South Pacific hearsay of Venice. All day birds perched there; now the last flight wheeled away, the rush and clatter of their wings like a supernatural breathing.

Mrs Lake stood still, gazing, her neck taut as a girl's. 'Oh Don!' she cried. 'The pigeons!' Nostalgia etched every line of her, and Mr Lake stood quietly, understanding. He knew the way of it – some idiotic little thing could jolt him back to England as easily.

'Where are we off to?' she enquired; coquettish, although not a moment before she'd had the look of a child whose balloon has gone forever. They wandered on, their pace and interest suggesting there was nothing new and nothing expected from the surroundings. It was briefly cool, and the mosquitoes hadn't yet arrived. As the street lights came on, they turned by mutual consent and went back to the hotel.

As Mrs Lake came from the shower that night, fastening her cotton robe, she said to her husband, 'Do you find me attractive still?' He said, 'Of course I do. It doesn't change. You look the same to me.'

'Do I?' she asked, very surprised, for he did not look the same to her. She did not believe him, though she was pleased at what he said. Their lovemaking that evening was fond and unspectacular. Mr Lake found to his dismay that his worry over the next day's ministerial luncheon was interfering with his carnal interests. Fortunately his wife knew him well enough to effect a happy conclusion for them both.

'I love you dearly, Amy,' he said before he settled to sleep. Though she would have liked to stay, it was far too hot to think of cuddling up and she went back to the other bed. She checked the time and wound her folding traveller's clock; she had bought it in Hong Kong, years ago, and it was still as good as new.

Mrs Lake preferred the early hours. She felt most alert then as she went quietly on her own to attend to letters or do a little study on the terrace still wet from night showers. That peace established the routine of her day. After she saw Mr Lake off to his ministerial manoeuvres she did her housework which, in one room, did not take long. She had no windows to wash, no spring-cleans, no seasonal wardrobes to sort or appliances to have serviced. In the opinion of her relatives at home, she was a person to be envied.

She filled the hand basin and whisked suds to a business-like froth. She never let anyone else handle Mr Lake's laundry. She rinsed and rinsed till no trace of soap remained. She carried the washing, wrapped in a towel, to the terrace. There she fastened the expanding clothesline to the two hooks she'd fixed and pegged out, smoothing wrinkles, picking off lint, untangling the long socks.

Beds made, dishes done, Mrs Lake set off for town. The walk was a familiar one and she smiled at the taxi-drivers lounging by the rank and waved to the Indian vendor who sold sweetmeats on the corner. She went to the market and bought two avocado pears, a pineapple, a pawpaw and a handful of beans from her favourite stall. The owner wrapped her shopping in newspaper and she reached into her handbag where forethought catered for a range of eventualities (a folding rain-bonnet, a collapsible straw hat, a dome-away carry bag). She took out the kit, undid the domes, packed away her purchases and paid. She dropped the change with a rattle in the tin of a blind beggar who squatted at the market entrance and went on to the supermarket. There she clicked her tongue at the price tags of tinned salmon and olives, bought a bag of sugar, a bottle of vinegar and a loaf of bread. The kit seams looked stretched as she returned to the accumulating heat. She should have done her lighter errands first, she thought. Her face felt wet. The local women in their bright cottons maintained an air of freshness – she had no idea how.

Wearing the straw hat and trudging a little, she queued at the post office, despatched her letters home and finally walked to the newspaper office at the far end of town. There she made a donation to the fund for the children whose parents had died that week, rescuing their family from a house fire.

She was glad to head back to the hotel. She shifted the kit from hand to hand. There was a funeral at the Methodist church and she stood in the sun, her bag on the ground, waiting while the bearers carried a cloth-draped coffin down the steps. She watched quietly, making one of those journeys people do make, in the blink of an eye, when some passing event detaches itself from generality and plunges like a sword. The hearse drove away. She lugged the kit up the hill and gratefully opened her door. She drank two glasses of water, went to shower and change all her clothes and put away the shopping. That's that, she thought, with a sense of accomplishment. It was not quite ten o'clock.

*

The dog which yesterday had barked was barking still as she organized herself and her study books on the shaded terrace. Its energy and faith were boundless. I expect they are training it, thought Mrs Lake, who had an Englishwoman's horror of unkindness to animals and a lot of experience that not all people shared her feeling. With effort she detached herself from the barking and opened her text on Japanese script. In Tokyo last year, en route to a World Bank conference with Mr Lake and anticipating temples, lakes and gardens, she'd had to come to terms with skyscrapers and hurtling trains. The disappointing fragments did not deter her. She bought a *Teach Yourself* language course and the Penguin edition of Japanese verse. Asia was nothing if not patient – and she had time to spare for the search.

Memorizing the *kana* and tracing the *kanji* in prescribed stroke order were peaceful disciplines. For basic mastery a reader needed to know two thousand *kanji*; the Chinese aspect of the script. Mrs Lake had now learned sixty-two ideograms. The pursuit of such a goal, even its unlikely attainment, somehow pleased her, aligning her with a child's perspective where each moment has its own permanence. When she tired of study she would imagine Japanese children, their hair cut straight, gazing out of schoolroom windows at the endless sky.

Now she scanned her book of verse. The words were spare and approached the blank page with the hesitant self-disclosure she imagined of the Japanese.

> Was it that I went to sleep
> Thinking of him
> That he came in my dreams
> Had I known it a dream
> I should not have awakened.

There is an attitude of acceptance even in loss, thought Mrs Lake. Still the dog barked.

As she cut open the avocados and sprinkled them with salt and vinegar, the hotel receptionist tapped on her door and handed her an envelope with English stamps. 'A letter from home, madam,' he said, smiling wonderfully. She recognized her sister's handwriting. A premonition invaded her. She sat down to slit the envelope. Inside there was a letter, and a Christmas card which enfolded a linen bookmark embroidered in cross-stitch; grubby, like sets of table linen she'd worked herself as a girl, laboriously picking and restitching. She read the message on the home-made card. *Dear Auntie, thank you for the green silk pyjamas. They are the right fit. Mummy has made the cake and we are icing it today. We have a super tree. I'm sorry our present is late but french knots take ages. The stamps from the Philippines are stuck in and look very nice. When are you coming for another visit? Love from Althea.*

Her sister's note was as brief. *We have only just brought ourselves to sort through Althea's things. The enclosed was meant for you, Amy. I send it, as a keepsake, though I expect for you, as for us, reminders of grief are of doubtful value. It is too soon for me to look back acceptingly. She was a lovely little girl. I miss her every day. You were here with us this time last year. The church is a mass of lilies but I'm afraid this year the message of Easter is lost on me.*

Mrs Lake sat there, a bookmark and an open letter in her hands. How can I believe Althea is dead? she thought. I know it's true. They sent a cable. I opened it and read of the accident, there in that bright foreign city. I still have it as proof. But was there really a funeral? Could they have buried Althea? What flowers were there in December? I tried to pray for her of course but prayer needs an image and how can I imagine Althea under snow when I see her so vividly, running on the lawns of Greenwich, her cheeks so rosy, her fair hair tossed about? We went through the Royal Observatory and laughed at the funny old instruments for viewing the stars. We saw the shell of the old oak where Elizabeth the First used to play as a girl. We ate our picnic near the river where the *Cutty Sark* is moored. Althea asked me to send her stamps from the Philippines and I promised I would. We shared our sandwiches with pigeons.

Oh! thought Mrs Lake, it was wrong – wrong! – that I wasn't at her funeral.

A feeling of displacement and anger moved her and she picked up the telephone and demanded a connection with her husband's office. A detached receptionist explained Mr

Lake was at lunch. Mrs Lake remembered the ministerial meeting and put back the receiver.

There was a knife and a spoon and a glass in the sink. She rinsed and dried them and put them in their proper places. She fetched in the washing, removed the clothesline and put away her books. Then she sat, quite still, like a painting framed by walls. She had the art of managing small spaces but today a vacuum threatened. Others had homes, babies, a place in the community – at least a friend to telephone. Where is my world? she thought despairingly. I am dependent and waiting, no better than that poor wretched dog.

Mrs Lake snatched her bag and went out into the slaying day. She strode down the hill towards the town. 'I am capable of walking,' she said rejectingly when the drivers smiled and offered their taxis. She ignored the sweetmeat vendor and pushed through lunch-hour shoppers, elbowing her way. The store windows appeared to offend her. Their owners, hovering in doorways, eyed her and did not invite her inside. She crossed side streets without looking and drivers blasted horns aggressively. She marched straight on.

She saw two local girls come out of the arcade. They wore knickerbockers and brief tie tops and their lips were coloured purple. Confused, feeling her anger rearrange itself, she stopped, thinking, don't imitate us. It was very hot. She felt in her bag for a handkerchief to wipe away the sweat on her face. Just then a boy darted out from the arcade and held a garland out to her.

Cutting him short, she said brusquely, 'I don't want it.'

'Fresh beautiful *lei*,' inveigled the boy, waving it under her nose so she saw the browning blossoms and smelled their sickly scent.

'I don't buy dead flowers,' she snapped, exhausted by beggars everywhere who thrust their claims at her.

'Fresh this morning!' he argued, used to tourists with fat wallets and uncertain resolve.

Mrs Lake snatched the *lei* and shook it in his face. 'Look at it! It's dying. You push your dying wreath at me and expect money. Do I look such a fool? Do you think the English wave dead flowers at strangers? Why are you here? You ought to be at school. Don't you go to school? And don't tell me a pack of lies . . . '

The boy, staring as though she was mad, pressed through the shoppers and was gone. Breathing fast, very flushed, the hot pavement dragging fluid to her aching feet, Mrs Lake stood and people stepped aside to avoid her. The flowers, so carefully strung, expired their foreign sweetness. Their cool, browning touch had the texture of death and she let the *lei* fall. It was all he had to offer, she thought; what am I doing here?

White Soracte

ANNE TARRANT

I was born on the windy slopes of Wellington, and when I think of my childhood now, I see my father sitting by an open window in our hillside home, breathing in the sea air that blew constantly from the Pacific Ocean.

At first, broom bushes and a rug on the spare section were my deep rabbit burrow. My bedroom under the tiles smelt warm and dusty like a bird's nest. In endless summer I ate my sugared carrots outside on the steps, or crawled through a forest of fennel. By the gate there waited a winged boy; the wind blew his scarf over my eyes as we flew together along the crest of the hill, above the harbour.

My father made concrete steps and paths in the garden, and a seat with my name on it – DIANA – in chips of white shell; trellises and hedges sheltered it from the south. The sticky grey leaves of the hedge plant looked as if they had been sprayed with salt and hid grey berries oozing a poisonous dark red jam. That was native *Pittosporum*. My father also planted hydrangeas and arum lilies, my mother's flowers.

My mother bought me a school uniform; it was blue, my favourite colour, and it had white collars and cuffs that snapped on and off. She bought me a panama hat with tight elastic under the chin to hold it on in the wind. Next came air-raid drill; we lay on the tennis courts at school biting on Indiarubbers, while name-tags hung round our necks on pieces of string. Mine said *Diana Torrance* in black ink. An enemy was coming across the sea.

Voices spoke from the sky on short wave radio – Big Ben, Winston Churchill, Charles de Gaulle – and on medium wave from Australia, I heard the kookaburra. My father hung up a map of the world where many parts were coloured red; on those lands, the British Empire, the sun never set.

When I think of my father now, I often see him with a book in his hand. He is seated at the window – an open window – reading. With his dark suit and his white hair, he looks solid, and he smells richly of tobacco and bonfires. He sits upright in a straight-backed oak dining chair, one arm resting on the window sill, the other holding his book so that the light from the window falls on the pages. His head is slightly bent, but every now and then he raises it to look out, and then his lips move. From time to time he makes a note in the margin of his book with a pencil which he takes from his suit coat pocket, or lays a spent match from his matchbox between the pages to mark a place. Sometimes he murmurs to himself as he gazes through the half-open casement at the garden falling away below into the fresh breeze of morning . . .

The image of my father forms a luminous square to which the rest of my childhood is but a dark background. Illuminated and detached from its surroundings in a long distant past, this picture lights up like a colour slide in the beam of a projector, fragile but enduring. As though our grey house with its red-tiled roof, the hills of Seatoun Heights, the road along which I used to run to visit Aunt Molly, the flat streets of Miramar, all of Wellington even, with its various hours and seasons, had consisted of but one window in a wall overlooking a terraced garden edged with blue and pink hydrangeas, on a Saturday morning in early summer.

My father's lips move as he sits at the dining-room window, below which the hillside slopes down, step by step, in terraces, to the roof of the house below. As he raises his eyes to repeat a phrase – for he is learning this passage by heart – his gaze falls on the suburb spread out beneath: the flat red roofs and tram lines of Miramar, the plume of smoke from the gas works, the white curve of Lyall Bay. Farther away, the open sea is blue today; a fishing boat out on the water seems to stand still, while beyond it, half hidden by cloud in the far distance, float the mountain peaks of the South Island.

'Close the window, Humphrey.' That's my mother's voice. 'Humphrey, you're letting in a draught.' Yes, I'm sure that is my mother speaking. But my mother isn't there. She is along the road at her brother's place, the sailor-home-from-the-sea, who has perched his house on a cliff above the harbour. Beth is having morning tea in Newport Terrace with her sister-in-law, my Aunt Molly.

'It's cold, Humphrey. Do close the window.' Before leaving she must have said it. For on this Saturday morning the house really is full of draughts, the back door has just banged shut, the Indian weave curtains are flapping. The plume of smoke below in Miramar is leaning to the right in the southerly wind off Cook Strait. But London-bred Beth is not here, she's out visiting, and my father likes fresh air. A man of over sixty needs to breathe! He settles himself more firmly in his chair and fills his lungs with good cold sea wind.

And now my father's hand begins to beat time, as he directs his sharp blue eyes to the middle distance, where there is only brightness and light. What is he repeating to himself with such concentration? Why that inward look that seems not to see what he is apparently looking at, the ranges of mountains across the sea on the horizon, the Seaward and Inland Kaikouras, visible today under a band of light cloud? Lowering his eyes to the page, he runs the stem of his pipe along the lines as he reads, with marked metrical stress, drawing out the long vowels,

> u – u – – – u u – u –
> vides ut alta stet nive candidum
> u – u
> Soracte

My father lays the book of Horace's *Odes*, bound in worn brown leather, on the window sill, and turns to look over his shoulder at the clock. He is waiting for me to come home. His wife is having morning tea with Molly, she won't be back until noon, but I, Diana, should soon be here. He wants to discuss with me the translation of LIB I CAR ix, *To Thaliarchus*. Now that I have been taking Latin at school for several years, I ought to be able to appreciate Horace, he thinks. The clock on the sideboard shows ten past eleven. This clock has pillars of black marble, like an Egyptian temple, and a plaque from the Union Steamship Company to my grandfather 'in appreciation of long service'. The hour hand points to the Roman numeral XI.

'Young people should learn the classics,' my father used to say. 'It clears the mind.'

'Clutters the brain, more likely,' my mother would reply, 'with a lot of old silt.'

'Our daughter has a mind like mountain water. Every pebble it passes over shines and sparkles.'

'What nonsense,' said my mother. 'She's just a good average.'

Perhaps it is the morning light that exalts my father. There are times in Wellington when the air is so clear it enhances everything, the most distant objects are visible in perfect detail, the light shines, especially just before or just after rain, brilliantly on whatever you wish like a magnifying lens.

My father overestimated my knowledge of Latin. At school we were reading *Everyday Life in Ancient Rome*, in English, and reciting declensions, not poetry. In prose we translated, 'How many farmers did the soldiers kill in the fields near the town?' Turn that into the passive, girls, using the ablative. And yes, I could read the motto on my school hatbadge, LUCE VERITATIS, engraved on a silver scroll beneath the oil lamp. Was it Aladdin's lamp, I wondered, which when rubbed produces the magical LIGHT OF TRUTH?

The strange thing is, the more Latin I studied at school, the less patience I had with my father. How embarrassing to hear him proclaiming pentameters on a Saturday morning when everyone else's father was mowing the lawn or playing golf! I tended to agree with my mother that this passion for the past was foolish nonsense, and even slightly shameful, while what mattered was everyday life in mid-twentieth-century Wellington.

And yet, in spite of myself, the lines he recited have imprinted themselves on my imagination; they glisten even now like pebbles in the mountain stream of my memory.

> *vides ut alta stet nive candidum*
> *Soracte, nec iam sustineant onus*
> *silvae laborantes, geluque*
> *flumina constiterint acuto.*

When I got home, my father used to ask me my opinion: which version sounds best in English? Which is closest to the Latin? High with snow, deep in snow, white with snow?

You see how Mount Soracte stands white with snow.

But he would not be satisfied; he could never capture the energy and compression of the original, suggestive at once of the depth of the snow, the height of the mountain, and its whiteness. In that ode, Mount Soracte, seen or imagined once in winter long ago across the valley of the Tiber, rears its white peak forever against a pure blue Latin sky. And recalling it now all these years later, I see my father seated by an open window on Seatoun Heights – where the southerly wind blowing in from Cook Strait ruffled the pages of his copy of Horace's *Odes* – rolling on his tongue the musical Italian vowels, and seeing in his mind's eye – as I see him now in mine – not the unnumbered hills of Wellington, but the seven hills of Rome.

Allie, the tabby cat, emerges from the rustlings of grass on the spare section, where broom bushes used to be and now a house is built. She jumps down the bank on to the top lawn and sniffs the morning. She can see the light wavering over the line of trees at the foot of the garden, the great bowl of brightness that fills Miramar and Lyall Bay, she hears the faint cry of a gull somewhere in the blueness overhead. Then she sees the man at the window. She walks to the concrete step and rolls on her back.

It is thanks to this movement that my father sees her. She is a plain tabby cat with white paws that I brought home in a sack. Not knowing her history, or where she came from, we called her Allie, short for Aliena, the Stranger. She is not the only stranger to have come to Seatoun Heights.

Allie rolls on her back on the warm step, partly for her own urges, partly for the master who is looking at her. She has probably been wandering over the empty sections on this part of the hill and hunting for insects in the rank grass.

'Looking for cicadas or tomcats', thinks my father. 'She has her needs.'

Waiting for Diana to come, he goes to fetch a saucer of milk for the cat. One moment Allie is lying on her back in the sun, the next she is lapping milk in the red-tiled kitchen, purring loudly beside the coke bucket. With a leap, she has sprung on to the dining-room window sill, one paw on the open book, while the man takes his place again in the oak chair, to stroke her fur. He sits a little heavily with the weight of his years. It is better for him to get up from time to time to prevent his joints from stiffening. He could not now terrace this hillside for Beth, as he once did, when he first came here.

Diana's Saturday morning music lesson must be nearly finished, thinks my father. Soon she will be walking up the hill from Miramar. She will climb the long flight of steps with her music case, past the lupins, the lucerne, and the wild honeysuckle, past the wattle tree that, like him, came here from Australia. She will walk in the front door, place her music on the hall table, come into the dining room. Her cheeks will be flushed from hurrying uphill, her straight fair hair, in two plaits across the top of her head, will be escaping in wisps.

When Beth bought the house, before she met Humphrey, she was running away from her family. All the way from London she had sailed, with her botany degree, to teach in any New Zealand school she could find. It was from among the tree ferns and dug-out canoes of the Wanganui River that he had rescued her. But her family had followed her, the sea-faring family already uprooted in the previous generation. They too had built on Seatoun Heights, on the harbour side, three minutes' walk away from Beth. Beth lacked a proper sense of family. And she spent too much time with her sister-in-law.

My father strokes Allie as together they sit at the window. Today the sky and the sea are exactly the same shade of blue; gulls are wheeling over Lyall Bay; the fishing boat has moved a few inches to the right, behind the line of white surf.

A whirring rises suddenly from lower down the hill, through the grey-green screen of pohutukawa leaves, which at this season have decked themselves out with tufts of scarlet. The neighbour in the house below is mowing his lawn. My father understands that many people must go about their business, as he used to, while he now has time for his books.

He raises his hand to wave to Satchell through a gap in the trees, but realizes that he cannot be seen in this window reflecting sky and clouds. Satchell sought his help, years ago, with those steps that ended in mid-air. On that occasion, Pythagoras had come to the rescue with the theorem of the right-angled triangle. 'Gooday Satchell,' my father calls, hullooing down the bank, and 'Good morning, Mr Torrance,' he hears coming back to him faintly on the wind. He'd have a yarn with Satchell later, ask after that adopted daughter who disappeared, see if they had succeeded in tracing her.

'Beth will be along soon,' Molly's voice says.

My father hadn't seen her come. He must have been talking to Satchell as she walked around the side of the house. Or else he had fallen asleep. Allie has vanished from the window sill. He picks up the book of Horace's *Odes* and puts it in his pocket. Molly's face is below him, looking up at him as she stands on the step where recently the cat has rolled. How long had she been there? If he had dozed off, was it before or after she arrived? She is looking at him with that slightly teasing smile that never fails to annoy him. It is an expression that manages to combine mockery, charm, and veiled resentment.

'The dago,' he mutters between his teeth.

Molly's brown face is shaded by a straw hat tied round with a velvet ribbon and trimmed with daisies. She holds it on with one hand as she tilts her head back to look at him.

'I've come for some parsley.'

'Oh, Beth won't be long, then? Help yourself, Molly.'

Watching for the flush of red to rise in Molly's high cheekbones, he adds, 'If you like eating weeds, that is.'

Old sourpuss, she thinks, quickly hiding her hurt. She lowers her head so that the brim of her hat shades her face and from under it observes the suit, shiny at the cuffs, the frayed shirt collar, the head of white hair, the ageing but still strong body leaning forward in the oak chair, the book protruding from the pocket.

'Why would anyone want to spoil good soup with parsley?'

'It's not for soup. It's for scones. Parsley scones.'

'Good God, parsley scones! Well, don't give me any. I like plain food.'

'You and your bully beef! You don't know what you're missing.'

'Next I suppose you'll be offering me raspberry tea, or some other damned brew.'

'That'll be the day!' Molly cries, tossing her head back and bursting into a peal of laughter. How droll he looked sitting there in his dark suit on a sunny morning, making out that he was above parsley!

'By the way,' she adds, casually, 'I saw Diana.'

'Did you?' says my father in a more friendly way. 'So she's on her way home?'

'Oh, no.' Molly, turning away towards the herb garden, can hardly hide the edge of triumph in her voice as, over her shoulder, walking away, she calls out, 'She was going to the beach.'

My father shakes his head in irritation. Doesn't the woman think of anything but cooking and flirting? Those cotton dresses – a swirl of orange poppies, like a florist shop – swinging from the hips, that false smile. And all the time looking for ways to needle one.

And suddenly his annoyance is directed at me. What was Diana doing going to the beach instead of coming home after her music lesson? What was her mother thinking of, letting her wander off like that, like a hoyden? And what about him, sitting alone, with no one to share the beautiful lines of Horace, that held so much meaning for him?

So Diana was going for a swim. Young people nowadays were much too keen on exposing their bodies to the sun. Why this passion for sea-bathing? Diana, running down the zigzag to the bay with her bathing suit rolled in a towel, perhaps stuffed into her music bag along with the scales and arpeggios. For she hadn't been home to change. Or perhaps she wore the bathing suit to her music lesson, under her dress, and instead of paying attention to the pieces she was playing, *Für Elise*, or that lovely minuet by Mozart, thought all the time of warm sand between the toes, the splash of the harbour waves on bare skin. And then another idea struck him. Perhaps she had changed at Molly's place. Dash it all, he should have asked Molly where she saw Diana. Perhaps they were all in a conspiracy together, Molly and Diana, and Beth too.

Then my father's anger falls away and a dove of sadness settles on his shoulder. What could you expect from Molly, after all? Years of war work in the aircraft factory at Lyall Bay, her husband away on a minesweeper. And before that, raised in an orphanage in India, near – what was that place where the tea comes from, among the foothills of the Himalayas? Children like that, neither English nor Indian, cast adrift from both cultures, what chance did they have in the world? Molly had been offered the choice of nursing or domestic service, to be followed by marriage, and shipped off to New Zealand with nothing in her cabin trunk but a Bible, while her rightful dowry remained locked in the coffers of the orphanage director. Near Darjeeling, in the Himalayas. This was the story that Beth believed in, and that she and Molly talked of together. My father sighs. Perhaps it was true. But what could be done about it now? That wrong, if it existed, was too long ago and too far away. As far away as the snow-covered peaks of Kanchenjunga and Everest, which Molly as a young girl could see in the distance.

'I say, Molly, you haven't brought me another hedgehog, have you?'

Molly, returning with a basket of parsley and chives, looks up, startled, as she passes below the window.

'What hedgehog?' She is blushing again.

'The one you gave me wrapped in your handkerchief.'

'Oh, that. I thought you'd have forgotten.'

'Well, have you?'

'Of course not. It was a joke.'

'You gave me a hedgehog wrapped in your handkerchief for a joke?'

'Yes. It was a game, that's all. For fun.'

'I suppose that's the sort of game you played in Darjeeling.'

'What do you mean?'

'You must have played tricks like that on people at the school there.'

'Why do you say that?' Here I see Molly putting down her basket. 'Yes, I did sometimes. I liked a bit of fun.' And, emboldened, with her hands on her hips, 'Don't you? Didn't you ever get up to mischief when you were young? I'll bet even you had some fun once, Humphrey, in Australia.'

My father's past life in Australia was something I never thought about at that time. On Seatoun Heights everyone had come from elsewhere, it seemed the normal state of things; the past was talked about so rarely it might hardly even have existed. Sometimes, as with Molly, skin colour or accent betrayed a foreign origin, but this struck me in no way as remarkable. In a suburb of settlers, it is only the young whose first roots go down into the local soil. A Pearly King, swearing broadly in Cockney, drove the Miramar trams, while his daughters – Ruby, Pearl and Emerald – grazed their horses on a slope near by; across the road, at the top of a clay bank, a north-country wife and her two shy children waited each day for the return of the husband from Trinidad; my Scottish grandmother; my half-Indian aunt: these were our neighbours, a potpourri of Empire. I took them all for granted, without questioning their personal history, because they themselves so rarely referred to anything but the present. Was there some sort of unspoken pact to avoid talking of the past? Or to speak of it only, as my father did, in such a way that it seemed unreal, a mythology in which snakes and bushfires and boundary riders took the place of dragons and knights?

'You got up to all sorts of things in Australia, didn't you? Oh, I know you were a School Principal and all that, and a Very Important Person, not like me, but I also know,' and here Molly drops her voice to a soft hiss, 'that you were married.'

What does my father feel at this moment? I think there is a long silence, in which he hears the lawn mower, the wind in the hedges, the cry of the seagulls, the dry scratching of cicadas on the wooden trellis. He sees the tops of some distant pine trees waving in the wind.

'You left your wife. She and your children are still over there.'

Later, after Molly had gone, my father would wonder why he had not felt angry. To throw this thunderbolt at him out of a blue sky! But instead of anger, he feels suddenly tired. And, in a strange way, relieved. The day was passing, already it was nearly noon, soon the morning would be over. And the summer too, the summer was passing, from one day to the next.

'There was a divorce,' he says.

Of course he had guessed that Molly must know about this. It was inevitable that Beth would speak at last, perhaps at one of their intimate morning teas. He himself had advised telling her family right at the start, when they had first met. But Beth, with her English propriety, had refused, absolutely. In fact it had been a condition of their marriage that his first marriage should be kept secret. The letters he wrote and received from Australia were to be those of nieces and nephews.

Molly is silent. She bends down, takes a sprig of parsley from her basket and turns it slowly between her fingers, watching the curling green.

'Does Diana know?'

My father shakes his head.

Suddenly Molly is her usual self again. With a quick spring, she throws the stalk of parsley up through the open window on to the sill in front of him. Then she shoots him a sidelong glance that is at once meek and mischievous, ingratiating and spiteful.

'Don't worry. I won't tell her. I won't be the one to tell her.'

And before my father can express the rising anger he now begins to feel – good God, what was the woman insinuating? was this a threat of blackmail? Molly is already scooping up her basket and walking away with brisk steps along the path towards the corner of the house, where she turns and flings over her shoulder,

'Beth thinks you should.'

And then she is gone. He smells the smell of a summer dress, cheap perfume mingled with a woman's perspiration, the sharp scent of parsley and chives. He suddenly remembers how, when she raised her hand to her hat and tipped back her head to speak to him, when she first came, the dark damp hair under her arm had been visible in the fold of her short sleeve. Was Molly's person more important than what she had said to him? What was this weakness coming over him now in his old age that put him in the power of this small, brown, prickly hedgehog woman?

Diana was a child of his old age. She and her brother had replaced the others without knowing of their existence. That was not as it should be, he had always felt so. Did Beth mean to force his hand now, using Molly as her agent? What effect would this have on her daughter? He had great hopes for Diana. In her, blue eyed and vigorous as he himself had been, the river of youth ran down like a torrent in spring, when the snows have melted. That was what made him vulnerable.

You see how white Soracte towers deep in snow, the woods can scarcely bear the weight and the rivers are blocked by hard frost.
Drive away the cold with logs piled high on the hearth, and pour, O Thaliarchus, more generously a draught of Sabine wine.
All else leave to the gods . . . nor, young man, scorn light love and floral dance,
While morose and hoary old age spares your green youth . . .

Why did she leave him alone when he so much wanted to translate this poem with her? Now it was midday, the sea had taken on a hard metallic sheen, the light over Miramar was dazzling. The harbour bays would be glinting, luring people to the water. In his mind's eye he sees Diana descend the zigzag to the beach accompanied by a flock of birds. The birds are carrying garlands of flowers and leaves which they have plucked from the banks beside the path, for it leads down a cliff overgrown, riotously overgrown, with wild sweet peas. Green tendrils trail from their beaks as they fly just ahead of her; he hears her sandals thudding and skidding on the asphalt as she hurtles along, in her eagerness to swim.

But why would she go swimming alone? Having climbed the hill from one side, after her music lesson, why would she then go down the other, only to make her way back up the long, hot haul through the stifling scents of summer? Surely she was with someone? Or was meeting someone? Yes, that was it, someone was waiting for her at the beach, some boy perhaps. She has a tryst, behind the bathing shed, or under the pohutukawa trees beside the road. A local lad with sunburned ears, he waits, chewing on a stalk of marram grass, kicking the sand under the trees behind the bathing shed.

Girls now were so bold and free. But Diana is still a child. Beth shouldn't let her run wild like this. And she herself, Beth, so ladylike, modest, and reserved . . .

Did Beth really want him to tell her daughter now of his earlier life? After all these years of silence? How could he suddenly spring this discovery on her, fully formed, like Venus arising from the foam? Any moment now Diana would be here, with her music case and her wet hair and sandy bathing suit. How could he tell her now of the unknown sisters in Australia?

The rest leave to the gods, for when they have calmed the winds warring on the raging sea, the cypresses will no longer be stirred, nor the venerable mountain ash.

Avoid asking what tomorrow will bring, and whatever sort of day chance brings, put it down as a gain, and do not spurn light love and floral dance.

While morose and hoary old age spares your green youth. Now is the time for playing fields and town squares and soft whispers at nightfall at the agreed hour,

Now the sweet laugh of the girl hiding in the corner . . .

Reciting these lines by heart, does my father feel calmer, less agitated than before? He stares into the expanse of light over Miramar, and the oak dining chair creaks as he changes his position. He stays that way, sitting straight in his chair in his dark suit, while the morning reaches its full measure of dazzling sunshine.

No, he didn't ask me that day where I had been. He seemed not to notice my flushed cheeks and downcast eyes, or the bathing suit concealed in the ash-house; while I, sensing it hardly the moment to raise the subject of Larry or Ray or Des – and although longing to dance and sing and throw my arms around his neck – I managed to appear calm. And he didn't tell me, at least not then, about the other, grown-up family in Australia. It was only many weeks later that he untied the twine of his silence.

'Do you mind, Diana?' he asked me then. 'Are you hurt by my previous marriage?'

I looked out of the window and thought for a moment. I hugged to myself a growing happiness.

'No,' I said.

It's all long ago now – my father by the window reading Horace, Aunt Molly, the music lesson and the forbidden swim – remote in time and space. The people are dead, the grey house with the red-tiled roof sold, its contents broken and scattered. Why does that morning linger in my imagination?

The sun had now reached the top of the sky and was shining down on the window sill and my father's chair. The shadow cast by the house on the garden had crept out of sight without his noticing. The green fall of the hillside, broken by roofs, plunged down into empty space full of glare, where at eye level, but far out, a flock of gulls flew by.

As often happens at midday near the sea, the wind had dropped. The curtains hung limp, the treetops no longer stirred, the smoke from the gasworks stood straight up. But only briefly. The vast breath of the world, readjusting itself, paused, and then the plume of smoke began to lean over the other way, to the left. Now the wind was in the north, blowing out across Lyall Bay towards the snow peaks of the Kaikouras in the south. Foremost among them, Tupuae-o-uenuku, momentarily clear of cloud, raised its summit above all the rest.

My father took out his book of Horace and opened it at one of the places marked by a dead match. Now he would read another ode. He would finish the Soracte poem later, when Diana came home.

Carving up the Cross

APIRANA TAYLOR

They'd come to the marae where we worked building the house and learning. Hard work it was too. Bit of the old terrible Turk, as Gum liked to say. Lifting up those logs, some bigger than yourself, and shaping them to fit with nothing but your chisels and mallet. Heavy work. Lifting those logs. Fitting them, shaping them and getting them right. Bugger-all pay too. You'd not write home about it. Wouldn't be able to afford the stamps. But the house was a creation and it was good working and learning under the warm sun. There was bugger-all work going on when they showed up because the chiefs were up at the mill selecting more logs. We'd gone as far as we could without more logs. It wasn't just an ordinary house we were building. We got to the trees before they were milled into four-by-twos. They came down in the trunk still shaped as trees and we were building a house of trees.

It was strange that they should come here. A tall man looking at our work, and a nun. Most of the bosses were out. 'Tena koe,' I said, and then directed them into the other house because I didn't feel like talking and they looked like they wanted to ask somebody something. They walked quietly off to where I'd directed, and I pushed off in the other direction with the broom as I swept up the chips that'd flown off the trees we'd carved that morning. That's how I got my job for the day. Carving a cross.

Yep, a cross.

'Yes, a cross,' said Sister Hannah. 'He ripeka mo to matui hui. A cross for our hui.' She was a small woman with big round glasses, but young with a kind sound in her voice.

'It's our annual hui,' said Pitama. 'Many Maori Catholics from all over Aotearoa attend. The Cardinal will be there to open the hui and bless the cross. It has to be a big one. When the Cardinal comes onto the marae, the cross will be there and will stand on the dais behind the Cardinal when he speaks. We have to have it by Easter. That's when we hold our hui,' he continued. 'You understand. The cross will stand on the marae and be a central part of the whole conference.'

All agreed I'd do it. I liked the idea. I thought it would be interesting. Besides, I knew it was an easy thing to do. Just cut the timber, fit it and that's it. I could see it already. Leave the arms standing proud. Two hours later I'd finished the thing. Dowling joints and all. It stood leaning against a stack of timber beside the marae. It looked powerful. I'd shaped it a little with my tomahawk. Maltese style. But the cross seemed strange standing there because here was a place where you could once just stand and talk to your mates, and suddenly you're supposed to kneel and pray.

The chiefs came back with the timber and then left. We were often glad to see them go, because we just wanted to get on with it. Building this great creation of a house all about Tane the god of forests and more . . . the house was slowly developing its bones as we fitted each tree in place, using six-inch nails. The women were weaving the flax. We worked and worked and worked on the house.

The weeks passed and the house we worked on grew more and more. As for the cross, you couldn't help but notice it. It was a big cross. But piles of timber grew up around it just the same. And chips from the house, as we worked burying ourselves into the backs of trees with chisels, shaping and fitting the arms and the shoulders and the backbone, and from inside the house, selecting the ribs to fit.

When Sister Hannah and Pitama returned for their cross we hoisted it for them and they were very pleased with what they saw. It was simply made, yet had a look of strength and command about it, so even if the story that goes with the cross wasn't known you'd still feel this structure had something powerful.

We stood and looked up at the cross from beneath its slanting shadow and we talked about it. 'Must've been hard buggers who whacked 'em up.' We got on to talking about the house we were working on, fitting everything together, chisels carving . . . and yes, a carved cross would be a fitting presentation. And that's how that happened. We decided I'd carve a cross, or rather I volunteered for me and my mate Ben to carve a cross for them. Another cross. A carved cross, instead of this one. Sister Hannah warmed instantly to the idea and so did Pitama, in his own way. Being Maori like me, there was a big place in their hearts for wood carving.

We had to make another cross because to carve it the proportions had to be slightly different from the first. It was bigger. We couldn't work on it where we were. We took the cross by truck back to my flat and carved it in our own time. Every spare moment. That's how it had to be. Easter was a little more than a month away.

We carved and carved and carved. We couldn't get the beggar into the flat because it was too big. Nor could we get it around the side of the flat. So we carved it on the path in front of the flat. There was no section at the front of the flat, just the public path and then the road.

What did it mean, we wondered. We looked at the lizard we'd drawn, and thought that was a good idea. The lizard crawled down the cross towards the ground. It took us a long time to block it out. Towards the end of doing that I moved on to the top piece, where I carved Tane standing erect. My friend stood and looked. 'Why not put the tara of Hine nui te po right in the centre?' I said.

'Yes,' he agreed and began. Life born of death these things in the seeds blown . . .

I carved a thief on each side of the cross where the palms had been nailed. The wood was matai. A red wood. Pitama and Sister Hannah came to see how work was going and were proud of what was happening and understood.

During the time when Ben carved te tara o Hine nui te po, an old couple from either the Pentecostals or the Seventh Day Adventists had begun calling in order to preach to us. The lady was a kindly soul who liked just as much to have a chat and knit bootees for the young ones as to preach. Her husband was an unsmiling man who often said with a tense anger in his near-monotone voice, as he pointed at me, 'The Lord died for you.'

The tara that Ben carved was taking a long time for him to

shape. It wasn't obvious what it was at first. The Seventh Day Pentecostal old lady thought the cross was the most beautiful cross she'd ever seen, and she shone like golden light when she looked at it in the autumn afternoon sun. Her husband seemed to warm to this cross too. But as the days carved themselves by, and the tara of Hine nui te po that Ben was shaping became more obviously just that, I noticed the attitude of the Seventh Day Pentecostal Christian man changed. He looked at Ben's work and he shook with anger. His pursed, white-rimmed lips said it all. Then this Pakeha Christian man's white face went red. His wife, however, said, 'This cross is beautiful,' and was happy to stand there and admire the whole thing. Her husband was shaking even as he ushered her away. We smiled and waved goodbye. The husband tried to smile and wave but couldn't hide his glare of rage.

We laughed, Ben and I. We didn't care what the man thought. We were carving the story as we understood it. For here was Tane Mahuta who gained the light for mortals and here was te tara o Hine nui te po, the female organ, the gateway. The male and female element. There also as a sign of tapu was the lizard. Te tipua. This was the truth. Any fool could see that.

Io. Io kore matua. Io kore kanhoi. Io karu maha. Io kore kara. Io nui . . . these are but a few of the many names of God. We knew. We carved happily.

Three days from Easter and we were left with just the finishing touches. Sister Hannah told us the cross was actually going to be presented for the Cardinal's blessing. She thought the cross was beautiful and Pitama understood. We were all pleased. Sister and Pitama especially so, because look, here was the cross almost finished in time for the hui and everything was going according to plan.

Two days before Easter we trucked the cross downtown to the marae where the Cardinal would be welcomed and where he would bless the cross, which would then be placed behind the dais as a central feature of this hui. When we arrived at the marae with the cross, Father Priest was there to greet me and Ben and Sister and Pitama. He was a clean-shaven young Pakeha priest, his cheeks scraped raw with the razor. His hands continually templed in prayer. He was subordinate to Sister and Pitama in this matter. Sister and Pitama made the decisions. Sister always made the final decisions.

We stood the cross by a tree on the marae. Sister, Pitama and Father Priest left. Ben and I oiled the cross. Then we danced in front of it. The cross glistened in the sun. We took the cross down and put it away in the mission workshop.

I thought that night about the next day, when the cross would be presented and everything would happen. I remembered how I'd heard that older, traditional Maori carvers had been asked to carve this cross and they'd refused the job. And also that the house we'd been building would soon be opened and that it would be blessed at dawn. For the house had kept growing as we worked.

We'd made the backbone of the house strong. Everything fitted. The harakeke woven. Flax panels lined the walls. At dawn it would be blessed in the old way, but the opening of that house was still far away. Not like this Maori Catholic hui.

Early on the morning before the Cardinal arrived Ben and I were at the mission applying the finishing touches to the cross and oiling the wood. I noticed Father Priest standing in the distance watching us. He seemed frightened of us and so I waved and smiled at him. He reminded me now of Mr Seventh Day Pentecostal. When I waved, his red-necked shaven raw face went redder and redder. He was wringing his hands together in anxious prayer. He looked at us nervously and angrily. He managed a lemon-faced smile. Then he walked away, but from that time on I often saw him talking to people and pointing at us as we worked. I remember every woman that saw the cross said it was beautiful.

'No reira e te iwi, tino nui nga mihi ki a koutou, kua tae mai nei i runga i tenei kaupapa, ara ko te manaakitanga o te ripeka nei. Mahana ana taku ngakau mo koutou kua huihui mai nei i runga i te maumaharatanga o to tatau atua, me te pono o te atua runga rawa . . .'

This was how Cardinal O'Keefe began his blessing of the cross. He'd already been welcomed onto the marae. Now there were more than a thousand people massed about him as he turned and blessed the cross with holy water. All through this I noticed Father Priest darting amongst the people and stopping every few moments to whisper in their ears. We breathed more easily and relaxed a bit more when the cross had been blessed and the Cardinal had gone inside.

I'd just sat down to roll myself a cigarette when Father Priest came to talk to me. 'The kaumatua, Koro Taapapa, says that cross is to be taken down immediately,' he said.

'Eh?'

'You have displayed a lady's private parts on the cross of our Lord,' said Father Priest as though he couldn't believe it. It was hard for him to conceal his disgust and hatred for us. 'The kaumatua says', he repeated, 'that cross is to be taken down immediately and taken away.'

After that there came a long half-hour of whispered arguments and attempted compromises in front of the cross. I remember Father Priest had been talking to an old Maori man who was the kaumatua, Koro Taapapa. I went in search of Koro Taapapa. I couldn't find him. He'd slipped away somewhere.

The cross was taken down and taken away. Sister Hannah, Pitama and others had understood. I didn't care, though we'd worked a long time on carving this cross. I recognized this as just another giant slap in the face of the Maori by those who couldn't understand. We knew what we'd carved. What was wrong with them? Later I understood why the older, traditional carvers had no wish to carve a cross. The demands of those blind to the universal truth sullied the traditional carvers' art. When we carve, we carve . . . and bugger you. That's what they'd say.

I thought and I thought. Well, Jesus didn't fall out of the sky. And then I thought about that house. And Tane. And all that world. And I knew Father Priest and Mr Pentecostal and them were blind to its beauty and hated it 'cause they couldn't understand it . . . and perhaps it was best to tell them nothing about it. Strange, those people never spoke with us, only to and at us. I wondered what their problem was, and looked at what they'd done to Koro Taapapa.

The cross was taken down and away. Sister Hannah took it back into the hills up to her tribal lands near the river where she was born. I often wonder now I've learned more

. . . and more . . . about the chisel and to carve, how if . . . if I was asked again, would I ever carve a cross for someone?

  If I did, they'd still get the same story.

Pa Mai

APIRANA TAYLOR

'It's strange. Here's me, a Maori, drinkin' in the bar with you Samoans, and I've noticed something I never noticed before. Every time I go up to the bar to get a drink, that Pakeha bar girl slops my beer all over the place and just about throws the change in my face. And you know I get this feeling, Sione mate, that she hates serving me 'cause she thinks I'm Samoan.'

'You imagine things, Harris.'

'No, it's true. I don't get treated like that. I notice she treats all you Samoans like that. Imagine that, eh? You come all the way from Samoa to New Zealand and spend the rest of your life gettin' the beer chucked in ya face.'

'You know what I say, Harris? You Maoris came over here on your canoes. Then came the Palagi on their canoes, but we Samoans got smart. We waited for two hundred years and then flew over on Air New Zealand. Just left the taro plantations behind and flew over.'

'A bit like your uncle, eh? How long's he been over here?'

'A couple of days. Yesterday he said to me, "Nephew, I wish to buy you a drink." So we took him to the Harbour Point. You know, the new pub down by the beach. As soon as we got there, Uncle Fauma made a beeline for the bar. He wanted to show us New Zealand-raised Samoans he wasn't a country bumpkin Sa from Savai. "Excuse me," he says to the barman, "I would like to buy four whiskies, thank you." And the barman says, "Do you want them on the rocks?" Uncle Fauma looks out of the window at the waves crashing on the shore and then turns back to the barman and says, "Oh no. I think we will drink them in here, thank you."'

'It's stuff like that, Sione, what gets you fellas a bad name.

Makes people call Samoans ignorant.'

'True, and it's not ignorance really. It's innocence.'

'Reckon you're right, mate. Innocence. Reminds me of the other night.'

'Yes. We must've smoked at least an ounce that night.'

'And there's us sittin' in the lounge with eyes more red than Dracula's, and in walks your mother home early from church choir practice. "Sione. Sione," she says, "I know you been drinking the marijuana." And you start laughing and say, "Mum, you don't drink it. You smoke it." And whoosh, she clips your ears and says, "See, I told you. Now I know you been smoking the pots and the pans."'

'Yes, and do you remember the bamboo plant I had in my room?'

'Yeah.'

'Well, last night Mum threw it out.'

'Innocence, eh?'

'It's like, you know . . . I came out from Samoa when I was ten and apart from a few words, I couldn't speak English. Samoan is my mother tongue. I had to learn English at school.'

'That's a bit like what happened to us Maoris. I remember one of my uncles telling me about how it was when he was a little boy. He had to climb a barb-wire fence in order to get to school. As he did so he ripped his pants on a barb. He couldn't speak English very well and when the teachers asked him what happened to his pants he told her he smashed them. How did you find learnin' at school Sione? Was it hard?'

'Not really. It was actually just a case of having to learn English. There were two words I could never get right. They were *hungry* and *angry*. I couldn't tell the two words apart. There I was at school and the teacher looks at me and says, "Are you hungry?" Why should I be angry, I thought. So I look up at her and say, "Oh no, I'm fine thank you."'

'Samoa is a strange place. If you look in the Samoan hymn book, there's a song in there that doesn't say a thing about God or Jesus or anything like that. All it does is rave on verse after verse about what a beautiful place Samoa is. Let me tell you something. I had an uncle who was married. His wife died and he married again. Every evening at sunset the second wife got battered around the house, chucked outside and dragged into the middle of the village. Well, my oldest uncle went to the grave of the first wife and dug up the grave. He rearranged the bones. He put the shin bones up by the head, and floated the feet out to sea so the first wife's spirit couldn't move. Well everything was all right after that. The second wife didn't get chucked out or anything. The funny thing about it is the local church Minister found out about what my uncle had done and told my uncle off. And later the police came round and beat up my uncle for rearranging the bones. So that's the conflict. The old *wha* Samoa versus the new law.'

'It's like that with us Maoris quite a lot. We've got a lot in common. We're Polynesian. You say *paepae*, I say *paepae*. You have a *malae*, I have a *marae*. You say *malamalama*, I say *maramatanga. Ua malamalama.*

'Last night when we were on the grog, Saina says to me, "E Harris, pa mai le awhi." I laughed 'cause I knew what he said. We say pa mai te ahi, which means: Have you got a light? Cheers mate.'

'E Harris, pa mai te ahi.'

'Pa mai le awhi, Sione.'

The Kumara Plant

APIRANA TAYLOR

Poemurry, or sometimes Poormurry, is what I used to call myself. I didn't learn to say my name properly until I'd been to Maori language classes at night school for nearly a year.

My name is Pomare Hakaraia. It's a good name. I like it. Especially now I can say it properly. Sometimes I just stand in front of the mirror and say my name over and over. Pomare Hakaraia. Pomare Hakaraia.

In jail they called me Hak. It was Horse who first called me Hak. Horse and I done our time together and when we got out I went with him and stayed with the boys because I had nowhere else to go and because I wanted to patch up.

So that's how I ended up in a gang. I won't say which gang because I don't want people to think I speak for any particular gang. I speak for myself and it's not gangs I want to talk about, but sometimes I have to mention them just to help me talk about what I want to say.

Our President always said I wasn't one of them. I had to prospect for a long time before I got my patch. I stabbed a bloke and put a cop in hospital and ended up in the can doing lag number two before I got a letter from Horse saying I'd get my patch when I got out.

My parents drank a lot and used to beat me up and I think that partly because of that there is part of me that will be a gang member till the day I die. But not long after I got my patch I realized our President was right and most of me was not one of them.

It was during my third spell in prison I got interested in Maori things. We had a Maori minister. We called him Dog Collar. He was all right though. He didn't come across as being too holy. I felt I could talk to him.

From him I learned a little of the Maori language and what a *marae* is. He even told me the name of my tribe. Don't think of me as a brown-skinned Pakeha sitting in the can and suddenly turning into a Maori. I only went to a few of the minister's classes, but that was enough to get me interested.

Dark though I am I've never known much about Maori things. My parents never said anything to me about taku taha Maori. But as the minister talked I felt that he fed me something I need and I wanted more.

I remember once he talked about a chief who came from a small tribe. By the time that chief was an old man he'd made his tribe strong and powerful. That chief was an ancestor of mine and listening to stories about him made me feel proud.

In jail you're not allowed things like pot plants. But I wanted something to make my slot look better so I wrote and asked Aunty for a potato. I thought I'd put the potato in a dish of water and make it grow.

Well, when Aunty came she didn't bring a potato but in her bag she had some kumara so I asked her for one. She gave me a kumara and I put the kumara in a dish of water and soon shoots appeared on the kumara and then a stem and then leaves.

To me there was something simple, beautiful and Maori about that kumara. When my time was up and it was time for me to leave, a friend of mine asked me if he could have the kumara for his slot and so I gave it to him.

What I want to say is that somewhere in my life I've found an answer. I'm not even sure what the problem or question is. But I reckon I know the answer. I can't put in words exactly what the answer is. All I can say is that the answer is the kumara plant. *Tihei Mauriora*.

Ta Tatau

EMMA KRUSE VA'AI

I was eight years old when my father came home quite late one evening. As he came through the door, I noticed that he stooped a little and that his shirt had been rolled up and was stuck under his armpits. Hiding my curiosity, I went back to doing my homework, but noticed that when he sat down he winced and didn't lean back and stretch out in the comfortable and easy way he usually did.

'Are you all right, Manu?' I asked.

'Ia,' he replied haltingly.

I kept watching him until, impatient, he said, 'Be a good girl, Sarona, and get Mama's fan. OK?'

Knowing something unusual had happened, I went out and soon returned with the fan.

'Now,' he said, 'just fan my back. Ah! No, no – more gently!' And I wondered what terrible thing could have happened that caused a little fanning to give him so much pain. I slowed down my fanning and soon had it right.

'Good, good,' he said. He breathed in deeply, and then out very slowly as if letting the air leave too quickly might hurt him. As he did this, I thought to move round him and look at his back where I was fanning him.

'Uola – it's a picture!' I said, staring open-mouthed and feeling very confused at the lines and patterns. You know, we were always being told not to draw on anything – on the walls, on books – nor on bodies for that matter.

'Who did it – who drew the lines, Manu? Who put the picture on your back?' I asked him.

'Oh – just another – man,' he breathed.

'Why did he do it – and did he use a ruler? Will it rub off?'

'No it will never come off,' he told me, wincing, 'and keep

the fan going, my daughter – it eases the pain.'

At that moment my mother appeared, carrying my little brother wrapped up in a towel. 'There's your father, there's your sister,' she sang to the laughing Fatu as she came towards us. Then she paused as she realized my father was not responding to her. Two more steps, and then she knew.

'Why?' she asked, tight-lipped. Fatu was quiet and peeped out from the towel with one wide eye, almost as if he were frightened. 'Why have you made yourself suffer – why must you make me suffer?' she asked my father.

'I've begun it now and have to finish it.'

Nothing more was said between them that night, nor did they speak to each other throughout the rest of what became a very long month.

The following morning I woke late and felt mad with myself because my father had already left. I knew my mother was also mad with him but, unlike other times when she had been angry with the whole world, she seemed quiet and gently tired, and I very much wanted to put my arms around her.

'After school, come home quickly, Rona,' she said.

'I'll run all the way, Mama,' I told her as I reached up to kiss her, and then stooped to kiss Fatu who pulled my hair as Mama hugged me and pretended to straighten the back pleats of my school uniform.

After school my mother sent me to collect gogu and ti leaves. I collected quite a few from my Aunty Mele's tree and some from our old Fofo down the road. No one asked any questions – which made me feel a bit disappointed. I suppose everyone knew why I was collecting the gogu and ti leaves.

That evening my father was actually limping when he was brought home by his older brother. In fact, he could hardly stand up and had to be supported. My uncle said, 'Malo, Sala, be brave, it will be over soon.'

My mother's eyes filled with tears, but they didn't melt. She smiled stonily and thanked him for helping my father.

'Lots of cold water and leaves,' my uncle said, 'and don't dry his clothes in the sun – dry them in the shade. And don't sleep with him either!' he laughed.

My mother didn't laugh. She already had a bowl of ice

water and a cloth ready to ease the pain. 'He'll try to sleep and I'll stay awake,' she told my uncle, who kissed Fatu and me goodbye, then left.

That night, wearing nothing but his lavalava, my father slept on the floor on a bed of leaves. He slept face downwards and my mother sat beside him, spreading cold cloths across his back, pressing them gently, peeling them off, dipping them into cold water, and starting all over again. The only sounds that could be heard were my father's suppressed wincing and drawn-out breathing, and water trickling into a bowl when a cloth was squeezed.

For two weeks our lives revolved around my father. I gathered leaves and my mother kept the refrigerator well stocked with water. Of course, we lived in town and didn't have a proper Samoan fale which would have been cooler and better suited to my father's condition. As the days passed his 'tatau' spread steadily across his back, then moved forward and round his ribs, across his buttocks, and down onto his legs until it was just below his knees. His legs were tattooed one at a time and there wasn't much design on the front of them, which meant that in these places the tatau was mainly black and the needle pricks which drove in the ink were very close together.

For a while when his knees were being tattooed, my father could scarcely walk because the skin thickened into a tight, wet, sticky seal. Each step he took broke the skin and the whole process looked as if it were pure agony. As the tatau grew, so did the pain. He lost weight and strength, and he seemed to need support all the time – even for as simple a thing as getting up from a chair. I fanned him whenever I could. I wasn't used to seeing him so weak and helpless, and it was the least I could do. But I had to admit to myself that the designs were beautifully symmetrical, even if they did keep oozing, and had to be wiped with a cold sponge.

One day when my uncle had been called away to a meeting, Mama and I went to pick my father up. The car stopped about ten metres away from the fale. There were about six men there and my mother told me not to look, but just to talk to Fatu. I did talk to Fatu but I looked as well. One man sat away from the rest, leaning against one of the posts. He was strumming a guitar and singing. The others sat in a kind of circle around someone they were leaning over and looking down at. It reminded me of the day when my family was visiting my mother's village, and we sneaked over to the Women's Committee house to see a woman giving birth. We never saw anything, just a lot of women round the mother-to-be.

I said, 'Where's Manu, Mama?'

'He's coming soon, Rona,' she told me. 'Now be patient.' And then I saw a foot sticking out from the group. It was my father's foot and the men were holding him down. I started to cry, and Fatu started to cry too.

'Oi, Rona, stop crying,' my mother said as tears began to well up in her eyes too. 'Those men aren't just holding him down – they're helping him because of the pain the tattooing causes.'

'Then why doesn't he stop having it done? Why does he hurt himself so much?'

'Because he wants to have a pe'a,' Sala said slowly.

'Why?' I insisted.

'Because it's important to him,' she said quietly. 'Because if something's important to you, then you have to be prepared to endure all the pain and suffering that's necessary in order to get it and keep it.' I didn't really understand this because getting the salu from my mother for my various escapades was quite sufficient, and I couldn't see that any more pain was necessary.

The last part of the tatau was around the navel, and by that time the healing process had started in the areas on which the tattooing had begun. The patterns across my father's back now looked like grey welts because of the scabs forming on the cut skin. There was also a noticeable and distinctive smell – not unpleasant, but not entirely fresh either. It was the smell of a healing tatau.

Because the scabs were very dry and very itchy, the cold water treatment was abandoned and instead, grated coconut was roasted until it was hot, and then scooped onto a thin cloth which was tied securely into a ball. When hot oil was seeping through the cloth, the ball was pressed firmly onto the healing parts. This procedure seemed to give my father a great deal of relief.

After a while, everyone could see that between us we didn't have enough hands to look after my father, and that because of its European style, our house wasn't cool enough. My father decided to go home to his village where he could get better treatment. Once he was there, swimming in the salt water sped up the healing process, and his many young cousins sat with him in the airy and open fale. Some of them fanned him. Others kept a small fire going and roasted and shredded coconut over it. Because it was more comfortable for him not to wear any clothes, I knew the fale was no place for me, and made the most of the sea and my extended family until I had to return to our house with my mother, and go back to school.

When my father returned to us ten days later, he was so much stronger that he gave me a big hug and a kiss, and swung Fatu up into the air. After he had greeted us, he went into the kitchen and turned Mama round to face him. He held her very gently, and she seemed to cry very quietly for a long time.

Kerekere

JOSEPH C. VERAMU

Yesterday Penisamani Varasivitu, the headmaster of the Val-usaga District School invited me to have lunch with him at his newly-built teacher's quarters, constructed by the Government after Cyclone Meli. I had recently been posted to the school to teach Vernacular and Arts and craft and he was obviously very keen to let me know about the school and its environment.

'Do you like farming, Tarinava?'

'Yes,' I said eagerly. 'At Tavutavu Primary School I planted cassava, dalo and vegetables.'

I did not mention that this had been a lucrative part-time occupation after school hours and I had sold most of my produce at the local market. Many country school teachers had small animal husbandry or agriculture-based commercial ventures because they were expected to contribute financially to community projects and traditional ceremonies. Their salaries alone were too meagre for their domestic and community needs hence the extra economic activity. 'Well, I'm glad farming is in your blood,' he smiled. 'I like to see young teachers channel their pent-up energies towards macho things like that. It often keeps them out of trouble. You certainly can make quite a lot of money by planting yaqona. And don't tell me,' he added quickly, 'that you have no such aims. I expect my teachers to participate in community activities and sports too. I also want them to make a little extra pocket money for all the small contributions they make here and there. Education shouldn't just stop in the classroom. Anyway I don't believe all that rubbish that teachers should not have extra interests.'

I nodded.

'Yaqona is six dollars a kilo and the price is always rising. I admire you ambitious young teachers. That is the right spirit.' He paused. 'However, you must be very careful out here too.'

I told him quite frankly that I had bought a block of land in the city on loan and was especially keen to pay it off as soon as possible since the interest rates were forever climbing.

He nodded. 'Ambition, Tarinava has its own price though, as I have already hinted,' he said. 'Poor old Master Semati, Samisoni and Masikerei. I guess I'll just have to tell you about these things so you won't get into trouble. Mind you, these are just isolated incidents and don't happen often. But it's always nice to think about things like this, especially when we are waiting for lunch.'

His wife smiled from the kitchen but said nothing.

'It seems unusual to me that these teachers should have got into trouble for being industrious farmers.' I had intended to be witty but my voice unintentionally sounded sarcastic.

'You'll find out in good time, no doubt,' he said rather drily. 'But for your benefit I'll start off with Master Semati since his case was the most pathetic of all.

'Master Semati, who taught class four, hailed from Naitasiri, thirtyish with a slightly receding hair line. His students respected and feared him for at times, when he was morose, he would beat them. We had a problem, and we still have, of land. And since we did not have enough of it we were forever asking landowners whose lands were closer to ours to spare us some of their lands so the school could use it to plant root-crops and vegetables for our boarders and so that the teachers could plant for their own use.

'Since the land belonged to the Tawa clan who had more than a thousand acres, we did not feel it would hurt them to use an acre or two of their lands for our school needs.

'Master Semati however was very ambitious and wanted to plant a thousand mounds of yaqona and equal numbers for dalo and yams. He went to the Vasaki clan who gave him three acres of partly leached land on a valley to the eastern side of the school overlooking the Moto river.

'Master Semati who had also studied agriculture spent the first six months healing the sick land by putting in a lot of pig

259

manure which he purchased from a villager who kept a large piggery in an adjoining village. He created his own compost heap and supplemented this with some chemical fertilizer, NPK, I think. He dug many drainage ditches so that water would not wash away the top soil. He even planted plaintain and banana trees together with river-grass on the peripheries of the land to prevent further erosion.

'He worked so vigorously that the villagers began gossiping about him. They said that he was trying to store more of the riches of this world when inevitably they would rot unto dust. They said he was greedy and avaricious, somewhat like those roti-curry eating Indians who worship money. But Master Semati, being the pragmatist that he was, ignored their derogatory remarks. He said that the people were envious of him because they were not half as diligent as he. They had become complacent, satisfied with their small patches of cassava and in gathering around the yaqona bowl in the evenings, drinking themselves to exhaustion. His comments created some resentment among the people.

'His own problems however had just begun. The Vasaki clan members, seeing how well his yaqona plants and root crops grew, began to pester him daily with little requests for domestic goods which he was obliged to give. Gradually he began to understand the frightening implications of these requests.

'Virtually every day, Mesake, Jovilisi and Avaitia's children would come to Master Semati saying they had run out of kerosene, sugar or salt, tea or flour, and would Master Semati supply them with these needs. One day after Mesake's child had come requesting some foodstuff, Master Semati went to Mesake and politely told him that he was not very rich and would not be able to satisfy all his wants. Mesake told him obliquely that he would make a lot of money from using their lands and it was only fair that he helped him and other clan members in their small needs.

'When Master Semati explained that he had given a whale's tooth and had traditionally asked for land and had been granted the right to farm, Mesake hinted that such requests were usually not recognized in a court of law, should it come to that. If he, Master Semati, Mesake concluded, valued his crops, he should learn to be persevering and patient and satisfy the small needs of the landowners. Master Semati, choking with impotent anger, left Mesake's smelly leaking lean-to house made of rusting corrugated iron. He complained that the Vasaki clan had hundreds of acres of land which they didn't bother to use. He cursed loudly when one of the teachers told him that most people who owned a lot of lands were not usually interested in all that they had but in what outsiders showed interest in.

'Throughout the first year Master Semati was plagued with all sorts of requests. When Jovilisi's plump wife got pregnant again, Master Semati was besieged with requests for Red Cow Full Cream Milk. His students began to suffer, for Master Semati released his frustration through corporal punishment. This was an absolute taboo for teachers but he got away with it because none of his students was ever injured. The time came however when Master Semati could not bear it any longer.

'When Jovilisi's eighth child, Romuluse, aged ten, with boils all over his legs and posterior, on account of eating too much Japanese imported tinned fish, and who had a distinctly pungent odour since the Jovilisi family didn't believe in bathing, came in the morning asking for Bushells Blue Label Tea, Master Semati lost his temper.

'"Doesn't your father know that I spend money to buy all these things? Why can't he work for his family's needs? I'm sorry. As from this minute I will no longer give out any more food on charity."

'In the afternoon Mesake and Jovilisi came to see him.

'"Master Semati, we respect your wishes not to be bothered. We are sorry to see that a man of means cannot give a very small portion of what he has." He paused. "As from today, please do not advance by another inch on your farm."

'A day later when Master Semati went to clear weeds from his dalo patch he found that at least three hundred had been cut to pieces. A week later he found a hundred yam mounds upturned. His yaqona plants too began to die after being overturned or simply slashed.

'Nothing Master Semati did could stop the demise of his gardens.

'Last year he left the school in disgust vowing never to use land that had been leased in the traditional manner.' Master Varasivitu yawned and looked thoughtfully at me, 'I hope there'll be no repetition of this shameful incident.'

For Change

VILI VETE

Sione sat on a treek trunk surrounded by his newly harvested yams and vegetables. He kept slapping his thigh and shaking his head as if he could not believe that so much good fortune lay around him.

'There will be enough to pay somebody to help me replant the field with kumala and bananas,' he said, 'and to keep what we want.'

'I shall need to buy a new uniform for our son Tevita, a pair of trousers for you, and some cooking utensils,' Ana, his wife, said.

'Yes,' Sione said. 'There will be enough money for all this, you will see. God in His Mercy has given us another chance.'

'First the marketing,' Ana said, 'then the plans.'

Then and there, in a fever of impatience, they wove baskets for the yams and set to calculating quantities and prices.

As born farmers there was nothing to equal the deep satisfaction of a rich harvest. Later that night they went and offered their prayers at the church.

After the evening meal, Sione went straight to bed. Ana tidied up. The food scraps and banana leaves were put in a basket for the pigs. She then went to bed. She found Sione still awake. She knew he was calculating the profit and how they were to spend it. Ana stretched herself out beside him in the dim light of the kerosene lamp placed on the big chest in which they kept their valuables.

Sione turned abruptly towards her. Their hearts were full of joy. The silence was broken by the sound of a lali from the village. Sione reached out from under the tattered tapa and put out the light. In the straining darkness she felt his body moving towards her, his hands on her were trembling, and she felt her senses opening like flowers to his urgency. She waited for him to come to her.

Next morning, Sione went to market. The horse-drawn cart was laden with baskets of yams, talo, cabbages and bunches of bananas. The earth had yielded richly.

It was early afternoon when Sione started back home. He had sold all his crops. He was whistling, and ignored the hot sun. When he was passing the home of his village's 'eiki, somebody called out, 'Sione, Sione, stop a minute!'

Sione stopped the horse. 'What is it?'

The man came closer and said: 'I have good news for you. The 'eiki heard that you had a rich harvest. He sent me.'

'So, he sent you to congratulate me? Is that the good news?'

'No,' said the man. 'His son arrived yesterday from the city to spend his school holidays here.'

'That is good news for everybody,' Sione said warily. He was thinking of his own son, hoping to see him at home that day.

'Yes, of course!' the man said. 'The 'eiki wants every farmer on his land to produce a basket of yams. You are to bring a puaka toho for the celebration.' Sione didn't know what to say.

'What's wrong, Sione? Aren't you proud to be honoured with such a task? Every person here longs for that honour.'

'Nothing wrong,' said Sione.

He wanted to strike the man; he wanted to ram the words down into his throat. But he managed with great effort to control himself.

The man left. Sione drove on. When he reached home it was late afternoon. Ana came out of the cooking shed. Smoke had forced tears out of her eyes. She hurried to him as he jumped down from the cart.

'You are early, Sione! What happened? Did you manage to sell everything?' she asked. Sione didn't say anything.

'Sione, are you all right? Are you ill?'

Sione didn't answer her questions.

'Damn it!' he said loudly. 'I am getting sick of it.'

Ana was very surprised. She stared at him. For the fifteen

years of their marriage she had never heard him say such words. She thought that he had been drinking.

Sione quietly unharnessed the horse. He repeated the words. After tying the horse to a coconut tree he hurried into the house. Ana was worried. Sione called out that he was hungry.

Ana went to the nearest banana tree and cut out a leaf. She took it to the cooking shed and placed it in the middle of the earthen floor. She then took the paka from the fire, poured the water out into a kumete and distributed the food on the banana leaf.

From a box at the corner, she took out a big basin which contained lū that had been cooked in coconut milk. She put some in a coconut bowl and placed it on the opposite side. Sione came in, sat down on a dried coconut leaf, and faced her.

'You say the grace, Ana. I am not in the mood,' he said.

'Bless the food which we are about to receive, make it for our good use, for Christ's sake.'

'Amen.'

Sione started to eat. Ana watched him. He said nothing. There was a crushed look about him which spoke of the deep hurt he had suffered. He had always wanted to own his own land. Through the years there had been the hope, growing fainter each year, that one day he would be able to call a small portion of land his own. Now, even his son knew it would never be. Like his father before him. Ana broke the silence by asking what had happened. She was sure now that he was not drunk.

'On my way back I was stopped by Ohule, the 'eiki's matāpule. He told me that the 'eiki wanted our puaka toho for the feast to celebrate the arrival of 'Amanaki Lelei, his son, after his first term at secondary school.'

'So,' Ana said, 'we are finally honoured.'

'We are being robbed again.'

'What do you mean?' Ana said as she started eating.

'Ana, don't you understand? We, the eaters of the soil, toil from sunrise to sunset to get enough to feed ourselves, pay our son's school fees, and to have some for other purposes. But that 'eiki he does nothing, but just eat, shit, and sleep.'

Ana listened patiently. 'Last week we sent him the best of our harvest and your new tapa. This week he wants the puaka toho which we were going to sell and pay for Tevita's school fees. That old . . . '

'He is not human,' Ana declared. 'He has no love in him. He has always demanded our best, ignoring the needs of us poor creatures.'

The memory of their son, who was going to arrive at any moment, came to her mind. She thought about his future. This brought tears to her eyes, hot and bitter, flowing and flowing as if the very springs of sorrow had been touched in her body.

Sione listened to her but it was a sham; a poor, shabby pretence to mask his feelings.

'Well, what . . . ?' Their dog barked and ran outside.

'Somebody is coming,' Sione said.

The sound of the cart became louder and finally stopped outside the fale mohe. Sione stood up and, without a word, walked out with long, quick strides. Ana followed him.

Outside were two men on a cart. Both were dressed traditionally to show their status. They both leaped down. The one who was tall and burly did all the talking and the other one, who was thin and insignificant, stood silently and agreed with what his companion said.

'*Mālō e lelei*, Ana mo Sione.'

Sione didn't speak, his face was overlaid with misery and anger.

But Ana managed to speak up. She seemed to have completely forgotten her earlier comments. She now showed the typical island custom – eager to show any wealth and disguising hurt with an easy-going manner.

'*Mālō e lelei, ongo matāpule*,' Ana said. 'How are you?'

'*Sai pē*,' the two men replied, one after the other. And before they spoke of their visit, Ana spoke up again.

'Come in, come into the house and make yourselves comfortable.' She turned to lead the way, but the tall man stopped her.

'It's very kind of you, Ana, but because we are in a hurry I will explain the purpose of our visit.'

'Do not speak of your visit. We expected you. My husband

had told me. We are proud. Bring the cart to the other side of the cooking shed.'

She turned to Sione and commanded him to get the ripe bunch of hopa which was being kept for Tevita, their son. Sione slowly turned to do what he was told.

'Is that the pig?' asked the thin man.

'Yes, that big one,' Ana said, still watching her husband go.

'*Maumau mo'oni!*' he said.

'It's all right,' Ana said as she went close to the pig. 'We fed him up for two years now. We had intended to sell it to help finance our son's studies.'

'So, we had better leave it, and take another one,' the fat man said.

'No, you take it; you know our duty comes first, even though we are poor,' Ana said.

The two men looked at each other, and then acted immediately. They tied the pig's feet together and loaded it on to the cart. They both leaped up to go.

'Wait,' Ana stopped them. 'Sione! Sione! Hurry up!' Sione came with the kau hopa and lifted it up to the fat man.

'*Mālō 'aupito*,' the fat man said. '*Mo nofo ā.*' The horse moved and the wheels turned.

'*Mo ō ā*,' Ana replied.

As the cart disappeared, Sione went and fed the pigs and chickens. Ana went into the cooking shed to tidy it. She found that all the food scraps had been eaten by the pigs. She put the basin into the pot and hung them on a nail on a corner post. It was late evening. She felt hot and decided to bathe. She went to the fale kaukau and got the empty kerosene tin which they used to fetch water and went to the well.

When she went into the fale mohe, Sione was already in bed. She took the comb and a bottle of coconut oil from the pola of the wall, sat beside him, oiled her hair, and then combed and plaited it. Sione turned to her.

'Ana.'

'Yes? What is it?'

'You know, I was afraid.'

'You mean, you are afraid of me?'

'No, Ana, I am not afraid of you – I love you.'

'But what do you mean?'

'I mean, I was scared to say anything when the two mat-āpule were here.'

'Why?' Ana asked as she stretched herself on the other side of the lamp which was between them.

'I don't understand – probably I was very tired – but no – I hate them all.'

'Sione, I always found you a man of courage and love, but since this occasion, I noticed the change in you,' Ana said.

'Yes; Ana, you are right – but not enough courage, as those young educated people have – you know, it was in my mind since the birth of our son . . . '

'What was in your mind?' Ana asked.

'That one day, I would speak to the 'eiki of the village about it – but I couldn't – I couldn't because there is so much of our ancestors in me – so much tradition.'

'I don't understand what you are talking about, Sione.'

'I am talking about that fat man in the village and his authority. He uses it wrongly. I might call him a senseless, selfish person.'

'But, Sione, you forget that he owns the land.'

'And God owns us and the land,' Sione said. 'If we believe that there is a God – God of Love – who demands nothing for us but to love our neighbours as ourselves, then we should act likewise.'

'Then you are wrong, Sione, for you hate your neighbour, the 'eiki of our village.'

'That is different, for he was not asking but confiscating.'

'I can see what you mean now,' she said.

'Hard labour has taught me to think and understand, you know. I always think that more than half of the problems in our community are caused by misunderstanding. People sometimes say that white collar jobs are discouraging young people from farming, but I disagree. There were lots of tal-ented farmers who gave up farming because of that mis-understanding. They looked for other jobs or migrated to other places.' The memory of their son came into his mind.

He kept silent but Ana asked: 'Do you think that Tevita would like to be a farmer?'

'I hope not,' Sione said. 'Unless God helps those men

change from brutality to love and understanding our needs.'

'No!' Ana said. 'Not those old men. They are as hard as iron. We hope their successors are better.'

'Yes, yes,' Sione said. 'I hope that our son be changed too.'

'And be successful in his studies so he can get a job in town,' Ana said.

The lamp ran out of fuel and Sione put it on the wooden chest. Sounds of singing and laughter from the 'eiki's celebrations were heard.

Ana drifted into uneasy sleep. In her dreams, she saw her son sitting behind a desk, with a line of pens in his pocket. He was talking to two black men in a language she couldn't understand.

Paradise

IAN WEDDE

It was winter. The wind blasted from the south-west, straight off the pack ice, he imagined. The rain, with a rattle of hail in it, had soaked through his parka to his skin. Water was roaring in the storm drains. The fingers with which he held the mail felt like parsnips. He kept his head down and thought of double whiskeys and saunas. The addresses on the envelopes blurred and ran with wet. His trousers were plastered to his legs. He turned corners and shoved letters into boxes by memory and instinct, pausing from time to time to pick up rocks in anticipation of certain dogs: just let any mutt try him today. Wait till they think they've got you then let them have it, yiiii yi yi.

The corgi was worrying at his trousers and had got a few nips into his ankle as well. He marched up the garden path with the dog hanging on and snarling. Dingaling, knock knock. Blast of warm as the door opens. Is this your dog madam? Yes . . . He let poochie have the rock then booted the animal into the shrubbery. Let's call it quits now lady, I won't claim for the trousers. Back up the path, shreds of pant leg flapping. That made it even colder. Fuck them. Why all the mail, it wasn't Mother's Day. Half was Tisco Television Repairs accounts, the rest was Readers' Digest bullshit. The energy chocolate was so hard with cold he almost broke his teeth. Below him the city was invisible. Because he was so wet the walking no longer kept him warm. Sickie time tomorrow. It would take at least two days to thaw. Have a steam bath, lie in bed dreaming Gauguin, move the TV in, smoke dope.

He turned a corner watching for Honey, a killer Alsatian who hunted silently. The top letter in his bundle was for

270

Taimaile, ha ha ... the envelope plastered with gorgeous Samoan stamps, *tropique sensuel*: fish, butterflies, lagoons, all that. Handfuls of hail struck him in the face and froze on to the surface of his parka. Fuck, *oneone, one ... one ... oneone* ... The litany had a certain rhythm to it. Homage to J. J. Rousseau. He flapped on. Then it began to snow. Dear Oates, we miss you.

Peeking out at six the next morning before deciding whether to ring the post office, he saw the stars burning with cold fire in the firmament. The air was as still as ice. Moonlight lit snowy pine trees on the far side of the valley. Frost had set on the surface of snow in the yard. The crystals glittered in light from the kitchen door. His breath smoked out through the crack. Wow. Shut the door, turn on the heater, make coffee. He drank it listening to silly patter on the pre-breakfast programme, then slewed and crawled in the car to town. Along the roadside were abandoned vehicles 'of various denominations'. He pondered this phrase which had come so glibly to mind. From the left hand window of the car he could see the empty harbour, very still and moonlit, with channel beacons flashing green and red. Navigational aids for Li Po. Beyond the fluorescent pallor of the water was the peninsula wrapped in snow. It looked to him like an immense old samurai lizard crouched in patience until dinosaurs should once again rule the world, when man with his silly services would have bred himself out of survival. Gone out, and been some time, and not been missed. With avalanches of loose shale the ridges and peninsulas would rise on short legs, open ancient eyes, and taste the foul air with forked tongues.

Or, he now thought, as the car minced across icy satin, the peninsula was like a lady's thigh, very white. Next he saw a lizard crouched on a lady's thigh. Then *he* was here. Lady, lady, fold your thighs upon my ears. The water turns like a limb and the dry land rustles its claws. I'm ascetic at heart. Near town they'd dumped grit on the road. The car gripped and sped. Reality equals velocity as a function of direction. Inspiration: whatever comes out eventually and needs to be purified again. Why so luxurious then. Easy: the true voluptuary needs to be able to draw a clear bead on the target.

There has to be a bare firepath. The metaphor's formally not factually violent. Oh darling you're killing me. Summer pleasures are blurry and fun but their peaks lack piquancy.

Next question.

If survival's not enough, what is?

Oates, can you hear me?

What an immense relief to get out of the mailroom after sorting. He slipped on his dark glasses. The cold air poured down his throat. The light had a musical quality: it rang like burnished metal. The dark latticework of twigs of the Chinese poplars was in perfect focus. He felt extra sharp. There was a nice power in selection and discrimination: a buoyancy. Cleaning the teeth of your senses, keeping them brighteyed. Then wallow and don't miss a thing. Oboy!

To Taimaile he delivered letters smeared with *fauve* extravagance. It left him cold. He was digging the Pacific horizon from his high vantage point. Cortez: 'So that's what it's called.' Here and there the snow had melted, but mostly it was still thick with a frosted crust. Schools were closed. The dogs were playing with kids and mostly ignored him. He whistled and slid. The Four Square grocer gave him a cup of tea. The Catholic Bishop's sister gave him a whiskey and a slice of plumcake. He accepted a chocolate fish from a little boy, and a free packet of chips from the fish and chip shop. Everyone felt magnanimous and cheerful. Everywhere people were playing in the snow. A few businessmen with pissed-off expressions trudged to work. So their Ford Falcons wouldn't start. Let them hike off their flatulence, their greasy breakfasts.

Oh yes he was 'in a crowing temper', to borrow the phrase from a dear friend who'd recently used it with some bitterness. A few weeks ago he'd been toe-springing up the hill under crisp autumn skies when she'd whizzed past in her little car. He'd seen her hand make a brief vicious signal at the window. It had spoiled his day. He'd realized that his limber pleasure was solitary. Putting letters in boxes. Her car had disappeared downhill taking his joy with it like a little fluttering trophy.

But today sparrows scuffled shrilly where horse turds unfroze in sunlight. Below him the city glittered under a thin veil of coppery fumes. He was satisfied.

But he needed a leak . . . fortunately his route reached the limits of the city's outer suburbs. For some of it he actually walked beside fields of cows. The children in this fringe neighbourhood kept ponies. There was a long lane, petering out into an unsealed track, which ran steeply up a hillside among stands of large oak trees. He had to go some distance up this to serve a house situated back from the road in a spacious well-planted garden. With relief and pleasure he stood staling loudly into a frosty patch of snow, attempting to write his initials, or 'Oates': this obsession . . . Above the small port where he lived was a monument to Scott of the Antarctic. The expedition had sailed from there. Well, you needed signals like that. He was going to be poet. That was *his* raise on survival. There was this soft whine as though some bowel was about to barf loudly. He was just nine years old. He found himself thinking of Scott of the Antarctic of whom his dad had been telling him and of brave Oates. He imagined Oates going out and taking his pants down. It all came out in rhyming couplets like someone was making his finger crawl like Oates over white. How long does it take to take a shit in Antarctica, how long to write rhyming couplets at nine? Oh Oates was dead, frozen, and he was a boy poet, frozen also, aghast, the feat accomplished. 'Brave Oates' he called it and showed it to his dad who beat him with the back of a hairbrush. It was necessary to survive, he decided, remembering the lines that had been destroyed, tracks leading out somewhere he would return from soon. It was a fiction he clung to. Meanwhile steam rose through the crisp air to the branches of the oaks above which he could see the faultless blue of the winter sky. Everything was fresh and lovely after the rain and the gales. He whistled between his teeth, craning his neck to look up through the branches.

'Aie!'

Today's bringdown.

She was standing by the gate with a hand to her mouth, a Chinese lady in her late thirties.

Chinese?

Someone had moved and he hadn't even noticed. The last lady hadn't been Chinese, what's more she'd never come to the gate.

'What you-do, what you-do!'

'Excuse me,' turning away and swinging his stream with him. Behind him he heard the gritting of gravel under her heels. Reality. Looking back he saw that she was still there, in fact she'd moved closer. The last of his steam drifted away into the cerulean. The air, calm and cold, was filled with birdsong. There they stood. Between them the immaculate surface of the snow was spoiled by strafings of sour yellow. She pointed at this, mutely aghast, stamping forward on small feet, her body held rigid as though in formal preparation for some martial ballet. She was right, of course (he sensed that her outrage was aesthetic rather than scatalogical): he *had* ruined it, a crude barbarian squirting urine around the immaculate interior of this winter morning. He noticed how the blood had risen under the clear surface of her skin, a kind of emotional haemophilia, passionate vulnerability. Her aristocratic nostrils were pinched whitely together with rage or disgust.

She turned and marched back towards her gate. It was not a retreat. Her back was stiff with the pride of a formal victor.

'I'm sorry,' he said after her. Bugger it, good pissing spots were scarce. This one had been idyllic. Birds in the branches, a paddock on the other side where in summer the ragwort was a sullen blaze of flower heads. Worth the steep fifty yards' grunt to the single letterbox there, to stand pissing in sunlight as John Clare might have done in 1860 in Epping Forest

> I found the poems in the fields
> And only wrote them down

or Li Po in the courtyard of the Empress, leaning a dipsomaniacal elbow against exquisite marble, or more likely splashing his rice wine into the pond housing ornamental carp. These thoughts improved his spirits.

All the same, next day, he approached the lane without joy. The name he was delivering was Ngaei, a doctor. So he'd met Madame Ngaei, the wife of a Chinese doctor. It occurred to him that it was a good name for an acupuncturist:

'Ngaaeeeeiiii!!'

Ha ha. It was another pristine day. Shoving the doctor's

drug company handouts into the letterbox he cast a glance up the driveway to the house. There in sunshine he saw Madame Ngaei standing with the flaccid hose of a vacuum cleaner in one hand. She was singing.

Takem han
Ahm stlanga in paladeye

It was poignant enough to make him squawk with laughter. The door slammed. He felt ashamed and barbaric. He really liked her. The style and economy with which she'd registered her complaint had been lovely. He admired her sense of form. Also, an admission he suppressed, he was flattered that she'd seen his cock. He trudged down the hill with a sense of failure worrying at his trouser leg, which he longed to lug to her front door and confront her with:

'This your poochie (succubus) lady?'

Bam!

And facing her, his grossness annulled by this immaculate gesture.

He'd recaptured his pissing spot but he wouldn't crow again for a while, no, nor throw his head back! Oh, his self-esteem had been badly punctured! He was in love. What a lousy trade. In return for being allowed (by default) to piss, he was a victim of that 'formal violence' . . . ah fuckwit! . . . his morning monologues were now from the heart, as his car veered on the black asphalt, as he contemplated the moon's pale carpet rolled out upon the water.

Daily he trudged up the steep lane, shoved glossy pharmaceutical advertising material into the letterbox of Doctor Ngaei, and pee'd just down from the gate, sometimes into mud, sometimes into an ochre rivulet which coursed down the slope from a ditch further up the road, sometimes into snow, sometimes on to the loamy surface of the verge.

Inspiration! Purify me . . . Always he experienced a nagging sense of desecration. The muddy rivulet was beautiful before he augmented it. Seeds germinated in the rich loam. Frost crystals on fallen twigs were blasted by his stream. He observed the seasons with uncharacteristic attention. Within

275

the small enclosure of his woody urinal he watched the light grow softer and dimmer as the oaks put out leaves. Along the verge a variety of tiny flowers appeared, minute blue or pink corollas turning their faces upwards. With shame and despair he pissed on them. He couldn't help it. The moment he'd put the doctor's garish rubbish in the letterbox, his bladder ached with tension. Soon even spring had passed and the lane was filled with the honeysweet scent of gorse-flower. To this he added his own bitter fragrance. Bees and flies buzzed and hummed in the dense growth of the oaks whose leaves broadcast a constant spray of sticky sap. As summer advanced this secretion stopped and the flies turned their attentions to his staling ground. They were transformed from summer musicians into gutter communi-cators of pestilence. Again and again he imagined the blood rising under her perfect skin. He could no longer distinguish between her real outrage in the face of his barbaric intrusion last winter, and the passion with which, in his imagination, he saw her responding to his presence this summer. His daily desecrations were painfully fraught with hope. Burn-ing flowers with his hot urine, he felt 'love's tender shoot cracking the cold clod of his heart'. Ashamed, he continued to be flattered. His atavistic id continued to regard this daily ritual as a ceremonial of display. He imagined that the exquisite Madame Ngaei watched it from behind the trees.

His daydreams, fed by his own memories of travel, were filled with fantasies of her past life. He saw her as a young secretary with the Esso company in Hong Kong, riding the morning ferry from Kowloon across to Victoria Island, per-fect in a cheongsam, turning the heads of clumsy tourists. Sometimes he saw her as a nurse on the floating clinic in the Aberdeen inlet, surrounded by a chaos of sampans . . . or having dinner with a young doctor, probably Swiss, in the Tai Pak restaurant. Stimulated by images of food, his fan-tasies took on a sexual coloration. He saw her clitoris as a delicate morsel in a bowl of soup.

At night he awoke yelling from a dream of a lizard scrab-bling on dry claws up her white thigh.

When, now, he went to piss on the verge just down from her gate, he experienced a painful moment of paralysis before his stream consented to flow.

He trembled at the prospect of having to deliver a registered letter to her door.

He caught glimpses of her. Once she was in the greengrocer's when he delivered mail there. Her perfume was subtle and subdued. His senses culled it from the dying breaths of cabbages and mushrooms. He banged into the door going out.

He asked for, and got, a transfer. It was late summer. The verge was beginning to be covered by a mantle of dry oak leaves. He pissed for the last time. His water splashed where gallons had gone before. He knew this spot more intimately than any on earth. He'd observed how it was never the same from one day to the next. Madame Ngaei had taught him something.

'I may be some time.'

With relief and despair he walked off down the hill, into exile.

From the autumn garden the beautiful Madame Ngaei noted, in due course, his absence. She sighed with regret. It had become an amusement. The clumsy boy had been fetching and arrogant. From time to time she'd imagined his crude embraces. She'd occasionally enjoyed watching him pee. She'd stood in her hiding place in the garden with a hand over her mouth while she giggled. Now she stood in the front garden of her house, in the late summer sunshine. She was vacuuming. Under her breath she sang.

> Takem han
> Ahm stlanga in paladeye

On the far side of the lane, beyond the oaks which she could once again begin to see through as their leaves fell, the hill paddock was filled with a urinous frenzy of yellow ragwort. How barbaric nature could be. How she longed to be educated in its gross intrusions. How she hated winter which was coming fast.

Levuka

VIRGINIA WERE

Levuka is the capital of Ovalau, a large volcanic island East of Viti Levu. It used to be the capital of Fiji until the shift to Suva in 1881.

The pioneering atmosphere is still strong in this somnolent town of 1400, a perfect base for excursions into the mountains, along the winding coast, or out to the barrier reef 1 km offshore. Levuka is one of the most peaceful, pleasant and picturesque places in Fiji.

Ed the American walked along the beach, a small straw hat squatting on his head.

Anne followed him. Anne whose father cut his face out of the only wedding picture her parents had, stuck in the face of Al Jolson, a white guy who painted himself black, sang Mammy. Her mother cried. It was their fiftieth wedding anniversary.

Ed said, I want I want I want to be the laziest man in the world, I want to have the biggest collection of Hawaiian shirts in the world.

Anne said, but Ed, this isn't Hawaii, this is Fiji, and you've already got more shirts than you can wear.

You dip you dip you dip dip dip stick, we're tourists, we gotta look like tourists, and see they all wear those shirts; hibiscus flowers on a red background, hibiscus flowers on a green background.

But that's Hawaii Ed and you can buy them back home, this is Fiji Ed and we gotta have something Fijian, this is Lautoka.

Levuka Anne Levuka.

O.K., but it's still Fiji.

*

278

Ed took the small straw hat off his head and put it on a rock. He began to take off his clothes. Is it safe to swim here Anne? What did the guide book say about sharks, don't they like to hang just off the reef, I've heard that they like to feed on the small fish that live on the reef.

Every day we went swimming every day. The time we went snorkelling one boy jump over and caught one baby shark. Boy! I can't believe it. Can you believe that one boy just jump over and caught one shark?!

Ed said you have to talk slowly to them, and use lots of sign language. You have to repeat yourself, and then they understand.

They began to wade out along the reef and she took his hand to steady herself on the rough coral. He stumbled and she felt his weight on her arm. Watch out Ed!

The woman in the curry shop said come New Year we'll take action. If things haven't improved by New Year there'll be a bloodbath in Fiji.

She says we hate them. If we grow some food, some taro or cassava on the land, if we grow something they come along and they pull it out. On their land they grow nothing but flowers, all they want to do is eat and sleep. The Fijians get drunk on kava and they go mad.

An Indian will not do this, but if he is pushed far enough he will take out a knife and kill; he will kill someone.

This is the difference.

They were nearly on the edge now, the water was light turquoise. Suddenly there was fifty feet of water below them. They were over the edge . . .

Down there on the pale bottom dark shapes moved.

At first it was frightening, their breathing sounded quick and ragged in their snorkels, then it slowed.

They drifted, hardly moving their arms and legs and they let the current take them down the edge of the reef. Brain coral, sponges, delicate trees grew up towards the light. The

279

fish flickered below them, bathing in the tentacles of sea anemone, browsing in the coral.

Spots, whirling stripes, blue next to yellow, electric blue, curious eyes, long snouts probing the coral.

Nearby a Fijian woman waded with a basket along the reef. She moved with a mesmerizing slowness. Her dress was wet and it clung to her black skin. She had a line on a plastic reel which she flung out over the reef.

Ed said to the woman in the curry shop, if I was to ask you for tea, how would you make it?

The woman was confused.

He repeated it. He spoke very slowly as if to a child. With a teabag and boiling water, in a cup, or with tea leaves in a tea pot . . . ? If I was to ask for tea . . . ?

The tea was fifty cents.

Finally he decided he would have a cup. He sat down.

Anne said to her where will you go?

We will stay here, this is our home. We will send our children to school in Australia or New Zealand; we know that they will never come back but they must go, they must get an education.

The woman in the hotel who gave them their keys wore a frangipani behind her ear. Everywhere there were shells, big white clam shells in the garden, in the corridors, in the rooms, on the verandahs.

Sad Pacific music filled the hotel.

Where can I buy a souvenir where can I buy one of those carvings those wooden bowls where can I buy one of those necklaces? Shell necklaces, bones seeds teeth coconuts.

Pineapples are cheap, coconuts just fall from the trees. You can hear them at night. Crash! And the dogs barking the sound of the village drum. Bang!

Did you hear that Ed what is it I don't like the sound of that.

Don't worry dear must have been a drum.

Sounds like *drums!*

*

They left on the next flight to Suva. Their suitcases bulged with carvings, shells bones teeth seeds, and Ed's shifts.

Ed started praying when he saw the Indian pilot open his manual and read it, flick some switches and then study the manual some more. The turbulence began and he felt his heart in his mouth. It was going to be a rough ride back to Suva.

The clouds came down the mountains and it began to rain.

Notes on Authors

MARJORIE TUAINAKORE CROCOMBE (Cook Islands). Born 1930 in Raratonga, educated in New Zealand; worked for the Cook Island Education Department. Lived in Canberra, then Papua New Guinea. At the University of the South Pacific she was for a time editor of *Mana*, which fostered South Pacific writing. At present administers the Auckland University Centre for Pacific Studies.

YVONNE DU FRESNE (NZ). Born in the Manawatu in 1929. Teacher, author of two novels and two collections of stories. Much of her fiction reflects the immigrant Danish community in which she grew up.

VINCENT ERI (PNG). A graduate of the University of Papua New Guinea, he was for a time PNG High Commissioner to Australia and is author of the first Papua New Guinean novel, *The Crocodile*.

JANET FRAME (NZ). Born 1924, Frame is, together with poet Allen Curnow, New Zealand's most honoured writer – author of a dozen novels, four collections of short stories and one of poems, together with a three-volume autobiography collected under the title *An Angel at my Table* which was made into the Jane Campion movie of the same name.

MAURICE GEE (NZ). Born 1931. After an MA in English from Auckland University, he worked as a teacher, then as a librarian, before becoming a full-time writer. Has written children's fiction, television scripts and short stories in addition to the nine novels which have earned him his place as one of New Zealand's major writers.

VANESSA GRIFFEN (Fijian of Samoan-European ancestry). Born Fiji 1952 (both parents also Fiji-born); graduate of the University of the South Pacific, where she now teaches in the Department of Politics; and PhD from Sydney. She has published a number of stories, soon to be collected for publication.

EPELI HAU'OFA (Tonga). Born 1939, Papua New Guinea; graduate of the University of New England (Australia) and McGill (Canada), and PhD from ANU (Canberra). Currently Professor of Sociology in the University of the South Pacific, Fiji. Has worked in the South Pacific as anthropologist, as consultant to the Asia Development Bank and the World Bank, and as Private Secretary to the King of Tonga. He has published a number of anthropological studies and reports, and is the author of two collections of short stories.

SHONAGH KOEA (NZ) is a full-time writer who lives in Auckland. She has published one novel and three collections of stories.

JOHN KOLIA (PNG). Born John Collier, Sydney, 1931, of English-Australian parentage, he moved to Papua New Guinea in 1956, and was naturalized PNG citizen in 1975, changing the spelling of his name. Despite this, he sees himself as a writer in the English tradition and has been criticized by Melanesian writers as 'neo-colonialist'. He is a prolific writer with a long list of published fiction and non-fiction.

GRAEME LAY (NZ). Born in Foxton, 1944; graduated Victoria University. Has published two novels, two collections of short stories, and a travel book on Polynesia.

BILL MANHIRE (NZ). Born in Invercargill, 1946, graduated from University of Otago, one of New Zealand's most notable poets. Also teacher of Creative Writing, and Reader in English at Victoria University. Five collections of poems published, and two of short fiction.

OWEN MARSHALL (NZ). Born 1941, graduate of the University of Canterbury, schoolmaster. As a writer he has concentrated exclusively on the short story, publishing six collections, and is widely regarded as one of New Zealand's two or three finest practitioners of the form.

PHILIP MINCHER (NZ). Born 1930, retired engineer, has published two collections of short stories and one of poetry, and written several plays for radio.

MICHAEL MORRISSEY (NZ). Born in Auckland, 1942. Author of eight collections of poems and three of short stories. Anthologist of, and advocate for, 'the new fiction'.

RAYMOND PILLAI (Fiji Indian). Born in Ba, Fiji, graduate of the University of the South Pacific, where he taught English for a time, and of the University of Southern Illinois. Moved to Wellington in 1991 where he teaches English as a second language. He has published one collection of short stories as well as poetry and plays.

JOHN PUHIATAU PULE (Niue/NZ). Born in Niue 1962. Brought to New Zealand in 1964. His *The Shark that Ate the Sun* is the first published fiction in English by a Niuean writer.

JANETTE SINCLAIR (NZ). Born in Dunedin, spent part of her childhood in Fiji, and now lives in Wellington. 'Outlines of Gondwanaland' won the John Cowie Reid Award for 1988.

J C STURM (NZ Maori). Born 1927. Describes herself as 'half Maori, half Pakeha – retired librarian and grandmother'. She is also the widow of the poet James K. Baxter and has been writing short stories, articles and reviews on and off for forty years. First anthologized in World's Classics *New Zealand Stories, Second Series*, edited by C. K. Stead, 1966. Her published collection of stories is *The House of the Talking Cat*, 1983.

SUBRAMANI (Fiji-Indian). Born Labasa 1943. Holds a Personal Chair in the Department of Literature, University of the South Pacific. Has published a study of South Pacific literature, a study of 'the pursuit of Reality in fiction', and a collection of short stories.

MARGARET SUTHERLAND (NZ) has published three novels and two collections of short stories. A fourth novel has been completed. She won several literary awards in New Zealand before moving to Australia in 1986 where she now lives and works as a writer and music teacher.

ANNE TARRANT (NZ). Born in Wellington in 1932; lives in Dunedin. She is married to Professor of Geology, Douglas Coombs, and has three children. Has published a number of short stories.

APIRANA TAYLOR (NZ Maori). Born Wellington, 1955. Tribal affiliations Te Whanau-a-Apanui, Ngati Porou and Taranaki. Educated at Te Aute College. His publications include three collections of poems: *Eyes of the Ruru*, *3 Shades* and *Tangi Aroha*, two collections of stories: *Rau Aroha: A Hundred Leaves of Love*, *Ki te Ao: New Stories* and a play entitled *Te Whanau a Tuanui Jones*.

EMMA KRUSE VA'AI (Samoan). Born Apia, 1956. Educated in Samoa and New Zealand, trained as a teacher and is currently lecturing in English at the National University of Samoa.

JOSEPH C VERAMU (Fiji). A writer in both English and Fijian, his stories have been serialized in Fijian papers. Has published a collection of stories, *The Black Messiah*, and a fiction for children, *The Shark*. Formerly a schoolteacher, he is now lecturer in Education at the University of the South Pacific.

VILI VETE (Tonga). Born 1941. Principal of St Andrews (Anglican) School, Nuku'alofa, is the author of several stories and a two-act play.

IAN WEDDE (NZ). Born 1946, graduate of Auckland University, the most talented New Zealand poet of his generation, and more recently fiction writer, he has published eight collections of poems, one of short stories, and two novels.

VIRGINIA WERE (NZ). Born 1960. Studied photography and painting at Elam School, University of Auckland. Has published one collection of poems and short stories. Lives in Sydney.

Glossary

arapo	night time (literally: night road)
aroha	love
bedstemoder	grandmother
cassava	tapioca
dalo	Fijian for *taro* (staple food plant)
'eiki	noble
elavo	men's house
fale kaukau	bathroom
fale mohe	bedroom (separate house for sleeping)
fanau	family
fullah	fellow
hafa-kasi	half-caste
harakeke	flax
hui	meeting
kapu tī	cup of tea
karaka	NZ native tree producing edible berry
karakia	prayer
kau hopa	fruit tree, like banana
kaumatua	old person, elder
kava	ceremonial drink from part of the pepper plant
kēhua	ghost
kei were koe	lest you forget
koha	gift
kumara	sweet potato
kumete	ceremonial *kava* bowl
lali	large drum
lavalava	wrap-around skirt worn by male or female
lū	*taro* leaves
Magafaoa	family
malae/marae	open space in village for meetings
malamalama/	
* maramatanga*	clarity, understanding
matapule	orator
matau	our
matua	older person (parent, uncle or aunt)
mimi	urinate
mokopuna	grandchild
paua	shellfish

paepa	seat for orators
paka	lobster
papa'a	white, European
patupaiarehe	forest fairy, elf
pe'a	Samoan tattoo
pola	large feast
puaha	large
pūriri	NZ native tree
rami	squeeze
rami	loin cloth
rangatira	chief or high-ranking person
Sa	Samoan
salu	broom made of coconut leaves
suipi	Samoan card game
taku taha Maori	my Maori side
tangi	funeral
tangihanga	funeral rites, customs
tapa	patterned cloth made from tree bark
tarau	trousers
taro	staple food plant of the Pacific Islands
tātarā-moa	bramble, in English 'bush-lawyer'
tēnā koe	greeting
Tihei Mauriora	phrase to open formal speech – literally the sneeze of life
toho	pig
tōtara	NZ native tree
tui	NZ native bird
tupapaku	corpse
tūtae	faeces
weta	large NZ native insect
wha	four
whakapapa	genealogy
yaqona	Fijian for *kava* (ceremonial drink)